Augusta Klein

Among the gods: Scenes of India

With legends by the way

Augusta Klein

Among the gods: Scenes of India
With legends by the way

ISBN/EAN: 9783337153267

Printed in Europe, USA, Canada, Australia, Japan

Cover: Foto ©Andreas Hilbeck / pixelio.de

More available books at **www.hansebooks.com**

AMONG THE GODS

A GOPURA OF THE GREAT PAGODA, MADURA.

AMONG THE GODS

SCENES OF INDIA: WITH LEGENDS BY THE WAY

BY

AUGUSTA KLEIN

WITH FULL-PAGE ILLUSTRATIONS

WILLIAM BLACKWOOD AND SONS
EDINBURGH AND LONDON
MDCCCXCV

En memoriam

SORORIS NOSTRAE

QUAE OLIM NOBISCUM PEREGRINATA

NUNC DOMI NOS EXSPECTAT.

CONTENTS.

CONTENTS.

ILLUSTRATIONS.

The Author begs to acknowledge her indebtedness to Messrs Bourne & Shepherd of Calcutta, Messrs Wiele & Klein of Madras, and others, for permission to reproduce the photographs illustrating this Work.

AMONG THE GODS.

CHAPTER I.

IT is a cold and melancholy November morning in the year 1891. London never was smokier or smuttier in all its dingy life. A drizzling rain comes down unceasingly from the low and colourless sky, and the gloom of a chill and clinging fog is in the ends of the muddy streets. On a shadowy platform in Charing Cross Station, hard by the train for Dover, stand a father and his three daughters and his daughters' Welsh maid,—"an English family," saith a critic of their former travels, "whether real or fictitious we know not." This is really too bad! Pray, Mr Critic, how would *you* like to have it insinuated that you were a figment of your own imagination?

The travellers are already known to such as have perused their Palestine wanderings,[1] and their introduction need not be a lengthy one. There is Irene the tender-hearted, and Philippa the business-like, and Sebaste, who gathers much

---

[1] See "Sketches from Eastern Travel," 'Blackwood's Magazine,' 1892.

wool in the course of every day. There, too, presiding over a small mountain of rugs and handbags, stands Elizabeth of cheerful countenance. And now they have bestowed themselves in their train and set forth on their six months' journey.

Overland they travel as far as Brindisi, where lies beside the quay the good ship Britannia, looking very proud indeed of her 6000 tons. And late on a Sunday night she steams out to sea, carrying our travellers with her.

Now, forasmuch as the business of this present scripture is to describe the travellers' adventures in India and Ceylon, the sea-voyages thither and thence might with great propriety be omitted. But though sea-voyages in general may be but tedious things to write about, yet these particular specimens of that kind are so prosperous and so delightful that to pass them over in silence would be ungrateful indeed. Ungrateful, and, moreover, untrue; for the mental picture of India which, when the journey is done, will hang in Memory's echoing hall, must, with its brilliant hues, be framed for ever in the shining blue of foam-flecked seas and the radiant, cloudless glories of boundless and sunlit skies.

"Very poetical, no doubt," says Philippa dryly; but the tropics are too warm, I think, for such soaring flights of eloquence. How the flying-fish can go on as they do, I cannot imagine. Look at that little twinkling constellation of them. They have kept up with the ship for two minutes at least, and we are making sixteen knots an hour!"

Under the cool shade of a double awning the travellers, reclining in their deck-chairs, are looking languidly forth on a world of golden sunshine and bright-blue sea and sky. Truly a region of peace and quiet is the Arabian Sea on a hot December day! All through the glowing hours of sunlight the mind reposes in a delightful inactivity, revelling in the dreamy sense of having left far, far behind all the complicated problems and the intricate life of the land, and of having floated forth into boundless freedom where space and time are not. But when evening comes, it brings with it awakening and reviving, and then our travellers' eyes, gazing no longer on vacancy, are intent on the gorgeous pageant of a tropical sunset at sea, the like of which, even in Egypt or Nubia, they have hitherto never dreamed of.

It is not till after the sun has vanished below the horizon that the real splendours begin. Then a haze of luminous purple hangs from above, and beneath is an expanse of daffodil sky, and on all sides are gauzy veils of crimson and gold, now piled in folds of deepening colour, now waving and floating and dissolving in clear and rosy light. Gradually the arc of colour contracts, growing ever more intense, ever more definite in form, while from the central light stream forth great pencils of coloured rays. The daffodil hue is a glowing gold, and the gold is rose-colour, and the rose is crimson, each mirrored in turn on the burnished surface of the deep and waveless sea. The purple haze has dissolved into the clear, deep blue of the night-sky, wherein swims the new moon's delicate crescent, the radiant rim of the disc that the bright earth-shine completes with a soft, clear light unknown in northern climes. And now the great stars shine forth, and all the brightest of them cast each a distinct path of light across the shadowy waters.

To watch on such a night the rising of Sirius is to see a vision never to be forgotten. Like a flaming lamp he hangs over his own shining reflection, shooting forth his bright beams of prismatic light, a marvel to behold. Well may the Zarathustrian scripture call him "the bright and glorious star"[1] whom Ahura Mazda the Holy One hath "established as a lord and overseer above all stars." North of him shines forth Procyon, while Castor and Pollux preside in state over the hosts of the north-east heavens. Capella darts her coloured rays from far above the horizon; away to southward glows and scintillates the glorious Aldebaran; and Canopus casts his calmer beams in a gleaming path along the sea. It is a scene that calls to mind that strange similitude of Indian wisdom, which tells how the Supreme Being "having prepared all created things, hath inserted and united Himself to them, but is at the same time distinct from them all. Just as the figures of the stars appear in water, but, if any one seeks to extract a star from thence, it is absurd. Such is his essence."[2]

Strange and unnatural look the brilliant constellations; for many are new, and the familiar ones are fantastically out of position. Orion reclines on his back, Cassiopeia stands on her head, and the Great Bear, that generally well-conducted beast, is balancing itself on the end of its tail. But there are other things which make the night stranger yet. Contending with the splendour of the planets Venus and Jupiter shines the faint radiance of the Zodiacal Light in the west, and below in the water are the balls and streaks of soft, bright phosphorescence which float and dance backward from the prow of the ship; and there is that mysterious, starlit distance stretching away and away like a vast gleaming pavement whereon rests the mighty dome of the dark-blue, starry sky;

[1] From "The Vendidad," translated by James Darmesteter. Sacred Books of the East.
[2] From Halhed's 'Sheeve Pouran.'

while the summer lightning from beyond the utmost horizon
runs and gleams and flickers in weird and elfin light.

Long, long ago the shores of the western lands sank down
beneath the horizon. They are like some far-off dreamland
now, and what was once the land of dreams will soon rise up
from the sea, and will prove itself, for many a month to come,
brilliantly and dazzlingly real.

But we have had enough of the frame. Let us come to the
picture itself.

It is early on a Sunday morning, and the sun is rising in a
glow of liquid gold, when our travellers awake to find themselves floating at anchor on the smooth waters of Colombo
harbour. All around them is an expanse of sparkling blue,
and beyond, against the background of the golden sunrise-
light, lies the coast of that Fairyland of ancient story, Simhala,
the Island of Gems. Thickly fringing the water's edge stand
deep groves of coco-nut palms, luxuriant and graceful beyond
the imagination of those who draw from rainless Egypt their
notions of southern vegetation. Not all growing perpen-
dicularly, as is the manner of date-palms, but bending and
crossing one another in curving lines, the coco-nut palms
are a thousand times more beautiful and fairy-like. Truly
it is an alluring land, an enchanted island just risen in freshness and beauty from the depths of the shining sea.

This is that Kingdom of the Lion round which are gathered so many wonderful myths of immemorial Buddhist tradition. Of old, in the long-past days, no human beings lived
therein, but spirits and serpent-princes ; and theirs was all
the countless wealth of this the Sorrowless Land. Here, in
their great iron city the Râkshasi demons dwelt ; and when
merchants came to traffic with the friendly spirits, then

would come forth those demon-women to the sound of the
sweetest music, holding flowers and scents in their hands.
But those whom they enticed within the walls of their city
they "shut up in an iron prison," and devoured them every
one. After those days the island was inhabited by men not
wholly human, the fierce descendants of the Lion King, a
savage and cruel race who knew nought of mercy or pity.
They were small of stature and of black complexion, in form
like human beings, and having the hearts of lions.

But already our travellers are rowing ashore in a quaint
and curious boat propelled by oars which are poles terminating in discs of wood; and presently they find themselves in
good time for Service in the Fort Church, where even the
sweep and flap of the punkahs cannot dissipate the comfortable sense of home, latitude and longitude notwithstanding.

The travellers establish themselves in the Grand Oriental
Hotel. Grand it is not (except so far as mere size goes), but
Oriental it may fairly be called by virtue of its cool and
comfortable absence of furniture, its multitudes of amiable
lizards and majestic beetles, and the outlandish human
figures which haunt its airy corridors. With a view to
coolness, the bedrooms have no ceilings, and one gazes
upward to the roof of the house, which roof is so constructed
as to let in welcome air while excluding the terrible sunshine. Instead of a window are folding-doors, always wide
open, and leading into a shaded balcony. Thus one sleeps
almost out of doors, and is awakened in the morning by
the soft balmy air blowing across the coco-nut palms, from
whose leafy crowns the rising sun is just disentangling
himself.

When the glorious sunrise has been sufficiently admired,

one claps one's hands for *chota hazri*, which presently appears. *Chota hazri* (which signifieth Little Breakfast) is the daintiest refection of the day, consisting of Ceylon tea and fresh bananas, with other local delicacies. It is brought by one of the white-robed Singhalese folk,—a strange figure that, with its bare brown feet, makes no sound at all as it softly glides along. The face is dark brown, with a silky black beard and quick, shining eyes. The fine black hair is glossy with coco-nut oil, and, being long like a woman's, is twisted up into a neat little knob behind, while the top of the head is encircled by a narrow tortoise - shell comb of which the ends touch the forehead.

Now is the time for sightseeing, for later in the day the sun will be too powerful to be braved out of doors; and accordingly the travellers sally forth to see the town of Colombo. Walking in this heat is neither pleasant nor prudent, and, they therefore patronise the jinrickshas. Now a jinricksha is a light chair on wheels furnished with two small shafts between which runs a native, pulling the conveyance after him at a fabulous and exhilarating rate of progress. There are always dozens of these men hovering about the hotel door and anxiously waiting to be hired, so that there will be no difficulty in getting about the town; but to find the town is very difficult indeed—in fact, throughout their stay in Colombo our friends cannot honestly say that they ever have found it at all. With the exception of a small nucleus of native shops, it is so widely scattered as to be altogether intangible. Colombo extends over 6415 acres of ground, and consists chiefly of coco-palms, including also a lake and other natural features. Here and there one comes upon a house in wide grounds of its own, or a few native cottages, or a large park with a public building in it;

but everything is miles away from everything else, and no two points of interest lie in the same direction.

The travellers give up the town in despair, and console themselves by visiting the Cinnamon Gardens instead. As they approach the part of the Gardens devoted to cinnamon-growing, a spicy fragrance [1] fills the air that is everywhere and always strangely balmy and sweet. The cinnamon-plant is cultivated as a bushy shrub, every part whereof has a strong and delicious scent.

In the Gardens is an excellent Museum containing specimens of all the animals known in the island,—quaint, uncanny-looking beasts, and unfamiliar birds, and brilliant butterflies; gigantic buffaloes, and turtles, and sea-creatures innumerable. One can travel all over Ceylon within the Museum walls. Here are many skeletons of elephants, of whom the personal history is related by the intelligent Tamil Christian whose duty it is to do the honours of the Museum to visitors. One of the skeletons is that of a faithful and trusted elephant who spent thirty-seven years of his life as a Carrier in the service of Government, and died esteemed of all, at the age of fifty. Another is that of a "rogue" elephant—that is, an unfortunate beast afflicted with a monomania which impels him to make for any human creature who comes in his way, and immediately trample him to death. Well-conducted elephants are accustomed to go about in herds, but the furious "rogues" are excluded from all circles of jungle society, and rampage through the world alone, a terror to encounter.

More interesting than outlandish beasts are the models

---

[1] Bishop Heber was perfectly correct about the "spicy breezes," notwithstanding all that has been said to the contrary by contentiously-minded travellers unblessed with poetical noses.

representing types of the island's various native races with their proper costumes; and especially attractive are some resplendent specimens of native jewellery, among which is conspicuous the wedding-necklace of gold, which is fastened by the bridegroom on the bride's neck, and must never be removed so long as he lives.

The strangest objects in the Museum are the masks of native "devil-dancers" who are called in to dance before the sick, and who wear different masks (each more hideously grotesque than the others) for the different demons to be propitiated, and the various diseases to be cured. When the disease is hatred of an enemy, the "devil-dancer" covers his face with the appalling effigy of a demon whose terrific teeth and claws are in the act of crushing to death little human figures of wretched and helpless aspect. He then dances before the vindictive patient, and sticks pins into diminutive effigies of the ill-fated enemy in question.

Leaving the Museum, our friends pursue their way under the towering coco-palms with their far-off crowns of foliage overhanging the giant bunches of slowly maturing fruit. A very brown little boy waylays them with a couple of unripe coco-nuts, and the travellers, having purchased the same for two coppers, refresh themselves with the so-called milk, which is in fact a sweet juice not unlike that of a melon.

At length they return to the hotel for breakfast, and become initiated in the mysterious delights of prawn and pumpkin curry seasoned with chutnee and grated coco-nut, while overhead the great punkahs sweep to and fro, and all around a multitude of white-robed Singhalese waiters scud noiselessly over the polished floors, proffering in obsequious silence all kinds of dainties to everybody.

Every day spent in Colombo and its neighbourhood brings

to our travellers fresh impressions of the profuse and exuberant beauty of this wonderful hothouse country. The
roads, made of the red loamy soil, are of a rich crimson
colour, which contrasts picturesquely with the lively green
of the luxuriant vegetation. By the roadside grow Indian
tulip-trees (vulgarly so called) with their delicate yellow
flowers blushing crimson just before they fade; while here
and there is a flaming mass of the lettuce-tree's yellow-green
foliage, good to eat as well as to look upon. Everywhere are
thick groves and forests of stately coco-palms, with a rich
undergrowth entangled with bright flowering creepers which
hide the bushes with trailing veils of crimson and purple
blossoms. Gayest of all are the shoeflower-bushes covered
with large, lily-like blooms of the most luminous carmine hue
that heart of man can imagine. Here and there the darker
foliage of the bread-fruit tree relieves the dazzled eye, and
contrasts with the vivid groups of bananas that shade with
their broad drooping leaves great clusters of crowded fruit.

As they wander day after day among such surroundings
of enchanting and unfamiliar loveliness, the travellers find
themselves haunted by clouds of innumerable butterflies of
large size and many colours. Their assembling at this season
(when their life is nearly finished) is preparatory, saith
native tradition, to their taking flight for Adam's Peak in
the interior, whereon they will worship the footprint of
Buddha, and thereafter die content. For the Buddha came,
in the days of old, to visit the Isle of Gems and to war
against the spirits therein and the wicked serpent-princes.
And when he was come to the island he "planted one foot
to the north of the royal city," and the other many miles
away on the summit of Adam's Peak. To this day at the
top of that high mountain a footprint is seen in the rock,

ON THE GALLE ROAD, COLOMBO.

more than five feet long and about two feet and a half in
width. The Muhammadans deem it the trace of Adam's
foot,—of Siva's the Hindus fancy; but the Buddhists aver
and the butterflies know it to be Buddha's most sacred
footprint.

Perhaps the most beautiful road in the neighbourhood of
Colombo is the highroad to Point de Galle. Here and there
by the wayside are palm-thatched native cottages surrounded
with tall bananas; and overhead the thronging coco-palms
bend far across the road, making a welcome coolness of sun-
flecked shadow through which pass brightly clad natives,—
white-robed Singhalese; Muhammadans of Arab descent with
caps of plaited silk; turbaned, grave-faced Tamils; and
stately Buddhist monks clad in their graceful robes of the
sacred golden colour. Through many centuries, through age-
long changes, those yellow robes have endured, ever since,
in the third century B.C., the teaching of the Buddha was
brought by Mahendra, the mighty Arhat, from the far-off
land of Magadha to Simhala the Island of Gems. A Prince
was he of the royal house of Pataliputra, a younger brother
of the great Aśôka; but he banished from his heart all
worldly desires, that he might gain in their stead the "six
spiritual powers," together with the "eight means of libera-
tion," and the excellent fruit of Arhatship. In a moment
of time from distant Magadha he came to the Lion Kingdom; and here he taught to all the people the Buddha's
sacred doctrine. Then there fell on those that dwelt in
this island a true and believing heart, so that they builded
an hundred monasteries that were filled with 20,000 monks
"distinguished for their power of abstraction" and for their
eminent wisdom. From that day to this their order has
continued; and still, in their graceful robes of yellow, they

walk through the sun-flecked shadows of the road to Point
de Galle.

All things are strangely dream-like in these enchanted
regions, — always excepting the vigorous and interesting
Church-work which is carried on in Colombo with no
small measure of success. Tamil and Singhalese Services
for the many native Christians are a matter of course;
and there is much pastoral and evangelistic work, wherein it is necessary to use no less than four languages—
English, Singhalese, Tamil, and Portuguese. The inmates
of the prisons are not neglected, nor those of the pauper
and leper hospitals; and special attention is given to work
among the Tamil coolies. Open-air preaching, begun under
Bishop Claughton, is still carried on by the Clergy, and
is found to be a very valuable agency in gaining the
attention of the heathen folk who would never enter the
churches. Perhaps the most important branch of Missionary enterprise in Colombo is the educational work carried
on by various institutions, whereof one or two are visited
by our inquisitive friends the travellers.

Close to Christchurch Cathedral, surrounded by great
tropical trees and undulating lawns of rich verdure, stands
S. Thomas's College. It was founded by the first Bishop
of Colombo in 1851, and in 1864 was affiliated to the
University of Calcutta. Its object is the education of
high-class natives; and the foundation includes, besides
the College proper, a Divinity School for the training
of candidates for Holy Orders, and a Collegiate School
which contains[1] 300 pupils. There is also, in connection
with the College, a native Orphan Asylum for the plain
Christian education of twenty orphan boys. The boarders

[1] 1892.

number more than 100. Pupils are prepared every year for the Cambridge Local Examinations, and for those of the Calcutta University. The Divinity School is doing a most important work in training candidates for the Native Ministry, which is found to be as needful and as invaluable in Ceylon as in every other Missionary Diocese. It seems to be from the formation in the island of a Native Ministry that there dates that steady and progressive advance which has brought the number of Christians in Ceylon to 150,000. The Society for the Propagation of the Gospel alone supports in the Diocese eight Native Clergy as well as 200 lay agents. S. Thomas's College owes much to the liberal support of that Society,[1] and so do I know not how many other beneficent and useful institutions in Colombo and the rest of the island. Thanks to the S.P.G., a distinctly missionary character has been impressed on the work of the Ceylon Church, so that the labours of almost every Chaplain and Catechist have now their Missionary counterpart. Yet so unobtrusive are the Society's doings that one hears not much about them, seeing that in every place it identifies itself with the Church organisation already existing, and is content to be, according to its unvarying rule, "the handmaid of the Church, not a substitute for it." "We owe it to the S.P.G.," wrote the Bishop in 1881, "that we not only have Missions, but are a Missionary diocese."

The help which the Society has given to S. Thomas's College is in itself an important contribution to the Church's work in Ceylon ; for it is impossible to estimate the amount

---

[1] That other most useful and admirable institution, the Society for the Promotion of Christian Knowledge, also contributed £2000 to the endowment of S. Thomas's College.

of the widespread Christian influence emanating from this one centre of high and efficient education. All the pupils at S. Thomas's receive a Christian training, and these dark-faced students form a large and very reverent part of the congregation at the daily Cathedral Services. Heathen pupils attend the College for the sake of the secular education, but all alike are instructed in Christian doctrine; and many are thus led to offer themselves for Baptism—a step which often involves the sacrifice of every worldly prospect, and the casting off of the convert by all his heathen relatives.

Bishop's College, for high-class girls and for boys under ten, is also doing very good work. The standard of teaching is being raised year by year; pupils are prepared for the Senior and Junior Cambridge Local Examinations, and the school will soon begin presenting candidates for the Matriculation Examination of the Madras University. The course includes all the subjects of a complete High School curriculum, as well as careful religious instruction. Our travellers are present at the annual prize-giving, and a very pretty sight, on this festal occasion, is the schoolroom with its decorations of bright-hued flowers and its further adornment with the dark-brown, intelligent faces of the pupils and the smiling countenances of all their delighted parents.

One of the most charming sights in Colombo is S. Michael's School and Orphanage, over which preside some S. Margaret's Sisters sent out to Ceylon from East Grinstead. Of the fifty-six native orphans some are hardly more than babies, little dark-brown things with silky black hair, and wonderful lustrous eyes beaming with happiness and with very unmistakable affection for their kind and devoted guardians. Youngest and prettiest of all the brown faces is that of the Tamil baby, christened Dorothea, and now [1] three years old.

"Make a salaam to the visitors, Dorothea," says the Sister; whereupon Dorothea clasps her tiny brown hands over her face, and then removes them with a bow and a baby-smile delightful to see; after which the little round arms are held out to "Sister," and Dorothea is rewarded with a kiss.

Close by is S. Michael's Church, wherein the travellers are present one afternoon at a Native Confirmation, and are greatly struck with the reverence of the forty or fifty candidates and of the many other Native Christians present.

There are numberless other things (including the Tamil boarding-schools founded by the Church Missionary Society) which undoubtedly ought to be described; but it is time to leave the seaboard now, and to hurry our friends away into stranger and still more beautiful scenes, the interior regions of jungle-forests and towering mountain-peaks.

[1] Christmas 1891.

CHAPTER II.

KANDY AND NUWARA ELIYA.

THE journey from Colombo to Kandy is seventy-five miles long, and a wonderful journey it is. The railway is an engineering achievement such as is exhilarating for human creatures to contemplate, impressing upon their minds what very clever creatures they are. Kandy is about 1700 feet above the sea-level, and the scenes passed through in rising to that altitude form a succession of the most marvellous pictures, for northern eyes to look upon, that northern minds could imagine or desire.

The first part of the way, following the course of the Kelani-Ganga, lies through forests of tropical trees broken by verdant expanses of padi (padi, be it observed, stands to rice in the relation of sheep to mutton)—lake-like glades of soft, vivid green, bordered by exquisite groups of palms that stand out from the deep forest beyond in ever-varying combinations of light and shade and majesty of graceful form. The coco-nut palms predominate, but here and there is a group of slender areca palms, their straight white stems contrasting with the background of luxuriant foliage; and then there is the darker green of the bread-fruit trees, and the brilliant colours of flowering trees innumerable.

The moist and low-lying plains are left behind at length; the native cottages, thatched with palm-leaves, appear no more; bananas and coco-palms become less frequent; high into the sunlit air tower the rocky peaks of mountains rising from depths of pathless jungle into the shadowy recesses whereof even the glowing southern sunshine can never penetrate, and wherein prowl unseen cheetahs and elephants, and milk-white monkeys have their home, and lizards four feet long.

There is a majestic mystery about these jungle-forests, a wild beauty and exuberance of teeming life, a mazy and unintelligible intricacy, not to be described in words. The giant forest-trees rise in stately grandeur, and spread themselves abroad, glorying in the mighty glow of the tropical sunshine; but beneath their venerable branches lie unfathomable depths of undergrowth, tangled and massed together in formless wealth of verdure, and covered with brightly blossoming creepers. So weirdly beautiful is the scene, that one is tempted to fancy it belongs not at all to the present world, but to some allegoric land wherein all earthly things are ideally reflected. It is almost as though one were to look into some profoundly subtle mind, and to see the mighty thoughts therein, rooted deep in living ground, spreading themselves abroad and rejoicing in the light, and beneath them wild masses of formless, exuberant feeling, and wayward fancies lightly flinging here and there bright veils of rainbow colours, and to see all these instinct with one strong, unifying stream of life welling up with deathless energy from an unseen source, whither consciousness may not penetrate, and which only faith can reach.

B

"My dear," says Philippa, "we are higher than we were, but not quite up in the clouds yet! You had better dismiss your misty imaginings, and help me to capture this firefly, that we may investigate him by daylight."

The travellers have arrived, long after sunset, at their destination, and are wandering by moonlight beside the lake of Kandy. Great clumps of bamboo shoot high above their heads, spreading abroad their gigantic, feathery leaves; before them lies the gleaming lake, and all around them float countless fireflies, filling the shadowy spaces with twinkling stars of light. The air is soft and fragrant, and full of a multitude of sounds,—low chirpings and croakings and whisperings innumerable, telling of a wealth of numberless life unknown in the temperate zones.

Night in the tropics is a marvel of loveliness; but morning is lovelier still, and our travellers awake on the following day to gaze on a scene of unsuspected beauty which, every morning of their stay at Kandy, will be a fresh surprise of unimaginable, incredible delight. There used to be a swamp at Kandy, but the last of the Kandyan Rajas, in the beginning of the century, converted it into a lake with a little island therein crowded with tropical trees. Closely shutting in this lovely sheet of water, rise high hills covered to their very summits with the most exquisite foliage in bewildering variety of form and colour. Graceful coco-palms stand out in delicate loveliness against the cloudless sky, broad-leaved trees laden with strange fruits or flowers crowd around them, luxuriant bananas hang out their curving leaves, trailing creepers wrap themselves round the lesser trees and bushes in deep folds of living green, and on all sides bloom gorgeous flowers in wonderful profusion. One has but to wander forth and gather wild, way-

side flowers to obtain in a few minutes a glowing bouquet
of hothouse blooms, and many others such as English hot-
houses never dreamed of. Just overhead hang the great,
snow - white bells of the datura; trailing Ceylon "sun-
flowers" cover the undergrowth with brilliant masses of
gold; the rich orange of the lantana blossoms is scattered
thickly over their soft green foliage; the crimson shoe-
flowers bloom forth from their darker leaves; flowering
creepers clothe the banks with purple; and hundreds of
lesser blossoms show like burning gems in the luxuriant
wayside grass. Never again in all their journey will our
travellers see such flowers.

It is the combination of all this softer loveliness with
the grandeur of mountain scenery which gives to Kandyan
landscapes their magic and inexplicable charm. One afternoon's drive, wherein the travellers make, by the upper
road, the circuit of the lake, they will always remember as
an expedition made through some enchanted country or
perhaps in Elfland itself. The heat of the day is over,
and the reddening sunbeams slant softly across the summits of the hills, flooding the rich scene with a glow of
golden splendour. Far into the clear air rise the stately
heights; all around throngs a wealth of flowers, and sun-
flecked foliage stirred by the fragrant evening breeze; and
far below lies the lake, shining with that ethereal and rosy
brightness which belongs of right to lakes when the hour
of sunset is near. Fair and peaceful seem those radiant
waters; yet would any native tell you that beneath their
glancing ripples they hide a fearful mystery. Below that
sunlit surface, far down in the shadowy depths of the lake,
lies a gold-mine. No human hands may reach it, no human
eyes may search therein for gold. The dim recesses of that

far-off mine are ringing with the tools of demon workmen,
—an awful company who haunt the lake and dwell therein
at home. And year by year at this present time they seize
upon some human victim — some heedless one bathing in
the bright waters or launching a boat thereon—and they
drag him down to the depths below and gloat upon his
drowning struggles. Every year have they done so, and
the season is come round again; soon must one be drowned,
but who it shall be none yet can tell.

By way of improving their minds, the travellers seize an
early opportunity of visiting a neighbouring tea-estate and
manufactory; and here should follow an elaborate account
of tea-estates in general, an historical review of the circumstances which led in Ceylon to the supplanting of coffee by
tea, an economic dissertation setting forth the quantity of
tea produced and the amount of labour required, with a
minute investigation into the condition and prospects of the
coolies employed in tea-growing, and the manner in which
they and their families are housed and fed. Also there
should be given an exact account of the processes through
which the tea must pass,—of the picking and drying and
rolling and fermenting and firing and sifting, and so forth,
with many other matters of the utmost interest. But we
will omit that part.

Let us consider the tea-estate as having been thoroughly
investigated, and join our friends in their subsequent wanderings through that more poetic region, the great Gardens of
Peradeniya, the "Place of Guavas." They extend over
nearly 150 acres, and are encircled on three sides by the
Mahaweli Ganga, the largest river in Ceylon. Guarding the
entrance stands a majestic company of india-rubber trees,

planted in 1833, huge forest giants, with great snake-like roots that twist and coil in mazy folds far over the surface of the ground. And beyond lies a scene fairer than ideal dreams of what Eden may have been. Doré's drawings of the foliage of Paradise are poor and mean compared with this. Wide expanses of undulating, soft green lawns alternate with groves of palms and spice-trees, where mighty creepers climb and wreathe themselves to the very tops of the tall trees, clothing them with broad green leaves and blooms of gorgeous colour.

Down amongst the grass grows an abundance of the little "sensitive plant," whereof the tiny acacia-like leaves at the lightest touch suddenly shut themselves up and drop close to the stem, so that the whole plant seems to have withered in a moment. The travellers, who have seen in London one precious little specimen thereof nursed and guarded with the utmost care, smile a little when the native superintendent of the Gardens complains that this is a very bad weed and most difficult to get rid of.

Having sufficiently tormented the poor little leaves, they turn away to admire the grander things which on all sides claim their attention. There are coco-palms and date-palms and areca-nuts; jaggeries and katu-kituls; the royal palm from Cuba, the sago-palm and the durian; fan-palms and palmyras; cinnamon and allspice and cloves; screw-pines and Egyptian doum palms; white-blossomed Indian cork-trees; fern-trees and climbing ferns; aroids and ground-orchids; and climbing palms that grapple with the tallest trees. There is the upas-tree from Java with its deadly juice wherewith arrows are poisoned; and cacao-trees from the fruit whereof cocoa and chocolate are made; lignum-vitæ, and jak-trees, and calabashes; the fan-shaped travel-

ler's tree, hoarding its copious supply of water for thirsty
wanderers; red cedars, and candle-trees, and vegetable
ivory; mangosteens, and mangos, and alligator pears; and
nutmegs with their dark-brown fruit embedded in scarlet
mace. There is the double coco-nut, which puts forth but
one leaf in the year and lives for forty years before its stem
begins to appear, and yet will reach at length a height of
100 feet, and produce nuts that take ten years to ripen, and
there are beautiful Alexandra palms, and the gigantic talipot
that grows upward for forty or fifty years, and then, from
the stupendous height of its far-off crown of leaves, sends
forth one majestic flower said to measure 40 feet in height,
—a pyramidal, snow-white bloom like a gigantic spirea-
blossom of the richest luxuriance; but as the huge clusters
of fruit grow ripe, the vast tree withers and dies.

The river-bank is crowded with fantastic growth—sandal-
wood trees, and great tufts of feathery bamboos, including
the "giant bamboo" of Burmah, whose culms, shooting
upward at the rate of a foot in twenty-four hours, reach a
length of nearly 100 feet, spreading forth on all sides thick
fronds of dark-green foliage that the mighty sunbeams may
not penetrate.

But no enumeration of details can give the faintest idea
of the loveliness of these magic scenes, and a sorry failure
is theirs who try to copy the stately forms of Nature in
mean and sordid heaps of heavy, piled-up words! Moreover, some there are whose restless minds cannot long remain
satisfied with even the refined society of trees the most distinguished; and it is time that we should seek in the native
town interests of a more human kind.

The crowds that haunt the bazaars of Kandy are as varied
as those of Colombo. There are the grave-faced Tamils, and

BUDDHIST MONKS, KANDY.

the Singhalese with their tortoise-shell combs; an increased number of Muhammadan Moormen, the descendants of Arab traders; and many "Burgher" folk who trace their descent from the Dutch and the Portuguese. And everywhere in twos and threes walk the picturesque figures of dignified Buddhist monks. The head is shaven, and the right arm and shoulder are bare, but the rest of the figure is covered, down to the feet, with the flowing folds of the sacred yellow robe. Some of these robes are of silk, the fine soft texture thereof enhancing the beauty of the dull, rich, golden colour. In his right hand the devotee carries his begging-bowl, wherein he collects fragments of food for his daily meal, and in his left hand a palm-leaf fan to guard his mouth from flies, lest he should headlessly cause the death of the least of living things.

These monks have their abode in the famous Buddhist temple near the lake. It is known as the Dalada-maligava Temple, and therein is enshrined that venerable tooth which of old the Buddha himself, "in order to disseminate the true doctrine,"[1] left to be preserved in this country;—that relic of miraculous properties which is "firm as a diamond, indestructible through ages," ever "scattering its light like the stars or the moon in the sky," shining in the night of darkness "brilliant as the sun" himself.

To the temple our travellers repair after sunset on the night of the full-moon feast; and as they walk thither beside the gleaming waters of the lake, their thoughts elude the grasp of the Present, and wander away backward for nearly fifteen centuries, picturing that ancient worship of the Tooth which Fa-hien the Chinese pilgrim saw, and described so

[1] From the travels of Hiuen Tsiang, translated from the Chinese by Samuel Beal, B.A.

well. "In the middle of the third month"[1] the solemn
feast was held; and, ten days before, there moved through
the streets of the capital a great elephant with gorgeous
trappings bearing on his back one "dressed in royal robes,"
who loudly proclaimed the same, beating a great drum as he
went.

"Bodhisattva," he cried (for such was the title of the
future Buddha),—"Bodhisattva during three *Asankhyeya-
kalpas*[2] manifested his activity, and did not spare his own
life. He gave up kingdom, city, wife, and son; he plucked
out his eyes and gave them to another; . . . he cut off his
head and gave it as an alms; he gave his body to feed a
starving tigress; he grudged not his marrow and brains. . . .
Behold! ten days after this Buddha's tooth will be brought
out. . . ."

So all the people arose, and made the roads smooth, and
adorned them with gorgeous hangings, amassing merit for
themselves. Then, "on both sides of the road," the king
placed wondrous effigies of those 500 different forms wherein
the Bodhisattva has appeared. And when the Tooth was at
length brought forth and carried in high procession along the
middle of the way, then all the people went forth with great
store of flowers and incense, bringing it on its way with eager
devotion and the offerings of zealous worship.

Arrived at the temple, the travellers find its entrance
guarded by two pompous but not ungracious elephants of
stone, carved in relief one on each side of the gateway.
Above them stand two great brazen lamps presented by a
former governor of Ceylon, who, if he thereby enlightened
the Buddhists, must have somewhat bewildered his fellow-

---

[1] See 'Fa-hien's Travels,' translated by James Legge, M.A., LL.D.
[2] A fabulous number of years, hardly to be expressed in figures.

THE TEMPLE OF THE TOOTH, KANDY.

Christians, of whom there are many in Kandy. Passing the carven figures of two "door-keepers," the travellers cross an outer court, and begin the ascent of a flight of steps leading up to the verandah of the temple itself. Overhead they hear a loud voice holding forth with the utmost vehemence, and looking up they behold the extraordinary figure of a Buddhist devotee, who, with wild gesticulations, is haranguing the world in general. He has gone mad, and is addressing, in flowing Singhalese, a large phantom-audience visible only to himself.

The visitors now pass some white-robed Buddhist nuns, and then make their way to the octagonal tower which, with its pillared balcony and pointed roof, is the most picturesque feature of the temple buildings. Herein is an oriental library of Buddhist scriptures, a quaint treasure-house of ancient lore, like some scholar's wistful dream. The books are mostly written in Pâli on narrow strips of the talipot palm-leaf. The pen is a little iron stylus, with the sharp point whereof the letters are cut into the surface of the prepared palm-leaf, as demonstrated to the travellers by one of the yellow-robed devotees, who, resting the pen on the thumb of his left hand, slowly inscribes for their benefit a sentence in Singhalese. The leaves, when the manuscript is completed, are fastened together, and protected by narrow boards, or plates of metal. Many of these coverings are of silver or silver-gilt, adorned with exquisitely delicate chasings, and with rubies and emeralds set therein.

While the visitors, surrounded by the stately figures of the devotees, are admiring these beautiful works of art, a strange thing happens. Suddenly and silently, whence they know not, appears in their midst an elderly Buddhist monk whom the others regard with the utmost reverence. His mysterious entrance makes him seem like some long-robed apparition of gracious countenance; but he is in reality the chief and holiest of all the Kandyan Buddhists. In answer to the astonished questions of the visitors, they are shown an unsuspected trap-door by which this illustrious devotee has arisen through the floor of the library. Beneath is a narrow stair leading down to the room wherein he spends the greater part of his life. He greets the Father with courteous kindliness, but, being too holy to touch a lady's hand, gently refuses to take any notice of his daughters.

It seems that, having heard that the travellers have come all the way from England to visit the temple, he desires to show them some treasures of the library which visitors are not generally privileged to see. One of these is a dainty little volume containing some part of the Buddhist scriptures. It is of the same long, narrow shape as the other books, but is written, not on palm-leaves, but on thin plates of gold. Another treasured possession is a leaf from the sacred bodhi-tree of Anuradhapura, mounted in silver and presented to the temple by a distinguished Englishman,—a graceful and poetic tribute to the Buddha's memory. Unfortunately there are performances of exquisite grace and poetic merit which do an altogether astonishing amount of harm. The illustrious Poet who made this beautiful offering is openly claimed by the Buddhists as a convert from Christianity, and it would be hard to estimate the injury to the Christian cause arising from this one act of refined and delicate compliment.

Leaving the Library, the travellers descend to the interior of the temple itself, and find it crowded with worshippers, and ringing with the deafening minstrelsy of conches and tom-toms. Here and there stand flower-sellers, from whom the worshippers buy baskets of the beautiful "temple-flowers"—white, yellow-centred blossoms with a strong and delicious fragrance. These are reverently poured out before the images of the Buddha, and especially before the famous tooth-relic for the reception whereof this temple was builded. Buddha would doubtless have disapproved, since in his Godless scheme of philosophy is no room for worship of any kind; but the instinct of sacrificial devotion, it seems, is too fundamental a part of human nature to be got rid of so easily, and apparently Buddhism is, to the generality of unlearned Buddhists, neither more nor less than an atheistic idolatry. There is nothing to worship but relics and images, the Buddha himself having long ago passed away "with that kind of passing away in which no root remains."[1]

"If the Buddha," said King Milinda of old, "be escaped from all existence, then . . . any act done to him . . . becomes empty and vain. This is a dilemma which has two horns." Verily it hath, and not all the Venerable Nagasenas in the world have been able, from that day till now, to "tear asunder that net of heresy," to "make in that jungle an open space," or to show how Buddhist worshippers can consistently suppose that "Blessed One" of theirs to heed their offerings or hear their cry from the depths of voiceless, unconscious Nirvana, his heaven of non-existence.

"When I have passed away," said the "Blessed One" as death drew near, "think not that the Buddha has left

---

[1] From 'The Questions of King Milinda,' translated from the Pâli by T. W. Rhys Davids. Sacred Books of the East.

you;" but he added, in interpretation of that saying, only this, "Ye have *my words!*" He himself is gone whence he shall not return, and has left his followers comfortless,[1] save only for that one stern counsel, "Be ye lamps unto yourselves. Be ye a refuge to yourselves. . . . Look not for refuge to any one besides yourselves."[2]

All of which considerations let us commend to the notice of such as feel attracted by the lordly dogmas of "Esoteric Buddhism," and Theosophy falsely so called!

Meanwhile the crowd of worshippers in the temple presents, in the flickering lamplight, a strange and animated picture. It is impressive to see the devotion wherewith those who have made their fragrant offering humbly prostrate themselves before the beautiful objects of worship. The most charming of these are some sacred bodhi-trees delicately carved in silver and gold, each with its little Buddha sitting under it in the conventional attitude of meditation. The visitors are also shown an image of Buddha, cut out of a single crystal, which, when a light is placed behind it, shines with a dazzling brightness,—and they are told of another, carved from a single emerald, which they are not permitted to see.

Finally, they make their way toward that most holy chamber where, enclosed in successive shrines of jewelled

---

[1] It hath been written, by no casual or superficial observer, but by one of the greatest authorities on the Buddhism of Ceylon: "It is, I fancy, considered a mark of culture in England to say that Buddhism is very like Christianity, if not almost as good ; . . . Buddhism is not like Christianity either in theory or practice. In theory if like Christianity at all, it is like Christianity without a Creator, without an Atoner, without a Sanctifier ; in practice it is a thin veil of flower-offering and rice-giving over a very real and degraded superstition of astrology and devil-worship."

[2] From 'The Book of the Great Decease,' translated from the Páli by T. W. Rhys Davids. Sacred Books of the East.

gold, is treasured the sacred tusk, half an inch thick and an inch and a quarter long, said once to have adorned the jaw of the great Lord Buddha himself. A checkered history it has had since then. Concealed in the hair of the pious Princess of Kalinga, it arrived in Ceylon at the beginning of the third century of our era. Captured in 1315 by the Malabars, and borne away to India, and thence recovered, it eventually fell into the hands of a Portuguese Archbishop of Goa, who in 1560 pounded the same in a mortar and burned the dust thereof. From all of which vicissitudes it miraculously recovered itself, to repose at length in the peaceful splendour of its illustrious Kandyan home.

The narrow steps leading up to its abode are blocked with an eager crowd of worshippers, who, having reached an anteroom separated by two curtains from the inner chamber of the relic, are allowed to go no further, but must surrender their offerings to one of the yellow-robed community, who pours them out before the shrine. The English visitors, through the kindness of the Apparition of the Library, are admitted by another staircase into the immediate presence of the relic. Here is an altar covered with fragrant temple flowers, and behind it a glass screen, and behind that the splendid shrine of gilded silver which incloses six other shrines of gold placed one within another, and adorned with emeralds, pearls, and rubies innumerable. And within the smallest and last is laid up the bit of ivory for which are poured forth day by day the reverence and devotion of countless earnest worshippers. Other costly shrines there are whereof one contains a hair from Buddha's head.

While the travellers are regarding the beautiful display of precious metals and fine workmanship, and watching the constant accession of fresh floral offerings from the crowded

ante-room, some privileged worshippers of evident distinction
are solemnly ushered into the dim and silent chamber. The
party consists of a native gentleman of rank, his sister, his
wife, and his little son in the arms of a servant. The two
ladies, who are young and handsome, are dressed in rich
robes of white; splendid jewels surround their gentle,
bronze-hued faces, and their glossy black hair is adorned
with twisted pearls. Having presented their offerings of
flowers, they prostrate themselves before the shrine with the
utmost grace, and a rapt devotion that is touching to behold.
Their awestruck faces and earnest, lustrous eyes are the most
beautiful things to be seen to-night in all the crowded
temple.

Before leaving Kandy our travellers duly visit various
other objects of interest. There is the dagoba near the
temple,—a solid dome of masonry said to cover treasures
buried of old in the ground; and there is the thriving
Buddhist school; and close beside it, planted on a mound of
state, grows a venerable pipal or "bodhi tree"[1] with massive
trunk and luxuriant foliage of broad, heart-shaped leaves,
whereof each one terminates in a long, thread-like acumen.
These leaves are joined to their stalks in such a manner as to
cause them, at the least breath of air, to quiver with restless
motion, reminding our travellers of that faint-hearted
monarch of antiquity, the great King Hari-scandra, who
"being terrified, suddenly trembled exceedingly like the
leaf of the pipal-tree."[2] This Kandyan bodhi-tree is greatly
revered, and for every branch of it that falls to the ground a
funeral ceremony is solemnly performed. The fallen bough

---

[1] *Ficus religiosa.*

[2] From the 'Markandeya Purána,' translated by F. E. Pargiter, C.S.

is wrapped in a cloth and cremated, and the ashes thereof are buried.

There is, moreover, to be seen the Audience Hall of the ancient Kandyan Kings, adorned with pillars of carven teakwood. It is part of the palace builded about the year 1600 by Wimala Dharma.

S. Paul's Church is at so little distance from the Buddhist temple that the worshippers at the daily Services can hear the din of the temple tom-toms. Its congregations are large and devout, and the Church-work is carried on with vigour and success. The mission-work assumes to a great extent an educational form. The Industrial School for boys is a very useful factor in this kind of enterprise. It contains[1] forty-six boys, all of whom are Christians, with the exception of five who are to be baptised on Christmas Eve. One of these five once wore the yellow robe of a Buddhist devotee; and the story of his escape from the temple in a servant's dress, and his presenting himself for Christian instruction, is a romantic episode in native life. There are also vernacular and English schools wherein over 100 pupils are educated. Moreover, the Church Missionary Society has in Kandy a girls' boarding-school, and a College which, since 1878, has been affiliated to the University of Calcutta. Nor must we forget to mention another most useful Church-school for very poor children, conducted with expenditure of much labour and some money by a Burgher lady and her seven daughters, whose noble devotion to Christian work is stimulating to behold, and whose constant kindness to our travellers during their stay in Kandy is an instance of Christian charity of the warmest and most delightful kind.

S. Stephen's Church is served by a Tamil Clergyman

[1] December 1891.

("Father Barnabas") who has a congregation of 200 Tamil
Christians, all of whom have been baptised in S. Stephen's,
where all the Services are in Tamil.

It would be unnatural to dismiss the subject of Kandyan
Christianity without connecting therewith the well-loved
name of Archdeacon Matthew. His grave is in the Christian cemetery at Kandy; and if any one desire to know what
it is like to leave a loving memory behind, he should mention that name to any Kandyan Churchman he pleases, and
watch the expression of the countenance he is addressing.

At length the travellers set forth on their upward journey
to cold Nuwara Eliya, more than 6000 feet above the sea.
As far as Nanuoya, the elevation whereof is over 5000 feet,
they travel by railway, passing through scenery still wilder
and more grand than that below Kandy. The jungle-forests
grow darker and more northern in character, tea-plantations
abound on the bare hill-slopes, while the rocky mountains
grow ever bolder and more fantastic, until Adam's Peak
appears, rising in sheer and isolated grandeur to its height
of 7352 feet above the sea-level.

Gazing at that steep and terrible mountain-crag, our
friends recall strange Buddhist legends which in the course
of many centuries have gathered thickly round it,—old tales
of how the Rakkhasa demons brought sickness and fever on
this land of Lanka, and how the "divine sage" Kakusandha
journeyed hither through the air with 40,000 of his disciples,
and, perching on the top of Devakuta (the same is Adam's
Peak), subdued by his power the raging fever throughout
the Island of Gems; stories, too, of Konagamana, of eminent
wisdom, and other worthies beside, whose deeds were told
long centuries ago by that incomparable Thera, the wise

Mahinda, who in the hearing of thousands "poured out the sweet draught of his discourse."[1] And even now the learned may read them in that fifteenth chapter of the 'Mahavansa,' "composed equally for the delight and affliction of righteous men."

At length Nanuoya is reached, and there follows a five-miles' walk to Nuwara Eliya through cool mountain-breezes (such as seem unnatural so near the equator), blowing over dark rhododendron forests that cover the mountain-slopes. For rhododendrons are great forest-trees in these regions, and often reach a height of no less than 70 feet. So unfamiliar are the scenery and the vegetation that one may well believe that pious Chinese pilgrim who journeyed in Ceylon in the seventh century, and tells how in these regions are "high crags and deep valleys, . . . haunted by spirits that come and go;"[2] and scarcely would our friends be surprised were they to meet (as that pilgrim did in an island to the south of Ceylon) those men with the beaks of birds who live on the fruit of the coco-palm.

But we must hasten upward to Nuwara Eliya's grassy plain, whence rise the lordly mountain summits in the disguise of wooded hills.

Of our travellers' stay in this lofty region and all their experiences there, we will record but one expedition—that made to the summit of Pidurutalagala (called Pedro by Europeans), the highest mountain in Ceylon, boasting an altitude of 8295 feet above the sea. The walk to the top is about five miles long, and is achieved by our friends

[1] See the 'Mahavansa,' translated from the original Páli by George Turnour, C.C.S.

[2] From the travels of Hiuen Tsiang, translated from the Chinese by Samuel Beal, B.A.

before breakfast on a fresh and sunlit morning long to be remembered. Soon after sunrise they start, while the hoar-frost is still glistening on the lawn and on the full-blown arum-lilies that fill the air with fragrance.

Of the wonderful view which they hope to gain from the summit not a glimpse is visible on the way, for the narrow footpath is hemmed in by thick forests of rhododendrons,— a solid dark-green fence, broken only now and then by the blossoms of glowing crimson. But at length the topmost cairn is reached, and there lies spread out before them a vast, limitless prospect of such wild grandeur, such majestic beauty, as the eye of man may seldom look upon. Just be-side them, 2000 feet below, lies the green plain of Nuwara Eliya, a smooth-lawned valley nestled high up among the giant mountain-tops, its small lake, with smooth azure sur-face, gleaming softly in the radiant morning sunlight. On all sides rise the mighty mountains—some softly rounded and muffled deep in dark-green forests, others towering far off in rocky majesty, their solid masses transfigured and etherealised by wondrous rainbow hues — bright veils of purple sheen and floating haze of gold, and soft - blue slanting shadow. Twenty-three miles away to the south-west, towering above the nearer One Tree Hill, stands Adam's Peak, cutting the delicate sky with sharp edges of shelving rock. Southward, fourteen miles away, rises Kirigalpotta to its height of 7832 feet; south - eastward Namunakulakanda, at a distance of twenty - four miles, rears up his kingly head. Numberless other heights there are with strange, outlandish names;—a princely company clad in majestic light, lifting themselves up from shadowy depths of the jungle - forest that, one vast and billowy sea, rolls on in darkly disordered waves away and away

toward the mysterious blue of dim and infinite distance.
Only on the eastern horizon, seventy-five long miles away,
lies one radiant thread of light—the Indian Ocean's boundless plain.

Such is the view. It may be right to add that a cloud
is resting on Pedro's summit, so that of all this extended
prospect our friends see absolutely nothing.

Soon they must bid farewell to Nuwara Eliya; for Christmas Day is close at hand, and they have set their hearts on
spending it at "Nazareth," one of the most interesting Mission stations in all the South of India. On their way down
to Colombo they spend a delightful Sunday in Kandy, and
take this opportunity to attend one of the Tamil Services in
S. Stephen's Church. After the Lesson (read by a member
of the congregation) Father Barnabas moves down from the
Chancel to the Font, and there follows the Baptism of a Tamil
convert,—a lad of sixteen who has had to give up parents
and home and all worldly prospects for the sake of this good
confession. According to a Church custom among the Tamils,
a freshly-plucked rose is laid on the surface of the water.
Otherwise the Service is exactly the same as our own, and
the travellers find no difficulty in following with their English prayer-books. The worshippers, who, like their Priest,
are all barefoot—for to enter a church wearing shoes would
be the grossest irreverence—are attentive and devout; and
the singing is most hearty. The Service ends with a sermon
from Father Barnabas, delivered with so much eloquence
and such sweetness of gentle dignity that the travellers
seem to themselves to understand every word.

After the Service they are most kindly welcomed by
Father Barnabas, who speaks excellent English, and by

his wife and sons, who, understanding no European tongue,
converse in the universal language of friendly smiles and
pressings of hands and other signs of kindness. Mrs Barnabas, to do honour to the visitors, has donned her festal
Tamil robe of soft, rich, apricot - coloured silk, the colour
whereof well becomes her bronze complexion, and is relieved
by a veil of snow-white muslin wound about the head. The
beautiful wedding-necklace of gold is conspicuous, and she
weareth ear-rings and anklets, and toe-rings very many.
The travellers ask to be allowed to congratulate the newly
baptised; but he is shy and silent, and soon shrinks away
into the background, while Father Barnabas tells them many
things of Nazareth, where he himself was educated, and of
his interesting work here in Kandy.

This little scene is almost our travellers' last impression
of Ceylon. Next Friday is Christmas Day, and on the
Wednesday afternoon they embark at Colombo for Tuticorin on a certain small steamship, Amra by name, whose
vocation in life is to carry loads of Tamil coolies from
Southern India to Ceylon, and back again when they have
made their modest fortunes on the tea-estates of the island.

On the present occasion 400 coolies are returning to Tuticorin; but the English travellers see little of them, being
fenced in with a canvas screen on the little quarter-deck.
Too soon the faëry mountains of Ceylon fade away in the
distance, and the steamer is alone in a tumbling sea. Going
below is out of the question, and, mattresses being brought
on deck, our friends go into a kind of hospital ward instead.
Nominally reclining, they are in fact standing on their feet
and heads alternately; while overhead (or feet, as the case
may be) the blessed stars dance reels the long night through.
It is as when the gods and demons churned the ocean long

ago, with Mandar the King of mountains for a churn and the serpent Vasuki for a rope; when "the roaring of the ocean, whilst violently agitated with the whirling of the mountain Mandar, was like the bellowing of a mighty cloud."[1]

Good night, dear friends, good night!

[1] See the episode from the 'Mahâbhârata,' translated by Wilkins, quoted by Poley on the " Devimahatmyam."

CHAPTER III.

IT is about eleven o'clock in the morning of Christmas Even when, after some twenty-two hours' enjoyment of that rhythmic and vibratory motion which is the outcome and expression of the universal principle of polarity, our friends the travellers set foot on the much-desiderated, long-in-vain-looked-for, sometime-almost-despaired-of, now-at-length-with-rejoicing-attained-unto shore of India, whereon having landed, they find themselves too late for the morning train to Tinnevelli, and Nazareth for the present out of the question. Wherefore they reluctantly determine to spend Christmas Day in Tuticorin. Truly it is not a lovely place, nor in any respect famous except with regard to its pearl-fishery. Year by year are dragged from their peaceful homes, and in this place ruthlessly slaughtered, thousands upon thousands of unoffending oysters, of whom the greater number are altogether innocent of pearls, but must nevertheless fall victims to the grasping, undiscriminating greed of man by reason of those hypothetic pearls which they might contain, but don't.

Yet though Tuticorin, *quâ* Tuticorin, cannot honestly be called attractive, our travellers have only to take a wider view of their position in order to find themselves in one of the most interesting places of the East—to wit, in Southern India. To Christian folk the history of its extensive and prosperous Missions would alone indue it with interest enough.

From very ancient times there has been in this part of the world a Christian Church known by the title "Christians of S. Thomas," and claiming to have been founded by S. Thomas the Apostle during his visit to India. Many quaint Church legends there are concerning that same visit, all of which may be found in those Gnostic Acta Thomæ adopted by Catholic Christians in the fourth century. But forasmuch as the original is not unto every one accessible, we may be allowed, perhaps, to translate one of them here. Some there are to whom this, like all other such legends, may appear absurd, and therefore irreverent; but that is from want of education :—

The Apostles,[1] being assembled at Jerusalem, did cast lots for the regions of the earth, that each might go to that nation whither the Lord should send him; and India fell by lot to Thomas, who is also Didymus. But he would not go thither, saying, "I cannot go by reason of the weakness of the flesh; and how can I, being an Hebrew, journey to the country of the Indians and there preach the truth?"

And the Saviour appeared unto him by night and said unto him, "Fear not, Thomas, but go thou to India." But he was disobedient and said, "Send me elsewhither, for to the Indians I go not." And there chanced to be a merchant in Jerusalem whose name was Abbanes, and he was come from India, from King Gondophares, having received commandment of him to buy for him a carpenter. And the Lord met him

---

[1] Abridged from the Greek text.

as he walked at noon in the market-place, and said unto him,
"Desirest thou to buy a carpenter?" And he said, "Yea."
And the Lord said unto him, "I have a bond-servant that is
a carpenter, and I desire to sell him." And when He had so
said, He showed to him Thomas afar off. And He agreed
with him for a certain sum of silver. Then He took Thomas
and brought him to Abbanes the merchant. And Abbanes
looked upon him, and said unto him, "Is this thy master?"
And the Apostle answered and said, "Yea, He is my Lord."
And he said, "I have bought thee at His hand." And the
Apostle kept silence.

And on the next day, early in the morning, he prayed,
and said, "I go whither Thou wilt, O Lord." And he went
to Abbanes the merchant, and took nothing with him but
only the money of his price; for the Lord had given it unto
him. And they journeyed to India.

And when the Apostle came unto the cities of India with
Abbanes the merchant, Abbanes went to salute Gondophares
the King, and asked his pleasure concerning the carpenter
that he had brought with him; and the King was glad, and
commanded that the carpenter should be brought in. So,
when he was come in, the King said unto him, "What craft
understandest thou?" The Apostle said unto him, "The
carpenter's and the builder's craft." And the King said,
"Wilt thou build me a palace?" And he answered, "Yea,
I will accomplish the building thereof, for to this end
am I come."

Now the King was departing on a journey. And he gave
the Apostle much wealth, and departed. And from time to
time he sent him money and provisions and whatsoever
was requisite for himself and his workmen. But Thomas
took these things and distributed them, giving alms to

the poor and the distressed; and he brought comfort unto them.

And the King wrote and sent unto him, saying, "Tell me what thou hast done, or what things I shall send thee, or of what thou hast need." The Apostle sendeth unto him, saying, "The palace is builded, but there remaineth yet the roof thereof." And the King, when he heard that, sent unto him again gold and silver; and this also did Thomas distribute in like manner.

But when the King was returned to the city and found not the palace that should have been builded, he covered his face with his hands, and did shake his head a great while. And being very angry, he ordered both the merchant and Thomas to be bound and cast into prison. And he sought by what death he should destroy them. But when he had determined to flay them and to burn them with fire, in that same night the King's brother died. And the Angels took him and brought him up to Heaven, and showed him the places and the dwellings there, and asked him saying, "In which place wilt thou dwell?" And seeing a great and splendid palace, he said to the Angels, "I pray you, my lords, suffer me to dwell herein." But they said unto him, "Thou canst not dwell in this house, for this is thy brother's palace that was builded by Thomas the Christian." And he said, "I pray you, my lords, suffer me to go to my brother, that I may buy this palace of him." Then the Angels let his soul go; and as men were putting upon him the garment of burial, his soul came into him. And he said to the King, "I beseech thee to sell me that palace which thou hast in Heaven, that was builded for thee by the Christian that is now in the prison."

And immediately the King sent and brought out of the prison both the merchant and the Apostle. And he said unto

Thomas, "I beseech thee that thou wouldest make supplication for me and pray unto Him whose servant thou art, that He may forgive me all that I have done unto thee."

Then did the Apostle preach the truth unto the King and unto his brother, and they were converted to the truth of the Gospel.

And by reason of this legend S. Thomas is to this day represented in paintings with a carpenter's rule in his hand.

Would there were space wherein to set forth the more authentic and not less interesting doings of that later Indian Missionary, S. Francis Xavier, the "Apostle of the Indies," who in 1542-44 preached the Gospel at Goa, and to the fisherfolk on the coast, and in Travancore and elsewhere. But space we have not, and those who wish to know of him had best look him up in encyclopædias, and suchlike. Or if any have no great appetite for those dry bones, let them rather read, in Torsellino's Life [1] (published not in these matter-of-fact days, but in 1596), of his sweet, merry boyhood, and of his studious youth, and of that strange compassion for heathen India which haunted him so long; and of—— Nay, it cannot be helped, we *must* translate a little!

"For often in sleep it seemed unto Xavier that he was carrying upon his shoulders an Indian who was so heavy that he would awake from sleep exhausted by that weight. And the event afterwards showed that this thing was no freak of the mind in sleep, but rather a sign of what was to come."

For long afterwards Ignatius Loyola, his Superior, "with a cheerful countenance as his manner was, said unto him,

---

[1] 'De Vita Francisci Xaverii . . . libri sex Horatii Tursellini, e Societate Jesu,' Antuerpiæ, MDXCVI.

'Doubtless, Francis, God Himself hath intended for thee the province of India. . . . Go, follow thither His voice Who calleth thee.'

"Whereat Xavier, blushing like a maiden, and with tears of joy, replied, 'I am ready to do all things, for the sake of Christ.'"

And finally, would that we could relate the labours of that succession of modern Missionaries whose devotion has been crowned with such manifest and tangible results, and such far-reaching success, as the most unsympathetic mind can neither deny nor explain away.

But historic disquisitions must be left to mightier pens and more ambitious pages. Our task is rather to describe with faithfulness the scenes and incidents actually beheld by our travelling friends of the present day.

They take up their abode in Tuticorin at the delightfully primitive hotel, where the rain, finding its way through the interstices of the roof, obliges them to sleep under open umbrellas. The hotel is kept by some native Christians who are most anxious to please, and do all they can to make their stay a pleasant one.

The travellers attend their first Christmas Service after sunset, on the day of their arrival, in the chapel of the S.P.G. Missionary College, which bears the well-loved name of Bishop Caldwell, who founded it.[1] This College is doing an excellent work, and boasts 120 pupils, of whom 90 per cent are Christians. The standard of education is high, and students are prepared for the B.A. degree of the Madras

---

[1] All particulars of Mission-work given in this and the following chapters refer to the time of the travellers' visit (*i.e.*, Christmas 1891), unless otherwise specified.

University. There are also several outlying schools in connection therewith, bringing the total number of pupils up to nearly 700, exclusive of the boarding-school for girls, founded by Mrs Caldwell, which also has a good attendance. The boys of Caldwell College have gone home for the Christmas holidays, but there remain the members of the Tamil choir, who have been so carefully trained by the Principal[1] of the College that very few English choirs could sing more beautifully. To see the procession of Choir and Clergy entering the decorated church, while every voice joins in the most familiar of our Christmas hymns, is a strange and beautiful sight. The ordinary white cassocks have been replaced by scarlet ones in honour of the Festival, and the glowing colour brightly contrasts with the snowy surplices, and with the bare, brown feet which make not a single sound as they slowly move along. Very impressive are the quiet reverence and earnestness of the grave Tamil faces, and the devout sweetness of the singing. The procession is closed by the College Principal and a barefoot Tamil Clergyman who assists in the English Services.

At length the rainy night gives place to the warmth and light of a tropical Christmas morning. The choral Services of the English chapel begin at seven o'clock, and more beautiful or devout Christmas Services our friends have never attended.

Later on they are hospitably entertained at tiffin by the College Principal, who is also the presiding Missionary of the Tuticorin group of mission stations. The travellers have come to India with a great desire to see (among other things) something of Indian Missions; but forasmuch as to gain a general idea of those same Missions would be the work of

[1] The Rev. J. A. Sharrock, B.A., of Jesus College, Cambridge.

many winters instead of one, they will for the most part
confine themselves to visiting a few mission stations of the
Society for the Propagation of the Gospel. Working as it
does "on Church lines always, on party lines never," this
venerable Society has a very special claim on all who desire
unity for the Anglican Church both at home and abroad.
The Society disclaims any spiritual authority over its Missionaries, and any kind of interference with the rights of
Bishops abroad would be utterly contrary to its principles.
Every S.P.G. Missionary who is sent out places himself at
once under the authority and direction of the Bishop in whose
diocese he is to work, so that nothing like friction can ever
be felt between the managers of the Society at home and the
authorities of the Church abroad. This very simple and
natural rule is of the utmost importance; for the harm that
may be done by party feeling and disloyalty to Bishops
(and that in the very face of the heathen) is altogether
incalculable.

Our friends accordingly persecute their kind host with
innumerable questions, and learn much of the efficient
and prospering mission-work carried on by the S.P.G. in
Tuticorin and in twenty of the surrounding villages, and
very much, alas! about the want of men and of funds
whereby the work is sadly crippled and impeded. The
workers, including the native Clergy, are but very, very
few; but what has been achieved by their means is very
notable. All the pupils of the Mission schools receive
careful Christian instruction, and the native Christians belonging to this one Mission already number 1356.

In the afternoon our friends attend the Evensong and
Baptismal Service in the Tamil church, which is gaily
decorated in the native fashion with long, pendent garlands

of flowers. This church is the place of worship for 1000
Tamil Christians, and the congregations have been very
large to-day. The Tamils dearly love very early church-going,
and their Services began at three o'clock this morning. At
eight o'clock there was a congregation of 700, and a children's
Service was held at two. Now, at the last Service of the
day, most of the dark-brown faces look, for all their happiness, somewhat tired out. Not so, however, that of their
Priest, who receives our travellers with a kindly welcome
which is most refreshing.

The day comes to an end with English Evensong—not
Even*say*, but a beautiful Service of choral praise long to be
remembered.

S. Stephen's Day is spent by our travellers in a very
unfestival-like manner—that is, in the long journey from
Tuticorin to Tinnevelli and thence to Nazareth. As far as
Tinnevelli they travel by railway, taking eager note of their
first glimpses of South Indian landscapes. Beside the railroad
grow silver-green aloes, with here and there a great candel-
abra-like flower towering high into the air; and beyond
them stretches forth a boundless plain of soft green—wide
stretches of padi alternating with strange trees, Palmyra
palms, and feathery "umbrella-trees," and many more of
unfamiliar names.

On arriving at Tinnevelli, they are met by a very charming
greeting—a letter from the S.P.G. Missionary at Nazareth,
inviting them all to stay with him as long as they can, over
New Year's Day if possible. The delight of receiving this
kind welcome from one who is an entire stranger to them
(except that his name [1] is familiar to all who know anything
of Indian missions), can only be appreciated by those who

---

[1] Rev. A. Margöschis of S. Augustine's College, Canterbury.

have wandered about, in a homeless manner, through strange
and distant lands.   It is specially comfortable now that the
travellers are bidding farewell to all that savours of European civilisation, and intend to take up their abode in a
far-off native village.

The twenty-two miles' journey thither must be accomplished in bullock-bandies—quaint and original conveyances
wherein our travellers presently dispose themselves.   It is
now mid-day, and the bullocks—handsome and amiable
creatures with humps and soft dew-laps and sweet brown
eyes—being somewhat feeble-minded beasts, will take nine
hours to achieve the aforesaid journey.

At first the way is haunted by picturesque native figures
—men with variously coloured turbans, and women clad in
bright-hued *saris*, that most graceful of garments, which
consists of one broad length of cotton stuff twisted about
so as to envelop the whole figure.   First it passes round
the head (with one end thrown back over the shoulder),
then drapes itself in classical fashion, leaving one brown
arm free, and finally, fastened round the waist, falls to the
ankles in graceful folds.   And the colour thereof is very
commonly a deep crimson that is a feast to the eyes of
beholders.

But soon the path grows more lonely, and strikes out away
into the open country.   Bordering the red soil of the road
grow great banyan-trees, each one in itself a little forest,
with tasselled roots dangling in mid-air, or just reaching
the ground, or deeply planted therein and supporting a
straight, smooth, pillar-like stem whereon rests the parent
branch.   Hither and thither over the mighty trunks dart
numberless palm-squirrels with light-brown fur striped with
bands of black ; while in and out of the dark foliage above

flutter the bright, emerald-green parrots, filling the world with cries which here in the open air are neither harsh nor piercing, but merely sprightly and cheerful.

Beyond are broad expanses of padi, and streams, and great reservoirs of shallow water, and banana-plantations, and Palmyra palms innumerable. These last do not grow at Palmyra, and are quite unlike the date-palms of those regions. For these Palmyra palms (called by the learned *Borassus flabelliformis*) have fan-shaped leaves, and tapering stems which widen so suddenly at the base that they seem to be balanced thereon, and look like those rootless trees of our infancy which went into a box at night.

But the most interesting features of the landscape are the Hindu temples and demon-shrines and pillared manta-pams,[1] and, now and then, a native village of mud-huts thatched with palm-leaves. Slowly the afternoon goes by, and the sun sets, and the night is dark; but still the journey continues hour after hour, until it seems as if it would go on for ever and ever. But at length there breaks upon the still night-air the welcome sound of a Christian church-bell; and the next moment the travellers arrive at the Mission bungalow, and are received with the kindest and brightest of welcomes into an atmosphere of homelike rest and comfort such as words are too chilly to describe.

The next day, being not only Sunday but also the Feast of S. John, is the dedication festival of the Nazareth church, and the occasion of much rejoicing. The principal Service is at 8.30; and the travellers, coming out of their rooms into the verandah a little before that time, see a crowd of

---

[1] These buildings are "temple property," and serve as resting-places for the gods on their journeys of ceremony. Travellers also of all castes rest therein when none of their idol-majesties happens to be in possession.

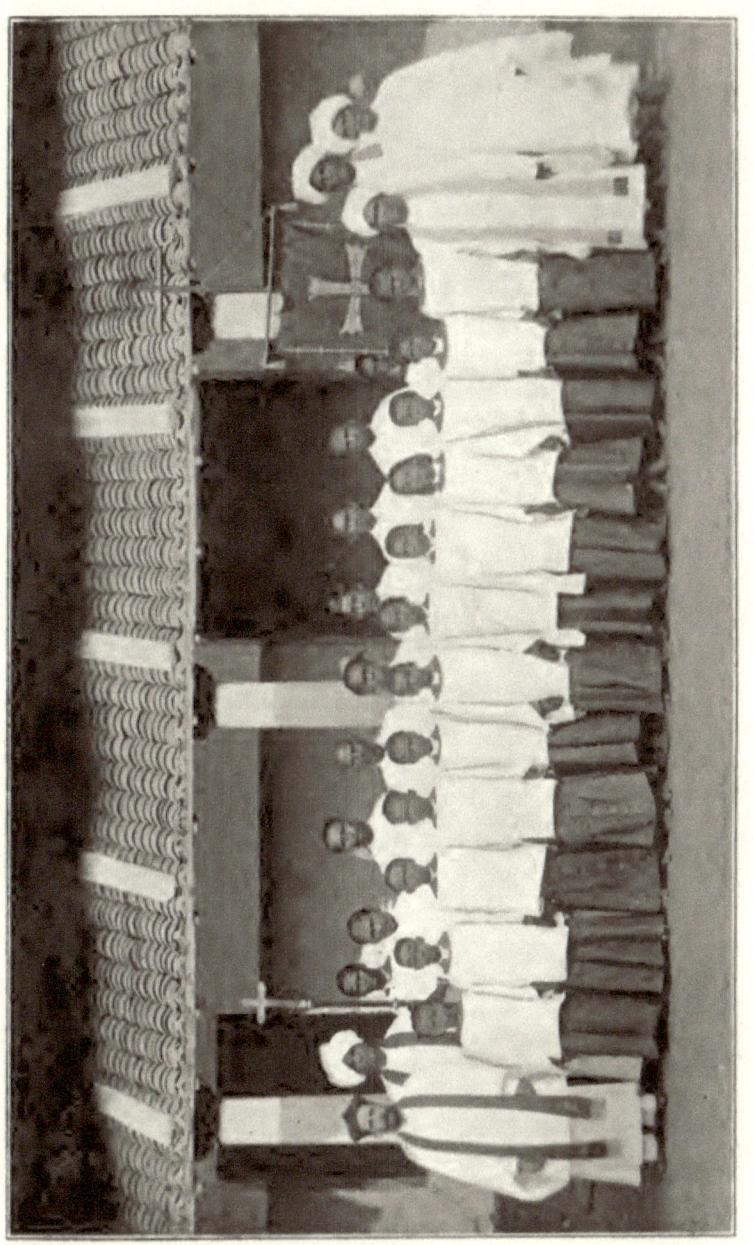

THE NAZARETH MISSIONARY, WITH FOUR NATIVE PRIESTS AND THE CHOIR OF S. JOHN'S.

dark-brown faces beaming with happiness—more than 500[1] of them. These are the pupils and teachers of the Mission schools and Orphanage.[2] The children have assembled to make their morning salutation before falling into procession and moving churchward. Each little brown hand touches the bronze-hued forehead, and there is a simultaneous cry of "Salaam! Salaam!"

Presently the procession is formed, and a beautiful procession it is. In front moves the uplifted Cross gleaming brightly in the sun; then follows the Choir, robed in white and scarlet, and chanting a Tamil hymn; and then the Tamil Clergy, the one white face contrasting strangely with all the dark-brown countenances around it. Finally, in order due, march the 500 children clad in their graceful, bright-hued garments, most of which were woven in the Industrial School hereafter to be described.

The procession moves all round the church, which is already half filled with the village-folk kneeling or sitting with quiet reverence on the stone floor, for all the Nazareth people are Christians. The church holds 1200, and, when the school-children have moved noiselessly to their places, it is quite full. All things are in festal array, and the church is profusely decorated with native garlands of sweet-scented flowers hanging down from above over the heads of the worshippers. So devout and reverent a congregation the travellers have seldom seen before. The Service is fully choral, and not one voice is silent. It is a little sad to "occupy the room of the unlearned," but the universal Giving of Thanks is the same in all languages; and it is easy to follow in the English Prayer-Book when one has once grasped

---

[1] There are 350 boarders and orphans, and 150 day-scholars.
[2] This Orphanage was the outcome of the great famine of 1877.

the fact that the Tamil version is necessarily about twice
the length of the English, from which it is translated. The
sermon is given by a very eloquent Tamil Priest, and is
listened to with a rapt attention which to behold would do
some English congregations good.

After Service the travellers return to the bungalow for
chota hazri; and there follow some delightful hours of
quiescence, during which they may revel at will among
the books of the Missionary's library. He is physician
and surgeon to his people as well as their spiritual Father;
and this explains the delightful jumble of scientific and
devotional works to be found among his books. Lives of
the Saints and Diseases of the Eye here associate on an
equal footing and in amicable contiguity, and so do many
other learned volumes not elsewhere found on terms of
intimacy.

When the heat of the day is over, the Missionary takes
his guests through the village. Although the people are
all Christians, they are very far removed from any European-
ising influences, and there is nothing on the surface to
distinguish Nazareth from a heathen village, except the
orderly cleanliness of the palm-thatched cottages, the bright,
intelligent faces of the people, the fearless happiness of the
children, and the church-tower presiding over all instead
of a Hindu temple or some sordid demon-shrine. It is
delightful to watch the beaming smiles and glad salaams
which greet the well-loved Missionary whithersoever he
goes.

The little brown boys and girls follow the visitors about,
watching them with wondering eyes of intense and insati-
able curiosity. Elizabeth, being very soft of heart where
children are concerned, presently begins to distribute sweet-

meats, to the general satisfaction. "They are so very good," she explains. "There was one tiny black boy near me in church who was too little to keep his eyes shut in the prayers, and so his brother, who was just a little bigger, put his fingers over them and kept them fast shut, *and his own too!* And just now I was going to give a sweetmeat to a child who had one already; but he shook his head, and showed me another who had none."

A large congregation assembles for Tamil Evensong, and afterwards there is a pretty scene at the Mission bungalow. The smallest of the orphan girls are admitted to be fed with bananas and generally petted. They are quite at home, and trip about over the matted floors, with their tiny bare brown feet, in a very frolicsome manner, their bright garments fluttering round them, and their lustrous black eyes overflowing with fun and happiness. The Tamils are a very handsome race, and the little girls are the prettiest of them all. The day comes to an end with English Evensong—the only English Service of the week. It is understanded by many of the people, since all the children learn English in school.

By seven o'clock next morning the church is again filled with reverently kneeling figures, and dark faces lit up with a quiet simplicity of earnestness that is very impressive. The travellers are eager to see the daily working of the Mission, and the Missionary devotes to his troublesome visitors so much time and pains that they do not know how to thank him.

He takes them first to the Dispensary, which, founded by Dr Strachan (now Bishop of Rangoon), is a great feature, of the Nazareth work, and wherein the Missionary generally spends three hours every morning prescribing for the in-

numerable patients who flock to Nazareth from far and
near. He has studied at S. George's Hospital in London,
and does all the dispensary work himself with the help
of one native assistant. During the present[1] year he has
treated the almost incredible number of 15,000 different
cases.

"There would be plenty of occupation here," says he,
"for a doctor who could give up his whole time to this
one branch of our work. The number of heathen who
are brought in this way under Christian influence is very
great indeed. At Trichendore on the coast there is a god
who passes his worst patients on to me to cure. The sick
people go to consult his oracle, and if he is puzzled what
to answer, he says, 'Go to Nazareth!' But my most serious
cases are those which have been treated already by native
doctors. When an arm has been broken, they tie it up
so tightly that gangrene sets in, so that, when the patient
comes to me, there is nothing to be done but instant am-
putation. They give the most extraordinary medicines too.
Quicksilver (in large quantities and unprepared) is a very
favourite one, and so are peacock's feathers!"

The Missionary sits at a table to receive his patients, and
presently there softly enters behind him one of the Tamil
folk with a large palm-leaf wherewith he surreptitiously fans
away the flies, very gently so that he may not know.

The patients do not understand English, and the Missionary
keeps up a running commentary upon them for the travellers'
benefit, who thus learn to distinguish the different castes,
with many other interesting matters. One of the sick folk is
a Brahman. His complexion is comparatively fair, and he
wears over his left shoulder the sacred cord which shows

[1] 1891.

that he belongs to one of the "twice-born" castes, and where-with he was solemnly invested when he was about to com-mence the study of the Vedas. The different castes, it seems, were separately created by "the truth-meditating Brahma," the "Lord of gods and creatures"; and the Brahman came forth from his mouth. His duty is threefold—liberality, study, and sacrifice. To kill a Brahman is the worst of all possible crimes, more dreadful even than the terrible sin of slaying a cow. The wise Queen Madalasa, when "with prattling words"[1] she spoke to her infant son Alarka ("as he lay on his back crying not unmelodiously"), could find no better wish for him than this, "Mayest thou meet thy death, my child, on behalf of cattle and Brahmans!"

Another patient, of lower caste, wears on his swollen leg a silver anklet which he has vowed to offer to one of the gods if he gets well. He has grown worse instead of better, and at last has come to Nazareth, where he obtains some medicine and a little quiet advice as to not applying to idol-gods in future.

A woman brings a tiny child suffering from a bad ear.

"Have you been careful," asks the Missionary, "to ram a stick well into the ear and screw it about to see what is the matter?"

"I have done so many times!" says the poor mother.

"Yes, and that is the reason why the child does not get well."

"I have to prevaricate a little," adds the Missionary in English, "or I should never be able to get at the truth!"

The more serious cases having been dealt with, the rest are left to the assistant; and the Missionary takes his guests to visit the Orphanage and schools. The threshold of one of

[1] From the 'Markandeya Purána,' translated by F. E. Pargiter, C.S.

the school-buildings is a large hewn stone. "That," says the Missionary, "was once a god. The boys think it fine fun to tread his godship under foot as they go in and out."

The teachers at Nazareth are, of course, all Tamils, and have almost all been educated at Nazareth. All of them—women as well as men—have passed the Matriculation Examination of the Madras University, and some have taken their degree. Nazareth has taken the lead in the higher education of Indian women. For seven years it has prepared its pupils for Matriculation; and teachers educated and trained at Nazareth may be found all over India in Government schools, carrying Christian influence whithersoever they go.

One of the most interesting of the Nazareth institutions is the "Art and Industrial School," wherein are most efficiently taught carpentry and blacksmith's work, tailoring, Indian and Muhammadan embroidery, weaving and lace-making, and drawing. The eleven looms of the weaving department manufacture all the clothes worn by the 350 children of the Nazareth Orphanage and Industrial and Boarding Schools. Orders are also executed for many outsiders. Moreover, the "tailoring" department is very flourishing, and each member of the church choir makes his own surplice and cassock. The pupils of the Industrial School are about 160, of whom about 50 are girls. Every one learns two trades at least. Carpentry is a great feature thereof, and the boys engaged in it can make chairs, tables, cots, desks, benches, and many other suchlike things. The present school was opened on November 14, 1887, when the Bishop and fifteen other Clergymen, English and native, together with the Nazareth Choir, entered the building in procession and held in it a Service of dedication. There seems still to linger about the place an echo of one of the prayers then used: "O Thou, who in Thy home at Nazareth didst sanctify earthly labour, grant that all these Thy children, who follow Thy holy example therein, may work with their hands the thing which is good." The motto of the school is ".Work and Pray." In 1888 the Government Inspector reported this to be " by far the best Industrial school in the division." The modest sum of £2, 10s. a-year is enough to provide for a boy or girl therein.

In the afternoon one of the teachers of the Nazareth Training School brings some of the elder girls to the Mission bungalow, and gives a model lesson in English for the travellers' benefit. The lesson is excellent, but the charming picture presented by the teacher and her pupils is more interesting still. The girls have adorned their glossy black hair with beautiful white flowers; and their pretty dark faces are beaming with intelligence and with a shy delight at the part they have to play. Their dresses are graceful as only Eastern dresses can be, and their bare brown feet peep out beneath them. But the most charming figure of all is that of the teacher. She wears a short jacket of purple silk, and soft flowing draperies of bright-coloured cotton reaching to the feet. Her intelligent face, moreover, has one of the sweetest expressions imaginable.

Shortly after the conclusion of this scene, there follows another still more strange. The travellers are standing about the room, admiring some Nazareth embroideries, when there enters a little crowd of Tamils—the chief men of the place, sent by the congregation to greet the English visitors.

" I think," says the Missionary, turning with a smile to his guests, " that they would like you to sit down."

When the visitors are duly seated in a row, one of the

Tamil folk brings forward a huge cluster of bananas, and lays it before them as a present. Then comes forth another swarthy figure laden with native garlands—thick, closely woven ropes of sweet-scented oleander-blossoms, white and pink and crimson, forming bright circles of delightful freshness, two or more whereof he suspends round the neck of each of the English folk, placing at the same time in their hands fragrant balls of snow-white blossoms. Then forth stands the oldest member of the congregation—blind and feeble, but of very kindly countenance—and makes a Tamil speech, thanking the visitors for coming to Nazareth, and offering them a very heartfelt welcome. When the Missionary has construed this little oration into English, and the Father's English reply into Tamil, he further narrates to the good Tamil folk some of his guests' former travels, and more especially their visit to that original Nazareth after which the Indian Nazareth was named. It is charming to watch the delighted interest of the good people when they hear of Jerusalem and Bethlehem and many other well-loved places.

Soon after this little ceremony, the travellers, still rejoicing in their fragrant adornments, are taken to see the school-girls' drill, and some of their very delightful games. Those which are accompanied with singing are the most attractive. Among them "Round the Mulberry-Bush" is conspicuous, but with certain unavoidable modifications, such as the banishment of "shoes" and "frosty mornings," and the introduction of Indian in the place of European customs. But far prettier than this Western importation is an exquisitely rhythmic native dance accompanied with a Tamil chant in a plaintive minor key.

After Tamil Evensong, the Choir and Native Clergy as-

THREE TAMIL GIRLS, NAZARETH.

semble in the verandah of the bungalow to say farewell
to the visitors, who, alas! are obliged to depart to-morrow
morning. The dark faces and the white and scarlet robes
make in the dim light an impressive picture, and the kind
Good-bye is very sweet indeed.

Then follows the pleasant evening meal, set out on a table
beautifully decorated (by the native servant) with flowers
and leaves, after the Tamil manner. The travellers take
this opportunity of showering all kinds of ignorant questions
on their kind host, who, with inexhaustible patience, tells
them all that is in their hearts with regard to the working of
the Nazareth Missions. He is the only white man within
twenty miles, and has under his care 12,500 native Christians, divided into seventy congregations. Six Tamil Clergymen work under him, and many Catechists; but the English
Missionary visits each congregation every quarter. The lone-
liness of this isolated position, for a mind of high cultivation,
and the terrible strain of responsibility, can only be realised
by those who know the dependence of the native character,
and the constant support required by all branches of such
work as this. It is sad to hear of the want of men and of
money which prevents the taking up of new and most hopeful work. "We are *afraid*," says the Missionary, "of the
outsiders who send asking us for Christian teaching. To
look after our own people is already almost more than we
can do."

The visitors now learn of many charming native customs,
whereof one is that of the offerings of the congregation
being made in kind. The mother of a family cooks rice
twice a-day for meals, and on these occasions she never
forgets to set apart a handful "for the Church." These
offerings are brought every month to the Mission bungalow,

and go to feed the Missionary's many orphan children, who, like all his people, always call him "Father."

But these are not the only contributions of the people, and the visitors are astonished to hear how much is done by even the poorest of the native congregations toward the support of their Clergy and churches. "Natives of India," says the Missionary, "do not believe in a religion which costs them nothing."

Another striking point in these Missions is the uncompromising manner in which are brought home to the people the responsibilities of the laity. "Evangelistic work," says the Missionary, "forms an integral part of the duty of every one who calls himself a Christian; and though most of our Christians are not qualified to 'go and teach,' yet each in his sphere can bear witness to the truth, and thus be a missionary."

Gladly, too, do the travellers hear in detail of that great Baptismal Service of a few years ago, when more than 300 converts were in one day added to the Church. Their conversion was brought about on this wise:—

The inhabitants of four hamlets not far from Nazareth were suffering from the raids of the Maravars, or thief caste, who plundered the defenceless people with the utmost cruelty. The sufferers appealed to the Missionary, who went to live with them for a week, and, by the prestige of his white face and well-known name, protected them from their foes. The impression which he then made was so great that the people asked to join the Mission, and were admitted as "hearers." After nearly two years' instruction and probation, the occasion was seized of a visit of the beloved Bishop Caldwell to make arrangements for their Baptism.

Round the foot of the rising ground whereon used to

stand the people's demon-temple runs a brook. Over this
brook was erected, as a necessary protection from the sun,
a canopy of white cloth adorned with flowers and fruit.
The Bishop, with eight other Clergy and the Nazareth Choir
in its festal robes of scarlet and white, stood beside the
water. A Tamil hymn was sung; and then, while the hundreds of worshippers knelt in silence, the Baptismal Office
began. The 303 converts (many of whom were children)
went down into the water, and were baptised. "It was
touching," says an eye-witness, from whose description our
own is borrowed, "to see the husband carefully leading his
wife down, parent lovingly holding his child, sons helping
their aged parents in. . . . Their earnestness was very
noticeable, and many uttered exclamations of thanksgiving
as they came up out of the water." "The ceremony," says
the Missionary, "took exactly an hour, and at the close the
venerable Bishop exhorted the people and gave them his
apostolic Benediction." Ninety-eight other converts, who
were unable to be present on this day, were baptised
shortly afterwards, bringing the whole number up to 401.

Our friends' last evening at Nazareth is brought to an
end by an event which, if only for the sake of its delicious
incongruity with all serious thoughts, shall be squeezed in
at the chapter's end. It seems that for months past those
boys who are advanced English scholars, and who have to
study Shakespeare for the University examinations, have
been learning "As You Like It" with a view to acting that
play at Christmas-time; and this evening has been chosen
for the long-expected representation. It takes place out of
doors, and the whole village has assembled to witness it,
sitting under the stars on the grass of the Mission compound.

The Missionary and his guests having taken their seats on chairs from the bungalow under a kind of extemporised canopy, and having been duly adorned with fresh and fragrant garlands, the proceedings begin with an exposition of the Play, given by one of the school-teachers in Tamil. This contains a summary wherein the Forest of Arden figures as "the jungle," and so forth.

Next are represented the Seven Ages of Man; and then follow scenes from the Play itself. All the actors have carefully whitened their faces and hands to a truly European complexion, and are clad in an imitation of European garments, probably sent forth by the "tailoring" department of the Industrial School. Most conspicuous of the performers is the Prompter, who, being in native costume and theoretically invisible, walks about among the actors proper, and pats the shoulder of whoever is to speak next. The action consists in sitting still on chairs or walking to and fro with the greatest rapidity, no compromise being allowed between these two extremes. All is done with the utmost solemnity, and the Play is followed by an address in English (with a somewhat strong Tamil accent) setting forth the Moral thereof. Finally the National Anthem is sung with a great deal more reverence than is generally shown in Britain.

The unwelcome morning comes too soon, and our travellers, having said Good-bye to their kind entertainer, once more dispose themselves in their bullock-bandies and set forth for Tinnevelli, attended by the salaams of the villagers whom they chance to meet by the way.

"I think," says Philippa, "that there ought to be established at Nazareth a Hospital for the treatment of those who suffer from the obscure disease of not appreciating Missions. Patients should reside there for a week or a fortnight, according to inveteracy of the malady. The course of treatment should begin with gentle walks in the Mission compound. The bright intelligence as well as the natural and healthy life of the school-children and orphans should be specially brought under their observation. Such as are convinced that Mission schools are conducted on sentimental rather than practical lines should be induced to study the sentiments of the Government Inspectors as set forth in their reports. By-and-by the patients would be strong enough for excursions to the outlying villages, and at length would be led to the discovery that the Nazareth Missionary is only one of many devoted labourers, and that the Christians in this Tinnevelli Division alone already number 150,000. When this bright side of the subject had been sufficiently impressed on their minds, they should gradually be allowed to perceive that what has been done is only a drop in the ocean of what remains, and to observe how the work is everywhere crippled for want of that sympathy and help from home on which so much depends. Their cure being completed, they should be shipped back home, and so make room for others."

This plan is eagerly discussed as the bullock-bandies jog pleasantly along through the early morning sunshine. And so Good-bye, O happy Nazareth!

CHAPTER IV.

TINNEVELLI.

Now doth it behove us to introduce one of the kindest of
our travellers' Anglo-Indian friends, the Superintendent of
Police for the district of Tinnevelli. Staying with the
Nazareth Missionary for a few days at Christmas, and thus
becoming acquainted with the wanderers, he invites them all
to his bungalow at Palamcottah, the European neighbour of
native Tinnevelli.

Hither having journeyed, they find that their kind host
has turned himself out of his own house to make room for
them, and himself intends to sleep in his travelling-tent
pitched in the garden. His guests echo with sincere gratitude that exclamation uttered long ago by the suppliant
Brahma, "This day is my very fortunate destiny in the
dwelling of assistance, and my happy fate in the abode of
friendliness."[1]

Many things do they learn from their hospitable entertainer, hearing especially of the great work done by the
Nazareth Missionary, and of his widespread influence, and of
various other such things whereof the Missionary himself is
not accustomed to speak. A great deal also do they hear

[1] From Halhed's 'Sheeve Pouran.'

about the working of the Police Department. At breakfast-time, on the morning after their arrival, come tidings of a great temple robbery; before tiffin an old lady telegraphs to say that she is to be murdered to-night; and so on.

"We have a good many burglaries," says the Superintendent; "but very often the robber and the robbed are the same individual. If you have an enemy whom you wish to get into trouble, the method is to hide some of your property in his house, to dig a hole through the mud-wall of your own, and then call in the police. Unfortunately the police always discover that the hole is wider on the inside of the wall than it is outside, and must therefore have been made from within."

Soon after their arrival our friends are taken by their host to visit the Hindu temple of Tinnevelli, a great Dravidian pagoda, the like of which they have never seen before. Notice has been given of their visit, and they are honoured with a state reception.

"I hope they do not imagine we have come to pay a state call on Siva!" exclaims the anxious-minded Sebaste.

"By no means!" is the answer. "You will not be allowed to go anywhere near the central shrine where his godship resides, and they will demand a sum of 10 rupees to pay for the purification of the temple after its profanation by our unholy Christian feet!"

Thus reassured, the travellers submit with a good grace to the ceremonious welcome prepared for them. Brahmans arrayed in white come forward and load their honoured necks with freshly woven garlands of fragrant oleander-blossoms. Limes are solemnly placed in their hands, and they are, further, sprinkled with perfume. And now ap-

proaches with lordly gait and benevolent countenance the
temple elephant, clad in scarlet, and full of conscious dignity,
yet not above being fed with limes and bananas. Like "the
noble elephant Supratika," he wears a bell which swings from
side to side and loudly rings as he walks. This personage,
having been solemnly introduced to the visitors, proceeds to
lead the way through the mazy courts of the pagoda. Next
advances a dignified company of temple Brahmans, and after
them, marching backward before the travellers, moves a band
of temple musicians loudly playing on conches and tom-toms.
Then follow the much-begarlanded visitors, and behind them
marches a row of native orderlies keeping at bay the turbaned crowd which follows with intense curiosity this solemn
oriental procession.

"Look at our host," whispered Philippa. "How submissively he wears that great garland of flowers! They say that
Greece subdued her conquerors. It looks as if India were
doing the same!"

Now doth my pen falter, and fear to approach the task
set before it; for how shall so feeble a thing trace out the
majestic lines of a South Indian pagoda? That at Tinnevelli, covering a little more than ten acres of ground, is far
from being one of the largest of Indian temples; yet as the
travellers, surrounded by their train of dark-faced attendants,
wander through its hypæthral courts and vista'd corridors of
sculptured pillars, its weird, shadowy halls, and forests of
fantastic columns, it seems to them an endless labyrinth of
mysterious and unintelligible intricacy, wherein on every
side the unfamiliar architecture is alive with grotesquely
hideous forms of gods and demons innumerable.

Wonderful is the effect on the mind of these archaic
trabeate buildings where never an arch may intrude! But

most extraordinary of all the astonishing forms are the tall *gopuras* or entrance-towers which our travellers here see for the first time, but which, at Madura and Shrirangam, will reach still grander and more imposing dimensions. Now a *gopura* is an outlandish erection of indescribable strangeness. It is as though some solemn Egyptian pylon had on a sudden grown vain and frivolous, had mounted on a rectangular pedestal, and, stretching itself up to a giddy and disproportionate height, had finally covered its attenuated figure with exuberant masses of tinted sculpture—gods and heroes and monsters piled one on the top of the other in a soaring pyramidal tower.

The Tinnevelli pagoda is a double temple dedicated to Siva and his wife Parvati, and contains a nuptial hall wherein their wedding is yearly celebrated, as well as sacred tanks on which their idol-majesties make occasional excursions by boat.

Long do the travellers wander through the labyrinthine temple buildings, now threading their way through the dim forest of the Hall of a Thousand Columns, now emerging into glowing sunlight among groves of stately palm-trees. One flourishing tree is pointed out to the visitors as having been planted by an eccentric American gentleman who felt disposed to pay a compliment to Siva, and probably cared not much for the effect of such an action on the impressionable native mind. He would have done better, the travellers fancy, if, instead of planting a palm-tree, he had followed the example of those ancient sages who "hewed down the tree of selfishness with the axe of learning, which was sharpened on the whetstone of association with the good."[1] But the task was too great

[1] From the 'Markandeya Purána,' translated by F. E. Pargiter, C.S.

E

for his hand, seeing that, beyond a doubt, "the black serpent of ignorance" had bitten him.

Nor is that calamity astonishing in such a temple as this, haunted as it is with wild superstitions which imbue the very air with an impalpable, insidious taint of all-pervading paganism. Gradually the subtle influence affects the travellers' minds, and, as they pass on their way through the pagoda's courts and halls, they begin to recall strange legends of Siva and the fair Parvati.

No venerable Aryan gods are these, for originally Siva seems to have been an obscure Turanian deity; but he grew great and powerful in India, and the conquering Vedic faith could not ignore his claims. Wherefore the Brahmans invited him to enter their complex system, and to this day Siva and Vishnu are the most popular of India's gods.

Siva, saith the Purána devoted to his glorification, "hath five heads and ten arms. He is white as crystal, and shining, dressed in clothes and chains of ornament, and having a tiger's skin." "He dwelleth on the peaks of Kailasa and Himalaya."[1] "Whatsoever is seen is all the essence of Siva. Just as fire is in all times inclosed in wood; and just as clay may be made to assume all different shapes, yet at the bottom is the same clay. Such is the nature of Siva." Nay, the very creation of the universe is in great part owing to him, for Brahma's hand "was not equal to the completion of that arduous operation," and, smitten with "heart-corroding sorrow," he "rested his forehead upon his knees and began to weep." But "Siva said, 'Let not grief and sorrow come upon thee, but assume comfort, and turn thy thoughts to the

[1] From the 'Markandeya Puràna,' translated by F. E. Pargiter, C.S.

work of creation; for I will produce the creatures into
existence, and will wipe from thy countenance the dust
of affliction.'"

Parvati, like all Hindu goddesses, represents the ener-
gising principle of her husband's power. She is the Mountain's Child, the daughter of Himalaya, the peerless goddess,
beautiful as morning, and "all who worship her obtain their
wishes." Her wedding with Siva who shall describe? For
thereat were all the gods assembled. Thither came "Brahma
mounted on his goose," with all the Sages at his stirrup;
and "Vishnu in colour like a black cloud, with his four arms
and his yellow robe, and his smiling and his eyes like the
lotus, riding in pomp and power unrivalled with all his
devotees." Thither too came Vasuki, the King of Serpents,
with other illustrious snakes "dressed in superb chains and
habits of ceremony; and the seven mothers also came to
prepare the wedding." Then did the bridegroom "set forth
in all pomp and splendour from the Mountain Kilas,"
wearing the moon for a diadem. "The old world assumed
fresh youth, and the sorrowing universe recalled its long-
forgotten happiness. . . . The rosebud of the heart was full-
blown, and the garden of the soul of the sorrowful inclosed
the shrubs of joy. The dwellers upon earth stored the
casket of their ideas with the jewels of satisfaction. . . . The
joy of those on earth ascended up to heaven, and the tree of
the bliss of those in heaven extended its twigs to the earth.
Thus Siva set forth like a garden in full blow, and Paradise
was eclipsed by his motion."

Before leaving the pagoda the travellers are permitted to
see the temple jewels, spread out for their inspection on a
crimson carpet. He who knows not India knows not what
jewels are, and of all Indian jewels these temple collections

are probably the most splendid. They are in the shape of ornaments for their idol-majesties to wear on festal occasions. The rubies and emeralds are fair to see, but more beautiful still are the long strings of pearls and the rich headpieces of gold thickly set (as the Hindu scriptures have it) " with excellent gems, and shining with the splendour of suns innumerable."

The most uncanny of the temple treasures are the steeds of silver and silver-gilt whereon ride the idols in processions of ceremony, — strange monsters with human faces and lustrous, jewelled eyes, well in keeping with the weird interior of an ancient Hindu temple. Ancient it is not very, so far as date goes, having been builded by Visvanatha in the sixteenth century; but though Hindu temples do not, like those of Egypt, date from a very remote Past, it is to be remembered that here in the far East is, in the Western acceptation of the word, no Present at all.

Emerging at length from the temple, the travellers gaze with admiring eyes at two enormous teak-wood cars whereon the deities of the pagoda make a progress through the town at the great annual festival. Each car is as large as a house, and is covered with a profusion of strange carving. Thousands of enthusiastic worshippers, when the feast comes round, drag through the streets these gigantic erections. No doubt they typify that celestial chariot of the god " which shone like gold for Siva's mounting. Instead of the right wheel was the sun, in the place of the left wheel was the moon, and the stars were distributed about it by way of ornaments. In lieu of the canopy on the top of the chariot was heaven. The four Vedas were put as horses thereto, and the setting out of the chariot one would say to be the year of twelve months gracefully moving onward."

The next day is spent by our travellers in visiting the Tinnevelli prison, and in the more cheerful occupation of examining the church and schools of the Church Missionary Society's Tinnevelli Mission. And so comes the last evening at hospitable Palamcottah.

After dinner the travellers and their kind host sit out in the garden under the bright stars, surrounded with great crotons and other hothouse plants, while all the air is full of the multitudinous sounds of a tropical night; and many stories do they hear of tigers and cobras and suchlike— creatures which seem to play the part of ghosts in Indian conversation. Presently there silently emerges into the lamplight from the surrounding darkness an Eastern figure clad in white and carrying a basket of primitive kind. No sound is made by the bare brown feet, and their owner speaks not. Taking from his basket a number of fragrant and freshly woven garlands, he hangs them round the necks of the whole party, places balls of flowers in their hands, and pours rose-water on their unresisting heads. Finally, approaching the Superintendent (who has never seen him before), he makes an humble salaam. Receiving permission to speak, he launches forth into a flowing Tamil oration, which his hearer thus briefly translates for the benefit of the guests :—

"Thou art to me as a father. All good that is mine cometh through thee. I am one who is seeking an appointment as a ship's chandler. If I might obtain from thee a recommendation,—it is to this end that I am come."

The suppliant, graciously received, is told to come again in the morning, and, having once more sprinkled the company with rose-water, departs rejoicing.

CHAPTER V.

THE CITY OF SWEETNESS.

RISING early, and driving by starlight to the station, the travellers set forth for Madura before sunrise; but soon appears "the adorable sun, in appearance ruddy as the full-blown lotus-flower,"[1] and the landscape is overflowed and overwhelmed by the universal flood of glowing Indian sunshine—no pale and colourless light as of northern countries, but a living, tangible glory of rich and dazzling gold, wherein all the world is steeped and shines transfigured. The hot hours of the morning are beguiled by the conversation of a very charming travelling companion, an English Inspectress of Schools from Travancore, who gives our travellers a lively description of that outlandish native state, where wild black leopards range abroad, with other curious beasts.

"The Maharaja," says she, "who of course belongs to the Kshatriya or warrior caste, is entirely under the influence of the Brahmans, and shows them the greatest respect. They invariably cast his horoscope, predicting the exact day of his death; and on that day he always does die without fail, often, it is suspected, with a little assistance in the way of poison. We have many strange native customs quite

---

[1] Markandeya Purána. Pargiter.

distinct from those of other states. One of them is that the ladies choose their own husbands. When a young lady has made up her mind on this point, her mother sends to the mother of the selected youth a present of rice. If this is graciously received, no objection will be made to the match; but any disparaging remark as to the quality of the rice amounts to a rejection of the proposal. All inheritance in Travancore goes in the female line, and a married woman may at any time dismiss her husband. This last is a very common practice among the heathen folk; but it is not in use among those who have been educated in our schools, for, though we are not allowed to give any definite religious teaching in school, the effect of Christian influence is very great indeed. There are in Travancore some 500,000 Christians, and the Christian ideal of morality is exercising a very marked influence among the educated Hindus."

At mid-day the travellers arrive, and take up their abode in the station-rooms, which are the best accommodation for visitors that Madura affords. The native town is large, containing about 52,000 inhabitants, and, like Tinnevelli, is the capital of a district. This district contains more than 70,000 Christians.

Historically Madura is of the utmost interest. Whether it was really founded by King Kula Sekhara, "the Ornament of the Race," three hundred years before our era, let the learned decide; but ignorant imaginations may revel at will in the shadowy scenes of the centuries that followed—those legendary days of the Pandyan dynasty, when Madura was the royal city of unpronounceable monarchs whose very names are romances. What must not life have been like in the reign, for instance, of the Race-adorning Kulab-

hushana, or of Raja Shardula, the Tiger among Kings, of
Valour-mailed or Renown-adorned, or Ripu Mardana the
Grinder of Enemies? What delight to be governed by
the Moon-crested or the Chief Gem of the Race, or by
Surabhi the Cow of Plenty!

Manifold are the bygone wonders which our friends ought
to be pondering during their stay; but the air is close and
unwholesome, and cholera is raging, nor is the town redolent
now of those ambrosial drops which fell from Siva's shaken
tresses, a fragrant shower that gladdened the dwellings of
Madhura the City of Sweetness. A thousand people have
died already of cholera, and ancient grandeur is by present
miseries very effectually eclipsed.

Nevertheless the travellers betake themselves forthwith
to sight-seeing, and first visit the great palace erected in the
seventeenth century by that majestic builder, the Maharaja
Tirumala Nayak, and of late restored by Government. An
imposing building it is, and interesting as showing the Muhammadan influence which made the civil architecture of
these Dravidian folk such an absolute contrast to that of
their temples. The grandeur, however, is sadly impaired
by the extensive use of *chunam*, a fine stucco, consisting of
shell-lime, wherewith much of the stonework is covered.
The style is Moorish, with pointed arches. Passing an ar-
caded quadrangle, the visitors reach the Celestial Pavilion, a
pillared octagon wherein Tirumala sat enthroned and held his
State receptions. It is surmounted by a great dome whereof
the interior apex is 73 feet from the pavement below. Many
other halls and chambers there are, including that great Hall
of Audience, 120 feet long and 70 feet in height, which must
have witnessed many an animated scene when thronged in
days gone by with bright-robed Eastern crowds.

From the shadowy interior of the palace it is pleasant to return to the large and sunlit quadrangle round which its halls are built, and which covers an area of over 4000 square yards. The granite pillars of its surrounding corridors would be grand and beautiful were it not for the inevitable *chunam* wherein they have foppishly arrayed themselves; as it is, the visitors turn from their glaring pretension to admire the graceful and gleeful gambols of the wild but amiable parrots to whom this court belongs. Revelling in the sunlight, their long tails floating behind them, and all their brilliant plumage gleaming in the golden light, they sweep and flutter through the air, or nestle like living emeralds in recesses of sculptured ornament. O dragging, stumbling pen of mine, would they could teach thee their hidden spring of light and rhythmic motion!

Thanks to a kind friend to whom they bear a letter from the Nazareth Missionary, the travellers in a very few days become familiar with the principal sights of the place. One of the most attractive of these is the Teppa Kulam or Sacred Tank. Such artificial lakes are throughout India greatly venerated, and their waters (whatever their physical condition) are believed to possess a power of spiritual purification. That ancient king addressed to the wise Vidura the greatest of compliments when he said, "Sages like thee, my lord, are veritable sacred tanks!"[1] The Teppa Kulam at Madura is a beautiful rectangular sheet of water about 332 yards in length and 314 yards broad. It is surrounded by a low fence of stone, which has at the corners curious groups of sculpture, and is, moreover, broken by broad flights of steps. In the centre of the lake is an island-temple, its pyramidal and richly-sculptured *vimana* rising into sun-

[1] From 'Le Bhâgavata Purâna' ... traduit ... par M. Eugène Burnouf.

light from thick and verdant foliage wherewith it brightly contrasts.

Near to the lake is the Judge's house, and in the grounds thereof grows a banyan-tree of such enormous dimensions as to look like an optical delusion. Its exact measurements at present I know not, but in 1879 its circumference was already no less than 565 feet, that of the main stem being 70 feet. To wander about under its thick foliage while the fierce Indian sun is blazing on the world without is as though one had reached, like those sages of old, "the cool, dustless, thornless grove of perfect religious knowledge!"

Besides exploring various other temples, the travellers make a long visit to the Great Pagoda of Madura, the most famous, perhaps, in all the South of India. Once more they are received by temple dignitaries and adorned with freshly woven garlands of flowers, and once more the temple elephant honours their entrance with his benign and gracious presence. Huge and dignified is he as those four gigantic elephants who support the weight of the world, by the motion of whose heads the earth doth quake. "Even as the King of Elephants, slowly he moves along."

Meanwhile a sacred temple cow, wandering at will through groves of sculptured columns, watches the visitors with a gentle consciousness of her own superior sanctity. Be it observed by the way that the Hindu veneration for cows (which carries back our travellers' imagination to Isis and ancient Egypt) is one of the oldest and most interesting of Indian superstitions, and throughout the Puranas is very prominent. "Never," exclaimed a pious king of Indian legend — "never may I entertain one thought of hatred toward Brahmans, gods, or cows!" "There is a cow, my child," said the wise Queen Madalasa, setting forth the mystical side of the subject—"there is a cow who is the support of all things. She consists of the three Vedas, her horns are pious acts, and her hair the excellent words of the good. . . . Her feet are the four castes, she is the sustenance of the worlds; being imperishable she does not wane."

Preliminaries over, the travellers plunge into the depths of the gigantic temple, which, covering fourteen acres of ground, is an intricate world of mystery, more vast and mazy than all the buildings of Dreamland.

There was, in all probability, a pagoda here as long ago as Kula Sekhara himself, but the present buildings, say the learned, date for the most part from Tirumala Nayak's days,—which is absurd, for the whole place is manifestly antediluvian. To describe it would require not a neat catalogue of architectural terms, but a profound labyrinth of unfamiliar words covering a space large enough to contain the longest and most bewildering of those old Hindu Puranas which, with their quaint similitudes and exuberant richness of imagery, their archaic form and wild grotesqueness of fantastic detail, are the only likeness I know of the great Dravidian pagodas.

The temple jewels at Madura far outshine even those of Tinnevelli. Bright gold and countless sapphires, giant pearls and brilliant rubies, all wrought with strange skill into rich ornaments of various shapes, are reverently brought out and massed together in one gleaming heap of magic treasure such as the wildest of fairy tales might hardly dare to describe. Here too are the wondrous steeds, plated with silver and gold, whereon the idols ride in high procession, curbing their spirited motions with reins of twisted pearls.

These idols are Sundareshwar and Minakshi, who are in

fact Siva and his consort, the attributes and resulting names of those worthies being practically endless. The pagoda is a double one like that at Tinnevelli, but Minakshi's part therein is smaller than that of her husband. After the exhibition of the wonderful jewels (which must be touched and handled before one can quite believe in them) the travellers wander on through courts and halls and corridors of weird architecture, vainly endeavouring to understand the labyrinthine plan of the strange and unintelligible buildings.

The wall of the second court is adorned with five *gopuras*, and the outer wall has four (one in each side of the rect-angle) of still more gigantic proportions. The tallest, though left unfinished, reaches a height of 152 feet; but such numbers do not express much, because the tapering form of *gopuras* causes them to look much higher than can be inferred from measurements. Opposite to this chief *gopura* is that famous *choultrie* or pillared hall built by Tirumala Nayak as a resting-place for Sundareshwar when he deigned to leave the central shrine of the temple and to receive in a more public place the Maharaja's devotion. A wonderful building it is, 333 feet long by 105 feet wide, and crowded, from the terrific monsters of its façade to the inmost recesses of its vista'd interior, with what is assuredly the most un-earthly sculpture that the mind of man has ever imagined.

More marvellous still, perhaps, is the Hall of a Thousand Pillars, which, forming so conspicuous a part of Dravidian padogas generally, appears at Madura in a specially beauti-ful and elaborate form—a shadowy forest of rich and fan-tastic sculpture made, it would seem, by goblin builders in far-off days of old.

Curiously beautiful also is the "Tank of the Golden Lilies," a broad, rectangular piece of water open to the sky, but surrounded with an arcade the pillars whereof are of that form so common in Indian buildings but so strange to Western eyes,—a bracketed capital, and a shaft consisting of alternate cubes and octagonal prisms. The water wherein these pillars are dimly reflected is of a green colour appalling to see, but that does not affect its spiritual quality. Such water is always cleansing, and even Krishna's lotus-feet could receive no higher praise than the epithet "pure as a sacred tank." [1]

From the south side of this graceful Teppa Kulam are visible several of the huge *gopuras*, towering up against the sky,—great mountains of tinted sculpture that one can liken to nothing, unless it be to those hymns wherewith the Puranas are adorned, and whose stately forms are so strangely builded of piled-up epithets and wild, exuberant imagery. Hence too are to be seen the *vimanas*, or towers, which surmount the central shrines, one marking the abode of Sundareshwar, the other that of Minakshi, and both covered with plates of gilded copper that reflect the blazing sunlight with gorgeous and dazzling splendour. To those inmost sanctums no Christian foot may penetrate; but the central part of the temple, being the oldest, is as usual the least splendid, and all that is most beautiful the travellers may see.

In the course of their wanderings they find themselves in the nuptial hall wherein (as at Tinnevelli) their idol-majesties celebrate their annual wedding; and in another part of the temple they come upon Sundareshwar's summer-throne

[1] Bhâgavata Purâna.

whereon, through the hottest months in the year, when his inner shrine becomes oppressive, he sits in the open air, shaded from the sun by a graceful canopy of stone, and cooled by much cold water which his attendant Brahmans pour over him continually.

It is long before the visitors can tear themselves away from this fascinating place where every step brings them to some new object of extraordinary and astonishing aspect. Philippa and Sebaste, wandering away by themselves, come suddenly on a scene so mysteriously horrible that they will long be haunted thereby. Before and above them is a grove of columns to which a flight of steps leads up, but beside the steps and beneath the pavement of the colonnade is a low door which, standing open, reveals a deep, abysmal hall whereinto no ray of daylight can ever penetrate, and which seems fit only for "night-walking goblins" to dwell in. The opaque darkness whereof it is full is made visible by the dim rays of ghastly lamps which, engulfed in the absolute blackness, show nothing else at all, unless the strange impression that the impenetrable gloom is inhabited by gliding figures arises from some faint and passing glimpse too dim for the mind to grasp. The two travellers are far from being nervous or hysterical persons, but there hangs over that abyss of darkness an unintelligible fear which there is no explaining away. Perhaps the hideous and repulsive demon-forms which swarm throughout the temple sculptures have insensibly affected their minds with a superstitious horror, or perhaps . . . But let us change the subject now.

On leaving the temple, the travellers go on to the little Anglican Church which stands in the midst of the native town, and wherein are held both English and Tamil Services. The beautifully-arranged interior is decorated with flowers in honour of the festal season, and the mighty sunshine without fills the chancel with a subdued, golden glow of soft and peaceful light;—a bright picture to be hereafter remembered as the last impression of Madura.

CHAPTER VI.

TRICHINOPOLI.

Soon the wanderers are again speeding (at the moderate rate of Indian railway trains) through the vast plains of the quiet Indian landscape, now rich with the vivid green of the padi-fields that in a few months' time will be bare and brown and dry. It is six o'clock on a Saturday night when they arrive at Trichinopoli, and are welcomed at the station by two of the kindest of all imaginable faces, whereof one belongs to the Principal[1] of the S.P.G. Trichinopoli College, and the other to dear Mrs Principal, than whom a sweeter hostess was never known on earth.

Sunday is as usual kept by the travellers as a refreshing holiday from sight-seeing and heathendom. The heat is intense, and they are glad to find that the principal Service at the English Church is at 7 A.M., followed immediately by Matins at eight, after which there is, for Europeans, no more church-going till the delicious hour of sunset. The church is blessed with very reverent Services, and is made specially sacred by the memory of the beloved Bishop Heber, who died at Trichinopoli during a visitation of the

[1] Rev. T. H. Dodson, M.A. Oxon., late Fellow and Tutor of S. Augustine's College, Canterbury.

South Indian Churches, and was buried here in S. John's Church, on the north side of the Altar. After Evensong the travellers gather round the beautiful brass which marks his resting-place, while their thoughts go back to that 3d of April 1826 which, with its earnest devotions, its hard and most honourable work, and its sudden, quiet call to rest, made so happy an ending to that noble Christian life.

Soon after sunrise next morning the travellers set forth to cultivate "impressions" of things in general. As they drive past the native houses of the town, they may watch here and there the performance of the first ceremony of the day. Before any member of a Hindu household may go to the temple for worship, the mother of the family sprinkles with water the space of ground immediately in front of the door, and marks thereon with coloured powders a geometrical pattern, executed with the greatest accuracy and neatness. This ceremony is the woman's part of the daily worship.

Passing, by the way, the large Roman Catholic Church, the sight-seers go first to the Fort-rock of military celebrity, —one of those huge, isolated masses of granite which rise abruptly from the green plains of this very flat district like rocky islands in a waveless sea. The Rock, which is 236 feet high, is ascended for the greater part by a covered way which leads the travellers past the entrance to a Siva temple which they are not allowed to enter. Close to the door thereof sits Ganesh, the father of prudence and cunning, who rideth on a mouse. King is he over the goblins of mischief, and before every undertaking must he be propitiated, that the goblins hinder it not. Though a son of Siva and Parvati, he is a horrible little dwarfish creature, with the head of a two-eyed, one-tusked elephant. Not

F

always, saith the legend, did he present so portentous an appearance, for originally he was possessed of an ordinary head of his own, which Siva, being enraged, cut off; whereupon poor Parvati, being greatly distracted in mind, began to make havoc of the universe, and threatened to bring all things to speedy destruction. "I will in no wise desist," said she, "till Ganesh my son be restored to me." Siva, his wrath being appeased, agreed thereto; but when they sought for the head of Ganesh, it could not anywhere be found. Then said Siva, "My counsel is that we take for Ganesh the head of whatsoever beast shall come hither in the morning from the land of the North." And in the morning came that way an elephant having one tooth. So the elephant's head was made fast to the shoulders of Ganesh, and Siva, by mystic *mantras* of the Vedas, did cause him to revive. And the grief of Parvati was assuaged.

At length the travellers reach the little *mandapam*, or pillared pavilion, which crowns the precipitous rock, and find their climbing well rewarded by the view which they thence obtain. A vast green plain, broken only here and there by granite rocks, stretches away to the great horizon-circle, whereof the radius may, by a simple calculation, be found to be almost twenty miles. For let h represent the height of the observer's eye, and r the radius of the earth, and x the distance from the eye to the horizon; then it is evident that $x^2 = h^2 + 2rh$, that is——

"My dear," says Philippa, sternly approaching with the inevitable guide-book, "you are not observing the features of the landscape."

And truly it is not a landscape to be neglected. Dimly seen in the eastward distance rise the Tale Malai hills, that reach, at their loftiest point, a height of 1800 feet. Other low ranges show in faintly pencilled outlines against the far-off northern sky, but the vast sweep of the horizon is scarcely broken again. Southward the beautiful Golden Rock rises from the soft, green carpet, and south-eastward of that are the French Rocks, the sight whereof carries back our travellers' imagination to those famous fightings of Chanda Sahib's days, with their glorious display of that military heroism beside which less showy virtues are all so poor and mean.

Turning northward again, our friends discover the river Kaveri, that sacred stream, the daughter of Brahma, to whose far-off source Ganges herself doth year by year resort, journeying thither through subterranean ways that she may be purified of her children's iniquities which they leave in her cleansing waters. And, sleeping in the embrace of Kaveri's encircling arm, lies Shrirangam's far-famed island, from whose dense forest-trees gleam forth the giant temple buildings.

Westward lies the old town of Wariur, and almost at the travellers' feet, beyond the line of the now demolished wall wherewith the Rock was fortified, lies the Sacred Tank, at the south-east corner whereof still stands the house of Clive.

Stretching along the southern side of the Tank stand the buildings of that great Missionary College which is so striking a feature of the work in Trichinopoli of the Society for the Propagation of the Gospel. The College and its affiliated schools contain[1] no less than 1403 pupils (the majority of whom are Brahmans); but there are many other S.P.G. schools in the surrounding villages, and the total number of pupils who are being educated by the Mission is

[1] 1892.

2020. The students of the College are prepared for the degrees of the Madras University, to which it was affiliated in 1883 as a First-Grade College. There is also at Trichinopoli a large Jesuit college; but in a city which, with its suburbs, has 90,000 inhabitants, is room and to spare for them both.

Now the great efficiency of the S.P.G. College, and all its successes in secular education, are they not written in the Government reports? But as for its moral and religious influence, it is altogether incalculable. Numbers of heathen students, attracted by the high-class secular teaching, are being brought by it under Christian influences, and the attitude toward Christianity of the educated classes of Hindus is undergoing a fundamental change full of hope for the future. Higher education the Natives of India are bent on having; and, thanks to institutions such as this College, they are gaining it to a great extent through Christian teachers,—a fact the importance whereof to the future welfare of the country it is impossible to overestimate. Hindus of the highest castes are often quite inaccessible to ordinary evangelistic mission-work, but in the colleges and high schools of the Society they are familiarised with the fundamental truths of the Faith, and are brought day by day into intimate contact with the Christian character and modes of thought in the persons of their teachers. Thus prejudice is disarmed, aspirations after higher things are awakened, and the leavening process is begun. It is that hard, quiet work of seed-time, wherewith outsiders commonly show their sympathy by asking where the sheaves are.

Descending at length from the Fort-rock, the travellers drive away in the Shrirangam direction, and, crossing the Kaveri bridge, plunge into the cool shade of the island's crowded trees. Soon they reach the outer wall of the great pagoda, which, covering an area of more than 163 acres, is by far the largest in India. The outer courts are filled with trees and native houses, and the great temple buildings, though probably none of them can boast an earlier date than A.D. 1700, look as if they grew there. The pagoda is planned in seven rectangular enclosures, one within another, with the temple proper in the centre of all; the enclosing walls being each adorned with four *gopuras*, one in the middle of each side, the size diminishing as you approach the central shrine. But the building was interrupted by the French occupation in the middle of last century, and most of the largest *gopuras* are left unfinished. A pathetic incident of the seizing of the pagoda is recorded by Crawfurd. One of the temple Brahmans, he says, addressed the intruders from the top of the great outer gateway, entreating them not to force an entrance to the sacred precinct, and when they persisted, threw himself down in despair, dashing out his brains on the pavement far below.

The Shrirangam temple is dedicated to Vishnu, who, like Siva, seems to have been originally a local god,[1] but, like him, was adopted by Brahmanism, whereby was formed the Hindu Triad, or triple manifestation of the Deity, under the attributes of Brahma the Creator, Vishnu the Preserver, and Siva the Destroyer. For what saith that holy book of the illustrious Markandeya? " The primeval all-prevading Spirit hath obtained the names of Brahma, Vishnu, and Siva. As Brahma he createth the worlds, as Siva he destroyeth them, as Vishnu he holdeth him still. Brahma is the quality of

---

[1] See 'Encyclopædia Britannica,' article "Brahmanism." The elder or Vedic Vishnu is a very different person from the Vishnu of the Puranas.

activity, Siva that of darkness; Vishnu, the lord of the world, is goodness. These are of the Self-born, the several manifestations."

In Vedic times too there was a similar triad of gods; for mythological systems, it seems (like Platonic metaphysic, and thought and speech generally), have a way of building themselves up on a triad of underlying principles,—a fact which, since it seems dimly to anticipate a great Truth of Revelation, has sadly puzzled some Christian folk, who consider not that Truth is one, or that mankind has ultimately not many lights to lighten it. Which subject (involving only the Higher Pantheism and one or two other small matters) it were scarcely fitting to treat in so profound a work as this.

Entering the pagoda, the travellers are soon absorbed in the study of Vishnu's praises as set forth in the sculptures thereof. As Siva at Madura, so Vishnu here is supreme over gods and men. He is "the most choice, the most venerable, and the immortal; than whom there is nothing more minute, than whom there is nothing more immense,— the unborn one, the root and the beginning of the worlds." "The universe exists in Vishnu: he is the cause of its continuance and cessation: he is the world."[1] "Mounted on a white elephant he rideth forth to victory;" in the universal deluge he reposeth in the depth of the waters, reclining on Sesha, the hooded snake that hath a thousand heads. The praises of Vishnu "are even as a ship on the ocean of existence; the lotus of his feet is the refuge of the soul."[2] His avatars are such as the hearing of Credulity herself may hardly receive.

[1] Vishnu Purana. . . . Translated by H. H. Wilson, M.A., F.R.S.
[2] Bhâgavata Purâna. Burnouf.

Arrived at the *gopura* in the second wall, the travellers
study, on the ceiling thereof, a painting wherein is set forth
the boar-incarnation of Vishnu, which came to pass on this
wise: There lived in ancient days one Hiranayakah, the
Giant of the Golden Eye, who, having by his austerities
gained favour with Brahma, made request for himself that
certain noxious beasts should have no power to harm him.
The names of these beasts he thereupon rehearsed, but the
hog he omitted to name. Then said Brahma, " Thy desire is
granted, O Hiranayakah." And when he had obtained this
power from Brahma, the heart of Hiranayakah waxed exceeding froward so that he wrought much evil; and in
the end he did even seize upon the Earth with his mouth,
and carry it into the sea. Now when the Earth was sunk
down into the deep waters of the sea, Vishnu came forth
from the nostrils of Brahma in the form of a little pig that
was but an inch in length; and he grew to be a mighty
boar of the stature of an elephant. " Fire flashed from his
eyes like lightning, he was radiant as the sun, and he strode
along like a powerful lion." His feet were the four Vedas,
his eyes were day and night, his joints were the different
ceremonies, his snout was the ladle of sacrifice, his mane was
all the hymns of the Vedas, and the illustrious Sages sought
shelter amongst his bristles. Then this great boar, " whose
eyes were like the lotus," did give battle to that wicked one
Hiranayakah, and for a thousand years they fought together,
and Hiranayakah was subdued.

Then said Vishnu, " Surely the Earth lies hidden within
the waters," and forthwith plunged into the ocean. " Then
the goddess Earth, beholding him thus descending, bowed in
devout adoration, and thus addressed the god: ' Hail to thee
who art all creatures! Lift me now from this place as thou

hast upraised me in days of old.' Then the mighty boar, whose roar was like the thunder," "repelled the water with its snout; and lifting out the Earth like a lotus with one of his tusks," "he set it on the top of the ocean, where it floats like a mighty vessel." [1]

On through the temple buildings wander the travellers, guided and followed by a group of intelligent, bright-eyed Brahman boys, each of whom bears on his forehead the mark which shows him to be a follower of Vishnu. This is a conventional representation of Vishnu's footprint, and consists of three perpendicular stripes of pigment, the central one red, the two others white and meeting in a white curve between the eyebrows. Followers of Siva (who constitute the other great Hindu sect) wear three horizontal white lines on forehead and breast;—a less striking badge than this of Vishnu which strangely alters the whole character of the face, and gives to the brightest countenance a look which is almost horrible.

Once more the visitors find themselves in a world of strange sculpture, wherewith their eyes grew gradually more familiar, till even those pillars of the Hall of a Thousand Columns, which consist of wildly rearing horses bearing riders on their backs and trampling with their hoofs upon the heads of rampant tigers, seem only natural and congruous among such weird surroundings. At length a point is reached than which no Christian foot may penetrate further. Here the travellers come to a stand, and gaze wistfully into the depths of dim and lamplit halls, striving if haply they may gain a glimpse of that central shrine where reign in perpetual darkness those two most honoured idols, the golden statues, adorned with splendid gems, of the

[1] Váyu Purana, quoted by H. H. Wilson.

PILLARS IN THE HALL OF A THOUSAND COLUMNS, SHRIRANGAM PAGODA.

Serpent with seven heads. But all they can see is a gulf
of dismal twilight, whence ring the wild, unholy strains of
joyless native music.

Ascending now to the temple roof, they gaze abroad at the
mighty *gopuras* and far-extending walls, and then turn their
thoughts to that famous temple of Jumbukeshwar, which,
being scarcely more than a mile distant, it assuredly behoves
them to visit before leaving the island. But "Time the destroyer that bringeth ill to all" has consumed three hours
since sunrise, and the glorious sun, in that mighty chariot of
his 9000 leagues in length, that is harnessed by the hours to
the seven steeds which are the seven metres of the Vedas, is
already high in the eastern heavens, and with his flaming
weapons striketh faintness into the hearts of all. Heat can
be easily borne by those who are strong, but tropical suns
have a mysterious power which seems to have nothing to do
with mere temperature, so that (as our travellers discovered
long ago on the Nile) one may be shivering in a cold north
wind, and yet not dare to stand in the sunshine for warmth.
Wherefore our friends creep out of the temple in a subdued and humble manner, and betake themselves home to
breakfast.

Spare days are scarce, so that ere long comes the last
evening of our travellers' stay in Trichinopoli, and their
farewell visit to those kind friends who have made that
stay so pleasant. The dinner-table is haunted by tropical
insects, who fly in at the open door from the verandah
to disport themselves in the lamplight. Each lamp has an
attendant lizard attached to it, who, when the lamp is lit,
crawls feebly forth in a thin and starving condition, and
who, at the end of the evening, having feasted on a vast

assemblage of insects, slowly returns to his home, so extremely fat that he can scarcely drag himself to bed. These apparently harmless creatures were probably human beings once, but in that former life of theirs they did not behave well. For what saith that sacred book of the great Muni, Markandeya? The man who stealeth pulse, when he next is born on earth, shall become a small house-lizard.

Meanwhile our travellers learn many things about the work in Trichinopoli of the S.P.G., and more especially about its educational aspects. Never before have they realised how comprehensive is the Society's educational method in India. Not only does it establish High Schools, Seminaries, and Colleges for the higher classes, but there are also boarding-schools for native Christians, middle-class schools, and village schools without number, not to speak of industrial schools and orphanages.

The visitors are eager to hear more of the Trichinopoli College, and their questions elicit, casually and by the way, some sad facts as to the want of proper accommodation for the rapidly expanding work and the lack of funds which cripples and impedes it, bringing on all the workers much wearing anxiety. Such things, however, are kept in the background by the kindly Principal, who, being determined to make his visitors happy, will not allow the introduction of any disheartening subjects.

"So you saw some acting at Nazareth?" says he. "Here, too, our native students are accustomed to act in the College hall the play they are preparing for examination, and on these occasions we have large audiences of the English residents and the native gentry. With regard to costume, the students have the most original ideas; chiefly they are convinced of the necessity (for whatsoever character) of a modern English suit, a walking-stick, and a pair of well-blacked English boots. Our last play was 'Julius Cæsar,' and I had the greatest difficulty in persuading Cæsar to wear anything but an English coat and trousers. The boots, too, were relinquished with the utmost reluctance, and nothing in the world would induce him to part with his walking-stick. In the middle of the play a dreadful thing happened; for Cæsar, accidentally dropping his walking-stick, quite lost his presence of mind and hastily picked it up (as is the native fashion) *with his toes!*

"Calpurnia, however, was a far stranger figure than her illustrious husband. The young man who took her part wore an unfortunately short dress, reaching only to his knees; stockings he had none, but he insisted on wearing an enormous pair of English boots. Calpurnia began by sitting on her high seat in the native manner—that is, with her feet tucked away out of sight, and nothing visible in the way of legs—but in the middle of an important speech she suddenly recollected that to sit cross-legged is not fashionable in Europe, and on a sudden there shot forth into public view two dark-brown legs terminating in black boots of the largest size imaginable.

"Another year we had 'King John,' which went off very well indeed, except for a somewhat disconcerting catastrophe at the beginning of the fourth act. Hubert and his attendant villains had never worn boots before, and did not realise that to walk in them requires practice. The consequence was that when they simultaneously rushed on the stage (each flourishing his inevitable walking-stick) they all three suddenly tumbled down together."

It is not till long afterwards that the travellers discover how much of the prosperity and efficiency of the College is owing to the indefatigable energy of the present Principal; but they gather from many accidental indications that he is greatly revered by the students.

"I get the most amusing letters from old pupils," he says, "written in very fluent English, but all showing the ineradicable native taste for high-flown language. They frequently address me as 'My Lord,' and I have lately received two exceedingly grave and respectful letters, of which one begins 'Honoured Enormity!' and the other *Spanking Sir!*'"

The travellers would gladly listen for hours to such reminiscences; but it is growing late, and if the lizards are allowed to eat any more *puchis*, they will certainly be ill. Besides, our travellers have to make an early start for Tanjor to-morrow; and so at length Good night!

CHAPTER VII.

TANJOR.

IT is eight o'clock on a glorious Indian morning when the travellers, after two hours' journey in a south-easterly direction, alight from their train at Tanjor, and are met with the kindest of welcomes by the three Missionaries who carry on the work of the Tanjor Mission of the Society for the Propagation of the Gospel. The Travellers' Bungalow not being at present available, our friends can spend only one day in Tanjor; but their kind hosts undertake that they shall have seen all the sights before they depart by the evening train for Madras.

First of all they must visit the famous pagoda, and thither they proceed forthwith. Arrived at the outer gateway, they hear within the sound of tom-toms; and a temple Brahman meets them with a request to wait till the "service" is over. This same service, as the Missionaries explain, is not the ordinary temple worship (which took place much earlier in the morning), but a movable ceremony which begins whensoever Christian visitors are seen approaching, and has been instituted with the special object of keeping them waiting a little, and thereby asserting the superior dignity of the Hindu religion. By the time our travellers have grasped this some-

what subtle point of oriental symbolism, the service is concluded, and they are allowed to enter the temple.

A beautiful pagoda it is,—no bewildering aggregation of
gradual and aimless growth, but builded (for once) on a
consistent and intelligible plan of the utmost simplicity.
Passing under the outer *gopura*, which reaches a height
of 90 feet or thereabout, the visitors follow the straight
passage which leads across the first enclosure, and, passing a second *gopura*, enter a cloistered, rectangular court
800 feet in length, and see before them the stately pile
of the temple proper, its gigantic *vimana* towering far into
the clear air,—a mighty pyramid of sculpture, 190 feet in
height.

Hitherto the sculptures have been such as belong to
Vishnu's sect of Hinduism; but the inner court belongs to
Siva, and the first object therein which the travellers come
upon is a great monolithic image of Nandi his sacred bull,
the "Sovereign of quadrupeds." Under a pillared pavilion
he reclines at ease, a majestic image 16 feet in length and
more than 12 feet high. Sleek and shining is he by reason
of the oil that is daily poured upon him; and proudly he
holds up his head, knowing himself to be no common block
of granite, but an image of miraculous qualities. In days
gone by, saith the legend, no larger was he than a man's
thumb; but slowly he grew and grew till he reached this
giant size; and thus he remaineth, waiting in dumb and
stony calm till the day be come when the British rule shall
cease in the land of India; and thereafter he will slowly
wane, and dwindle ever more and more, till he reach that
former size of his, and therein shall he continue.

But that stupendous central shrine, dating at least from
the beginning of the thirteenth century, and so grand in the

severity of its sculptured ornament,—wherewith shall I describe it? What mighty phrases, what words of ponderous dignity, should be heaped and builded together in one towering pile of massive, imperturbable solemnity, a mountain of stately eloquence!

Other small shrines there are, notably that richly decorated abode of Subrahmanya, which, later and more florid in style than the central temple, is said to be unsurpassed in all the South of India. A very estimable personage is Subrahmanya (whose name means "Good to Brahmans"), being a son of Siva, and a brother of Ganesh. Chiefly famed is he for that great battle of his with the wicked and presumptuous Tripurasura, by whose violent deeds the universe was disquieted. For ten long days they fought; and Tripurasura was subdued, and troubled the world no more. Many festivals hath Subrahmanya, for every twenty-seventh day is dedicated by his worshippers to his honour; and year by year some of his special followers take part in a very remarkable ceremony which consists in seeking out a place frequented by snakes, and there depositing for their delectation an offering of milk and eggs,—a remnant apparently of that mysterious snake-worship, of very ancient times, about which we know so little.

Having explored the pagoda, the travellers are hospitably entertained at breakfast in the Mission bungalow; and presently there enter two or three native salesmen, who, perceiving by some occult means the presence of possible buyers, have brought for their inspection some very beautiful specimens of Tanjor art-work. The most magnifical of these are certain large, round salvers of brass, richly encrusted with wondrous adornments—wilds legends of Hindu mythology, elaborately wrought in silver and copper, the two metals mingling together in the same composition with exquisite effect of contrast.

Eagerly meanwhile, and with the most unconscionable pertinacity, do the travellers catechise their kind and patient entertainers, demanding to know all imaginable details concerning this important and very interesting Mission. The Christians in the Tanjor district number more than 78,000. Of these the greater part (as in other South Indian districts) belong to the Roman Church, which has been at work in Tanjor since early in the seventeenth century, whereas the Society for the Propagation of the Gospel only began its labours here in 1825.

The most interesting feature of the S.P.G. work in Tanjor is S. Peter's College, which since 1874 has been a First-Grade College of the Madras University. The Priest[1] in charge of the Tanjor Mission is also the Principal of the College; and he delights his troublesome visitors by giving them much interesting information about mission-colleges in general, and this one in particular. One striking fact is the preference of even heathen Natives for institutions wherein secular and religious education go hand in hand, and their distrust of those purely secular Government colleges wherein the principle of religious neutrality has been pushed so far that, while the education they provide undermines the belief in Hinduism, not only is no other religion taught in its stead, but even the universal doctrines of justice and morality are sternly excluded from the curriculum. Very interesting is that report of the Educational Commission of 1883, wherein it is written: "The evidence we have taken shows that in some provinces there is a deeply-seated and widely-spread desire that culture and religion should

[1] The Rev. W. H. Blake, B.A., of Trinity College, Cambridge.

not be divorced, and that this desire is shared by some representatives of native thought in every province. In Government institutions this desire cannot be gratified."[1]

The Tanjor College is open to all castes and creeds. Of its students 75 per cent are Brahmans; other Hindus form 10 per cent, and Christians 15 per cent. The curriculum includes the subjects appointed for the examinations of the Madras University, as well as religious instruction which all the classes receive. The present number of students in the College is over 200; while the High School and Middle School attached to it bring the total number of pupils[2] up to 564.

Here, as in all the Society's schools, the principle is strictly adhered to that all pupils "should be instructed in the doctrines of Christianity, but that the privileges of the baptised should ever be kept distinctly in mind," and definitely put forward.

The Society is now at work in thirteen of the neighbouring villages, while the Tanjor College and thirteen branch schools are doing excellent mission-work on educational lines, their total number of pupils[2] being 1576. At Vediapuram, about five miles from Tanjor, the Society has a branch Mission which has two Clergy and thirteen lay agents working in eighteen villages.

Many are the incidents that might be told of such work as this, and many are the facts which might be given to illustrate the untiring energy of the workers, their anxieties and hopes and successes, and the wearisome crippling of the Society's efforts through lack of the necessary funds. Yet fear not, O my readers! Too well I know your accom-

[1] Quoted in the Classified Digest of the Records of the S.P.G., 1701-1892.
[2] In 1892.

plished minds to offer them any such mean refection of
inartistic details.

After tiffin the travellers seek the Palace of the late Raja,
the ladies hoping to obtain an interview with those secluded
Princesses, the Tanjor Ranis. The Palace (the greater part
whereof, say the learned, was built after the founding in
1675 of the Maratha dynasty of Tanjor) is inferior to that
of Madura, and has nothing to boast of but a comfortless
and sordid magnificence such as nightmares might like to
inhabit.

In one of the Palace courts the travellers encounter two
great elephants, who live herein, eating a great deal, and
costing much to keep. The Ranis ride not upon them at
all, nor ever so much as see them, yet can they nowise dis-
pense with these necessary adjuncts to the dignity of their
position. I have heard that even in Europe such private
elephants are not unknown.

In another part of the Palace the visitors come upon a
group of Pariahs, poor and wretched past all description.
They are assembled round a heap of plantain-leaves, from
which they are gathering grains of rice—the soiled remains
of a meal given to poor folk by the Ranis' munificence. The
Pariahs are of course not allowed to eat with caste-people,
and miserable indeed is their share of this oriental pauper
meal.

Arrived at the Telugu Durbar-hall, the travellers are called
upon to admire a white marble statue by Flaxman representing the Raja Sarabojee (or, more correctly, Sharfoji), the
pupil and devoted friend of Schwarz the German Missionary.
He stands with the palms of his hands together and the
fingers closed,—an attitude which, associated in Western

minds with the saying of prayers, is in India a common sign
of respectful greeting. The statue is placed on a granite
platform, the sides whereof are adorned with sculpture scenes
from those wars of Hindu gods and demons " waged in former
times for the full space of one hundred years," [1] when the
great-cheeked demons, their eyes red with wrath, furiously
fought with powerful weapons and cruel arms against the
immortals, and by their invincible arrows were eventually
pulverised.

Not far off is the large and most interesting library, containing 18,000 Sanskrit manuscripts, and many more in
other Eastern languages. Thence the visitors go on to the
Maratha Durbar-hall, wherein they behold some rich robes
belonging to the late Raja, a state haudah or elephant-saddle,
and other relics of bygone splendour.

But more beautiful than all these are the Ranis' jewels, set
forth, in another part of the Palace, before the dazzled eyes
of our English travellers. Such large and brilliant gems
they have heretofore neither seen nor imagined. The diamonds (as always in the native jewellery) are cut, not in
facets, but flat, so that they are almost devoid of brillancy ;
but the great emeralds and pearls, and above all the rubies,
are marvels of sheeny lustre. They are most wonderful ;
" in the praise thereof," [2] as the Hindu scriptures say, " the
tongue of panegyric is struck dumb, and the foot of invention
becomes lame on the plain of their encomiums."

Presently the three English ladies are summoned to the
presence of the Ranis, and forthwith plunge into the recesses
of the labyrinthine Palace. Groping their way up a dark stone
staircase, and passing sundry sordid little idols, they finally

[1] See the 'Sapta Shati,' translated by Cavali Venkat Rámasswámi.
[2] Sheeve Pouran. Halhed.

emerge on a terrace, and thence enter a dreary room where three of the nine princesses are sitting in a row ready to receive them.   There are also present two of the Ranis' nieces, young married ladies, one of whom holds a brown baby, of about eighteen months, who is dressed solely and entirely in very splendid jewels. After mutual salaams the visitors are invited to sit in an opposing row in front of the Ranis, and there follows much cheerful if not very profound conversation, carried on through a lady-interpreter.

The Ranis spare no pains to make their visitors happy, pursuing that object by feeding them with Indian sweet-meats, and finally by playing to them on an ancient instrument, of quaint device, constructed on the principle of the guitar.   After this the visitors are invited to sing, where-upon Irene rises to the occasion, and makes the echoes ring with the strains of "Home, sweet Home."   It is a strange picture, — the shadowy background of the dreary palace interior, the light faces and summer dresses of the English visitors, and, opposite to them, the dark and aged counte-nances of the sadly-robed Princesses, who listen with unre-sponsive attention to the song which they cannot understand.

At length the visitors rise to take leave, and are graci-ously dismissed with many speeches of oriental compliment. Emerging from the Palace, they betake them to the Siva-ganga Tank, a large sheet of very brown water which is specially holy, being supplied from no less a source than the far-off Ganges herself, who, saith the legend, flows to this place through a subterranean passage. It is late in the afternoon, and the softened radiance of the westering sun streams over the animated scene in a glory of glowing colour.   This is the hour of water-drawing, and long pro-cessions of dark-eyed women, with their vessels of gleaming brass, glide down to the water's edge, the members of each several caste descending by a separate staircase of stone. Many of the water-drawers are poor, but all are adorned with jewels of silver and gold, the form in which all Indian women keep their savings. Their slender, brown arms are loaded with bracelets; nose-rings, ear-rings, and necklaces abound; and even the bare feet are often adorned with elaborate toe-rings of silver, brightly contrasting with the dark-brown skin. Their richly-coloured robes are worn with a grace such as only Eastern folk can command, and their glossy black hair is crowned with freshly gathered flowers. Only here and there a girl-widow, muffled in coarse, white garments and bereft of the jewels which are a necessity of life to Indian maidens, creeps sadly down the steps and fills her jar in silence.

The travellers, as soon as they can make up their minds to turn away from the charming scene at the Tank, go to visit the now disused chapel builded by Schwarz in 1779, and chiefly remarkable for a monument of white marble erected to that Missionary's memory by his pupil and friend the Raja of Tanjor. Its sculptured relief, the work of Flaxman, represents the Raja taking leave of Schwarz, who lies on his deathbed. To Indian folk the composition must be sadly spoiled by the unfortunate blunder whereby the artist has represented the Raja as greeting the Missionary with the left hand,—a terrible insult in oriental eyes. The monument bears an inscription in English verse, the composition of the Raja himself. It is an affectionate and childlike tribute to Schwarz's memory, ending with the touching if artless lines :—

> " May I, my father, be worthy of thee,
> Wishes and prayeth thy Sarabojee."

After this the travellers repair to the Mission Church, a reverently appointed place, as mission churches ought to be, with no stagnant "week-day" atmosphere, but air kept fresh and stirring by its daily Tamil Services.

There follows a bright evening meal at the Mission bungalow; and then, through the soft starlight of an Indian night, the travellers are accompanied by their three hosts to the station, and finally, safely stowed on cushioned shelves, are whirled away to the northward, with rattling and roaring and bumping the long night through.

CHAPTER VIII.

MADRAS AND THE SEVEN PAGODAS.

THE travellers awake to find themselves nominally at
Madras, but really in an enchanted fairyland of verdure.
There are soft expanses of sunlit padi; there are thronging
trees of many kinds with graceful palms predominating;
there are sweet flowers and golden sunshine; but as for the
city, it is not easy to perceive, being so rare a substance that
it has to be taken on trust. Black Town certainly is a
fairly solid nucleus, but to find it is a matter of time.

It seems that at Christmastide Madras is full of visitors
(who seem to be mostly palm-trees), so that our friends
can find no better place of abode than the Kapper House
Hotel, a lonely and desolate mansion standing sadly on
the sea-shore three miles from everywhere. Herein they
make themselves exceedingly comfortable, though rather
pressed for room, the hotel being crowded with a large
and distinguished company of rats. These are under the
supervision of a little black-and-white kitten, who is very
nice and amiable, but is generally, in self-defence, pre-
tending to be asleep. Of course she could devour the
rats if she chose, but she refrains, from pity, believing
with Alarka, that wise King of ancient story, that "there

is not so much pain when a cat eats an unselfish sparrow or mouse"[1] as when she kills some larger creature whose self-consciousness is more highly developed. The only danger is that the rats may be of a different opinion.

The travellers are zealously waited on by the good native Manager, whose white turban is for ever roving about in search of something to please them. What pleases them most is the abundance of lovely eucharis lilies wherewith he decorates the table at meal-time. These are of no more account hereabout than the commonest flowers with us, and very refreshing it is to find them laid in fragrant masses on the table-cloth at every hour of refection.

The pleasantest apartment of the house is the broad, shaded terrace on which the upper windows open. Seated hereon the visitors can gaze forth over the sea, and listen to the never-ending thunder of the surge as the great waves of the Indian Ocean come foaming down on the sandy shore. Sometimes the desolate scene is enlivened by the lordly equipage of the Maharaja of Mysore, who is staying in Madras on a visit, and, with syces and out-riders of imposing grandeur, drives forth at evening to take the air.

There are other diversions too, for our friends make this spacious terrace their reception-room, and many are their callers — turbaned personages with dark faces and flowing robes, bringing all the riches of Indian embroidery for the visitors' gracious inspection. The embroideries are charming. There are richly worked tassoes, and soft, snowy Indian silks embroidered with delicate needlework dear to the feminine heart. Then there are wondrous squares of more gorgeous colours,—rich, mazy arabesques of gold-thread

---

[1] Markandeya Puráua. Translated by F. E. Pargiter, C.S.

mingled with delicate silks. Western minds might learn much from the study of oriental art-work. How different from these Indian embroideries are our prim, conventional designs that one sees to the end of at the first glance and tires of at the second,—which lead on to nothing, which have nothing to hide! How mean and vulgar they look to eyes that have but once lost themselves among the labyrinthine traceries of form, the dazzling harmonies of colour, that these Eastern workers delight in! Here is intricacy without confusion; mystery without vagueness; exuberant wealth of fancy with exquisite purity of outline; buoyant freedom and absolute harmony; fanciful elaboration of ornament and vital unity of design.

At first the travellers, dazzled by these magic splendours, are almost afraid to make any purchases lest they should prove but faëry treasure, and, when brought beneath the grey skies of the North, should suddenly turn to tinsel. But this is a groundless fear. Rich and beautiful as the embroideries look in the glowing light of India, they will be far more resplendent and more to be marvelled at when set in the subdued colouring of dull and cloudy England.

Perhaps the most beautiful of the Madras embroideries is that which consists of richly massed and delicately wrought gold arabesques wherein are skilfully set sheeny beetles' wings of an intensely lustrous green, shading off into red when the light changes. These jewel-wings give wonderful definiteness and life to the whole, the green and the gold contrast delightfully, and the design is a very charming one from every point of view—except perhaps the beetles'. Here and there, no doubt, some exceptional and high-souled beetle might be willing to shorten his life for the sake of becoming part of a long-lived work of art; but with the ordinary run

of beetles — the kind of beetles one meets every day — I
believe that such an ambition would have but little weight;
and the question arises, whether there is not an inalienable
right appertaining to beetles and others——

"My dear," says Irene soothingly, "here is an amiable
juggler come to entertain us."

He is a Maratha, and comes from Mysore. His swarthy
countenance is more wily and secret than any one's face can
be who is not a juggler. His skill is something frightful.
European conjurers might perform tricks resembling his;
but then they stand on platforms, with tables in front of
them. This personage (after a humble salaam) seats himself
on the pavement at the very feet of the travellers, who, lean
over him as they will, and watch him as closely as they can,
may never penetrate the mystery. Can he have cast a
"glamour" in their eyes?

There are many strange things in India, and the jugglers
are one of them. It is very easy to explain the basket-trick
—for those who have not seen it; but those who have are
fairly puzzled. A story is told of two gentlemen—an Englishman and an American—who once determined to solve the
mystery. One of them, being an artist, took sketches of the
several stages of that performance; the other took photographs. On comparing notes afterwards, the artist was
found to have clear representations of the events seen;
but of these the plates of the photographer showed nothing.
This is interesting. Unfortunately the extremely dogmatic
"theosophist" tract wherein this story is set forth does not
make it quite clear whether the photographs showed nothing
at all, or only nothing remarkable. In the former case it is
just conceivable that there may have been something wrong
with the camera.

Now doth it behove us to conduct our readers to visit the public buildings of Madras, and to give them by the way an accurate and exhaustive account thereof. We should discourse, for instance, about the palace of the Nawab of the Carnatic, Government House, and the Fort; and about that towering lighthouse 125 feet high, with its brilliant light visible fifteen miles from land. But public buildings are toilsome things, and there are sunstrokes and mosquitoes about.

It behoves us also to give a condensed and masterly sketch of the city's history. We should begin with its foundation in 1639, and plod conscientiously through the years down to the present time. But it is too hot for history.

Something vague and legendary, perhaps, would be more refreshing. Let us betake ourselves to that quarter of Madras which is called St Thomé, and seek out the traditional scene of S. Thomas's martyrdom. This is an eminence known as the Mount, and crowned with a church. The "Mailapur" of the martyrdom of S. Thomas has been with great probability identified with Mihilapur, which is St Thomé.

Now the death of the Apostle came to pass, saith the legend, on this wise:—

The blessed Thomas preached the Gospel in the city of King Misdaios, and many women believed; and Tertia also, the King's sister, was converted unto the truth. Then the King was angry, and commanded that Thomas should be cast into prison. "And the Apostle,[1] when he had broken the Bread and given thanks, gave it to Ouazanes and to Tertia and Mnesara, and to the wife and the daughter of

---

[1] Abridged from the Greek text.

Siphoros, saying, 'May this Eucharist be unto you for salvation and joy, and the health of your souls.' And they said, 'Amen.' And there was heard a Voice saying, 'Amen. Fear ye not, only believe.' And the Apostle, when he had so done, went away with joy into the prison. . . .

"And Misdaios sent for the Apostle Thomas and set him before him; and he asked him, saying, 'Art thou a bond-servant or free?' 'I am a bond-servant,' said he, 'of one only Master over whom thou hast no authority.' And Misdaios said unto him, 'Hast thou fled from thy master, that thou art come hither?' But Thomas said, 'I was sold of my Lord into this land, that I might save many, and by thy hands depart from this world.' And when the Apostle had so said, Misdaios sought how he might slay him. . . . He took him therefore and went out of the city, and there went also with him armed soldiers. And when they had walked one mile, he delivered him unto four soldiers and one officer, and commanded that they should bring him unto the mount, and slay him with their spears, and so return back unto the city. And when he had so commanded the soldiers, he also departed into the city.

"And when Thomas was come up into the mount, to the place wherein he should be slain, he spake and said unto those that held him and to the rest, 'Brethren, hearken ye unto me at this time also, even now at the end. For I stand at the point of the going out from the body. Let not therefore the eyes of your heart be blinded, neither let your ears be made deaf. Believe in God Whom I preach, and be not guides unto yourselves in the hardness of your hearts.' . . .

"Then the blessed Thomas went apart to pray; and when he had kneeled down, he afterward arose and stretched forth his hands toward heaven, and spake these words :—

"'My Lord and my God, my hope and my confidence, and my Teacher who givest me boldness, Thou wilt be with me even unto the end. . . . Thou hast made me to hunger in this world, O Lord, and hast filled me with the true riches. . . . Let not the seed of the corn that I have sown be destroyed from out Thy field. Let not the enemy, with his tares, catch it away. . . . Thy vine have I planted in the earth; she hath sent down her roots to the depth, her shooting forth on high is spread abroad, and her fruit is upon the earth. . . . Grant unto me therefore, O Lord, that in quietness I may pass hence, and that in joy and peace I may ascend and stand before my Judge. But the evil one, the Accuser, let him not behold me. Let his eyes be blinded through Thy light which Thou hast made to abide in me.' . . .

"And when he had thus prayed, he said unto the soldiers, 'Come ye, fulfil the bidding of him that commanded you.' And the four men came near, and pierced him with their swords; so he fell down, and died. Then all the brethren wept; and they brought goodly raiment and much fair linen, and they buried him in a royal tomb wherein the former kings were laid.

"Now the Apostle Thomas, when he was departing from the world, had made Siphor a Presbyter, and Iouzanes a Deacon.

"And it came to pass, after many days, that one of the children of Misdaios the King was smitten by a demon, and no man was able to heal him, for the demon was very grievous. Then Misdaios considered the matter, and said,

'I will depart and open the tomb, and when I have taken up one of the bones of the Apostle of God, I will hang it upon my son, and he shall be healed.'

"So Misdaios departed to the sepulchre of the holy Apostle; but when he had opened the tomb he found not the Apostle there, for one of the brethren had taken him away by stealth and carried him to Mesopotamia.

"Then did Misdaios take dust from the place where the body of the Apostle had lain, and he put it upon his son, saying, 'I believe in Thee, Jesus Christ, through Thine Apostle Thomas, and with undoubting faith I confess the Father, the Son, and the Holy Spirit.' And when he had so spoken he put the dust about the neck of his child. And immediately the child was made whole. So Misdaios also, the King, was joined with the other brethren, and he bowed the head beneath the hands of Siphor. Then said Siphor unto the brethren, 'Pray ye for Misdaios the King, that he may obtain mercy, and that his sins be forgiven him.' They all therefore rejoiced with one accord, and offered prayers in his behalf. And the Lord Who loveth mankind, the King of kings, gave unto Misdaios also hope toward Himself, and joined him unto the company of those that had believed on Christ, giving praise to the Father, Son, and Holy Spirit, to Whom belong power and worship now and always and even for ever and ever. Amen."

The Apostle is said to have suffered martyrdom in the year of our Lord 68, on the 21st of December, the day which we still keep holy as the Feast of S. Thomas. For the fact that he visited India we have very ancient authority;—it is referred to by Abdias at the end of the first century, and S. Jerome gives the name of the town where he died—but how

far we may trust the legendary details of his work I will not
undertake to decide, preferring rather to contemplate the
undoubted and very tangible facts of Christian Church-work
in Madras at the present day.   There is a very special
reality about the Anglican Cathedral with its bright and
beautiful Services, and about other churches too.   There are
schools and orphanages and other useful institutions. Good
work is being done here by the Society for Promoting
Christian Knowledge; and the Society for the Propagation
of the Gospel is likewise hard at work, one of the most
interesting features of its operations being the Theological
College in Sullivan's Gardens.   This was opened in July
1848, so that it is coeval with S. Augustine's, Canterbury.
It is doing a most useful and very necessary work in training
native Catechists, and candidates for Holy Orders.   A large
number of the Native Clergy working in the South of India
have received in this College their theological training.
Only matriculates of the Madras University are received as
students, and the theological course takes three years, at the
end of which time students are presented for the Oxford and
Cambridge Universities' Preliminary Examination of candidates for Holy Orders.   In this examination native students
of the College have for ten years past taken honourable
places.   In 1886 its candidates were more successful therein
than any corresponding body of men from any other institution.   The S.P.C.K. assists the College with an annual grant
of Rs. 1080.   The Church Missionary Society also has a
Divinity School in Madras.

From the standpoint of this cathedral city the travellers
look abroad over the Diocese ; but so wide a panorama, com-
prising so many centres of Roman and Anglican Church-
work, is at first confusing to the mental eyes, and our friends

choose out for special study only the branches supported by
that great Missionary Society whose methods, as aforesaid,
they have learned to regard with special confidence and
sympathy. As long ago as 1881, the Society for the Propagation of the Gospel had in its schools (which are under
Government inspection) no less than 13,207 pupils, of whom
3598 were girls; and since those days the work, though
short-handed and further crippled for want of funds, has
gone on and prospered. The aim of the Society is here, as
everywhere, to establish a Native Church which in due time
shall be capable of standing alone. The educational method,
though so important an instrument, has never been independent of evangelistic work, and from the beginning the
school and the congregation have been developed side by
side. In about 1000 towns and villages of the Diocese the
Society has established congregations of native Christians;
the number of baptised Christians in these missions was, in
1881, 37,706, and the number of catechumens 20,083.

The C.M.S. is also hard at work, and in the Madras Presidency (including Haiderabad and the other Native States)
the total number of Christians, Catholic and sectarian, is[1]
1,642,030.

But our travellers begin to grow weary of Madras, and
nothing will serve but a romantic expedition to the rock-
temples of Mavalivaram, otherwise known as the Seven
Pagodas. Archæologically this is doubtless the most interesting place in Southern India; its rock-hewn temples
are the earliest examples we have of Dravidian art, seeing
that before them wooden architecture alone was known in
the South;—and the delightful part of it is that the place is

[1] 1892.

thirty miles from Madras, and that there is no road to it. It can be reached only by means of the East Coast Canal, and the journey is best made by night.

The requisite preparations are intrusted by our friends to one Chinasami, a darkly handsome personage, arrayed in white and red. His snowy turban becomingly frames a countenance of like colour with an ancient copper coin, and possessed of a pair of large, lustrous black eyes full of quick and wary intelligence.

It is eight o'clock in the most lovely of all imaginable nights when the travellers drive forth into the moonlight to begin the journey. The first six miles thereof may be accomplished in a carriage, and a wonderful drive it is. The cool-rayed moon (as the Hindu scriptures call her) is shining as she never shines outside the tropics. Brilliant and lovely is she as when long since (so the Indian legends tell) she first rose, from out the sea of milk, "with a pleasing countenance, shining with ten thousand beams of gentle light."[1] Wonderful are the effects of light and shadow as the magic glory falls on the clustering palm-trees, glancing on the smooth curves of the drooping leaves till all their delicate lines shine out in radiant pencillings of silver.

Yet even such moonlight as this can scarcely dim the lamps of the stars shining out from the deep blue of the night-sky in sparkling multitudes, even as they shone in the eyes of that Indian poet long ago who sang of blessed Suka, the princely sage, "greater than the greatest of men,"[2] shining forth in the midst of the other sages, "even as the

---

[1] Wilkins, 'Episode from the Mahâbhârata,' quoted by Poley on the "Devîmahatmyam."

[2] From 'Le Bhâgavata Purâna ou histoire poétique de Krichna,' traduit et publié par M. Eugène Burnouf. Paris, MDCCCXL.

divine orb of the moon shines forth surrounded with her train of planets, with constellations, and with stars."

The air is soft and sweet, and the deep silence is broken only by the shrill, musical chant of the syces, as they cry in a monotonous, ever-repeated cadence to warn all way-farers that a carriage is approaching. It is a pity that such a drive should ever come to an end; but end it does at length by the moonlit waters of the canal, whereon floats a native boat stored with the necessary provisions, and attended by the dark figures of the coolies who are to tow it through the night. Under an arched covering thatched with palm-leaves the requisite number of mat-tresses have been placed in a row. Hereon the travellers recline, shaded from the dangerous moonlight, but enjoying, at each end of their shelter, a wonderful view of deep-blue, starry sky. The boat glides smoothly on its way, the lapping water makes soothing music in the stillness, and every one falls asleep.

The awakening is a merry one. The night has suddenly departed, and all the world is aglow with sunshine. Why did that wise Queen Madalasa say that a man "should not gaze up at the orb of the sun at sunrise or at sunset"? Assuredly one cannot do so at any other times,—leastwise in India. But there is not much leisure for gazing at present, for, while the boat still glides over the smooth waters, Chinasami, in that small space allotted to him and the chickens in the bow of the boat, is diligently preparing *chota hazri*, which he presently serves up with the utmost solemnity; and scarcely is this ceremony concluded when the travellers find themselves at the end of their journey.

It is a strange place. There are palm-trees, and there is smooth, green grass, whereon are scattered great fantastic boulders of grey granite, which are just the right material for rock-temples.   Leaving their provisions at the travellers' bungalow, the visitors set forth to enjoy a delightful day of archæologic study.   They speedily find themselves in the fifth or sixth century of our era, and surrounded with beautiful little shrines and temples hewn out of the living rock and adorned with sculpture-figures of real artistic merit, contrasting strangely with the degraded Indian art of the present day.   Such are the oldest works; but there are others of somewhat later date already showing the hideous coarseness wherewith anything connected with Hinduism inevitably becomes infected.

Our friends first make their way to the temple by the sea-shore, probably the oldest structural temple of the Dravidian style that we know.   It stands on the very brink of the sea, which seems to have much encroached since it was builded.   The surf beats on it now with increasing violence, and is slowly defacing the sculptures thereof.   The legends tell of a whole city, once great and populous, but now lying silent and forgotten beneath the relentless waves.

These lonely temples are all deserted now; there is no one to defend them from the profanation of Christian feet; and the travellers may wander at will through the ancient chambers, even to that dark and innermost cell once so jealously guarded with fear and awful mystery.   This shore-temple was dedicated originally to one Maha Bali (whom our friends will presently meet with again); but he was not allowed undisputed possession of his domicile, and the travellers, on entering the northern porch, find themselves confronted with Siva and Parvati carved on the wall in high relief.   They are old acquaintances now: like the pious Nared of old, the travellers have already given ear "to the history of Siva's origin and of his marriage with Parvati, as delivered oftentimes by the learned Sages."[1] They have heard tell of "the splendour of his essence which is exempt from all the accidents of darkness and light, of heat and cold, of beginning and ending;" and the legend hath been told them of how it was he who first brought this perishable world from the "closet of invisibility," from the "veil of nonentity," and made it to appear at length "on the theatre of manifestation." Wherefore these "wanderers in the path of novelty" pass him by, to seek in the inner chambers of the temple for less familiar deities.

But they find them not. Only in the western vestibule reclines the "pre-eminent Vishnu," "the universal soul, the immeasurable, the eternal, the changeless." He is 10 feet 10 inches long. Of old he was approached, no doubt, by crowds of eager worshippers, crying as they came into his presence, "Om! Reverence to the adorable Vishnu!" but now he lies alone in the dark, while the passing centuries heed him not.

Not far from the temple the lord Vishnu appears again in the form of a tall, rock-hewn figure with the head of a bull and an amiable expression of countenance.

Thence the travellers wander on from one old, rock-hewn shrine to another,—small but beautiful temples cut from the hard granite in the archaic forms of trabeate architecture, designed with an exquisite sense of proportion, and showing in each laboured line a wonderful exactness and finish. Especially light and graceful are the curious pillars, whereof the lower part of the shaft consists, in many cases, of a conventional but terrific lion seated on his haunches and grinning horribly, with gigantic ears and wildly curling

[1] Sheeve Pouran. Halhed.

tail. These amiable beasts (evidently, say the learned, of wooden origin) are specially interesting as being characteristic of the Seven Pagodas, but found nowhere else in India.

Then the visitors make their way to the modern Brahman village, with its palm-thatched huts, and its palm-surrounded temple dating probably from the twelfth or thirteenth century. Not far off is a melancholy group of rock-cut figures representing the goddess Durga with seven attendant maidens. This same Durga, it seems, is but another form of Parvati, the wife of Siva and the active manifestation of his power,—the goddess "who resides in all the world as a form of effulgence,"[1] "the remover of difficult limits," "the ample, the mild, and the austere."

The next piece of sculpture which the travellers meet with is a rock-cut family group of three very charming monkeys. The father-monkey is searching with the utmost solicitude in Mrs Monkey's fur, while she, in her turn, is tenderly nursing the baby. The execution is delightfully natural, and it is hard to believe that so many centuries have passed since those monkey worthies sat for their life-like portraits.

As soon as they can make up their minds to part from this amiable family, our friends wander away to the sacred tank, with its quaint little *mandapam* in the centre reflected in the smooth water; and thence they go in search of the most extraordinary piece of sculpture that Mavalivaram can boast of—the great scene popularly supposed to represent the Penance of the heroic and mythic Arjuna. It is carved in high relief on the face of a rock 43 feet high and 96 feet long; and it is a wonder to behold. It contains a multitude

[1] From the 'Sapta-Shati, or Chandi-Pat,' translated by Cavali Venkat Rámasswámi, Pandit.

of figures, most of them fully life-size,—men and gods, a snake-deity and his wife, harpies, elephants, lions, deer, monkeys, cocks, and so forth. Three elephant-cubs are specially attractive. The so-called Arjuna himself, that illustrious ascetic, father of Pandu and ancestor of all the Pandyan kings, is a prominent and impressive figure. He is represented as employing himself in religious austerities and "performing exceeding adoration." With arms extended above his head he standeth continually on the great toe of his left foot. So extreme is his leanness that all may see how he hath "tormented his existence with a variety of mortifications."

If there is one thing that Hindu gods cannot in any wise resist, it is the cumulative effect of self-inflicted austerities in those who worship them,—witness the case of those three sons of Tareke who thus conciliated Brahma: "Standing[1] for an hundred years upon one foot they continued absorbed in prayer; for a thousand years they subsisted altogether upon air; . . . for yet another hundred years they stood with their arms lifted up to heaven. So, when their devotion had thus exceeded all limits," they obtained the goodwill of Brahma, "the cloud of mercy was full distended, and the sea of benevolence overflowed its banks."

Even so did Arjuna, the friend of the "Blessed Krishna," conciliate Siva, so that when Muki, that wicked demon, came in the form of a boar to hinder the ascetic's devotion, the mighty deity went forth against him, and did shoot at that boar with arrows until he miserably died.

"Very pretty, no doubt," says Philippa, dryly; "but, as a matter of fact, that good ascetic up there has only in modern times acquired the name of Arjuna."

[1] Sheeve Pouran. Halhed.

"Philippa, that is too bad! It is of no use trying to tell romantic legends if you knock them on the head in that way!"

"Perhaps," says Irene, cheerfully, "she has something better to tell us instead. Give us a lecture on archæology, Philippa, and see if you can make us understand what this extraordinary scene is about."

"It is about serpent-worship, my dears,—that ancient *naga*-religion of prehistoric times which meets us in so strange and unexpected a fashion in the study of Indian art. Please to observe how the strange and crowded figures in this scene are engaged in worshipping that great *naga*-king in the middle, who rejoices in a snaky tail, and whose head-dress is formed of the hoods of a seven-headed cobra. The lady beneath him is his wife; and she also ends in a serpent-tail, but her head is canopied by three cobra-heads instead of seven. Now the important point to notice——"

"But, Philippa, dear, it is so hot! May we not leave the sculpture now, and explore that old cave-temple near it? See how cool and inviting it looks, and what a delicious shelter it will give from this terrible glare outside."

The temple is hewn into the rock to a depth of 40 feet. Its façade is about 50 feet long, and very impressive are the weird lion-pillars standing out, row behind row, against a background of mysterious darkness. The travellers wonderingly explore the shadowy interior, and then, emerging again into the light, seek out the neighbouring Varaswami Mandapam, the "Temple of my Lord the Boar."

Herein are two scenes carved in relief, of which one represents the Varaha or Boar-incarnation of Vishnu, wherein, as we have already set forth, he once saved the Earth from the abyss of waters. Long ago was that story

told by those four learned birds, even "Pingáksha and
Vibodha and Supatra and Sumukha, the sons of Drona,
the noblest of birds," who "dwell in the Vindhya range,
in a cave of the noble mountain, where the water is very
sacred, with their minds subdued." And "they all addressed
Jaimini the disciple of Vyása, resting himself, with his
fatigue mitigated by the breeze from their wings." And
the birds spake, and said, "This is the third form of
Vishnu, which is assiduously intent on the preservation of
creatures; it destroys the haughty demons, the exterminators
of righteousness. . . . Whensoever, O Jaimini, the wane
of righteousness occurs and the rise of iniquity, then it
creates itself."

It is represented here as a human figure with a boar's
head. In its company is Lakshmi, Vishnu's bride, the
goddess of beauty and good fortune. Indispensable is she
to his working and his power. For what said the sage
Parasara to Maitreya the best of Brahmans? "The bride
of Vishnu is the mother of the world; . . . Vishnu is meaning, she is speech; . . . he is righteousness, she is devotion;
he is the creator, she is creation; . . . Vishnu is the personi-
fied Sáma veda, the goddess lotus-throned is the tone of
its chanting. Vishnu is the moon, she is his unfading
light; . . . he is the ocean, Lakshmi its shore; . . . she
is the creeping vine, and Vishnu the tree round which it
clings."[1]

The other scene represents the Dwarf Avatar, that fifth
form of Vishnu which he assumed on this wise:—

There lived of old a mighty King whose name was Maha
Bali; and he was puffed up with pride and neglected the
offerings of the gods. Then came Vishnu unto him as it

---

[1] From the 'Vishnu Purana,' translated by H. H. Wilson, M.A., F.R.S.

had been a dwarf, small of stature, and very contemptible to look upon. And Maha Bali said unto him, "Come, tell me what gift I shall bestow on thee!" Then Vishnu made humble petition, and said unto him, "I pray thee that thou wouldest give me so much land as I can pass over with three steps." Then Maha Bali laughed aloud, and said, "Thou shouldest have asked some greater thing." But Vishnu answered and said, "Thus much sufficeth for thy servant. I pray thee therefore that thou wilt swear to give it unto me, and that in ratification thereof thou wilt here pour water on mine hand." And lo! as the water touched his hand, the dwarf began to grow; and he became very tall and mighty, so that at the first stride he covered the earth, and at the second stride he covered the heavens, and at the third he would have taken unto himself the nether world also, but being compassionate he thrust Maha Bali down thither with his foot, and hath suffered him to reign therein even unto this present day.

This legend dates from ancient Vedic times, and some perceive therein a mystic signification, saying that Vishnu is none other than the sun, and that those three great strides of his symbolise the sun's three stations at his rising, his noon, and his setting.

The travellers have much more to see; but at this point of their wanderings the heat of the sun becomes overwhelming, and they are fain to creep back to the travellers' bungalow to rest and eat tiffin. They find there a compatriot who has come, like themselves, for a day's archæological sight-seeing. Fresh from an important Native State, he has many strange things to tell.

"Our last Maharaja," says he, "had not an exalted idea

of British dignity. The English Resident, when he called at the palace, was obliged to enter barefoot, and had a delightful experience of oriental politeness. The Maharaja, with his attendants, would enter the room in which he was waiting, and, seating himself as though no one were there, would take no notice of him for several minutes. Then he would ask three questions: 'How is my sister the Queen of England? How is my brother the Prince of Wales? Are you and your wife in good health?' These questions having been answered, the mighty despot would rise to his feet, whereupon the Resident was instantly hustled out of his presence. This was endured until the old Maharaja died. On the accession of the new one, the Resident caused great excitement by entering his presence with his boots on. Happily this new prince is only a child, and can be taught better manners."

At length the hottest hours are over, and our friends set forth again, and betake them to that interesting group of rock-temples, commonly called the "Raths," an assemblage of five small shrines guarded by a large elephant and a terrific lion, both hewn, like the temples, from the living granite-rock.

Of all the works at Mavalivaram these are the oldest; and nothing in the place can compare with this little group of temples for architectural interest. Herein, as Dr Fergusson has taught us, we seem to have the germ whence Dravidian architecture sprang, and a key to its intricate 'problems. Hinduism is the religion set forth in the sculpture of these rock-hewn shrines; but their forms are undoubtedly Buddhist, wherefore we know (or at least Dr Fergusson does) that their authors must

THE RATHS AT THE SEVEN PAGODAS.

have migrated hither from the Buddhist regions of the
North. Two of the Raths are rock-cut copies of Buddhist
viharas or monasteries, and these are the rudimentary
beginning of all the stately *vimanas* wherein South Indian
pagodas rejoice. To this day, it would seem, the Southern
Hindus are building temples of Siva and Vishnu, towering piles on whose terraces may still be traced the forms
which, long centuries ago in the distant North, were the
cells of Buddhist monks. Other two of the Raths are of
oblong shape. These, it seems, are copies of ancient Buddhist temples, and from them have sprung to their giddy
height the lofty Dravidian *gopuras*. One of these oblong
Raths is specially interesting as showing the disastrous results of exactly copying in solid rock the form of a wooden
original. The interior is only partially excavated, the work
having been interrupted, apparently, by the settling of the
massive roof, whose enormous weight the slender supporting pillars found themselves unable to uphold. Whereupon
there ensued a terrific crack, cleaving the temple in two,
and great masses of the sculptured granite, breaking at the
shock from their places, fell crashing down to the ground.

. This strange little rock-temple is popularly called Bhima's
Rath ;[1] but concerning that same Bhima our travellers, notwithstanding their legendary enthusiasm, can recall but very
little. He was the son of Pandu, it seems, of the ancient
Lunar Dynasty, and with his club he struck down Duryod-
hana, the chief of the Kuru princes; but whosoever would
know of his further exploits, let him read them for himself
in that " stream of Vyasa's words which has descended from
the mountain of the Veda, and has swept away the trees of
bad reasoning, wherein the melodious sounds are the geese,

---

[1] The names of the Raths are only modern inventions.

the noble story is the splendid lotus, and the words are the expanse of water," even in "that precious and long story of Mahabharata."

Long time do our friends linger about these fascinating little temples; and then they walk south-westward until, about three-quarters of a mile from the Raths, they arrive at a precipitous rock wherein is hewn a temple of Durga known as the Yamapuri or Mahishamarddani Mandapam. As they enter it their imagination is recalled (for the last time on this day) to the grotesque fairy tales of Indian legend; for here (opposite a sculpture-scene wherein Vishnu reclines on Sesha the monarch of serpents) is a relief representing the victory of the great goddess Durga over that wicked buffalo-demon "Mahishasur of ample heroism, who repulsed the army of the gods,"[1] so that "the whole multitude of the deities were cast out from heaven and wandered on the earth like mortals." Then came Durga the imperishable, riding on her lion Kesari, the gift of Himavant. And "the lion of the goddess, being enraged, swiftly shook his mane and marched against the army of Mahishasur, like fire against a forest." Then the mighty demon "enraged tore up the earth with his hoofs and cast down the highest hills. . . . He lashed the ocean with his tail, and made it to overflow everywhere. The clouds were dispersed by his long horns, the mountains and sky were blown into a hundred pieces by his breath and sighs." "Being highly endowed with bravery, he furiously hurled mountains with his horns at the goddess." But Durga, the Matron World, was more mighty than he, and at length she "pulverised him with her strong arrows."

Having sufficiently contemplated this exciting scene, the

[1] See the 'Sapta-Shati, or Chandi-Pat,' . . . translated by Cavali Venkat Rámasswámi, Pandit.

travellers proceed to climb up the rock to the little structural temple which crowns the summit thereof. On the top of the temple is a lighthouse, and from the top of the lighthouse our friends gain an extended view of the neighbourhood,— tropical trees and ancient shrines, fantastic rocks and gleaming waters, all lit up with the softened evening sunshine.

Thereafter the travellers descend to their boat, and, once more reclining under their palm-leaves, float softly away Madrasward through the swiftly deepening night.

CHAPTER IX.

FROM MADRAS TO CALCUTTA.

THE good ship Cathay, which is to take our travellers to Calcutta, after keeping them waiting for five days, appears at length on the 11th of January. From the end of the pier our friends watch the passage of their luggage through the tumbling surf. The surf-boats wherein it is conveyed are picturesque native vessels sewn together with coco-nut fibre and painted red. A more solidly constructed boat would not last long among the Madras breakers.

The travellers themselves are taken off from the pier, and presently rejoice to stand again on a genuine fragment of England, to see white faces around them, and hear the sound of their native tongue. The most interesting people on board are a mission party of five sent out (with the help of S.P.G.) by the Dublin University. They are on their way to Chota Nagpur, where they will be a welcome and much-needed addition to the Bishop's staff of workers. The five Clergy are all graduates of Dublin University, and one of them is a physician and surgeon as well. There is also a lady who has had long experience as a missionary-nurse, and who looks after the younger Missionaries' health with a motherly care delightful to behold.

Unfortunately the passage out has been terribly stormy—one boat has been lost and two damaged—and all this is the fault of the Missionaries, it being a law of nature well known to seamen that "one Parson on board means bad weather, two bring a gale, and three a hurricane." However, there is no denying that they are a great acquisition to the society of the Cathay. Their daily Services in the saloon give a homelike atmosphere even to the Bay of Bengal, and their delicious Irish humour is the brightest thing on board. Long will be remembered an encounter between one of them and a certain facetious personage who considers that his rank entitles him to the exercise of a certain amount of insolence. "Do you know you are speaking to a Baronet?" he demands of one of the Missionary Clergymen. "I don't know about your being a Baronet," answers a quiet voice with a soft Irish accent expressive of the utmost politeness and a deep, bubbling spring of suppressed fun, "but I know that ye haven't the manners of a gentleman." The poor Baronet will take long to forget that gentle set-down, and will ever after uphold with vehemence all vulgar saws about the incapacity of Missionaries.

To come into contact with the energy and life of real workers, though humiliating to mere holiday-makers, is very refreshing too; and it is invigorating to hear something of the thorough and efficient work carried on with such devotion and blessed with such wonderful success in the far-away diocese whither the Missionaries are bound. Fifty years ago the people of Chota Nagpur—an aboriginal, non-Aryan race known as Kols—were sunk in the grossest vice and ignorance, slaves to drunkenness and terrifying superstitions, as miserable a people as one could easily imagine. In 1845 four Lutheran Missionaries were sent out to India by Pastor Gossner of Berlin, and began to work in Chota

Nagpur. For five years they laboured, enduring much hardship and suffering, and not a single convert did they make. But in 1850 four Kols came to the Mission-house at Ranchi and said that they had seen some of the Scriptures distributed by the Missionaries, that they had read in them of Christ, and that they wished to see Him. These four became the first converts to Christianity, and their baptism was followed by many more, until the native Christians were counted by thousands.

In 1869 the Missionaries and 7000 of their converts presented a petition to the Bishop of Calcutta, asking to be admitted into the Anglican Church. Bishop Milman granted their request, and in April of that year he visited the district to hold a Confirmation, and to bestow Catholic Ordination on the Missionaries.[1] The Mission was affiliated by the Society for the Propagation of the Gospel, and has greatly prospered ever since. According to the ordinary method of that very wise Society, the work was placed on a sound educational basis, mission schools were efficiently organised, and arrangements made for the training of native Clergy and Catechists. The Rev. J. C. Whitley, transferred from Dehli in 1869, threw into the work all his great powers with the most entire devotion, labouring with the German Missionaries on terms of the deepest respect and affection; and on March 23, 1890, after twenty-one years' strenuous and successful work, he was consecrated as Bishop of the new Diocese of Chota Nagpur.

Terribly short-handed as the workers have been, and hindered too by want of funds, their work has grown and pros-

---

[1] Of the three German Missionaries ordained by the Bishop, only one, the Rev. F. Batsch, had been among the original four. Two had died, and one had been obliged by ill health to return home.

pered, so that there are now among the Kols 12,519 baptised
members of the Anglican Church, about half of whom are
Communicants. There are 20 Clergy, 60 Readers, and a large
number of Catechists. These are no mere surface results.
Rapid as the growth has been, the work is all most thorough
and searching. The people are required to give liberally in
support of their churches and schools, Church discipline is
strictly enforced, and the native candidates for the Ministry,
after many years of careful training, have to pass a severe
examination before being admitted to Holy Orders.

For those who can remember the wretchedness of the old
days, it is strange to visit the Chota Nagpur of the present,
where in more than 500 native villages Christians assemble
daily, at sunrise and sunset, for Service in their own tongue ;
where education is growing and ignorance retreating, and
where is good hope that, if Christians at home will give the
prayers and the help that are so urgently needed, the whole
nation will at length be added to the Church.

To study such histories suits well with the quiet leisure of
a tropical day at sea ; but when the glowing sunshine is gone,
and there reigns over all things the magic enchantment of an
Indian night, then all that has practical reality must needs
be ignored and forgotten. Then doth the aged Metaphysician
discourse of Absolute Existence and Universal Truth, and
the world of troublesome particulars is as though it had never
been. Then doth the full moon ride aloft on her three-
wheeled car, and the ten horses thereof "that are sprung
from the bosom of the waters "[1] are all "of the whiteness of
the jasmine." Then the glassy expanse of the sea shines
with so strange and mysterious a glory that one must perforce
believe that saying of Parasara the Sage, who set forth of old

[1] From the 'Vishnu Purana,' translated by H. H. Wilson, M.A., F.R.S.

I

how " day or night retires into the waters according as they are invaded by darkness or light; it is from this cause that the waters look dark by day, because night is within them; and they look white by night, because at the setting of the sun the light of day takes refuge in their bosom."

The voyage from Madras is very smooth sailing, and in all respects delightful. Not the least amiable of the passengers are the cockroaches, of whom, as always in hot climates, there is a considerable company, and who have a particularly endearing way of crawling over one's pillow at night. No wonder they wish to be sociable, seeing that they too were originally human beings. Unfortunately in that former existence they were ill-advised enough to filch oil from their neighbours, thereby bringing upon themselves that dreadful condemnation which Markandeya, the Immortal Sage, pronounced in ancient days, " He that stealeth oil is born a cockroach."

It is quite disappointing to arrive (on the evening of January 14) at the mouth of the Hugli, and to realise that but ninety miles of the pleasant journey remain. The passage of the Hugli, with its shallow waters and shifting sand-banks, is not one to be attempted at night, and the Cathay lies at anchor until six o'clock the next morning. Slowly, as she proceeds, the low banks converge, and there come into view the dense jungle-forests of the swampy Sunderbans where tigers and fevers range at large. This is the busiest and most important of all the Ganges' mouths; but so desolate is the scene at first that our travellers can think of nothing more cheerful to rehearse than the Five meritorious Kinds of Suicide, whereof one, saith Hindu legend, is to cut one's throat at Allahabad (where the Jamna and the Ganges meet), and another is to betake oneself " to the

extremity of Bengal, where the Ganges discharges itself
into the sea through a thousand mouths,"[1] and there, wading
into the water, to enumerate one's sins and devoutly to say
one's prayers till the alligators come and eat one.

But as the day wears on and Calcutta draws nearer, many
ships go by, and the flag of each vessel is flying half-mast
high. The newly arrived Cathay knows nothing of any
occasion for mourning, but presently the news is signalled to
her by a passing steamer, "The Duke of Clarence is dead."

It is evening before the travellers can land; and they drive
away from the quay through the horrible, smoky night-fog
for which Calcutta is famous. Nor can even daylight impressions indue the city with great attractiveness. Calcutta
is terribly modern—for the greater part of the seventeenth
century Kalighat and the neighbouring villages were still
mere collections of native mud-huts; the public mourning
has cast a gloom over the city, and the travellers, were it not
for a certain Major-general—that kindest of kind friends—
would gain but a colourless impression thereof. Thanks to
him, they are admitted, soon after their arrival, to a large
meeting of Natives assembled in the Town-hall to vote
addresses of condolence to the Empress and the Prince of
Wales. More than 5000 are present, and our friends, from
their seats on the platform, have an excellent view of that
sea of native faces, and an excellent opportunity for studying the physiognomy of Bengal. If judged only from their
aspect here in Calcutta, the Bengali folk would not, in the
matter of good looks, compare favourably with the Tamils.
The complexion is lighter, the features are less regular, there
is much more vivacity of manner, and far less dignity of

---

[1] See the conclusion of the 'Ayeen Akbery' . . . translated from the
original Persian by Francis Gladwin.

bearing. The whole assembly is composed of men, for native ladies have, of course, nothing to do with public matters. The Lieutenant-Governor of Bengal presides, and the other speakers are certain dignified Maharajas, who, resplendent with jewelled turbans, address the meeting in very creditable English. The speeches are full of loyal feeling, and the memorials to be sent to England—"the humble and loyal Addresses of the inhabitants of Calcutta in meeting assembled"—set forth in the language of sincere sympathy how the grief of the Royal Family "is shared by millions of hearts throughout the Empire"; but the proceedings of the meeting look, to English eyes, somewhat formal and cold. All is done in accordance with a previously settled programme, the 5000 listeners take no part whatever, and but very few can hear what is said, since all the dusky Princes speak only to those on the platform.

During the whole of our travellers' stay in Calcutta the daily papers from England are full of joyful prognostications and of the preparations for wedding festivities. To read them with the knowledge in one's mind that the cable has brought, is a taste of what life would be like if prevision of the future were often possible.

On January 20 the travellers attend, in S. Paul's Cathedral, a memorial Service held nearly simultaneously with the Prince's funeral Service in England. The crowd is great, and the thousands of worshippers are clad in mourning, the officers appearing in full-dress uniform. The organ is supported by a military band, and the playing of the Dead March is most solemn and impressive. The choral Service, like all the worship of the Calcutta Cathedral, is very beautiful and devout.

Indeed, so striking is the spiritual aspect of the Cathedral that the material building is not so distressingly prominent as it otherwise might be. Still, considered in itself apart from its sanctity, the building is so hideous as to be actually terrifying. They would never dream of building such a thing now; but the fact is that, as Dr Fergusson points out, there used to be no architects in India, and the church-building was carried on by *military engineers*. The Calcutta Cathedral is builded in what that same authority defines as "the Strawberry Hill form of Gothic art." I would describe it if I could, but the subject is too painful; one can but turn away with a shudder.

Turning away from the Cathedral, one strays naturally into the Maidan, a wide, grassy plain bordered on the East by the European houses of Chowringhee, and on the West by Fort William and other things of that kind. This is the great breathing-space of Calcutta. Herein, during our travellers' stay, the Commander-in-Chief holds a grand review of volunteers, and an impressive spectacle it is. The horses are beautiful and spirited, the Maidan is a capital galloping-space, and the horsemanship is worth looking at.

The most delightful day of sight-seeing enjoyed by our friends at Calcutta is that whereon that most thoughtful of major-generals places at their disposal, for an expedition up the Hugli, a delectable little steam-launch which rejoices in the name of Firefly. Being unable to accompany them, he sends as their guide one of his zamindars, an imposing personage who is undoubtedly the most handsome Native in Calcutta. His dignified countenance—of comparatively light complexion—is adorned with a luxuriant beard and moustache of fine silky black, and with a wonderful pair of shining dark eyes. His costume is an oriental uniform of white and scarlet and gold, such as dazzles the eyes of

beholders. Even from a merely æsthetic point of view, such
a personification of brilliant colour is a considerable addition
to the pleasure of the day's impressions.

With most exhilarating speed the Firefly darts forth into
the broad stream, parting the sunny waters with the sharp
edge of her prow, whence two rushing curves of spray, with
mirthful roaring and dashing, fleet ever sternward, and vanish
in her foam-flecked wake.

But the bright and animated scenes of that morning on
the river what words can describe? What shall we say of
the stately river-side buildings, of the wonderful architecture of the temples, of the green luxuriance of the trees?
How can we set forth the sights at the burning ghats,
where the murky clouds of smoke from the funeral pyres
float far through the clear air, and where the dead man's
friends, clad in sordid robes, are bathing in the River
below to wash away the pollution of having touched the
corpse? Above all, what pen could move lightly or swiftly
enough to set forth the multitudinous energy, the thronging
life, of the varied and crowded shipping? Why will not
my words sparkle and flash with the dancing waters, or go
puffing and fuming along with the busy steamers, or come
lumbering down with the clumsy grotesqueness of those
quaint and formless native boats piled high with the produce of Upper Bengal? Why cannot they catch the merry
turmoil of the spray, or rush by with the sound of the wind,
as the Firefly darts on her way? What is the use of words
if they won't reflect one's mind? Some folk *make* them do
it; but those are they whose spirits are blessed with such
intense and exuberant life as will burst through any barrier,
and so can subdue unto itself even the thorny obstructions
of language, the hardness of stubborn words. When will

the day come, I wonder, when language shall be superseded by (or leastwise develop into) some higher mode of expression that shall use, not the lifeless symbols of convention, but forms which shall be vitally one with that which they perfectly symbolise? Yet even now, may be, we have the germ of such future expression; and methinks that germ is rhythm.

"My dear," says the Father, "you have had twenty miles of wool-gathering; but here we are at Barrackpur, and you would not like to miss the Viceroy's country-house."

Leaving the Firefly at his Excellency's private landing-place, the travellers wander away through the park, and marvel at the beauty thereof. Landscape-gardening in India is a wonderfully easy matter, and the sight of an English park full of tropical trees and flowers is one to be long remembered. The direct path from the River to the house has been converted into a delightfully shady alley by means of bamboos planted close together on each side and bent over during their growth so as to interlace with one another and to form an arched covering of dense, luxuriant verdure,—a grateful protection from the fiercely glowing sunshine. The house—built by Lord Minto and enlarged by the Marquis of Hastings—is adorned with flowering creepers, bright masses of purple and orange blossoms dazzling as the sunshine itself.

Before leaving the grounds our friends visit Lady Canning's tomb—a white-marble sarcophagus placed under a spreading tamarind; and they also see the sombre memorial-hall—a melancholy thing, with not a single Christian symbol about it—builded by Lord Minto in 1813 as a tribute "to the Memory of the Brave who gloriously fell in the Service of their Country during the conquest of the Islands of Mauritius and Java, in the years 1810, 1811."

Ten miles more of rapid steaming up the River bring the Firefly and her passengers to Chandarnagar. Settled by the French in 1673, twice captured by the English and twice given back, the little town at the present day is a delightful picture of wholesome whitewash and prim French neatness. The most conspicuous feature is the large church built by some Missionaries from Italy in 1726. But there are many English residents here, and an Anglican church as well as the Roman one. The travellers land for tiffin, and then, when the hottest hours are over, again embark on the Firefly, and float gaily down to Calcutta.

They have not yet half done their duty by the city's "objects of interest." There is the Fort to see, and that terrible place where the Black Hole once was; and there are the state apartments of Government House to explore, and the Mint, where one watches the transformation of bullion into shining pice and rupees.

Specially interesting is the Indian Museum in the Chowringhee Road. One thousand one hundred and seventy native visitors enter it every day on the average,—and well they may. Herein our travellers contemplate weird sculpture from ancient temples, and some fragments of the original bodhi-tree at Buddha Gaya, said to be that under which Gautama sat on the night wherein he attained to Buddhahood. Most interesting of all is the famous Rail from Bharhut, a grand specimen of early Buddhist sculpture, dating from about 200 B.C. In another part of the museum are antiquities of earlier date in the shape of a megatherium or two and other notable fossils. Here the travellers learn what the megaloschelornis was like, the megalonyx and the glyptodon, the amphicyon and the machairodus, and the gigantic Siwalik cat.

Returning to the India of the present day, the travellers bethink them of their great desire to see something of the home-life of the native gentlefolk of Calcutta. Accordingly the sisters appeal to a kind friend who is working, in connection with the Zenana Society, among the Muhammadan ladies, and in her company pay a round of calls. The last house they enter is by far the most magnifical,—a large and costly mansion of such dreary and sordid grandeur as is depressing only to think of. They are received by the eldest son of the house, an intelligent youth of about seventeen, who is on the eve of departure for England, where he is to finish his education. His three little brothers, who wear sparkling caps of Indian embroidery, entertain the visitors while he goes to tell his mother of their arrival. To reach the zenana the travellers have to ascend a staircase and thread their way through some very dusty passages; but they finally emerge into the presence of the lady of the house, a handsome woman much adorned with jewels. Near her sits her sister, whose robes of fine white muslin, and the fact that she wears no ornaments, show her to be a widow. There are other lady relatives who have come to bid the son farewell, and the room presents a richly coloured picture of dusky faces and beautiful native dresses. The visitors are courteously welcomed, are presented with Indian scent, and are further entertained with the somewhat childish and personal conversation wherein Muhammadan ladies delight. The missionary lady acts as interpreter, and, thanks to her, the visit is a pleasant and interesting experience.

The travellers, who have come to India with a pardonable desire to learn something of the Indians, are not a little astonished and amused at the vulgar contempt for all things

native which they meet with now and then in the European
society of Calcutta.   "You have no idea," says some one in
the garb of a gentleman to one of our friends at a dinner-
party—"you have no idea of the scorn and derision with
which we look on the natives.   To treat them like human
beings is out of the question,—they are far too detestable for
anything of that kind !"

It is a change from this kind of talk to visit the Oxford
Mission - house, whither our travellers repair one Sunday
evening to hear an English lecture given in the hall thereof
for the benefit of educated Hindus.   Here is no suspicion
of contempt on the one hand, or of anything like sentimental
weakness on the other; but the gentle directness, the stern
simplicity of those who speak the truth in love.   The Missionaries are all honours men from Oxford, and their chief
work is among the most highly educated of the Natives.
Of these, when our travellers arrive, a large audience of
men has already assembled, and throughout the lecture
they listen with the greatest attention.   This is one of a
course of Sunday evening lectures, and its subject is "Life
as a School."   Nothing could be more scholarly than the
quiet, lucid development of the argument; and the merest
outsider can appreciate the wisdom whereby the method of
exposition is adapted with wonderful tact to the subtle,
metaphysical mind of the educated Bengali.   Beginning
with the burning question of political freedom, and arguing
that it is useless until moral freedom has been first obtained,
the Lecturer likens the training of life to that of a school.
The first lesson to be learned therein is the recognition of
individual responsibility to God, and the teacher is Conscience.   Then follows a masterly piece of psychological
analysis, wherein is vindicated the authority of Conscience

as a primary and ultimate faculty which makes uncondi-
tional claim to rule all other powers of the soul. Strenu-
ously is combated the doctrine of fatalism as making moral
freedom impossible, and the tendency of the caste system
to destroy the sense of personal responsibility is gently
and fearlessly touched upon. Much more there is of well-
reasoned Christian philosophy, and the lecture ends on
this wise :—

"Do not think that we Christian missionaries have come
to make you Christians. No; but we come to arouse your
consciences that *they* may bring you to Christ. If any number of you were to become Christians from interested motives,
that would be no happiness to us or to our Master. That
you may be true Christians some day I pray and long; but
above all I long now that you may be true men, true to
the light that is in you, the light of Conscience, the Light
that lighteth every man that cometh into the world."

The lecture is followed by a short Service, the few Native
Christians present coming forward to join in it, and many of
the others staying in their places to listen. Then the travellers are invited to see the rest of the Mission-house, and
they forthwith seize the opportunity to ask all the troublesome questions they can think of. The Mission, it seems,
was founded in 1880, its chief object being to work among
the educated Natives. Its Superior is the Rev. H. White-
head, M.A. (of S.P.G.), who, like this evening's lecturer, is a
late scholar of Trinity College, Oxford. Five other Priests
(all Oxford M.A.'s) are working under him, and there are
three "lay brothers" as well. Every day after 3 P.M. some
of the Missionaries are at home to receive inquirers; and
many are the educated Hindus who present themselves,
some of them real seekers after truth, others coming, in the

first instance, rather with the purpose of showing off their fine English and their subtle powers of argument, and only gradually to be won from the display of captious dialectic to the exercise of earnest inquiry.

Besides this, there is plenty of educational work; for not only is there in connection with the Mission a boarding-school for Native Christian boys, but the Superior has now undertaken, at the request of S.P.G., the direction of Bishop's College, which, affiliated to the Calcutta University, and giving a sound general collegiate education, has for its special object that indispensable part of all sound Missionary effort, the training of Native Clergy, Catechists, Schoolmasters, and Readers. This institution, with the schools attached to it, contains 147 Native Christians, and the work it is doing is most useful and important. It has twenty-one scholarships for maintaining theological students who are preparing for work in the Mission-field.

Moreover the Oxford Missionaries are carrying on much hopeful work among the dwellers in the melancholy Sunderbans, those unwholesome marshes about the mouth of the Hugli, where for half the year all the country is flooded, so that one goes from village to village in a rudimentary boat that is the hollowed trunk of a tree, while the tropical sun pours down his merciless and stifling heat. Missionaries have to go everywhere, but theirs are the only white faces that haunt those dismal regions; yet the Christians in the "Tollygunge and Sunderbans" district are 3455, and the number of catechumens is 1484. Twenty-five mission schools have been established, and their scholars already number more than 700.

As for the rest of the Church-work in Calcutta, it is, in spite of all difficulties and anxieties, living and prospering.

The educational part of it is specially vigorous, and the schools are too many to mention.

During their stay in Calcutta the travellers endeavour to gain some general idea of Anglican Church - work in Bengal, studying especially the doings of the Society for the Propagation of the Gospel. Whereupon they become aware that in Bengal (including Chota Nagpur) the Society is now [1] at work in 632 native villages, and has established 85 mission schools wherein are being educated 2468 pupils. The two Bishops have working under them, in connection with the Society, 32 Clergy (of whom 20 are Natives) and 198 lay agents. The Society has now in connection with its Missions in this part of India 17,457 Christians, of whom 8243 are Communicants.

But our friends have not long time to spend on such cheerful objects of study; soon they are plunging back again into the murky atmosphere of heathenism, and devoting a morning to a visit to one of the burning ghats by the River, where the Hindus burn their dead,—a place of fear and mourning, where, as saith the ancient scripture, "the colour of the smoke - trails from the funeral piles spreadeth gloom over the regions of the sky, and where the night-roaming demons are joyful through the delight of tasting carrion." [2] Truly a forcible similitude is that of the precept of old which saith, "A man destitute of truth should be avoided even as a burning ground!"

To this particular burning ground are brought, on an average, twenty - four bodies a - day. When the visitors arrive no funerals are in progress, but the wood-fires are burning in readiness. Presently a man appears carrying the bodies of two little children wrapped up in a bundle.

---

[1] 1892.   [2] Markandeya Purána. Pargiter.

It seems that in the case of such young children no kind of funeral ceremony is used. The man who brings the bodies is only a servant, and he proceeds to throw them on to one of the fires as though they were a couple of logs. The travellers' thoughts wander away to the poor mother, not allowed to come to the burning ghat, but sitting at home with the consolation of believing her little ones to be safe in the clutches of Yama, the Lord of Death, who sitteth enthroned "surrounded by hundreds of deformed, horrible, and crooked diseases, his mouth gaping with projecting teeth, his countenance dreadful with frowns."

But this shall not be our last impression of Calcutta! Let us rather accompany our friends the travellers to the beautiful gardens which stretch along the right bank of the River a little below the city. To call them (as they do) the Botanical Gardens is absurdly incongruous. It is painful and ridiculous to be obliged to refer to such an enchanted region of verdant delights by so hopelessly prosaic an appellation. These gardens are like that lovely place that Tareke found of old, "a pleasant and beautiful spot in the wood Madhu, adorned with verdure and blossoms."[1] They are like that sacred grove which Rama once beheld, "fascinating beyond compare," wherein he "listened to the copious, pleasure-inspiring, love-soft, beautiful, ear-delighting, melodious songs poured forth from the mouth of the birds, and saw the trees there loaded with the weight of the fruit, and bright with the blossoms of every season—mango-trees and hog-plums and pomegranates; jujubes and almond-trees; citrons, jak-trees, and plantains; Palmira palms and cocoa-nuts, and delightsome bignonia-trees in blossom; with lakes, beautiful and placid, crowded on all sides with the lotus."

[1] Sheeve Pouran. Halhed.

THE GREAT BANYAN TREE, BOTANICAL GARDENS, CALCUTTA.

Wandering at random, the travellers find themselves entering at length the deep forest-shade of that far-famed banyan-tree, the largest they have ever seen, or ever will see. Its vast corona covers an acre of ground, the central trunk has a girth of 51 feet, and nearly 200 lesser stems support the mighty branches with their continuous roof of luxuriant foliage. The tree is only one hundred years old; but it seems by a metaphoric yet vital symbolism to reflect some age-long growth. As one wanders on into the green depths of shadow, there comes over the mind a sense of some living fund of energy, ever spreading farther from its birthplace, yet finding everywhere a new birthplace for itself, everywhere a home and rest; ever drawing fresh supplies from ever more distant sources; with many roots in many places, yet never losing in the multitude of off-shoots the essential unity of its central life. One thinks of a Vine one has heard of, stretching out her branches eastward to the far-off River, and westward to the boundless sea——

"Sebaste," says Philippa suddenly, "who is it 'whose eyes are in the ends of the earth'?"

"Ah, well, it does not so much matter about the outside eyes. It is the eyes of the mind, Philippa!"

"And where, pray, were the eyes of your mind a moment ago?"

"They were far beyond the ends of the earth, at all events. They were in the world of symbolic truth, Philippa."

"Indeed! And what symbolic truth does the banyan-tree elucidate?"

"For one thing, methinks it sets forth the true spirit of travel; not that dissipated cosmopolitanism which seems to leave part of the mind in every place it visits until there is nothing left but a mindless gulf filled only with a collection of multitudinous impressions, but the spirit that takes all impressions into its own unity, and that has the patience to stay in each place long enough to pierce through the varying outer crust and get down to that substratum of vital truth which underlies all the multitude of superficial appearances!"

"What a nice long sermon, Sebaste! You should have preached it to the American gentleman who sat next to me at dinner last night. He had arrived the day before, and was leaving by last night's train. He had seen, he said, 'all that was necessary.' I did not ask him what he thought of the Oxford Mission; I knew that he had never even heard of it. It makes me quite restless only to think of him! Father dear, we have been half an hour under the banyan-tree! Don't you think we have seen 'all that is necessary' by this time?"

Whereupon our friends move away to seek out a wonderful collection of orchids,—an assemblage of exquisite blooms many of which seem to subsist on nothing but air,—and well they may, for assuredly they are far too ethereally delicate for any more earthly food.

Then the travellers wander back toward the entrance through vistas and groves of palm-trees; and as they go they talk with eager hope of Darjiling and the Himalaya.

CHAPTER X.

DARJILING.

In a hot and glowing afternoon the travellers set forth on the northward journey to Darjiling perched high among Himalayan snow-peaks 367 miles away. For a while, as the train speeds onward, the smooth, green plains of Bengal glide past, with lovely groups of trees and palm-thatched native cottages lit up by the mellow radiance of the softly westering sun; but too soon the swift darkness blots all things from view, and the travellers have nothing but stars to look at until, about 8 P.M., they arrive at Damukdiya on the southern bank of the Ganges.

The River here is nearly three miles broad, and the current is so strong that the steamer must make a considerable *détour* up-stream, which takes time. Wherefore the wanderers hope that this, their first introduction to the main stream of holy Ganges, will be no hurried meeting, but a peaceful gliding over calm and starlit waters, with time for much exalted musing, for the telling of Ganga's ancient legends, and for recalling the dreams of Indian poets in days of old. Is not this the River in whose pure waters the seven Sages " practise the exercises of austerity,"[1] wreathing their

[1] Vishnu Purana. Wilson.

K

braided locks with her swiftly flowing streams? Nay, are
there not some who tell how this sacred River, "heard of,
desired, seen, touched, bathed in or hymned day by day,
sanctifies all things," so that "those who, even at a distance
of a hundred leagues, exclaim 'Ganga! Ganga!' atone for
the sins committed during three previous lives;" and how
from the mountain Meru she takes her divided way, flowing
forth to the four quarters of the earth to accomplish its
purification?

With expectant minds filled with such dreamy fragments
of legendary lore, the travellers leave their train and hasten
on board the boat. To find that it is a steamer is of
itself a shock to the poetic mind; but, as if this were not
mortifying enough, the deck has been roofed over and
screened round with ridiculous, impertinent, idiotic awnings
through which not one ray of starlight can penetrate. The
apartment thus formed is artificially illuminated, and in the
middle of it is a dinner-table. It is pitiful, but true, that
round this last odious object the travellers are obliged to
dispose themselves, and (chained to their seats by courtesy to
the other passengers) to remain in that humiliating position
during the whole of the transit, while course succeeds to
course in an unfeeling and despicable manner until the Sara
Ghat, the northern landing-place, is reached. Whereupon
our friends must hurry to the train that awaits them, bestow
themselves on shelves therein, and go rattling and bumping
away through the plains of Upper Bengal.

But if the night is dark and noisy, the morning brings
dewy freshness and a glory of golden light. Gladly awaking from uneasy slumbers, our friends alight at Siliguri for
rest and *chota hazri*. Then, wandering forth, they find
themselves in the very presence of the mighty heights of

Himalaya. Around still lie the rich, green plains, the smooth, low - lying level broken only by luxuriant groups of tufted vegetation; but rising abruptly from that sea of verdure, towering far overhead in stupendous masses and peaks, yet clothed to the very summits with dense tangles of jungle-forest, the great outer spurs of the range rise far above and beyond the flight of puny words. Yet these lesser giants do but nestle at the feet of Kinchinjanga's shining heights, whose vast snow-fields lie far, far above in the heart of the clear blue sky. Though our friends may now almost be compared with Nared, that ancient worthy who " traversed " of old " with the foot of curiosity the surface of all the earth ";[1] yet in all their wanderings they have never seen the like. To stand on a flat, unbroken plain but 300 feet above the level of the sea, and thence to lift up one's eyes to a great mountain-summit whose snow-fields are shining in the morning sunlight at a height of more than 28,000 feet, is not a frequent incident of life, or one to be lightly forgotten.

One is astonished no longer at the wildness of those ancient legends that cluster round the mighty Himalaya—"Himachal," as they called him of old. Benign and amiable he always was, but never seemed his countenance so kindly or so venerable as on that festal day long, long ago when Parvati, his lovely daughter, was wedded to Siva the three-eyed lord, the " compilation of all perfections." Then did the great Himachal, " exerting himself in preparations for the marriage," " arrange himself with all the other mountains and their wives and children, arrayed in chains and fine garments, to wait upon Siva " the bridegroom. And when Siva, with all the multitude of his lordly train, was yet at a

---

[1] From Halhed's 'Sheeve Pouran.'

distance, "the mountain Gendemadher [1] was despatched to meet him, and Himachal himself sat still awaiting his arrival;" but "when the procession came nigh at hand, then Himachal hastened forward to meet" the bridegroom, and affectionately "took him in his arms." Siva had need to be a god, I fancy, to survive that giant embrace.

Eager to ascend into the piled-up heights that rise before and above them, the travellers set forth on their further journey by the so-called Himalayan railway, which should rather be called a steam tramway, were it not that both words are far too miserably commonplace to be used in connection with so exciting and so romantic a mode of travelling. The rails are laid, on a 2-foot gauge, along the side of the wonderful mountain-road, said to be one of the finest in the world, which was made at the cost of £6000 per mile. Seated in an open car, protected from the sun, but with nothing to interrupt the glorious views, the travellers hurry along toward the mighty wall of the mountains, speeding through the verdant plain of the Tarai, where the morning sunshine lights up the strange landscape so that it is a wonder to see. Here and there, springing high into the air like forest-trees, spreading abroad gigantic, fern-like fronds, the exquisite lines of their curving culms half hidden in the depths of feathery foliage, rise the luxuriant clumps of bamboo, while often the eye is startled by I know not what gorgeous trees all ablaze with crowded blossoms of vivid orange and crimson.

At first the rich soil is partially cultivated; but soon all signs of human life are gone, and the travellers find themselves entering on that wild tract of marshy jungle which lies at the very foot of the stupendous mountain-chain. High

---

[1] This is Mr Halhed's spelling, for which I am not responsible.

overhead wave the giant grasses, and all around is a marvellous
tangle of rankly luxuriant growth. It is a rude and uncouth
region, where tigers and elephants live, and the rhinoceros
roams at large,—such a region as the wise Nârada sought of
old, "an impenetrable wilderness full of reeds and bamboos
and canes, of tufts of grasses and plants with hollow stems,
a wilderness that was very great, terrible, and fearful, wherein
serpents dwelt and jackals, and frogs and owls."[1] Therein
did Nârada the wise sit him down beneath a pipal-tree, and
"attaining to the summit of inaction, became drowned in the
flood of blessedness." But what happened to him after that,
if any desire to know, let him read thereof in that venerable
poem, the 'Bhâgavata,' "which fell to earth from the lips of
Suka, even as it had been a fruit falling from the productive
tree of the Law, a fruit whereof the juice is none other than
Amrita" the elixir of life. As for me, I must hurry away
after those troublesome travellers of mine, who are now
plunging deep into the shadows of the primeval forest that
wraps in sombre stillness the steepest mountain-slopes.

Fostered by the great heat and by the heavy rains of
these eastern regions of the Himalaya, the jungle-growth
of the forests is a wild profusion of exuberant vegetation,
a mighty tangle of verdant life, such as overwhelms the
dullest mind with an ever-rising, irresistible tide of wonder
and exultation. Stately tree-ferns and wild bananas mingle
in the undergrowth's mazy pomp; high into the golden
sunlight rise the thronging forest-trees, their stems clothed
with the dense mosses, the orchids, and other parasite plants
that love this humid atmosphere; the relentless scandent
trees grapple with the forest giants, and rear themselves

[1] From 'Le Bhâgavata Purâna,' . . . traduit . . . par M. Eugène
Burnouf.

up beside them, and seize them with relentless grasp, and slowly strangle the very life that seemed so strong; while, most wonderful of all, the mighty creepers twine themselves in folds of living verdure about the larger trunks, and mount upward to the topmost branches, wrapping them deep in cloudlike shadow, and descending thence in bright cascades of rich and lovely blossoms.

Beautiful and delightful are the fair gardens of the earth, wherein each stately plant stands free with space and air and sunshine enough for full and harmonious development; lovely is the order of art, wherein all things are distinct and definite, with no secret mazes of intricate perplexity nor ever a shadow of deepening mystery. We love those peaceful parks wherein none can lose his way, the graceful groupings of chosen trees, and the smoothness of tended lawns; but oh! who cares to think of them in the midst of primeval forests? Who would not rather choose to plunge into these abysses of solemn shade, and lose himself in the dim world of the boundless jungle, where from tree to tree, from thicket to thicket, the giant trailing plants fling ever their tangled wreaths; where all things are twined and massed together into a profound, inextricable unity; where all the multitudinous growth seems stirring from its inmost depths with the wildness of buoyant and undivided life? We love the fair poems of the world, the thought-gardens that men have planted, with all their grave and ordered groupings of perfected and harmonious forms; but oh! how different a poem must be from the forest of the poet's mind! Carefully and with loving zeal doth he labour, bringing out choice plants to set them each by itself where it may most perfectly develop on all sides, and where it may best be seen; but methinks, when his work is done, he will not linger long, but flinging wide the gate for the public to enter, will gladly turn him back again to wander away and away into the lonely depths of that pathless forest whither we may not follow.

"Yes, I like that!" exclaims Philippa. "It reminds me somehow of one of those old Indian similitudes that you are so fond of quoting, Sebaste: 'Even as a path overgrown with weeds, such is the speech of the ignorant, which conveys no certain meaning.'"

"My dears," says Irene hurriedly, "do, pray, observe how quickly we are mounting. In every seven miles we rise more than 1000 feet."

"The making of this railway is one of the greatest engineering feats ever achieved," says Philippa didactically. "Sebaste, you should observe what extraordinary curves we describe. They think nothing at all here of curves with a radius of only 70 feet. Of course the wheels are constructed on the bogie system, and turn under the carriages."

"Yes, Philippa," says Sebaste submissively, "it is very interesting and improving. Here we are at a reversing station. Will you expound it, please?"

"It is a device," answers Philippa, "for rising to a higher level where the slope is so steep as to make a curve impossible. The engine pulls and pushes alternately, and the train describes a figure like the letter Z, the only difference being——"

"Philippa, *look* at the view!"

Indeed no one can help looking at it. The travellers have now reached a height whence they are able to look abroad over the mighty billows of the heaving jungle-sea, away to the dim expanse of the boundless plains lying far below, and already shrouded in delicate haze through which gleams like silver the Mahanadi's winding stream. Every moment the view grows broader and grander and more over-whelmingly wonderful. In an ever-increasing multitude the great mountains assemble, gathering themselves together in lordly companies, towering to greater and yet greater height as their stupendous slopes are less foreshortened; while slowly the vast plains sink down, and vanish out of sight.

Already the heat of the lowlands has given place to the freshness of mountain air when the travellers arrive at Karseong, a Himalayan village perched, above a deep valley, in close conjunction with a tea-plantation. But still our friends have ascended only a very little way the lower skirts of the mountains. Here they are only 466 feet higher than the summit of Ben Nevis, and very low down in the world they feel themselves to be as they gaze up to the snowy peaks still so far away. Withdrawing thence their eyes to fix them on nearer things, they are struck by the altered looks of the Natives. The type of countenance is now un-mistakably Mongolian,—a wonderful change from the solemn faces of the plains. So many are the hill-tribes which haunt these heights of British Sikim that our friends are fairly bewildered. Most numerous, perhaps, are the Bhuteas.

"One might suppose from their name," remarks Philippa, "that they all came from Bhutan; but the natives of Bhutan are called Bhatanese,—a distinction that must be carefully borne in mind."

"Well, Philippa, where *do* they come from, then?"

"Some of them come from Bhutan, but many also from Tibet, and some live here in Sikim. If you were to give a little more time to study, Sebaste, you would not need to be a walking question-mark."

The Bhutea men wear their hair in long pigtails; and their

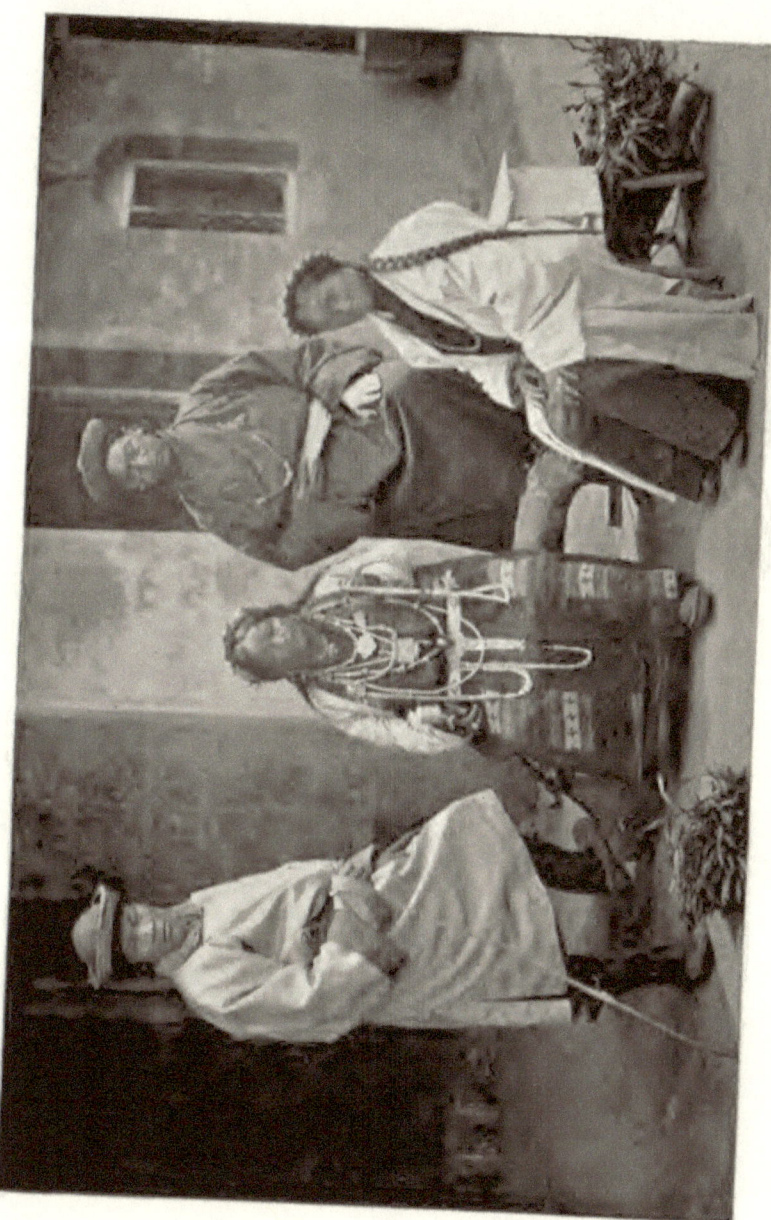

BHUTIA MEN AND WOMEN, DARJILING.

flat faces, cocked eyebrows, and oblique, slit-like eyes are
further reminders that China is not far off. Their turned-up
caps, moreover, have an unmistakably Chinese air, and so
have their thick-soled shoes conjoined with leggings, which
last are a delectable patchwork of green and scarlet and
blue. The rest of their attire is a full blouse-like garment
gathered in at the waist with a hidden girdle, and reaching
as far as the knee.

As for the women, they are wild-looking indeed, but
undoubtedly picturesque. Their faces would often be very
handsome were it not for the thick, red-brown pigment
wherewith they relentlessly adorn them. It may be a protection from the cold; but on the whole I incline rather to
regard the custom as a necessary concession to fashion; for
these rude people of the mountains are in some things almost
as barbarous as certain less distant tribes.

Some of their fashions, however, are in excellent taste,
notably the way in which the women dispose their plentiful,
silky, black hair. It is parted in the middle, and in some
cases flows loose over the shoulders, but more often is braided
in two long plaits, while round the head is sometimes worn a
beautiful silver coronet. They all carry their savings about
with them in the shape of ornaments; and the most sordid
of threadbare robes is always relieved by some delicate piece
of Tibetan silver-work adorned with rare chasing and with
turquoises set therein. The large pendent earrings are
specially admirable, and so are the beautiful little silver
cases wherein charms are carried. The charms are various,
sometimes being the nail-parings of some one of the " Lamas,"
as the Buddhist priests call themselves in Sikim and Tibet.

Very noticeable are the strength and activity of the Bhutea
womankind. It is said that one Bhutea lady once carried

up on her back, from the plains to Darjiling, an English visitor's grand piano. Our travellers, during their stay at Darjiling, will not have an opportunity of seeing the instrument; but that is no argument for its non-existence; and in any case, as an American gentleman once remarked, "It is a great mistake to spoil a good story merely for want of facts."

Soon the travellers are again speeding on their way, still struggling upward with ever greater depths beneath them of precipice-guarded valley. Only by looking downward can they in any wise realise the heights to which they attain. All around still flourish the teeming masses of the immemorial forest. Where in northern countries begin the regions of perpetual snow, still the giant peaks and ridges are overflowed and overwhelmed by that troubled ocean of fathomless jungle-growth; still the unfamiliar trees deck themselves out in faëry vesture of mosses and blossoming creepers; still far above and beyond are the colder tracts of scanty vegetation which border the dazzling snows.

The whole ascent to Darjiling takes about seven hours; and the afternoon is wearing away when the travellers arrive at Ghoom, a quaint little native village set on a ridge 7372 feet high. Curiously the people assemble to gaze on the white-faced visitors. A wonderful group they make, those shaggy mountaineers; but most wonderful of them all is an aged Bhutea lady—the most striking old lady our travellers have ever seen. Her wild locks are tangled and knotted so as to be a marvel to see, and she weareth a multitude of charms and other mysterious things of curious and magical appearance. She is known as the Witch of Ghoom, and is assuredly most uncanny. She is specially polite to our travellers, and entertains them with much discourse which it is a pity they cannot understand.

Thence the journey continues for four miles more to the scarcely less exalted Darjiling, a cheerful collection of scattered houses with an English church presiding, all brightly lit up by the pleasant afternoon sunshine. No sooner have our friends arrived than they are pounced upon by pig-tailed coolies, assisted each into a rickshaw, and pulled up the narrow footpaths that lead to their novel abode. A delightful lodging-place they find it, in the court whereof are displayed for sale a collection of leopard-skins, little stuffed bears, and other hunters' spoils from the neighbourhood. After sunset these curiosities vanish, and in their place comes a company of live jackals, who yelp and whine and wail the long night through. Our travellers feel much flattered at being thus assiduously serenaded.

More strange and bright are the days spent in Darjiling than days that children dream of. To live for even a little while so far above the ordinary world, is a delight to be long remembered. The view from Darjiling of the Kinchinjanga range is perhaps the grandest on earth, and never will our travellers forget the sight to which they awake on the morning after their arrival. All transfigured by the morning light, the mighty, forest-clad mountains.tower up from the depths range beyond range, till the last gigantic ridge seems to stand out against a background of soft and hazy sky. But yet above and beyond, far, far removed from earth, shine forth from the midst of the sunlit heavens the radiant snow-clad heights. They are forty-five miles away, yet, though viewed from a height of 7200 feet, they seem to tower overhead and to dominate all the world. Floating on shadowy haze, islanded in the blue depths of the cloudless northern sky, and reflecting from vast fields of snow the glowing sunrise light, they belong not at all to this dim world of ours.

Exalted and pure and perfect as some momentary cloudland glory, yet are they steadfast and strong as the very ground beneath our feet,—like some dream of ideal longing realised beyond all hope, found true and unchangeable for ever.

But the delightful expeditions which the travellers achieve, how shall we ever relate them as brightly and merrily as they deserve? On these precipitous mountain-ridges is no room for roads or carriages, and the paths are narrow and winding. Walking would be pleasant enough, but the air is at first difficult to breathe, being so rare that one cannot obtain enough oxygen without such rapid respiration as, in violent exercise, becomes panting pure and simple. Wherefore our friends have recourse to some amiable Tibetan horses, sprightly little creatures who are always ready to be off, and who, being well accustomed to mountaineering, trot gaily along the edges of the precipices with never a start or a stumble.

To rise before the sun, and, mounting one of these willing steeds, to fare forth and away in the first flush of the daybreak among Himalayan heights and depths,— such joys what pen can describe? The mountain-air is pure and keen, the mountain-path winds onward through forests of magnolias and rhododendrons and Himalayan oak-trees, where he dews lie thick on the trailing plants and the delicate ferns and mosses. Far overhead the changeless snow-peaks shine, and beneath one's feet lie the dim abysses of the vast and yawning valleys. From 5000 to 6000 feet deep they are said to be, and the eye is scarcely able to fathom their awful and mysterious depths. There are many valleys in the Himalaya—great dislocations of the earth's crust—into any one of which, as saith a great authority of scientific and sober mind, the whole of the Alps might be cast "without producing any result that would be discernible at a distance of ten or fifteen miles." Well doth that same authority lament that for these great things we have only little words to use, and that in writing of Himalayan mountains we must needs, even as though our subject were the little giants of Europe, talk only of peak and valley, of range and spur and ridge!

But if mere dimensions even are too much for words to express, far less can be told how the immensity of Darjiling scenery affects our travellers' minds. Humiliating (is it not?) that so merely relative a thing as size must assuredly be should so deeply stir our feelings,—that what would seem to be in itself nothing in the world should overwhelm our very souls, so that, as the eye springs up to the radiant heights or plunges down and away to the shadowy depths beneath, the mind is perturbed with wondering awe and a struggling, exultant joy. But then are not *all* our impressions in some sense relative? The beauty we see in a landscape, is it of its stocks and stones? Is there any such phenomenon as what we call light except there be an eye to see it? The beauty of a poem, is it in the printed page? Nay, surely not, but rather in the author's thought, and (by means of the material medium) in the mind of him who reads it. How humiliating that paper and lines of ink should affect our hearts so strongly! Nay, rather how convincing a proof that there is a mind behind them. Only let us not think that the cosmic writing is made up of such mean and lifeless symbols as these conventional alphabets of ours, symbols that have no essential or vital connection with that which they mechanically symbolise!

"Sebaste, take care! You will be down the precipice! Your pony *will* always walk with one foot over the edge."

"Philippa, I can't help my pony! He is far more to

my mind than the majority of human beings, who go jogging
along in the ready-made paths and keep always to the
middle of the way."

"My dear," says Irene gently, "try to tell us calmly what
you object to in human beings."

"They are ungrateful, Irene, and irreverent and stupid !
They *will* not recognise the vitality of the world or treat
it like a living thing. It is bad enough to look upon books
as we do—to use them, as ancient temples have been used,
as mere quarries to hew our thoughts from, nor ever to
realise that there are human spirits behind them; but surely
it is a thousand times worse so to treat Nature itself. It is
strange how men will criticise and pass judgment on beautiful scenery, nor ever dream of the eternal Spirit behind
it, infinitely transcending all glorious self-expressions, yet
through them reaching out to our spirits that we may know
and love and worship——"

"So that is your new and untrodden path, Sebaste ! "
exclaims Philippa. "If you were to read your Keble a
little more carefully, perhaps the originality of your ideas
would not strike you so forcibly. But that is the way with
this younger generation——"

"Why, Philippa, are you my grandmother, then ? "

"Don't interrupt me, my dear. I was about to point out
the persistency with which the young people of the present
day are accustomed to dress up old truths in the newest
possible fashions, and then to trot them out as their own
inventions, being led thereto by such a morbid fear of ortho-
doxy, such a weak desire to seem original, as passes my
understanding."

"My dears," says the Father, "the ascent of Senchal is
scarcely a fitting occasion for acrimonious discussions."

Indeed it is not. The travellers have reached the summit at length, and, standing at a height of 8163 feet, look northward and eastward over the massive ranges of Sikim and Nipal, and upward toward the frozen snows of Everest's faroff peak. Surely through all the day no mist or haze or shadow may reach his shining crown; yet between our travellers' eyes and those ever-sunlit snow-fields a curtain of cloud is drawn. Wistfully and long do they wait, if perchance they may catch one glimpse of that rounded summit whereon no foot of man may ever tread, but the height whereof man hath notwithstanding measured, pronouncing the number of feet therein to be 29,002. But if Everest be the highest peak in the world, he exceeds by only 846 feet the majestic Kinchinjanga, who, being so much nearer to British Sikim, is a far greater and grander feature in Mount Senchal's panorama. Yet even as our travellers gaze, his glorious heights have receded, and swiftly the mountain-haze is rising and spreading abroad, blotting out all the varying hues of the vast landscape with one uniform, transparent tint, till the great mountain-ranges are all one sea of watery blue, rolling in liquid masses toward the rock whereon the travellers stand—mighty waves, tossing up their crests to heaven, as though they would overwhelm the solid land and sweep the world away.

Wild fancies are apt to haunt the mind while it is still in the strange commotion stirred up by the first amazing glimpse of Himalayan scenery; but let it not be thought that these fanciful travellers of ours spend all their time in dreaming. Exhorted by the inexorable Philippa, they repair to the weekly market held in Darjiling (whereto the many hill-tribes flock from many miles around), and there improve their minds by ethnologic studies. There are pig - tailed

Lepchas and hardy Nipalese, and Limboes and Bhuteas beside, and I know not how many more. It is impressive to see a strong Bhutea woman come trudging down the mountain - paths, carrying her market produce in a great funnel - shaped basket which, resting on the back of its bearer, is kept in position by a band of woven grass passed across her forehead. And the jewellery they wear on market days is astonishing to behold,—great necklaces of gold, and other delights too many for me to describe.

Here, too, our friends become familiar with the sight of those Buddhist prayer-wheels which hitherto they have but vaguely heard of. Now a prayer-wheel commonly consists of a metal cylinder revolving at the end of a wooden handle. Within is a roll of manuscript, and without is engraved a mystic formula. As the cylinder revolves, the words, it would seem, are by some mysterious centrifugal force projected into space, to the great advantage of all concerned. Among the busy groups of marketers moves an aged Bhutea lady, who, twirling her prayer-wheel over their grateful heads, earns many an honest copper. Very convenient must be this method of saying prayers by proxy, with never a moment's interruption of pressing worldly business.

On another day our friends climb down the mountain to a little Buddhist temple where they are politely received by an affable red-robed Lama. A cheerful race are the Lamas, much given to trumpeting on dead men's thigh-bones and performing in musical wise on drums which are human skulls. This particular gentleman has under his charge at the temple many prayer-wheels of wood, some of them 8 or 10 feet high, with large and mysterious letters piously painted thereon. Near each hangs a bell, and from the wheel projects a stick which maketh the bell to ring at every revolution. And each time the bell is struck the Lama chants aloud, "Om Mani padme hum," which meaneth (so the learned aver) ostensibly and literally, "Ah, the jewel is in the lotus!" but intrinsically and symbolically (though one might not think it), "The self-creative force is in the Kosmos." In Tibet (so our travellers are assured) such wheels take the form of water-mills, and windmills also there are for the meritorious grinding of prayers.

Hard by this same temple the travellers contemplate some sacred trees of the law. Now a tree of the law is a staff of bamboo whereunto is attached as a flag a length of cotton or silk, and on the flag are inscribed those same magical words, "Om Mani padme hum." One of our greatest authorities on Buddhist lore thus sets forth the purpose of these very curious erections: "Whenever," saith he, "the flags are blown open by the wind, and 'the holy six syllables' are turned towards heaven, it counts as if a prayer were uttered; a prayer which brings down blessings not only upon the pious devotee at whose expense it was put up, but also upon the whole country-side." [1]

At length comes the last day at Darjiling, and the last expedition must be made. "We will go," say our travellers, "to the top of Tiger Hill."

A hill it calls itself advisedly, for it is but 8514 feet high, and the mountains hereabout are very different things. Early our friends set forth, and merrily ride away through the sparkling morning dews. Reaching Senchal, they pass him by, and so press gladly on to the farther and higher point. As they reach it, the snow-clad peaks to the northward are still glowing in the early sunlight.

[1] From 'Buddhism.' By T. W. Rhys Davids, M.A., Ph.D. (S.P.C.K.)

I had meant to tell so many mountain-legends of India among these stupendous heights! "There is a fair and stately mountain," saith one,[1] "and its name is Meru; . . . and it stands, piercing the heavens with its aspiring summit, a mighty hill inaccessible even by the human mind!" I should have liked to tell that story. And Mandar, too, the King of Mountains, and Vindyachel who of old was despised, but who by devout observance attained to an excellent height, so that the mountain Sumeiru might never more boast himself against him—— But no, it may not be. In these exalted regions the air is too pure and bright for the heavy and sickly exhalations of old Hindu mythology! I dare not tell such vanities in face of those shining heights —so far away in distance and in unattainable glory, yet towering so high overhead that they seem to have drawn near in their radiant might as though with a spiritual presence.

Well hath Plato told us how, in that ideal world above us, whose sea is our misty air, whose air the glorious ether, there are islands that lift themselves out of our grosser atmosphere into transcendental light! But even Plato's stately cadences seem not majestic enough for the unimaginable heights, the solemn abysses, of Himalayan scenery. Such grandeur no words can reach, unless it be those of that ancient Psalm of ours:—

> "In His hand are the deep places of the earth;
> The strength of the hills is His also."

But already the mountain-slopes are overwhelmed in billowy seas of cloud. For a little while the shining peaks on high seem floating hither and thither above the heaving

[1] Wilkins, 'Episode from the Mahábhárata,' quoted by Poley.

surface, then slowly they sink and vanish, away from mortal ken.

Next morning Darjiling itself is deeply wrapped in mist, and sadly our friends set forth to journey back to Calcutta. Through the day they descend, gliding and rushing and plunging downward with a swiftness and an impetus that are delightfully exhilarating. "It makes one feel," says Sebaste sentimentally, "like one of the heavenly bodies." Soon the clouds are left far above, and the sunshine glows warmer and still more warm. Wraps are thrown off one by one, until at last the hot, heavy air of the plains has closed in overhead, and our travellers arrive at evening in beautiful Siliguri.

All the night they travel southward over the plains, reaching the Ganges' northern bank in that strange "interval between day and night" wherein, as the ancient legends tell, "the terrific fiends called Mandehas attempt to devour the sun." Still the glittering stars fill the dome of the deep-blue sky; awnings and dinners are happily absent; and, as the travellers glide from the bank over the unruffled expanse of water, they may star-gaze as much as they like, recalling the strange astronomic lore wherewith Hindu scriptures abound, —how on Dhruva, the pivot of the atmosphere, the seven great planets rest, and how all the celestial luminaries are bound by aerial cords to the steadfast polar star.

But soon the stars grow dim, and red in the eastern sky appears the sudden dawn. Above that rosy glow the crescent moon is gliding, and our travellers must needs repeat one more quaint Indian legend,—how, when Ganga flowed down from heaven, she encompassed the orb of the moon, who, bathed by her holy stream, hath thence derived her lustre.

Ever more brightly the sunrise glows, its glories clearly mirrowed in the River's glassy surface; and before the southern bank is reached, all the world is transfigured in a flood of golden sunshine, a radiance of spiritual loveliness which to behold, methinks, might do the Materialists good.

CHAPTER XI.

THE CITY OF FLOWERS.

AFTER their return from Darjiling our romantic - minded travellers tarry not many days in commonplace Calcutta. Bihar, with its treasured memories of the Buddha, its ancient sites and its venerable traditions, attracts with an irresistible spell their eager and restless minds. So forth they fare at evening, and begin their rapid journey to the capital of ancient Magadha, the royal city of Pataliputra, which Alexander's conquering generals called Palibothra, and which has long since descended from its former glories into unpretending Patna.

With the Buddha and his teaching the city is intimately associated, for this is that Pâtaligâma where he tarried long ago and taught in the village rest-house. In the Book of the Great Decease[1] it is written how "when the Blessed One had stayed as long as was convenient at Nâlandâ, he addressed the venerable Ânanda and said, 'Come, Ânanda, let us go to Pâtaligâma.'" And when Ânanda had answered, "So be it, Lord," "the Blessed One proceeded with a great company of brethren to Pâtaligâma." And "the dis-

[1] See 'Buddhist Suttas,' translated from Pâli by T. W. Rhys Davids. Sacred Books of the East.

ciples at Pâtaligâma" heard of his coming, and they prepared for him the rest-house, setting up therein a water-pot, and fixing a lamp of oil. And the Blessed One, when he had washed his feet, "entered the hall, and took his seat against the centre pillar with his face towards the east. And the brethren also, after washing their feet, entered the hall, and took their seats opposite the Blessed One against the eastern wall, and facing towards the west. Then the Blessed One addressed the Pâtaligâma disciples," and pronounced the discourse which tells of the fivefold loss of the evil-doer, and the fivefold gain of him who doeth well. So "when the Blessed One had thus taught the disciples, and incited them and roused them, and gladdened them far into the night with religious discourse, he dismissed them, saying, 'The night is far spent, O householders. It is time for you to do what you deem most fit.' 'Even so, Lord!' answered the disciples of Pâtaligâma, and they rose from their seats, and bowing to the Blessed One, and keeping him on their right hand as they passed him, they departed thence." At that time "the Blessed One, with his great and clear vision, surpassing that of ordinary men, saw thousands of fairies haunting Pâtaligâma. And he rose up very early in the morning, and said to Ânanda, '. . . Among famous places of residence and haunts of busy men, this will become the chief, the city of Patali-putta, a centre for the interchange of all kinds of wares.' "

All night, in an unpoetical railway train, the travellers speed north-westward, and at early morning they arrive in Patna's civil station, which calls itself Bankipur. Herein they find but one interesting thing—namely, the far-famed Golah, the acoustic properties of which extraordinary build-

ing are probably more astonishing than those of any other
in the world. It is an enormous oval dome more than 90
feet high, and having at the base a circumference of 426
feet. It was built in 1783, and was intended for a granary;
but, as it remained empty of grain, many ghosts have chosen
to make thereof a permanent place of abode. The properties
of the building as a whispering-gallery are something magical and appalling; but it is in the centre of the circular
space, beneath the apex of the giant dome, that the spirits
do mostly congregate. To stand there in the dark (for the
Golah has no windows to light it) is a strange and awesome
experience. Every word, however softly uttered, is caught
up by a hundred phantom voices and repeated, here and
there and far away, by all the ghostly crowd. Each step
is followed close by thronging footfalls of an invisible multitude, and if any one dare to be merry, the vast space
rings with a veritable tempest of unearthly and thunderous
laughter. One mocking ghost there is who follows the visitor about, repeating over his shoulder every remark he
makes; and that one goblin voice it is which dictates to
all the others.

Emerging from the Golah's haunted gloom, the travellers
drive away to the city of Patna. After the sordid squalor
of Calcutta's make-believe native quarters, it is delightful
to be plunging again among the animated crowds and the
vivid colours of a genuine native town. Along the southern
bank of the Ganges it lies, stretching, with its suburbs, to
a length of no less than fourteen miles. Through the principal street our travellers drive, gazing at the bright and
unfamiliar scene with a half-incredulous wonder. To-day
is a Hindu feast, and all the dark-faced inhabitants have
come forth in festal array, gladly mingling together on

foot or scudding hither and thither perched by twos and threes in swiftly moving *ekkas*, those smallest and quaintest of two-wheeled native carriages, which only to look at is refreshing. The houses, moreover, and especially the picturesque "shops" of the bazaars, are gaily decorated with bright-hued garlands, so that well may the town be called, as of old, Pataliputra, the City of Flowers.

But presently, through all the glamour of the Present, the Past begins to assert itself : for this is no mere modern city, and beneath the light that plays on the surface is a depth of bygone years. For a moment, as the travellers gaze, the bright scene swims before their eyes, and, when they again see clearly, all things are wonderfully transformed. Twenty-two centuries have ebbed away, and present once more are the vanished days of the ancient Maurya Dynasty. Gone are the modern houses, and in their stead rise palaces and temples such as befit a royal city. Curiously archaic in form are the buildings, and, splendid though they be, they are all and only of wood, for the days of building in stone have scarcely begun in Magadha, or anywhere else in India. Instead of the modern bazaars with their humble lines of shops, rise antique storehouses full to overflowing with all the riches of the East, whose owners are yonder wealthy merchants treading the streets with jewelled turbans and robes of precious stuffs. Nor is there now the rattling of wheels, but high on the backs of elephants move through the city in solemn state great nobles and mighty princes.

Truly a splendid race are these Maurya Kings of old. At their head is seen the founder of the Dynasty, the powerful Chandragupta, who from B.C. 325 reigned in Pataliputra over a far-extending empire, and whom, after the example of the ancient Greeks, we still call Sandracottus. But greater than

he, and emerging more clearly into the light of history, arises
his grandson, the "Sovereign of Elephants," the mighty Asoka,
beginning in 272 B.C. his long and prosperous reign. He it
was who exalted Buddhism to a place of honour, making the
land to "glitter" with the sheen of the Yellow Robe; and
about the year 250 he held in the city of Pataliputra the
third great Buddhist Council, and from that time Buddhism
prevailed in India for nearly one thousand years. The
legendary history of that great convocation, if any desire
to know, let him read it in "the fifth chapter of the Mahávansa, entitled 'The Third Convocation on Religion,' composed
alike to delight and afflict religious men."[1]

In that sacred book of the Mahávansa are many strange
things told of Asoka, the Lord of Chariots. He it was who
"put to death one hundred brothers minus one," and thereafter reigned supreme over the land of Jambudípa. No
need was then in Pataliputra to snare game for the
royal household; for the elk and the wild hog and winged
game also of their own accord resorted continually to the
kitchens of the King, and there expired on purpose. Asoka's
herdmen were tigers, and wild boars were his shepherd-dogs.
The mystic Nagas, those mighty serpent-princes, brought
from the naga wilderness medicinal drugs to the great King's
court, and fine clothes of seamless fabric, "of the colour
of the sumana flower." A great company of parrots also
waited on the King, bringing daily from the marshes of
Chaddanta 900,000 loads of the hill-padi that grows in those
regions. And when the padi was brought to the city, an
army of mice received it, and they husked it daintily
without breaking the grains, so that there was rice enough

---

[1] See the 'Mahávansa,' translated by G. Turnour, C.C.S., and L. C. Wijes-
inha Mudaliyar.

and to spare for all the great King's household. Willingly
for him laboured honey-making bees; "singing birds of
delightful melody, repairing to the monarch, sang sweet
strains;" and day by day a band of bears worked with
hammers in his arsenals.

He it was, saith Buddhist tradition, who caused to be
builded in the midst of the city that royal palace, those
mighty halls, which remained, long centuries after his time,
the wonder of all beholders. Their giant walls and massive
gates no human hands could have reared; and the rich
carving that decked them and the cunning work of inlaying
were such as no mind of man hath devised. For Asoka was
very powerful, so that many spirits obeyed him, and they, the
ancient legend avers, were the great King's skilful architects.

But as our friends wander in search of those magic
palace-towers, they suddenly are made aware that the tide
of Time is returning; and already the rolling centuries have
engulfed the splendours of the Maurya dynasty, driving the
travellers back till at length the shore on which they stand
is very near the 400th year of our era. Still Buddhism
reigns supreme, and everywhere along the streets walk
monks in their yellow robes, for there are monasteries in
Pataliputra that are "very grand and beautiful," and the
number of monks in this one city is six or seven hundred.
As the travellers gaze around them astonished and knowing not whither to turn, one of the yellow-robed brothers
approaches, and accosts them with a sign of kindly greeting,
as though he would be their guide. No bronze-hued countenance is his, like the Indian faces around him. His face
is light and broad, his eyes are narrow and inclined at an
angle, and when he addresses the wondering travellers he
uses the Chinese tongue.

"I also," says he, "am a stranger in this city of Pataliputra, nor for many days beside my shadow have I seen the shadow of a friend! I am come hither as a pilgrim from the land of Han to search among the Indian monasteries for the holy Books of Discipline; and the Faithful call me Fa-hien, the Illustrious Master of the Law."

The travellers return his oriental salutation, and gladly intrust themselves to their new friend's learned guidance.

"You have done well," he says, "to visit Pataliputra now at this present season; for this is the eighth[1] day of the second month, the yearly festival that the Believers keep with pomp and great rejoicing. I will lead you to a convenient place whence you may behold, if it be your pleasure, the great Procession of Images."

So they follow him far through the populous city, and by the way he tells them many things which, but for his visit to Hindostan, neither they nor the world would have known.

"This city," says he, "has long been obedient to the holy teaching of the Buddha. Herein have dwelt many holy ascetics! In this place was the home of that great professor of _mahâyâna_ whose name was Râdha-sâmi. He had much wisdom, and an excellent discernment, and a good understanding in all things. The King of this country reverenced him greatly, and humbly did him honour, nor ever presumed, when he went to greet him, to seat himself beside him. And if, in his love and reverence, the King took his hand in his own, as soon as he let it go the holy ascetic made haste and poured water upon it to cleanse it. But here is the place of which I spoke, and this way the procession will pass."

[1] See 'Fa-hien's Travels,' translated by James Legge, M.A., LL.D.

Holding his begging-bowl with his left hand beneath a fold of his yellow robe, Fa-hien lifts his bare right arm and points along the stately street, where the pageant is seen approaching. Surrounded by a crowd of eager devotees, towering high overhead, a vast erection looms into view. On a four-wheeled car it stands, built up in five storeys with bamboos tied together. It is more than twenty cubits high, and has the form of a Buddhist tope. It is a moving mountain of gay colours, for over the bamboos of which it is constructed is wound white cloth of Kashmir painted in many hues with quaint and mystic designs. In each of its four sides is a niche wherein sits an image of the Buddha with the figure of a "Bodhisattva" standing in humble attendance. Other images there are, brilliant combinations of gold and silver and lapis-lazuli, flashing and glittering in the sunshine. Over them hang gorgeous canopies, while round them flutter many-coloured silken streamers.

As the great car is dragged slowly past, Fa-hien explains to the wondering travellers the nature of the erection.

"It is upheld," he says, "by a king-post in the midst, with poles and lances slanting from it, and over all is wrapped, as you see, that silk-like cloth of hair."

Before the car, and after it, and around it, presses an ardent crowd, each dark face strangely lit up with an expression of enthusiastic devotion. They come mostly from the surrounding country, and have but lately entered the city. Many of the crowd are monks, and the rich golden hue of their sacred robes harmonises well with the more brilliant colours of the laity's festal array. All the worshippers carry in their hands fresh garlands of fragrant flowers; sweet clouds of incense rise and float around the moving car, while full-voiced singers and skilful musicians fill all the air with the plaintive strains of weird and ancient melodies.

So the tall mountain rolls on its way, and is followed by another as vast as itself, and then by another, and yet another, till the wildly fantastic but dazzling procession would seem to have no end. There are some twenty cars in all, each different from the rest; and round them all the eager crowd moves on, the strange music rises in rapture and falls in wistful cadence, and the incense-cloud is made more fragrant by the scent of the countless blossoms.

As the pageant slowly passes, the good Fa-hien explains to the travellers such things as they desire to know; but when the last great car rolls by, the sound of his voice seems hollow and strange, the lines of his kindly face grow dim, and, as the sunshine falls on his yellow robe, it seems as though its graceful folds were ready to melt in mist. With a shadowy gesture of farewell, he joins the moving throng. The numberless figures grow less distinct, the music sounds faint and muffled, and all the rich and gorgeous pageant is blurred in a coloured haze. Surging back in irresistible might the flowing tide of the centuries sweeps with it our helpless travellers, till it casts them finally high and dry on the humdrum shore of the Present. Vanished for ever is Pataliputra, and they find they have relapsed at unawares into the town of modern Patna.

"It is actually time for tiffin!" exclaims Philippa indignantly, "and we have spent the whole morning in woolgathering. We must visit the opium-factory to-morrow, and try to improve our minds!"

Accordingly our friends spend a long morning in that interesting establishment, and become acquainted with all the processes through which the juice of the poppy must pass before it is ready to be sold as opium. First they are introduced to the opium - poppy itself—*Papaver album somniferum*, as the botanists call it—and behold the delicate fork of metal wherewith the cultivator scratches the poppy-heads of his plants to allow the juice to exude; then they behold the great chatties full of the dark - brown opium as it is brought in from the country; and afterwards they become initiated into the mysteries of testing and cleaning and drying and packing. But nearly three hundred years ago Mr Finch, that worthy traveller and merchant, sketched out the process whereby the opium-drug is obtained; and his quaintly simple account of the matter is more attractive than a long discourse.

"We passed," saith he, " through the pleasant and fertile country of Malve, where there's also a vast deal of Opium. They give the Heads of Poppies two or three scratches, from whence distils a Tear, which at first is white, but afterwards congeal'd by the Cold, turns a reddish Colour; but 'tis a great deal of Pains they bestow in this Business, for a small Matter of Profit; for the Heads are small, and drop their Tears very sparingly."

CHAPTER XII.

THE TEMPLE OF THE BODHI TREE.

THE city of Patna, however interesting, is regarded by our friends the travellers as not much more than a stepping-stone whereby to reach that most famous and most interesting of all the sacred sites of the Buddhists which lies sixty-four miles to the south of it; and soon they are devoting a long day's work to the visiting of Buddha Gaya, the place where, nearly twenty-five centuries ago, Gautama attained to Buddhahood. Rising long before it is light and driving by starlight to the station, the travellers set forth on the three hours' railway journey which is to bring them as far as Gaya, the nearest point to the Bodhi Tree at which railways have hitherto arrived.

Trains are sadly incongruous with the dreamy scenes of the East. Yet it must not be supposed that Indian railway carriages are such odious objects as our own. The broad eaves shading the windows from the sun, the longitudinal arrangement of the seats, and many other small differences of construction, combine to give them an unfamiliar air which might make them susceptible, in competent hands, of even poetical treatment. Above all, the multitudinous passengers are more than capable of putting to flight all

dull and gloomy shadows of the sordid commonplace. The
Natives are great travellers, and the number of them which
can be packed into a single compartment is a never-ending source of astonishment. So many are they that the
railway officials do not individualise, but treat them; so to
speak, in the aggregate. To open the door of a carriage for
Natives of low degree is too much trouble, and, if the door
be locked, they must enter or leave by the window. Very
curious is it, when the train is approaching a station, to see
hanging out of its windows the shoes (with brown feet within
them) of the passengers who intend to alight. Natives of
higher position receive, of course, far greater consideration;
and when secluded ladies travel, there is much unavoidable
ceremony.

. Most delightful of all are the extraordinary scenes at the
stations, where the platforms are crowded with strange figures in stranger costumes, and dark faces with lustrous eyes,
framed in the resplendent hues of cunningly twisted turbans.
One might write a whole book on the beauties of Indian
turbans. Little can they picture them to themselves who
draw their notions of oriental costume from Algeria or
Egypt or Syria. Here in India the textures are finer, the
colours much more delicate and varied, and the twisted coils
piled one on the other in a far more imposing fashion, while
the inner end of the stuff hangs down behind in a graceful
manner, protecting the neck from the sun. The most wonderful thing about these Indian turbans is the way the glow
of the sunshine falls on their soft and intricate folds,—the
brilliant hues where the sunbeams rest, the cool shadows
that nestle between, the magic and shifting lustre of tran-
sient reflected lights. Often the fine Indian muslin is so
slightly tinted as to seem white when unrolled; but when

the turban is deftly twisted and coiled about the wearer's head, then (like the petals of a half-blown rose) its folds accumulate colour—creamy yellow or delicate purple, tender coral or soft moss-green,—and many other rich hues there are, but they have no names in the West.

Numberless and splendid as are the turbans which our travellers behold on this present railway journey, there appears (at a station) one which outshines all the others, —an exceptional and astonishing turban, which must be more particularly described. It is of soft, rich Indian silk, and the colour thereof is a glowing purple of wonderful depth and beauty. It is twisted around the head that wears it in piled-up folds of stately and solemn splendour; but the purple silk has a narrow edging of gold,—just one brilliant thread of light that follows all those mazy wreathings in and out, now hidden away, now darting forth again, like a sunbeam run mad.

"Ah," sighs Sebaste, as the train moves on, "there was an artistic principle involved in the folds of that turban!"

"A poor sort of principle," says Philippa. "I have no patience with those who mistake crooked ways for artistic methods, who go twisting and coiling about, and can never express with straightforward simplicity that which they desire to teach."

"Nor have I," exclaims Sebaste, firing up; "and I have no patience either with the wind or the trees or the rivers, that waste their time in making such useless, murmuring noises when they might be preaching us sermons. What a pity the birds don't sing in articulate language, telling us what it behoves us to do and to think, and insisting on what they have to teach until they oblige us to listen! What a pity the flowers don't turn round upon us and

M

honestly tell us our faults; and oh, what a good thing it would be if the stars were arranged all over the sky so as to form letters and words, and nice little verses of hymns!"

"My dear," says the Father, "you will have leisure at some other time for rearranging the stars. At present we have more earthly things to look at,—native villages, and rice-crops, and those gleaming patches of white, which are the opium-poppies in flower."

So the train speeds on its way until, some three hours after leaving Bankipur, our friends arrive at Gaya, the place where Gautama is said to have practised for six years the most astonishing austerities, living each day on a single hemp-seed and a single grain of rice. Here they alight, and, disposing themselves in a gharry, set forth on the seven miles' southward drive to Buddha Gaya and the Bodhi Tree.

"Philippa," exclaims Sebaste presently, "I will forgive you all your views on Art if only you will amuse us now with some of the Buddha's legends. What was that dusty old Buddhist volume that you were studying so diligently last night?"

"It was the travels of Hiuen Tsiang," says Philippa, —"leastwise a translation of them."

"And who was Hiuen Tsiang?"

"He was a Chinese Buddhist monk who visited this part of the world A.D. 629; and he wrote his travels in a much fuller and more business-like way than your stupid old friend Fa-hien."

"Dear Fa-hien!" exclaims Sebaste sentimentally, "I shall always like him best. He was such a kind, soft-hearted old boy. Do you remember how the tears filled his eyes when he told us how long it was since he had seen the land of Han?"

"Ah, but you know nothing about Hiuen Tsiang!" says
Philippa. "You should read what Chang Yueh has written
about him! 'His illustrious ancestors like fishes in the lake,
or as birds assembled before the wind, by their choice services in the world served to produce as their result an
illustrious descendant. . . . At his opening life he was
rosy as the evening vapours and round as the rising moon!'[1]
The description of his wisdom and learning is truly astonishing; and yet, when the time came, he 'embarked in the
boat of humility and departed alone.'"

"I am sure he was a terrible prig! But what has he to
say about Buddha Gaya? Why did Buddha come to this
particular place, or choose this particular bo-tree to be
'enlightened' under?"

"Hiuen Tsiang says that he first thought of obtaining
enlightenment on the top of the mountain Pragbodhi, but
was dissuaded by the mountain-deity, who was afraid of the
consequences to himself. So the Buddha (he was only a
Bôdhisattva as yet) descended the south-west slope; and
half-way down he came to 'a great stone chamber,' and sat
him down therein cross-legged. And another deity 'cried
out in space' that this was not the place for him 'to perfect
supreme wisdom,' and directed him to go south-westward
till he came to this pipal-tree. So Bôdhisattva rose to depart; but a dear old dragon who dwelt in that cave was
greatly distressed, and said, 'This cave is pure and excellent.
Here you may accomplish the holy aim. Would that of your
exceeding love you would not leave me.' So Bôdhisattva, to
appease the dragon's grief, 'left him his shadow,' and so departed. And long centuries after the Buddha had passed
away from existence, his shadow still remained in the depth

[1] See 'Buddhist Records of the Western World,' by Samuel Beal, B.A.

of the mountain-cave.   But Bôdhisattva went south-westward
till he came to the Bodhi Tree; and beneath it he sat on a
diamond throne, and there attained to Buddhahood."

But at this point in Philippa's edifying discourse the
gharry comes to a stand, and the ancient temple of the
bo-tree is seen towering against the sky. The dignified
and handsome face of a native gentleman looks in upon
the travellers with a courteous greeting, and they are told,
in excellent English, that they are "all invited." Alighting
from their gharry, they perceive that some festivity is in
progress, and that a far-spreading, gay-coloured canopy has
been erected as a protection from the sun for the benefit of
European visitors. At the time of our travellers' visit the
temple and the site of the bo-tree are still in the hands of
Hindu *mahants,* a monastic college whose principal function
(if report speak true) is the fleecing of Buddhist pilgrims.
The chief *mahant,* it seems, has lately died; and to-day his
successor is being solemnly installed in his stead.

Eating their tiffin in the shade of the canopy, the travellers became acquainted with an affable Bengali barrister
who speaks English with more ease and fluency than
most Englishmen have at their command. Perceiving that
they are strangers to the place, he offers to show them
the temple, and under his kindly guidance they valiantly
brave the noonday sun and set forth on its exploration. It
is a towering pyramidal pile, massive and straight-lined,
reaching a height of 160 feet. It used to be considerably
higher; but the crowning *kalas* has been worn away by the
weather, and presents but a deplorable vestige of its original
graceful proportions. The temple in its present form is,
among Indian temples, absolutely unique, being a copy (as
the learned aver) of a *vihara* of nine storeys; and it was

completed (as a Burmese inscription sets forth) A.D. 1299 by
Buddhists from Burmah. But this was only a restoration,
and the temple still retains many of the features which distinguished it in the beginning of the sixth century, when
Amara the Brahman had rebuilded that ancient *vihara* of
Asoka's, which may have replaced a still earlier building
dating from the times of the Enlightened himself. Since
1880 the building has been again restored at the cost of
80,000 rupees. Our travellers are not learned in architectural
technicalities, but, as they gaze on the results of this last
restoration, they find themselves instinctively and involun-
tarily shuddering. How different now does the building
look from that stately and richly decorated *vihara* that
Hiuen Tsiang beheld,—a towering pile of "blue tiles covered
with *chunam*," having many "niches in the different storeys"
filled with "golden figures."

With a regretful sigh they enter the temple, and are confronted, in its principal chamber, by a great gilded figure
of the Buddha, sitting enthroned in the somewhat painful
attitude of conventional meditation. He is adorned with a
robe of state, various offerings are placed in his neighbourhood, and over his head is suspended a votive umbrella.
Other chambers there are, and other figures of Buddha; but
the whole interior of the building has a sadly modernised
air, and the visitors soon wander out again into the sunshine,
and begin to examine in detail the more interesting exterior
features.

Along the temple's northern side runs a narrow platform
of masonry raised to a height of 4 feet above the surface of
the ground. It is 50 feet long, and is called, as the affable
barrister remarks, Buddha's Promenade. Here it was that
"the Blessed One," the "Storehouse of Virtue," having ob-

tained enlightenment and "realised the bliss of Nirvana," spent seven whole days walking up and down in meditation, eastward and westward; and at the points where he set his foot are sculptured ornaments of stone, commemorating those miraculous blossoms which sprang up under his footsteps.

Passing along by the Promenade and coming round to the north side of the temple, the travellers attain at length to the site of the Enlightenment itself, "the steadfast spot chosen by all the Buddhas, the spot for the throwing down of the temple of sin," [1] the place of the Diamond Throne, overshadowed by that "monarch of the forests," the venerated Tree of Wisdom.

The present tree, alas! is but a puny descendant of the original pipal—an infantile, inadequate thing that is very disappointing to look upon. From its branches hangs a long strip of paper with strange characters written thereon. This is somebody's horoscope suspended here that the sacredness of the place may bring good fortune to him whose life it foreshadows.

"I had hoped," sighs Sebaste, "that the real bo-tree might still be in existence. At least Fa-hien said that 'in Central India the cold and heat are so equally tempered that trees will live in it for several thousand and even for ten thousand years!'"

"Fa-hien was a credulous creature," say Philippa. "If you wish to hear the true story of the Enlightenment, you should go to Hiuen Tsiang!"

"But I thought Hiuen Tsiang spoke of a Diamond Throne under the bo-tree, and I don't see one here."

"No, you can't exactly *see* it, but it is there all right, and it reaches down for I don't know how many thousands of

---

[1] From 'Buddhist Birth Stories,' translated by T. W. Rhys Davids.

miles, to the very limits of the Golden Wheel. Only, toward the end of the Age, 'when the true law dies out and disappears, the earth and dust begin to cover over this spot,' so that the throne is no longer visible. This place is the centre of the world; all the Buddhas who preceded Gautama sat on this Diamond Throne to obtain enlightenment, and so will all future Buddhas also. 'When the great earth arose, this throne also appeared,' and 'when the great earth is shaken, this place alone is unmoved.'"

"But, Philippa, have you nothing to tell us about the Tree of Wisdom itself? It is easier to believe in than diamond thrones, and we have its descendant to look at while you are telling its history."

So Philippa tells many things of the ancient bodhi-tree, —how its leaves "remained glistening and shining all the year round without change," but used, when the Nirvana-day came round, to wither and fall on a sudden and then in a moment to revive; and how Asoka, in his unbelieving days, raised an army against the Tree, and cut through its roots and divided the trunk and chopped the branches small, and ordered a fire-worshipping Brahman to burn them there and then. Whereupon the Tree sprang up again in a night, and was never a whit the worse.

Then there is that strange legend to tell of the branch that was sent by the converted and pious Asoka to the far-off land of Lanka, the same is Simhala and Ceylon. For Asoka, the Ruler of the World, collected much gold, and caused to be made thereof a vase "nine cubits in circumference, five cubits in depth, . . . and, in the rim of the mouth, of the thickness of the trunk of a full-grown elephant";[1] and he filled it with scented soil. Then, having

[1] From the 'Mahavansa.'

caused the road from Pataliputra to the bo-tree "to be swept and perfectly decorated," he came with more than a thousand kings, and set the precious vase on a golden chair beside the Tree. And "using vermilion in a golden pencil," he therewith made a streak on the branch. And forthwith the bo-branch "severed itself at the place where the streak was made" and "rested on the top of the vase." And a hundred roots shot forth from its stem "like a network," and descended into the fragrant soil till the branch was firmly planted, whereupon the great earth quaked, "and, from the fruit and leaves of the bo-branch, brilliant rays of the six primitive colours issuing forth, illuminated the whole universe." Then the Ruler of the World, the Delighter in Donations, intrusted the great bo-branch to the Princess Sanghamitta, his daughter, renowned and profoundly learned. He bestowed also eight vases of silver and eight vases of gold wherewith to water the same. And he caused it to be embarked in a vessel on the river Ganges together with Sanghamitta his daughter and her eleven attendant nuns. And "departing out of his capital," he preceded that vessel on its way, marching with all his army through the far-reaching Vinjha Wilderness.

When they came to the shore of the ocean, Asoka-raja disembarked the great bo-branch, and made thereto with devotion an offering of all his empire. Then, having placed it with its attendants in the royal ship prepared for it, he "stood on the shore of the ocean with uplifted hands, and, gazing on the departing bo-branch, shed tears in the bitterness of his grief. In the agony of parting with the bo-branch, . . . weeping and lamenting in loud sobs," he "departed for his own capital." But Sanghamitta, the pious Princess, came with a happy and prosperous voyage to

Simhala, the Island of Gems.   So the great bo-branch was planted at Anuradhapura, and to this day it is growing there, the most ancient tree that we wot of.

Such legends do the travellers recall as they linger in the noonday silence around the Bodhi Tree; and more especially they remember the great scene of the far-famed Enlightenment itself.   But that story hath been told us of late years in so poetic and idealised a form, that I hardly dare to rehearse it as it appears in the original legends.   It is one thing to hear of spiritual conflict, of heroic virtue and triumphant holiness, and another to read in the Buddhist scriptures how Gautama "sat himself down in a cross-legged position, firm and immovable, as if welded with a hundred thunderbolts," and how Mara came against him mounted on his elephant named "Girded with Mountains" that was 250 leagues in height, and with him a mighty host, and hurled at him great mountains that changed, as they reached his presence, into "bouquets of heavenly flowers," so that the mighty elephant "Girded with Mountains" fell down on his knees in worship; or how, when the "Great Being," the "asylum of mind and memory," had at length obtained enlightenment, "the ten thousand world-systems" shouted for joy, and "lotus-wreaths hung from the sky," while the great ocean became sweet down to its profoundest depths, and the rivers were stayed in their course.

And already the business-like Philippa announces that it is time to be moving on.

"As we cannot see the Diamond Throne," says she, "let us try to find that other seat of dignity, the Throne of the Seven Gems.   It is not far from the bodhi-tree, and on it the Buddha sat 'after he had arrived at complete Enlightenment.'   Hiuen Tsiang speaks of it; but he adds to his account the pathetic remark, 'From the time of the holy one till the present is so long that the gems have turned to stone.' "

Before leaving the bodhi-tree the travellers admire, placed in a niche of the temple wall just opposite the tree, a venerated image of the Buddha which gleams brightly in the sunlight by reason of the gold-leaf wherewith pious-minded pilgrims have adorned it.   Then they wander vaguely about, seeking near the temple for the Throne of the Seven Gems, and reluctantly coming at length to the conclusion that from the time of Hiuen Tsiang to the present is so long that it has altogether disappeared.

But they find, for their consolation, many interesting fragments of ancient Buddhist sculpture, including stone Buddhas innumerable, whereof many, as the barrister explains, have received the incongruous names of various Hindu gods.   Most attractive of all are the remains of that sculptured rail of stone wherewith Asoka surrounded the *vihara* which he had builded.   Fascinating indeed are the sculptures thereof, for they are the earliest specimens we have of the art in India, and show it as yet untouched by any foreign influence whatever.   Very prominent therein is that ancient and mysterious worship of Trees and Serpents, the indigenous religion that Buddhism found and took to itself and assimilated.

Having viewed the world from the temple's roof, and having finally said farewell to the ancient pile and their courteous guide, the travellers betake them to the neighbouring "College" of the *Mahants*, where, in honour of the solemn occasion, a great feast is at present in progress.   As they cross the outer court of the building they perceive that preparations are being made therein for the State-durbar

which will here be held to-night by the new-made Chief
Mahant. A great canopy has been erected, and beneath it
several dark figures are at work, like the attendants at Siva's
wedding, "spreading abroad the carpet of congratulation and
arranging the banquet of bliss." [1]

Making their way to the crowded inner court, the visitors
behold a wonderfully animated scene. The roofs of the
surrounding buildings are crowded with oriental banqueters,
and, as they enter, they are surrounded by a crowd of
swarthy *Mahants*, who all wear the holy salmon-coloured
robe of their order, but show faces which look by no means
holy. Farther than the entrance of this inner court the
travellers may not go ; and, when they ask to see the Chief
Mahant, they are told that he has just begun to eat, and
will go on eating till evening—an assertion which, it is to be
hoped, need not be taken quite literally.

Retiring from this festive scene, the travellers drive back
to Gaya, and seek out that older part of the city where is
the famous Temple of Vishnu Pad, the honoured shrine of
the footprint of Vishnu, the lotus-eyed lord of the world.
Even in a day devoted to Buddhist studies, a little Vaishnava sight-seeing is not very incongruous; for is not the
Buddha recognised by Hinduism as the ninth avatar of
Vishnu ?

As they wander through the temple precincts, the visitors
meet several sacred cows, who pass them softly by with a
sanctimonious air; and presently they come upon a strange
scene which they will long hereafter remember. An old,
white-haired man has come to perform, for the benefit of the
souls of his ancestors, the solemn rite of *sraddha*. Specially
acceptable to those venerated *pitris* is this offering when

[1] Sheeve Pouran. Halhed.

duly made in the sacred city of Gaya. Long ago it was written in the book of the illustrious Markandeya, "Flesh of the rhinoceros, . . . turmeric and soma juice, and a *sraddha* performed at Gaya, without doubt yield the *pitris* endless satisfaction." This present hour, moreover, is likewise propitious; for in that same book it is written, "Just as the time of the waning moon is dearer to the *pitris* than that of the waxing moon, so the afternoon pleases the *pitris* more than the forenoon."

The old man has chosen in the temple court a place, according to the ordinance, that hath neither been looked at by dogs nor scorched with fire, and that hath not been "made hot with the words of enemies and wicked men." He has brought with him a number of little cakes of rice, which he places one by one on the pavement, sprinkling each as he sets it down with a few drops of water. A friend sits near him on the ground, holding a paper whereon are written the names of those ancestors who are to be nourished by these sacred "morsels of the *pitris*." Over the ceremony presides a handsome, bright-eyed young Brahman, who, as each cake is sprinkled with the water, recites some mystic formula in a monotonous rhythmic chant. Very sacred is that duty which the aged worshipper is performing, and his beneficent *pitris* will reward his devotion by bestowing upon him "long life, wisdom, wealth, knowledge," and "final emancipation from existence." Slowly, with touching earnestness and reverence, he goes on with the mysterious rite, too deeply absorbed to notice anything else; but the young Brahman turns on the travellers his mocking, merry, black eyes, that say more plainly than words could speak it, "Just look at the silly old fool!"

The Brahmans of Gaya, commonly called Gayawals, are

notorious for their unbounded rapacity. Strictly do they enforce that ancient Brahmanic maxim, "Men of understanding must give gifts to Brahmans; whatever is most desired in the world, and whatever is prized at home, . . . must one who hopes for immortality give to a Brahman endowed with good qualities." Many stories are told of the methods in use among the Gayawals for the fleecing of their hapless victims. Year by year to the sacred places of Gaya and its neighbourhood come pilgrims whose number is said to be between 100,000 and 200,000. The Gayawals meet the trains that bring them, and take the pilgrims in charge; and even if they be rich on their arrival, they are likely to depart in poverty and deeply involved in debt. Terrible is the scene enacted when a wealthy sinner has come, seeking in holy Gaya to rid himself of his guilt. Then do the Gayawals gather round him, and tie fast his trembling hands with a garland of sacred flowers. Nor will they loose him from that inviolable bond until, after many prayers and unavailing lamentations, he has vowed away his gold.

With such things as these in their minds, the travellers are not disposed to give any smiling answer to the lustrous, quick, dark eyes that, from this present Gayawal's face, so merrily appeal for their sympathy.

Leaving the strange little group, they wander on through the temple precincts till they come to the door of that inmost shrine where Christians may not enter. Within is a depth of baffling darkness; but, as they strain their eyes to see, they at length discern, let into the chamber's pavement, that sacred plate of silver which bears the print of Vishnu's lotus-foot that has power to save its devotees from "the woes wrought by the fear of existence." Seated on the pavement around it are the dimly seen figures of silent and motionless worshippers offering garlands of flowers, both fresh and sweet, to the mystic and holy footprint.

As they return from the shrine on their way to the entrance of the temple, the visitors perceive that the aged worshipper has finished his offering, and is now undergoing the concluding ceremony of having his scanty locks shaved from his head, while around him sit two or three of the temple Brahmans reciting with imperturbable countenances " sacred *mantras* of the Vedas."

CHAPTER XIII.

BENARES.[1]

VARANASI, holiest of cities, bright-robed daughter of Ganga, whose "pure" stream has mirrored for ages thy lordly palaces and gorgeous temples, how shall we rightly celebrate thy wonders? Most ancient of India's cities, whosoever would traverse the plain of thy history, the feet of his imagination are lamed. How shall we speak of the dim and far-off days when those patriarchs of our race, the Vedic Aryans, made of thee their home and their stronghold? Nay, in that more distant age when "Time the Destroyer" was yet unborn, wast not thou the first of all the earth to arise from the universal waters; and in the terrible deluge did not Bhagván support thee on his trident so that the waves devoured thee not? Art thou not the home of Siva himself, who performed in thy neighbourhood unheard-of austerities, and ordained in thee his own worship for ever?

No, let us hope not quite for ever; but at present this city is the centre and heart of Hindu idolatry, a fact intimated to our travellers as early (on the first day after

---

[1] Banáras is the correct form, but in the case of so familiar a name we may be allowed, perhaps, to conform to the vulgar usage.

their arrival) as the serving of *chota hazri*, which makes
its appearance on resplendent trays of Benares brass-work,
exquisitely chased with mazy arabesques, from the intricacies whereof peep forth a multitude of queer little gods,
who, with impish persistency though in varying forms,
will haunt our English friends throughout their stay at
Benares.

The sun, with flaming locks, drawn by those "seven ruddy
steeds, the daughters of his chariot," is already filling all
things with the dust of his rays when the travellers, with a
humbler equipage, set forth to see and to wonder. Strange
figures, to Western eyes, are their coachman and syces. They
are clad in the most brilliant orange that mind can imagine,
their dusky faces framed in dark-blue turbans. But by far
the most majestic figure of all is that of the Pandit Pursotum
who sits beside the driver. Assuredly our friends will be
for ever grateful for the excellent guidance of that "tiger-
like man." If there were any more complimentary epithet
than this, I would give it him with pleasure. A fine and
solemn face hath he, with large, lustrous eyes, and a bushy
beard of glossy black, which he has carefully trimmed
"facing eastward or northward" according to the ordinance.
He is dressed in white, with the exception of his very becoming turban, which is of rich, gold-coloured silk. Being
learned in the Hindu scriptures, he obeys with exactness that
precept of the wise Queen Madalasa, "One should neither
dress unbecomingly, nor speak unbecomingly. One should
be clad in pure white raiment."

"Surely," whispers Sebaste, "such a picture as that has
no right to expose itself to the glare and the dust out of
doors. I feel inclined to address to him that pathetic
question asked of old by the subjects of the exiled Hari-

scandra, 'Alas! O King, what will thy very youthful, beauti-
ful-browed, fine-nosed face become when injured by the dust
on the road?'"[1]

Thus attended, the travellers drive away through the
shade of tamarinds and nîm-trees, alternating with dazzling
sunshine; but they see nothing as yet of the native city,
which is at some distance to the south-east of the canton-
ment. They presently pass Queen's College, a Government institution wherein Pursotum learned his Sanskrit
and that excellent English wherein he explains objects of
interest passed on the road. Queen's College is an imposing erection, perhaps the finest Gothic building in India
(what the others are like it were possibly unwise to inquire); and our travellers behold it now to the best possible advantage, the last example of Gothic art they have
seen being that architectural nightmare, the poor, dear
Cathedral in Calcutta. Our friends will explore the college
another day, will be dazzled by the brilliant flowers of which
the garden is full, and will there admire an hypæthral
museum consisting of ancient carvings from Sarnath and
elsewhere. They will also be introduced, at the garden
fountain, to a stolid-looking, ungenial personage, their first
Indian Alligator.

But for such attractions they have no time at present,
preferring idol-temples and heathenish ceremonies to any
number of sober-minded Colleges.

They presently meet a little procession, at the head of
which rides, on a white horse, a youthful bridegroom gor-
geously arrayed. On his head is a shining crown of tinsel,
from which hang strings of white flowers, covering his face
like a veil. One of his relatives walks by his side, shading

[1] Markandeya Purána. **Pargiter.**

N

him from the sun with an oriental umbrella, while various other friends follow, also on foot, holding up banners and other curious devices constructed of tinsel and of all the colours of the rainbow. But the little bride is sitting at home, and has no share at all in this great pomp and grandeur.

"Pursotum," exclaims Philippa presently, "what in the world are those curious packages carried about slung to bamboos? We have met two or three already, and there is another—a neat parcel wrapped up in a crimson cloth. What is it?"

"That," says Pursotum, "is a private lady."

And a secluded lady it really is. Belonging to a high caste, she may not walk abroad like her humbler sisters, but must make herself up into a parcel and be carried by two of her servants. On a little square of basket-work she sits, to the four corners whereof are attached small and slender bamboos, which, meeting over her head, are firmly tied to the large bamboo above, that rests on the men-servants' shoulders. Fitting closely round the four small bamboos is a covering of crimson cloth. The lady sits of course in the native fashion, with feet tucked away out of sight, so that, when the covering is drawn down, not a vestige is visible of her or her dress. Our travellers, on one occasion, are much distressed at seeing one of these compact little parcels left to itself in the middle of the road, the "private lady" inside not daring to lift the covering to see what has become of her servants.

These and many other curious sights make short the way to our friends' present destination, which is the temple of Durga. Durga, the Inaccessible, the Terrible One, is, notwithstanding such attributes, the most popular of goddesses,

and her annual festival, the Durga *puja*, is celebrated with
great rejoicings and the sacrifice of goats innumerable.
Many forms hath she, and manifold powers. In the mansion
of the virtuous she dwelleth as the goddess of riches, as the
deity of misfortune in the abode of the wicked, and as Intelligence in the heart of the wise. How can her form be
described, which is inconceivable? She is great, heroic,
ample—the destroyer of the giants. Revered is she by all
the deities; the magnificent sages faithfully prostrate themselves to her. She is the beneficent mother of the whole
universe, the sovereign of the world. So at least sang Indra,
the Suras, and Vanhi the god of Fire, as they hymned her
victories over the giants.

The Inaccessible she assuredly proves herself to-day, noti-
fying to our travellers, through her attendant Brahmans, that
they may in nowise enter her temple unless they honour her
by first removing their shoes. Unfortunately our friends
have a scruple on this point. "A good deal of harm has
been done," a Missionary in the South once told them, "by
European Christians who submit to having their shoes removed when entering the Hindu temples. The Natives say,
'The Sahibs go into their own churches with their boots on,
but they take them off when they come to Hindu temples.
They know that our temples are holier than theirs!'"

Happily the visitors can see, as they stand on the threshold, the whole of the interior; and a very graceful interior
it is. Absolutely different are these "Indo-Aryan" temples
from the great Dravidian pagodas of the South. Here are
no more vast halls, pillared corridors, forests of fantastic
columns, abysmal vistas of gloomy shadow; but a single
cloistered court, and in the centre a single shrine approached
by a small and curiously wrought pavilion, and surmounted

by one of those curvilinear spires, or rather elongated domes, which are characteristic of all temples built in the "Indo-Aryan" style. As usual, this almost conical dome is stained with ochre to a deep claret colour (the sacred hue wherewith no private house may presume to adorn itself), and is further embellished by brilliant points of gilding. Just beneath it sits the Goddess, peering out of her dark recess with greedy eyes to see if there are any goats in prospect.

But Durga herself is of secondary importance to the visitors, who have come to call not on her so much as on the monkeys, sacred to Hanuman, whom she hospitably allows to make their home in her temple and its surrounding trees. Most amiable creatures they are, with thick coats of glossy, brown fur, and humorous faces charming to behold. There are only about a hundred of them, Pursotum says, but they look far more numerous, resembling that little pig of nursery celebrity who "ran about so fast that nobody could count him."

A peculiar cry is uttered by one of the temple servants, who scatters on the ground grain and sweetmeats for their delectation, and instantly a crowd assembles. Old monkeys and young monkeys, monkeys small and monkeys large, with a rush they gather together, swinging themselves down from the overhanging trees, dropping from the walls of the enclosure, galloping round unsuspected corners, grinning at the would-be intruders, and eagerly falling to on the dainties prepared for them. This is very condescending, considering how holy they are; but natural too, for was not Hanuman himself—that giant Monkey-god who leaped across the strait betwixt India and Ceylon, and defeated an army of 80,000 men—was not he so eagerly desirous of goodies that he once mistook the sun for a sweetmeat, and accordingly swallowed it?

The travellers walk round the outside of the temple, and examine the giant tamarinds wherein the monkeys love to disport themselves, and one of which has a hollow trunk specially set apart by them to be the babies' nursery.

"Two years ago," says Pursotum, "there used to be 5000 monkeys living here."

Pursotum, being a devout believer in their holiness, does not add that these same 5000 monkeys committed such ravages in the neighbourhood that no one could live in security for miles around their temple; nor that they even penetrated as far as the railway station, where they plundered the newly-arrived sacks of rice, to the lamentable loss of the owners thereof. The European officials, who dared not slay so sacred a beast for fear of a riot in Benares, showed great tact in dealing with this dilemma. They prepared, on the trucks of a train, a feast of nuts and sweetmeats; and when a large company of monkeys had assembled to partake of it, the train was put in motion, and the monkeys, steaming forth into the jungle, were never heard of more.

"There seems to be a fine garden over there," says the Father, when the monkeys have been sufficiently admired. "Who lives there, Pursotum?"

"The Swami Bhaskaranand Saraswati lives there. He is more holy than any one in India."

"Is he a Brahman, then?"

"He was so once, but now he is greater than Brahman. He is Swami."

"But what makes him so holy?"

"He does not eat any meat,—nothing but vegetables and milk. And he does not wear anything; only, when Sahibs and Memsahibs go to visit him, he will wear some dress."

"May we go to see him, then?"

And Pursotum shows the way forthwith. The travellers enter a garden luxuriant and lovely as only an Indian garden can be. The narrow, paved walks are raised a foot or two above the carefully irrigated beds where flourishes a crowded growth of tropical vegetation. Far-spreading trees make a delicious shade beneath their thick foliage; flowering shrubs fill the air with perfume; vivid banana-leaves hang broad and graceful in sun-flecked shadow; brilliant flowers grow close to the ground; the air is full of rustlings and murmurings innumerable, and of a cool and fragrant freshness delicious beyond imagination.

"Here," says Pursotum, "is a statue of the Swami."

The statue, which represents the aged saint sitting in an attitude of meditation, is of white marble. Round its neck hangs a garland of yellow flowers, fresh and fragrant.

"The people worship this statue," explains Pursotum. "The Swami himself will not receive them now, because they trouble him with asking him to give them many things. Whatever he promises to any one, he receives immediately. If he promises riches, a man will begin to grow wealthy at once, and within a month he will be very rich. He can also give sons, or good health, or anything. There was a native regiment here that was ordered to go to the war in Burmah, but they feared, and did not wish to go. And they came to the Swami, and bowed down to him, and wept, and said that they would never again see their homes or their families. Then the Swami touched each of them with his hand, and told him that he would come home safely. And every one that he touched did return perfectly safe. See, he is coming to meet you."

Attended by two reverent disciples, the old man approaches. His dress consists of a single robe of soft, white

Indian silk, tied round the waist, and falling in rich folds below the knee. It has a many-coloured border, which Pursotum reverently touches in token of respectful greeting. A gentle, kindly old man he is, with none of the arrogance that one would expect in a personage thus idolised, but only a mild self-complacency, so innocent and childlike that it is impossible to be very angry with him for his folly in allowing himself to be worshipped.

Deeply versed as he is in Sanskrit learning, the Swami knows not a word of any Western tongue, and the conversation is carried on chiefly by Pursotum, who sets forth the merits of the saint, appealing to him for confirmation of his statements. It seems that this peaceful hermitage is the present of a pious Raja, but that all gifts in money the Swami absolutely refuses. Large fortunes have been offered him by wealthy Hindus, but have been invariably rejected. One Maharaja once offered a large sum (five lacs of rupees, Pursotum says!), begging him, if he would not keep it, to distribute it among the poor. "Do thou thyself distribute," was the answer.

The Swami assents to these facts with a delighted smile of the utmost simplicity. Being further asked what is his age, he says that he is sixty-five,—which is very old for India.

"Tell him," says the Father, "that I am eight years older than he."

"Thou," answers the humble Swami, "art in all things greater than I! I pray thee that on thy return to England thou wilt remember me. If thou or any of these thy daughters should write a book, let my name be inserted therein."

Dear old Swami Bhaskaranand Saraswati! Thy name is

not exactly a handy one, but assuredly we would squeeze it
in, were even the page too narrow to accommodate its rolling
syllables.

The Swami next says (Pursotum interpreting) that when
the visitors arrived he was about to eat, and that he now
desires that they will themselves eat in his garden. One of
the grave and pious disciples retires to fetch some of the
Swami's food — a charming concoction of potatoes, fruit,
honey, and various herbs, set out on a platter made of
leaves neatly stitched together. A little of this refection
is placed by the aged saint in the hand of each of his
visitors, who, having happily left European notions far behind them, are not troubled by any conventional hanker-
ings after plates or spoons or forks.

Before taking leave, the Father, knowing the native enjoyment of such ceremony, presents his card, which the Swami
places on the top of his own head by way of expressing his
thanks. Then, taking the Father in his slender, bare, brown
arms, he gives him an affectionate hug, and, moreover,
bestows upon him one of his own Sanskrit works, as well
as his biography, likewise written in Sanskrit, and a picture of himself, wherein he appears, according to the precept, seated, in the exercise of devotion, on the sacred
khás-khás grass, calm, and free from all desires, maintaining a difficult posture, restraining his breath, "keeping his
head, his neck, and his body steady, without motion, his
eyes fixed on the point of his nose, looking at nothing
else around."[1]

Finally, plucking some flowers for each of the travellers,
the kindly Swami bids them farewell. While the English
visitors place their hands in his, Pursotum's yellow turban

[1] Quoted in Crawfurd's 'Hindus.'

bows to earth once more, as he devoutly touches, first the Swami's bare feet, and then his own forehead, with an earnest reverence that is impressive to see.

At length the travellers drive away, and are soon plunging into the heart of Benares city on their way to the Golden Temple. In a short time they are obliged to alight from their carriage, for only on foot may one penetrate the intricacies of the narrow and sinuous streets. Wonderful streets they are, — deep, winding clefts between the tall oriental houses, bordered with the quaint recesses that call themselves shops, from which gleam forth whole armies of little brazen gods, with here and there a stone figure (and an excellent likeness) of Swami Bhaskaranand Saraswati, destined for some temple or shrine.

Here and there a shop is devoted to prayer-bags. To say one's prayers in a bag seems to the Western mind a curious notion; but not so to the Hindus, who love, when praying, to thrust the right hand, holding a rosary of sacred beads, into one of these gnomon-shaped receptacles of brightly coloured cloth quaintly embroidered to represent the head and neck of a sacred cow.

Then there are shops full of oriental sweetmeats manufactured of milk and sugar, and so tempting to behold that our travellers wistfully approach. Whereupon the turbaned shopman, sitting cross-legged amidst his piled-up wares, will beg them not to touch; for the touch of a Christian, or even of a Christian's shadow, would make his dainties unfit to be eaten by pious Hindus.

Most attractive of all are the flower-shops, overflowing with fragrant garlands, or rather *ropes*, of flowers—purple and white and orange and yellow—piled up in masses of gorgeous colour, and destined to be bought by pilgrims and hung round the necks of idol-gods, or wreathed in solemn devotion about Siva's idolised symbol.

But the shops by no means monopolise all the rich hues of the glowing scene. The private houses, too, make a brave show, being decorated with native wall-paintings —sky-blue elephants and other cheerful devices—executed on occasions of domestic rejoicing, such as a wedding or the birth of a son.

And far more wonderful than all else is the ceaseless stream of brightly-clad figures flowing for ever along the narrow, winding ways,—an ever-moving, variegated procession inextricably mixed up with the sacred hump-backed cows, who stray about in a harmless and amiable manner throughout the whole city. To buy a cow and let her go loose to live in the temples and streets is a very meritorious act indeed; and the gentle creatures meet with the utmost deference and respect from everybody.

"The municipal authorities," saith the author of 'Picturesque India,' "at one time used to kidnap them darkly at dead of night, and turn them loose on the opposite shore of the Ganges, but they generally swam back, and turned up holier than ever."

Holier, indeed; for did not even that wicked and bloodthirsty cow who gored to death in ancient days her master's son, and thereupon turned from white to black through the guilt of her crime—did not even she, when she had thrice plunged in a sacred river, come out as white and fair as ever she was before?

Slowly making their way through the crowd, the travellers arrive at a small temple of Siva wedged into a corner of the street, and richly adorned with elaborate sculptures. The presiding Brahman allows our friends to enter, shoes

notwithstanding; and they eagerly explore this tiny abode
of that "chief of the gods" who contriveth all things for
the good of the world, the immortal Five-faced Lord, whom
when the Devas hymned they pathetically exclaimed, " Verily,
what power have we to perform thy worship? Verily,
what means hath an atom without hand or foot to open
its mouth in praise of the all-illuminating sun, and what
strength hath the grovelling ant to spread the carpet of
argumentation for the exalted praise of Solomon?"[1]

Facing the symbol of the god reclines in stony dignity
Nandi, his sacred bull, "the Sovereign of all quadrupeds,"
and Siva's constant companion. On the wall hangs an
appalling picture of the goddess Kali, the Dark One, a
terrific form of Durga (assumed, say some, with a view to
frightening the wicked into reformation), and the spouse of
Time, the Bringer of Evil, the Sovereign of all things, who
himself is but a form of Siva, the God of a Thousand Names.
Frightful is she to look upon. She wears a necklace of
skulls; one cobra forms her girdle, and another, coiled
around her throat, supports with its venomous head her
long, rough tongue. In one of her four hands she holds the
head of a demon freshly hewn from his gigantic shoulders,
while in another she brandishes a scimitar. Gazing at her
hideous portrait, one can vividly imagine that memorable
battle of hers when "the terrific-faced Kali furiously fell
upon the giants, wrathfully swallowed up her enemies, and
chewed the chariots with her teeth."[2]

Rather hastily retreating from the presence of this heroic
lady, the travellers presently approach a very holy object
indeed, the Gyán Kúp, or Well of Knowledge. Crossing

[1] From Halhed's 'Sheeve Pouran.'
[2] From the 'Sapta-Shati.' Cavali Venkat Rámasswámi, Pandit.

a court wherein reclines a colossal Nandi coloured a brilliant red, they enter a colonnade adorned with light and beautifully ornamented Hindu pillars, and in the centre thereof discover the Well. Its great sanctity arises from the fact that Siva (or at the least his symbol) was once thrown into it, and is to this day reposing at the bottom, communicating to the water above him a marvellous power for cleansing from guilt even the greatest criminals on earth. The opening of the Well is almost entirely covered, but with what material remains a mystery, seeing that the covering is altogether hidden from view by masses of bright flowers thrown upon it by pious worshippers. At the narrow aperture sits a Brahman ladling out the water (in return for copper coins) to a crowd of pilgrims, each of whom receives the precious liquid in the palm of his hand, drinks three drops (throwing them into his mouth with the fingers of his other hand), and reverently deposits the rest on his head. An old woman addresses our travellers, exhorting them (says Pursotum) to buy some of the water for themselves, and assuring them that they will gain from it great benefit.

Resisting her persuasions, they leave the Well, and so reach at length the far-famed Golden Temple dedicated to Bisheshwar, the Poison God, the blue-throated, Uma's lord, who is another form of that "adorable three-eyed god of the gods," Siva himself. For once on a time, when the gods and the demons, in their search for Amrita the water of immortality, had churned the ocean more than enough, a deadly poison came out therefrom "burning like a raging fire, whose dreadful fumes in a moment spread throughout the world, confounding the three regions of the universe with its mortal odour, until Siva, at the word of Brahmâ, swallowed the

fatal drug to save mankind, which remaining in the throat
of that sovereign god of magic form, from that time he
hath been called **Nil-Kant**, because his throat was stained
blue." [1]

Two of the temple's domes are **covered** with thin plates of
gold, **the gift of** Maharaja Ranjit Singh **of Lahore**; and dazzlingly do they shine and glow in the sunlight, with astonishing if somewhat barbarous splendour. The **travellers**, having
contemplated them from the upper **storey** of a neighbouring
house, descend to the threshold **of the** temple, which they are
not permitted to cross, **but whence they have a good view of
the** crowded interior. Sacred **cattle, grave and dignified**,
with dew-lapped throats and gigantic humps, slowly **munch-
ing garlands of sacred** flowers, **look out on the visitors with**
supercilious solemnity, knowing **that they may not dare to**
enter. Standing opposite the entrance, **the travellers watch
with wondering minds** the ceaseless **streams of devout pilgrims entering and leaving the temple.**

All the worshippers carry large garlands of bright flowers,
which, **when they** have **been placed around the symbol of
the** god within, they **receive back, and piously wear in his**
honour. The earnestness and **devotion of the pilgrims are**
touching to see. On leaving **the temple many of them press
their** foreheads against the **stone doorpost, looking backward,
as they** do so, toward **the central symbol. Most of them
carry** brazen trays whereon **stand tiny cups (also of brass),**
one filled with **rice, another with milk, another** with **Ganges
water; and every** little **god whom the worshipper passes
must be treated to a taste of these delicacies.**

**Over the doorway sits Ganesh, hideous to behold with his
elephant's head and** fat little figure, taking **toll from all who**

---

[1] From Wilkins, quoted by Poley on the "Devimahatmyam."

enter,—a grain of rice, or a flower, or a drop of Ganges water. Being the Father of Calculation, he is not to be trifled with, since he keeps strict account, no doubt, of the offerings that are his due.

"Philippa," says Sebaste presently, "why is your dress so much besprinkled with Ganges water and grains of rice? Are they pelting you on purpose?"

"Oh, how dreadful!" exclaims Philippa, in dismay. "Here is a poor little god whom I have been eclipsing!"

And there indeed, let into the wall, is an ugly little idol, who scowls at Philippa with a very malignant countenance,— and no wonder!

Retreating along the narrow street, our travellers pass an uncanny-looking representation of Sanichar, the Regent of the Planet Saturn, who is worshipped on Saturdays, and who consists, apparently, of a round face of silver from which depend garlands of flowers. The next moment they arrive at the Temple of Annapúrná, the Goddess of Plenty, whose special duty is to supply Benares with food. The temple is about 170 years old, and contains some fine and delicately tinted adornment of sculpture. Sacred cows innumerable appear in all directions; and a splendid peacock is parading about the paved court, while the peahen sits aloft on the roof of the shrine attended by flocks of pigeons.

Philippa and Sebaste, lingering with Pursotum just within the entrance, have a good view of a train of pilgrims who presently arrive laden with great garlands of yellow flowers. Round the central shrine they move in procession, and finally enter it. Having seen the goddess decorated with their offerings, they emerge and approach an old priest, who marks each one on the forehead with a bright crimson pigment applied with the thumb. When the pilgrims have departed, the garlands which they left with the goddess are brought out, and the aged priest, wishing to pay a compliment to his English visitors, takes some of the wreaths, and approaches to hang them round their necks.

Our friends have often submitted to being thus decorated where there was no idol in the case, and have learned that to refuse a garland is a very great insult. The dilemma carries back their imagination to the days of the early Church, and if they were disposed to accept Annapúrná's gifts, those words of S. Cyprian would be sufficient to deter them,—who, speaking of those Christians who refused to participate in idolatrous ceremonies, exclaims, "Frons cum signo Dei pura *diaboli coronam* ferre non potuit, coronæ se Domini reservavit!"[1]

The visitors accordingly give the old priest to understand that, being Christians, they must decline the honour. Accepting this reasonable excuse, he gives the garlands to the sacred cows instead, who, independent of scruples, placidly browse thereon. He moreover tells our travellers (through Pursotum) that he is an hundred and six years old, with other matters of interest.

Thence our friends go on (past a hideous figure of Ganesh, coloured with vermilion, and having silver hands and face and feet) to the temple of Sákshí Vináyak, the Witness, built in 1770. Herein certificates are given to pilgrims who have duly performed the circumambulation of the holy city of Benares.

Next they visit the temple dedicated to Usanas, the Regent of the planet Venus, wherein are many women praying for goodly sons. Of this same Usanas our travellers can recall but little, save what is written of him in

[1] S. Cypriani Liber de Lapsis, c. ii.

the book of Markandeya the Sage,—how, when the army of the Daityas were fleeing before the face of the gods, he called unto them with valiant words, and said, "Ye must not go, turn ye back; why run ye away, ye feeble ones?"

Many other temples and shrines are visited, including that mysterious Well of Fate, into which whosoever looketh at mid-day and seeth not his face therein reflected shall assuredly die within six months. The number of temples in Benares (irrespective of smaller shrines) has been computed at 2000 at least, so that the visitors have plenty of sights to choose from. Nowhere better than here can Hindu idolatry be seen in its most attractive aspect. But, in all conscience, even the brightest, most picturesque, most superficial view of it is saddening enough. There is no rest or comfort among such scenes, unless it be in the words of that daily prayer of the Anglican Church in India, "Grant that all the people of this land may feel after Thee and find Thee."

Our travellers end their first day by driving out to Sarnath to visit the ancient *stupa* which marks the place, in the far-famed "Deer-park Garden," where the Buddha preached that first great sermon of his, which was the beginning, they say, of his "turning the Wheel of the Law." The mango-trees are just bursting into bloom, and they, together with nîms, acacias, and tamarinds, pleasantly shade the road. As for the venerated erection itself, the description thereof we will not attempt. Its rugged and cumbrous mass would find but scant accommodation in the final recess of a chapter already long drawn out; and even that sorry refuge it would be obliged to dispute with many another homeless subject.

THE GOSAIN TEMPLE, BENARES.

Not till after many days do the travellers begin to grow familiar with Benares, and to regard its animated scenes as realities rather than dreams. Most dream-like of all is the wonderful river-side life which they contemplate in many delightful boat - excursions on the broad, smooth waters of venerable Mother Ganges. But that ancient and majestic personage may not unreasonably, methinks, demand a chapter to herself.

CHAPTER XIV.

MOTHER GANGES.

FROM the Roof of the World she comes, from the Dwelling-place of Snow, from Himachal's icy cave 10,000 feet above the sea. Thus much I know; but that former course of hers, that origin yet more remote, who shall tell of it with certainty? Yet hath it been told in ancient days, and what was told is this: From Vishnu's lotus-foot she sprang, from the very nail of his great toe, and she fell in her rushing course on Siva's tangled locks, and thence to the roof of the world flowed down; and so to men at length descended her excellent stream, "the home of sages, the abode of geese and cranes," the world-purifier, the wife of the sea. And lower still she went, to the infernal world itself; and, flowing thus through the three regions of the universe, she is called the Three-wayed River.

On earth, saith the legend, she first appeared in answer to the prayers and to reward the austerities of Bhagirath the pious, who desired by a libation from her sacred stream to liberate the spirits of his ancestors, and make sure their wellbeing for ever. But, as she first flowed over the earth, her stream engulfed the place of Dschani's sacrifice, and he in his wrath swallowed up the waters; nor, until the gods had humbly prayed him, did he allow the river to flow forth again from his ears.

Again she threatened to overflow the earth; but Siva, besought of gods and sages, rolled back her torrent from mouth to source, and imprisoned it in a tuft of his own long hair. Yet once again she appeared; for when Gotama the Sage had been entrapped into the frightful crime of slaying a cow, Siva loosed Ganga from his head that he might bathe therein and be purified, and Ganga "at the prayers of Gotama flowed down like a torrent from the Gûla-Tree which grew firm on the mountain Brahmagiri, whither all men went to bathe. But when Gotama's accusers arrived there, Ganga vanished at their approach, saying, 'If the good and bad were favoured alike there would be no use or advantage in goodness.'" [1]

Honoured is she through all her course of 1500 miles, but nowhere more than at holy Benares, where day by day she is worshipped with offerings of rice and milk and flowers, and honoured by thousands of bright-robed bathers, until she seems to have donned such festal array as that wherein she appeared at Siva's wedding long ago, when the Rivers and the seven Seas, and all the sacred Places of Pilgrimage assembled together, as well as the sun and moon, and many other notabilities.

All the religious energy of Benares has for its heart and its centre the bank of the Ganges. If the life of the streets is vivid and intense, it is concentrated and a thousandfold intensified in the scenes by the river. Thither move for ever processions innumerable. Sometimes it is a wedding-train, with music and rejoicing around the central palanquin wherein the bride and bridegroom sit, going to

[1] From Halhed's 'Sheeve Pouran.'

pour milk and flowers into the sacred stream; sometimes a moaning chant fills the air, as the funeral of some pious Hindu creeps onward to the burning ghat, whence the ashes of the departed will be carried away by the holy waters, and his soul fly straight to a fabled heaven. And scarcely less solemn are the funerals of the sacred cows, each of whom, when she dies, is tied by the hoofs to a stout bamboo, and, borne on the shoulders of pious-minded men, is brought to the River and cast therein.

Not long after their arrival in Benares the travellers find themselves standing one morning at about seven o'clock on the Dasashwamedh Ghat (a *ghat*, be it observed, is a landing-place, generally consisting of a great flight of stone steps leading down to the water's edge). All around is a thronging multitude, lively and picturesque beyond the wildest imaginings. Below lies the broad expanse of the River, "embrowned with the unguents of the celestial nymphs," but sparkling in the sunshine, and fringed with a silent and devout assemblage of solemn pilgrim-bathers. The men throw off their outer garments before entering the water; but the women wear their usual dress, the all-enveloping *saris*, and very impressive is the sight of their long-robed figures wading slowly into the water and solemnly dipping below the surface.

Having thrice offered to the ascending sun a shower of drops from the holy stream, the worshippers emerge from the River, nourishing with the water that drips from their clothes the souls of their respective ancestors. Then, wrapping themselves in dry garments, they gather round the Sons of the Ganges. These personages are Brahmans who, shielded from the sun by huge, round umbrellas of bamboo resembling gigantic mushrooms, sit on the steps of the ghat, ready to be-

stow on bathers a mark on the forehead signifying that they
have left all their sins behind them in the purifying waters
of the River.

A little higher up sit "Veda-skilled Pandits," reading
aloud the Sanskrit scriptures, and expounding in the vulgar
tongue. Around these dignified professors the people next
assemble, sitting on the sunlit steps in compact masses of
many harmonious colours. Our friends approach one of the
Pandits, who, to judge by the size of his attentive congregation, is a very great favourite. . Cross-legged he sits on a
seat of dignity. Round his neck hang many fresh and
bright-hued garlands, and before him is a heap of offerings
—flowers and fruit piled up for his acceptance by his devout
and reverent hearers. Like the illustrious Muni Markandeya,
with a loud, clear voice he speaks, devoid of the eighteen
defects.[1] Pursotum's serious countenance, framed in its
twisted folds of yellow silk, turns in silent attention toward
the aged speaker.

"Tell us what he is saying, Pursotum." And Pursotum
interprets:—

"One God there is, and one alone. Many are the deities
ye worship. All these are but His servants; for God Himself is One."

Strangely sound such words here in idolatrous Benares;
but no one can hope to understand anything of Hindu religion who does not recognise that the system is, theoretically,
a pantheistic one. Not to speak of the Vedas, which set
forth the ancient and purely Aryan religion, the doctrine
of Pantheism is continually implied even in the popular
and comparatively modern Puranas. Unfortunately, both in

---

[1] *I.e.*, in reciting he shaketh not his head, he pronounceth not indistinctly,
he speaketh not through the nose ; and so forth.

India and elsewhere (with the exception of some learned Philosophers and other exalted beings of that kind), men don't seem able to get on without worshipping something, and something other than the impersonal abstraction of a merely pantheistic creed; nor is it within the power of every ordinary mortal to rise to the sublime heights to which that King of ancient times attained, who, "reducing the five elements to the three qualities, and these to the unity of their principle, merged that principle, with all that it constitutes, in the Soul, and the Soul in Brahma the immutable and absolute existence."[1] Accordingly the religion of the ordinary Hindu is Polytheism in its most degraded form, for all that the learned Pandits may solemnly preach to the contrary.

As the travellers turn away from the much-decorated sage, Pursotum points out two small suttee monuments marking the spots where widows have been burned on the pyres of their dead husbands.

"It is sixty years ago," say Pursotum, "that there was the last suttee in Benares."

Absurd stories are not very congruous with so horrible a subject; nevertheless, if any one desire to read of the mythical origin thereof, let him look in the Siva Purana, and he will find that the word is derived from the name of Sati, who was none other than Parvati the wife of Siva. When Sati's father affronted Siva, she burned herself by reason of vexation; and the place of her death became so holy that "all who come there with pure faith and sincere devotion obtain all their desires, and many have cut off their tongues and heads and bestowed them in devotion, and in a moment have received fresh heads and new life" through the virtue of that sacred place.

[1] See 'Le Bhâgavata Purâna,' . . . traduit . . . par M. Eugène Burnouf.

RIVER-SIDE TEMPLES, BENARES.

And whosoever desires a description of the suttees which took place constantly at the beginning of the century, let him read it in Crawfurd's graphic Sketches, and not demand it of me.

The travellers leave the monuments, and, having regarded, from a respectful distance, the Smallpox Temple where those who have recovered from smallpox go to give thanks to Sitla the goddess thereof, they return to the water's edge and embark on one of the quaint and shapeless things which call themselves boats hereabout. On the roof of the cabin they sit, and, as their turbaned oarsmen make way slowly up-stream through many floating garlands on their way to the sea, there unfolds itself before them one of the strangest scenes in all the world.

The city is built in a great bend of the River, where the bank reaches a height of about 100 feet. Up this steep bank is piled a fantastically beautiful mass of palaces and temples and shrines. Every Maharaja has a palace in Benares, whither the aged members of his family come to die. Strange and imposing piles they are. The lower half of those nearest the water consists of a solid mass of masonry, except for one narrow stair leading down to a doorway, which, in the wet season, is altogether submerged. Some of the palaces are stained a rich crimson, streaked and effaced by the River in flood-time until nothing is left but a suspicion of delicate colour.

But, surpassing even these in architectural interest are the temples with their sculptured pillars, and their conical domes, each consisting of a compact cluster of "curvilinear spires." Each spire of the cluster is stained a deep red and tipped with gold, the central spire rising above the lesser ones, an elongated, egg-shaped dome of wonderfully graceful proportions. A delightful contrast to these richly tinted buildings are the masses of green foliage which here and there appear where a pipal-tree or a tamarind finds room to grow and to flourish.

And everywhere from the summit of the bank to the water's edge descend the giant ghats. Cataracts of steep masonry are they, their broad steps bordered everywhere by shrines and temples blossoming forth beside them like gorgeous flowers; and wonderful theatres they make for the ceaseless movement and effective grouping of the animated crowds that haunt them. Down at the water's brink are the solemn bathers, while up and down the great steps move in procession the figures of water-drawing women in crimson *saris*, each bearing on her head a large, round vessel of shining brass, poised in equilibrium or steadied by a slender brown arm adorned with glittering bracelets. But the most wonderful part of the scene is the crowd of richer folk, who are clad in all the colours of the rainbow, and are for ever forming themselves into new and exquisite combinations of delicate and glowing hues. Most beautiful of all are the women's veils, thrown over the head so as to shade without hiding the face, and descending in soft folds of Indian muslin so fine as to look like silk. They are of a rich golden colour, and coral-pink, and crimson, and delicate moss-green, and the tenderest shades of cream-colour and purple and orange, often edged with a narrow border of silver or gold that gleams and glitters in the sunlight. The men are also brightly clad. And the turbans!—But on turbans we have discoursed already, and they must not again entangle us in their cunningly twisted folds.

The travellers in their boat ascend the River as far as the Ashi Ghat, where the city begins, and then drop slowly down-stream, past the "Empty Palace" where Chait Singh had his abode, and whence, when put under arrest by Warren Hastings, he escaped to Ramnagar across the River; past the upper Burning Ghat, past palaces and temples innumerable, and past the Dasashwamedh Ghat, at which they embarked. Close by it is the great Observatory builded by Raja Jai Singh at the end of the seventeenth century, and containing huge mural instruments for astrological observations,—Bhithi-yantras and Digansayantras, Chakrayantras and Yantrasasa-ments, with other uncanny erections.

A little farther down the River comes into view the Nipal-ese Temple, the most picturesque object, perhaps, in the whole of Benares, and an absolute contrast, with its successive storeys and slanting roofs, to all the other temples, although, like them, it is stained with the sacred dark-red colour.

Our friends at length arrive at the Manikarnika Ghat, near which they intend to visit Vishnu's Well. As they approach the shore, they are grinned at in a highly unman-nerly fashion by a hideous clay figure of the hero Bhîma. He faces the River, with head propped forward so that his staring eyes may watch the passing boats. Every year at flood-time the River washes him away, and he has to be modelled and painted afresh. He rejoices in huge black moustaches, which give him a very sinister expression of countenance.

On landing the travellers follow Pursotum round various corners and up a flight of steps, whereupon they find them-selves in one of the prettiest of the smaller temples in Benares. Beneath the pillared pavilion in the centre sits a solitary figure in the sacred orange-coloured robe which marks him as a *yogi* or Hindu ascetic. With a rapt countenance, and evidently unconscious of all around him, delivered from

the chain of outward things, " he is even as a lamp standing
in a place without wind, which wavereth not."[1] He seems
as if, like **Parîkchit** the King of the Earth, he had utterly
detached himself from the two worlds, and had undertaken
his last fast on the shore of the Ganges, that River of the
Immortals that is purified by the dust of Vishnu's lotus-feet.
It is of such as he that the ancient scripture saith: "Now
if a *yogi* is fed first, he can save . . . those who feast, just as
a boat saves in water, better than thousands of Brahmans."[2]
Pursotum regards him reverently, and presently says:—

"That is a holy man. When he dies he will not be
burned, but will be put in a stone coffin and thrown into
the Ganges."

"But I thought, **Pursotum**, that that custom was not
allowed any longer."

"It is not allowed to every one, but always to *yogis*. And
so it is to children who die under one year old: if their
parents are rich enough, they are put in stone coffins, but if
not, they are only made fast to stones and then thrown into
the River."

The conversation is interrupted by a polite flower-seller,
who suddenly throws some garlands of white flowers round
the travellers' hats, and has to be rewarded therefor. Then
they leave the temple, and find themselves before a wretched
hovel, at the door whereof sits a little group of men—some
of the most degraded and horrible of Hindu devotees. Their
heads are uncovered, their hair is matted together, they are
smeared with ashes, their faces are less than human,—dreadful faces such as are not to be seen in Christian lands—no,
not even in London.

Our travellers next pass an array of brass vessels covered

---

[1] Quoted by Crawfurd.   [2] Markandeya Purána. Pargiter.

with basket-work and decorated with sacred peacocks' feathers. They are slung to bamboos, and are destined to carry Ganges water to some far-off town. Little bells are attached to them, which will jangle as the procession of bearers moves away on its long journey.

The next moment they meet a procession of shivering figures, with water dripping from their drenched and clinging garments. They are coming away from Vishnu's Well; and there at last is the well itself—a picturesquely dirty tank with flights of steps on its four sides leading down into the water. Three feet is the utmost depth of the sacred liquid, wherein are standing devout pilgrims who pour milk and rice into the water, together with white flowers, which float thereupon, disguising its evil colour. A Brahman is presiding over the devotions, and makes each worshipper hold the sacred grass in his hand while he himself recites some mystic words in a low voice. Then, having received his fee, he dismisses them to dip in the Ganges, and thus complete the ceremony.

As our friends return to their boat, Pursotum points out the lower Burning Ghat, where two muffled corpses lie by the water's edge, awaiting the construction of their funeral pyres.

Re-embarking, they continue to drop down-stream, past the print of Vishnu's feet, and past Sindhia's Ghat—a vast mass of masonry slowly sinking down into the River and carrying a temple with it. They now arrive at the Ghat of the Five Rivers, where meet, they say, the Dhantapapa, the Jaranada, the Kirnanada, the Saraswati, and the Ganges. Of these five streams only the last is visible; but this is easy of explanation, since the other four, it seems, flow underground.

On the bank above stands the mosque of Aurangzib, with its two slender minarets that rise to a height of more than 250 feet above the River. Thither some of our travellers will ascend on another day, and, islanded there on high, floating in a sea of sunshine, with no companions save the emerald-green parrots who build their nests up there, they will look abroad over the River, away to the green belt of the open country, and the shadowy, far-away heights of the Chunar Hills; while from the deep and tangled maze of the crowded town at their feet will rise up to them the sound of many voices,—no rumbling din as of a Western town, but a shrill, restless, confused clamour, " the *cry* of the city," that goes up day by day unceasingly to the heaven of cloudless blue.

At present the sun is already too high for further sightseeing, and the travellers are glad to return to the Dasashwamedh Ghat, and thus end their morning's business.

In the afternoon of the same day Pursotum suggests a visit to Ramnagar, the palace-fort of the Maharaja of Benares. It stands a little higher up the stream than the city, on the other side of the River. There, says Pursotum, a festival is held to-day.

As their boat slowly makes way up the River, our travellers see on the Benares bank, a little above the city, two great elephants surrounded by a group of native figures. The elephants belong, it seems, to the Maharaja, and are presently to be conveyed across the River. Our friends have been introduced to many an elephant in the courts of the southern temples, but never before have they seen them as a natural feature of the landscape under the open sky. In these circumstances their clumsiness vanishes, and only dignity remains, so that it is quite an impressive sight to

see them marching along, continually flapping their enormous ears; and no longer does that seem a doubtful compliment of Rita-dhvaja, who spoke of the lovely Queen Madalasa
as "the fawn - eyed daughter of Gandharva, who observed
true religion, *whose gait was like the elephant's*": and one
begins to understand something of the pathos of King
Surath's complaint, who, having been driven out of his
kingdom, and wandering in the dreary forest, exclaimed,
"I know not the fate of my counsellors, or of my trained
elephant Surahasti."[1]

Very grand looks the fort of Ramnagar as our travellers
approach it, raised high above the River, which clearly
reflects its walls.

Other boats are also approaching, densely crowded with
brightly clad Natives, and on landing our friends find themselves surrounded by an animated throng of holiday-makers.
One of these is a snake-charmer, round whose figure great
hill-snakes glide and coil, thick and strong as that serpent
wherewith, as with a cable, in the universal deluge Vishnu
fastened the Rishis' ship to his own stupendous horn. On
the ground is a cobra with head erect and hood extended,
darting his tongue in fury at the unfamiliar visitors. They
are assured, however, that his poison-tooth has been ex-
tracted, and that he can bite no more.

Making their way through the outer courts of the castle,
the travellers enter at a doorway where stands on each side
an ivory elephant, while beneath them crouch terrific plaster
tigers, one of whom is having his whiskers painted.

The visitors wander through the state apartments, and
finally emerge on a balcony overhanging the principal en-

---

[1] From the 'Sapta-Shati.' Translated by Cavali Venkat Rámasswámi,
Pandit.

trance, whence a fine ghat leads down to the water's edge.
Standing by the small, white-marble pavilion wherein the
Maharaja prays, they obtain a bird's-eye view of this great
staircase of stone. On the steps sit many flower-sellers,
their large baskets overflowing with garlands; and from the
water's brink ascend in constant streams whole boat-loads of
Natives newly disembarked. Wonderful is the sight of this
crowd of Hindus in festal array, many of them clad in
satins and velvets finely embroidered with gold.

Each new-comer buys some flowers, and solemnly carries
them in a flat, round basket to the tiny temples perched
high up on the ramparts of the castle. Here the worshippers
move eight times round the shrine, and finally offer their
floral gifts. Many of them pause as they do so to trace with
their fingers on the walls or the pavement the letters of an
invisible name.

As our friends once more embark, the light is soft with
the glow of sunset, and each boatful of brilliant figures is
clearly mirrored on the surface of the shining water.
Before they have reached mid-stream the night is upon them,
and from many a palace in the city rings forth a hubbub of
native music,—tom-toms and other delectable instruments
filling the air with sound, as when the warrior-maidens of
old " sounded the trumpet, likewise the conches, kettle-
drums, and other instruments in the festival of war." At
sunrise and at sunset, at mid-day and at midnight, this wild
music is made in all the river-side palaces as an act of
religious devotion. Musical modes are gods in India, and a
Hindu will never allow that his unintelligible strains are
not far superior to any music of the sober and conventional West.

Now through the gathering darkness are seen the red

lights from the two Burning Ghats, and from each trails far through the air a dark line of shadowy smoke. The travellers cause their boat to pass close to one of them so that they can see the blazing pile, and above it the little company of mourners, distinctly visible, in the light of the fire, against a background of darkness.

As the boat approaches its destination, a tiny flickering light glides near it, floating slowly seaward. It is a little lamp fed with ghee,[1] and launched as a pious offering to well-loved Mother Ganges. Meanwhile the countless stars shine forth, and the travellers are reminded of that ancient King to whom it was said, "As drops of water in the sea, or as stars in the sky, or as showers of rain, as the sands in the Ganges . . . are innumerable, O Maha-raja, even so thy merit is in truth beyond reckoning."

As they drive away from the River the travellers meet a funeral. The muffled body of the dead man is slung to a bamboo resting on the shoulders of two of his relations, who speed along at a quick trot toward the Burning Ghat, chanting as they go in the vernacular, "Ram is great! Ram is great!"

"Pursotum," says Philippa, "when can we go to the Burning Ghat, and watch the funeral ceremonies?"

"You can go to-morrow," says Pursotum; and the next afternoon the travellers accordingly watch for more than two hours in that melancholy place "where stands in Benares the burning-ground, very dire with the close contagion of fear, and painful by reason of the sounds of lamentation." And these are the rites which they see:—

On a rough bamboo stretcher the shrouded corpse is brought to the river-side. It is first dipped in the water,

---

[1] Liquid butter.

and then laid on the bank, while the dead man's nearest relative begins to build the pyre with logs of wood laid crosswise. On this pile the body is placed, and the chief mourner, putting his hand under the wrappings, rubs it with the dust of sandal-wood, and lays pieces of sandal-wood beside it. Then he completes the pyre, piling up the wood over the body, but leaving still visible the muffled head and feet. Then follows a long pause while the chief mourner goes away to bathe in the River, and to put on a clean garment, and to have his head shaved. He next goes to a bamboo-hut (perched on a ledge of ground above the Burning Ghat) where lives the Domrá, a low-caste personage whose duty is to supply the fire for the burning. There is no fixed price, and a long bargaining takes place before the weary mourner returns with the fire smouldering in a whisp of straw. He now walks five times round the pyre, touching each time he passes it the head of the dead man with the burning straw. At the fifth circumambulation he sets fire to the wood near the feet of the corpse, and in a few minutes the red flames are blazing high in air. When the fire has burned for more than an hour, the chief mourner takes a long, pointed bamboo wherewith he beats and stirs it,—a process said to give intense pain to the soul of the dead. Finally he takes up on the point of the bamboo what looks like a charred piece of wood, and pitches it into the River. Then Ganges-water is brought and poured on the hissing flames until they die out in a white cloud of steam, whereupon the ashes are raked and washed down into the River, and the ceremony is over.

The relatives of the dead must now bathe before returning home, and the chief mourner will for thirteen days be considered unclean, and must cook his own food and eat by himself. On the thirteenth day he will make a feast for his relatives and friends, for on that day the soul of the dead will enter Yama's city that is "awful, made of iron, terrible in appearance." There Yama, the god of the dead, "with fiery red eyes, reigneth for ever with Death and Time the Destroyer." Terrible is the journey thither; for when a man dies, Yama's servitors, "terrific, carrying hammers and maces, hard-hearted," immediately bind him in cruel fetters and drag him forth to the southern region "which abounds in hundreds of holes, and which is heated by the blazing sun." And "being dragged about by those fearful ones, being eaten by hundreds of she-jackals, the evil-doer proceeds by an awful road. But men who give umbrellas and shoes, and who bestow garments, those men pass along that road with ease." Throughout this journey (which is a short and easy matter for those who die here in holy Benares) the dead man's soul is sustained by a daily offering of rice-cake and water, which gradually enables him to grow a new body instead of that which has been burned, slowly taking to itself arms and legs, until on the tenth day it obtains at last a head. Thenceforth the dead is worshipped as a *pitri* in the periodical rites of *sraddha*.

Such things doth Pursotum tell to the travellers as they stand on a high ledge by a sculptured temple, looking down on the funeral ceremonies of the gloomy burning-ground. But at length the fierce light of the day sinks down, and the River is a bright plain of rosy glass with rippling streaks of blue. And so farewell for a while, O venerable Mother Ganga!

CHAPTER XV.

THE CITY OF AKBAR.

BEFORE leaving Benares our travellers have an opportunity, such as they have hitherto never enjoyed, of seeing that most terrific of natural dramas, a protracted tropical thunderstorm. All day the still air has glowed with an almost unbearable heat. So long is it since rain has fallen that the grassy level of the compound is scorched and yellow, while the thirsty ground is cleft by long, gaping cracks, and the pipals and nims and tamarinds, covered with parching dust, hang down with a drooping hopelessness their dry and weary leaves. Even the sunshine has lost its life, and on the dusty earth it is poured, from the dead and colourless sky, in a cruel, blinding, glaring blaze that has no sense of pity.

But when the sun is near his setting, rolls up from the northern horizon a bank of inky clouds,—no freely floating masses such as we know in England, but a dense and solid wall of angry, blue-black hue. Swiftly, irresistibly it comes, swallowing up the sky; and forth leaps the lightning-flame —not yellow or steely blue, but of a lurid, rose-red colour unknown, so far as our friends are aware, in our feebler northern storms.

A thunderstorm at night so near the tropics is not a sight to be missed. Stay not within in lamplit rooms, but go out into the verandah and watch. It will give you a headache may be, but it is well worth that. Black and thick the night has fallen, hiding the world from view; but more awful than the deepest gloom are the moments of leaping light when the weird spell of the lightning calls all things forth in a moment into strange, unnatural distinctness. Then every colour is clear and vivid, every leaf on the frightened trees is plain for all to see. One would wellnigh think it day, were it not that all things, in their dazzled stillness, seem staring and stiff with terror, were it not that the sky in its dreadful brightness is of so livid and ghastly a hue. A moment more, and again the whole world is engulfed in the murky darkness, overwhelmed by the roar of devouring thunder and the floods of the rushing rain. Ever more fiercely rages the tumult, until the lightning-flashes are joined together, until the clamours of the storm-wind and the sound of the waters are all one with the din of the bellowing thunder that hurtles round the great vault of heaven with one unceasing roar of never-resting, unappeasable despair. So the turmoil rolls and crashes till the strength of the storm is spent, until the lightnings fade back into darkness and the thunder dies in silence, until Nature, as though she were wearied by her passionate burst of grief, at length sinks down exhausted and cries herself to sleep.

But next morning all is dewy freshness, and the earth has renewed her youth. Clear and blue is the radiant sky, and the sunshine's smiling brightness is gentle and sweet as the tenderest light of eyes that beam and glisten. Green blades are springing from the breathing ground, and the trees are stirring and quivering with the joy of their verdant life.

The brilliant parrots flutter among them, filling the air with their cries that blithely answer the Indian woodpecker's soft and bell-like note.

As the calm and peace that come with the dawn after long, dark hours of weeping; as the hope and the rest that the sick man feels when a wasting fever has left him, when renewed and cleansed from its inmost springs the tide of life flows back,—so are the gladness, the sweetness, and mirth that have come with the new-born day. For the dewy flowers, the broad green leaves, and all living things beside, are transfigured and full to overflowing of some bright, mysterious secret. They know it, they have heard it, but we may not hear just yet; and the trees, as the soft air stirs them, make smiling signals one to another, as though they whispered of us, "What will they say when they know it? What will they do? How will they bear such joy as they dream not now is in store? And soon they shall know, but we may not tell them yet. Hush—hush!"

Even as when we were children, in the bright and distant days, sometimes, when a birthday drew near, the elder faces around us were full of delightful mystery, and all the air was astir with a half-suspected secret that we would not know too soon,—so now through the world that lives and smiles is bursting the glory of some great good above all that we ask or think.

On such a morning as this the travellers leave Benares, and set forth on a 200 miles' north-westward journey into Awadh (or Oudh, as the vulgar usage hath it), that they may spend some days at Lucknow and Cawnpore in visiting the ever-memorable sites connected with the Sipahi Mutiny. But of the impressions of these days, of their meditations in

THE MEMORIAL WELL, CAWNPORE.

these places, our friends may be forgiven if they keep no
written record.

And now again the rich Indian landscape, with its strangely
beautiful vegetation and its boundless level of verdant plain,
is swiftly fleeting past, as our travellers pursue their way
north-westward to Agra, the City of Akbar.   Starting from
Cawnpore at 11 A.M., they arrive about tiffin-time at Etáwah,
which used to be the headquarters of the Thags, and doubtless would be still were it not for the British *raj*.

The historically minded Philippa is called upon for an
account of that amiable community, and a gruesome story
she tells: how they were bound together by devotion to the
terrible Kali, in whose honour it was their vocation in life
to strangle as many people as possible; how they had a
secret language, and signs whereby to recognise each other,
and an elaborate organisation; and how their method was
to make friends with well-to-do travellers, and remain in
their company on terms of intimacy and kindness, until at
an opportune moment they could strangle and plunder and
bury them.

When they attacked a company of travellers, every one of
them had to be strangled, that none might be left to give
information.[1]   Only, if very young boys were of the party, the
Thags would adopt them and bring them up to the craft.   In
the whole system of Thagi there was nothing, perhaps, so
horrible as the cautious and gradual education of these young
recruits.   It was so gently done; all danger of shocking their
minds was so carefully avoided, as step by step they were
insensibly promoted, until that proud day was reached when
the neophyte, solemnly presented with the noose, acquired

[1] See ' Asiatic Researches ' for 1820 (vol. xiii.).

the privileges of the fully initiate, and began his sacred career. The sacredness thereof must on no account be lost sight of. Each expedition began and ended with an impressive religious ceremony, and a number of omens were strictly observed, including the chirping of lizards. At the preliminary sacrifice a sheep was slain before Kali's silver image, prayers for success were devoutly offered, and there was a solemn dedication of the instruments of the art.

These instruments were three. The first was the noose of cord, for which might be substituted, in ordinary practice, a turban or any other length of cloth, provided that its colour was none other than yellow or white, which hues are sacred to the goddess Kali. The second instrument was the knife wherewith they used horribly to lacerate their victims' dead bodies, that the process of dissolution might go on speedily. The third was a pickaxe for the digging of graves. Not always had they all been needed, for in the good old days, long, long ago, the victims were left unburied, and Kali herself (following on the track of her pious devotees) devoured them every one. But once on a time it came to pass that a company of Thags had slain a man; and, as they were departing from the place, a young neophyte dared to look back, and he beheld the dark goddess in the midst of her banquet, and the dead body of the victim hung dangling out of her mouth. Then the goddess, filled with rage, did make declaration that never more would she deign to feast on those that the Thags should slay. Only so far she relented that she gave for a pickaxe one of her teeth, for a knife a rib of her own, and the hem of her robe for a noose.

After that, it seems, the Thags went on and prospered; and a great deal of business they did, especially in the hot

weather when men travelled by night. In this one district
of Etáwah were found in wells, during the years 1808 and
1809, sixty-seven bodies of the victims of Thagi. The numbers of the Thags were astonishingly large; but those outside
the Society had no means of recognising them, and the terror
of their unseen presence must have been awful. But then
their devotion, though doubtless mistaken, was certainly
most sincere; and it is a comfort to think that it matters not
what we believe so long as we act up to our convictions.

Through the hot afternoon the journey continues; the
sun goes down, and our friends arrive at Agra in the sweet
and dreamy stillness known only to those who have felt the
magic of an Indian night. The Zodiacal Light is faintly
gleaming, and, as they cross the Jamna, the starlight shimmers
on the broad stream, while Jupiter, wonderfully large and
brilliant, throws a shining path across the waters.

But with the morning comes eager haste, and astonishment of wondering admiration. Hindu architecture has
grown familiar enough to our travellers; but of Muhammadan buildings in India they have hitherto seen but little,
and their minds are ill prepared for the splendours of this
stately city of the Mughals. Faring forth in the cool, fresh
air of early morning, they betake them first to the palace-
fort which Akbar (in the sixteenth century) began to build,
and his magnificent successors finished.

Built of deep-red sandstone, its towering walls and its
mighty gates glow with rich, crimson colour. More than a
mile and a half is the circuit of those royal walls; their
height is nearly 70 feet; and they are crowned with strange
"beehive" crenelations which add much to the extraordinary impressiveness of the unfamiliar architecture. Surely

this is no common fortress builded by the hand of man!
It belongs not to this ordinary world, but rather, one would
think, to some Eastern fairy tale. Doubtless it was reared by
demon-builders long ago for some mighty magician to dwell in.
Nay, so mysterious is its oriental grandeur that one scarcely
believes it to exist at all, unless it be in some vague, metaphoric manner like that other fortress, of Indian allegory,
whereof spake of old those pious sons of the soul-subdued
Sukrisha. "Great,"[1] said they, "is the fortress which has
Wisdom for its rampart, and the bones for its pillars. . . .
It is enclosed on all sides with sinews; and there the
Sentient Soul sits firm as king. Two rival ministers hath
he, the Intelligence and the Understanding;" and four
enemies who desire his destruction, even Desire and Anger
and Covetousness and Folly. These four besiege the fortress,
and the Understanding betrays his king. Then doth the
Intelligence perish, and the Sentient Soul is subdued.

With minds still haunted by such old-world similitudes,
our travellers enter the Fort by way of the Elephant
Gate, and speedily find themselves opposite the entrance
of the Moti Masjid, the famous Pearl Mosque built by
Shah Jahan in 1648-1655. Ascending a high flight of
steps, they pass through a gateway of red sandstone lined
within with polished white marble; and so they find themselves in the shining marble court. A beautiful cloister surrounds it; in the centre is the marble tank for ablutions;
and opposite the gateway, raised by steps above the white
pavement of the court, is the lovely praying-place, its
cusped Saracenic arches retreating in stately perspective
to the cool shadows that reign within. From the roof
rise many light and graceful cupolas, and three great bulb-

[1] Markandeya Purána. Pargiter.

ous domes that curve upward against the cloudless sky in lines of perfect loveliness. Domes and cupolas, arches and pillars and court, all the building is of radiant white marble such as we know not at all in our cold and watery atmosphere.

One dreams that the Emperor who builded so beautiful a place of worship must needs have been pious and devout, and it is pleasing to recall that picture of him which his admiring chronicler has left us, who tells in florid Persian how, "at the close of night,"[1] "the sun which illumines the firmament in the universe of royalty and dominion, the moon that irradiates the sky of monarchy and felicity"— that is to say, the King—"with an attentive heart . . . offers up his devotions to the true Deity;" and "when the true dawn is about to appear, he, with readiness of heart and purity of mind, employs himself in reading the glorious and renowned Koran with perfect fluency and eloquence."

Long do the visitors wander in this enchanted precinct, penetrating to the *mihrab*, and admiring most of all the exquisite screens of marble fretwork behind which the ladies used to worship. Words are too clumsy and commonplace for these faëry webs of such delicately intricate design that one almost dreads to touch for fear of tearing them. The fairest lace is not more dainty, yet are they as fresh and stainless now as when first their makers wrought them three centuries and a half ago. Finally our travellers ascend to the roof, and look away over a great curving bend of the Jamna, to the white domes and minarets of that most lovely of marble tombs, the far-famed Taj Mahall. But that is the crown and the flower of Agra's splendours, and we must not describe it yet.

[1] From Mr Gladwin's translation. See the "Persian Moonshee."

Leaving the mosque at length, our friends betake them
to the great cloistered square which was the Carrousel or
Tilt-yard.　Herein is the tomb of Mr Colvin, the Lieutenant-
Governor of the North-West Provinces, who died in 1857
during the Mutiny, when Agra Fort was crowded with
refugees and besieged by the rebels.　A brass gun, taken
from the mutineers, is here to this day.

On one side of the grand court, and opening on to it, is
the Diwan i Am, the Hall of Public Audience, which seems
not to have been completed (in its present form) until the
twenty-seventh year of the reign of Aurangzib.　It is a
triple colonnade of red sandstone, with slender pillars and
cusped Saracenic arches; but all has now been so mercilessly
whitewashed (or leastwise painted white) that it is pitiful to
see.　Within, at the back of the hall, is a beautiful estrade
of marble, whereon, in solemn, cross-legged dignity, the
Mughal sat enthroned.　The Audience Hall is raised by
steps above the great court; and the Emperor's throne
commanded a view not only of those in his immediate
presence, but also of all the crowd without.

What saith our florid' chronicler concerning the great
Assembly held every morning by the Emperor in the stately
Diwan i Am ?　The prayers have long been finished; and
that distribution of presents is over wherein it was manifest
that "the hand of the Emperor is boundless as the ocean in
bestowing bounties, being the key of the gates of kindness
and liberality;" the Gracious Monarch has repaired to the
plain of the Jerokahdursun, where "the eyes of those who
entertain hopes and expectations" have been "brightened by
the light-diffusing countenance;" and now "the sun of the
heaven of prosperity and empire, the shadow of God, the
asylum of the universe, the splendour of whose instructive

front causes light and gladness to the world and to mankind," "increases by his presence" the splendour of the Hall
of Audience, "where the servants of the court stand ready to
enjoy the blessing of making obeisance."

Now the Emperor has taken his place, and there follows a
review of "fleet steeds, with inlaid and enamelled furniture,"
and "renowned elephants, resembling mountains, and decked
in complete trappings ornamented with gold and precious
stones. Then the princes of high descent, agreeably to their
respective ranks, have permission to be seated near the im-
perial throne. After which the following persons: Khans,
Omrahs, and Mirzas, . . . Ministers of State, viziers of high
degree, . . . gentlemen of the sword and of the pen, valiant
and cautious, . . . armour-bearers of great exertions, archers,
. . . dilapidators of mountains, and other respectable persons."
Meanwhile the behaviour of the servants is exemplary beyond
belief. "Struck with veneration and attachment on beholding the august countenance," they are "lost and immersed in
wonder and amazement. Notwithstanding they are so much
pressed together, they do not presume to converse one with
another, but, having closed their lips with the seal of
silence, and girded up the loins of obedience, completely
armed and accoutred, listen to commands inevitable as the
decrees of fate, and, in the road of obedience and compliance,
outstrip the lightning and the wind."

Then follows the reception of foreign ambassadors, and of
those "merchants and traders" who "from remote regions
resort to this court, the asylum of mankind, permanent as
the sky; and, opening their own packages, display bright
jewels, and the choicest piece goods, with other wares, arti-
cles, and things; and having derived immense profit, erect a
monument of fame, by spreading through all the quarters of

the earth reports of the virtue and renown of this immortal emperor."

There are also officers of State to be interviewed, and collectors of revenues, and so forth, who "on being introduced or on taking leave, . . . the Ministers of State having caused them to approach," "are directed to kiss the august feet; and some, through excess of favour, have the sacred hand laid upon their back;" while "other Omrahs and officers at a distance are honoured with especial notice by the bend of the eyebrow, or by a side glance from the august eye, the seat of favour and kindness."

When our friends have sufficiently feasted their imagination on the gorgeous spectacles that, in the days of their Sublime Majesties the Lords of the Age, the Diwan i Am must have witnessed, they wander on into the Palace, and presently find themselves in the Anguri Bagh, an oriental garden-square round which, in stately loveliness, stand some of the more private halls and chambers. Opposite to the visitors, on the other side of the garden, are the arches of the Khas Mahall. Within is a hall, but on the garden side is an open colonnade. The whole is of snow-white marble, wherewith richly contrast the gilded cupolas that crown the roof, resting on slender pillars. Beneath the flat roof, and supported by brackets, runs a broad, slanting dripstone, whereof the soft, luminous shadow reaches the topmost cusps of the Saracenic arches of the supporting colonnade. Along the bright pavement within lie the shadows of the pillars, and beyond are dim recesses of cool and shadowy gloom.

To the left of the Khas Mahall extends a faëry pavilion, between whose columns our travellers catch a glimpse of the River flowing far below. This pavilion, like the Khas

Mahall, is built of richly sculptured and snow-white marble, and is roofed with gilded plates of copper, which flash and burn in the sunlight. Other buildings there are, each more lovely than the rest. The brilliance of the sunlit surfaces, the soft coolness of the shadows, the mystery of the reflected lights, the contrasting splendour of the golden roofs, methinks the palaces of Fairyland could scarcely equal.

Turning to the left, the visitors make their way to the north side of the garden, and thence enter the Shish Mahall, the Palace of Glass, which is the most fantastic bathing-place they have ever seen. Ceilings and walls are all lined with numberless tiny mirrors, divided only by the mazy lines of intricate and graceful arabesques delicately wrought in stucco. No daylight can enter, and there is nothing to mar the extraordinary effect of the torch which our travellers carry, and the light whereof is thrown back from everywhere in multitudinous twinkling reflections. There is a wonderful device, moreover, whereby the water, as it flowed in its marble channel toward the bath, was made to descend in little cascades, behind which lamps were set to light up the falling drops.

Crossing southward the Anguri Bagh, our friends seek next the Jahangir Mahall, where they find themselves again surrounded by the quaintly beautiful but weird and unintelligible forms of Hindu architecture. Herein doth Philippa discourse on Jahangir in general, and in particular upon his rebellious behaviour to Akbar his princely father. He was fonder of drinking than of business, it seems, and during his reign the government was conducted by Nurjahan, his famous and strong-minded consort. Nur Mahall, they called her, the Light of the Palace, and a very wonderful personage she assuredly must have been. Those were

strange times; and we know something about them too, for
was not Mr Finch, Merchant, our own fellow-countryman,
staying at Jahangir's court, and has he not told us many
things of the wonders and splendours thereof? Best of all
his descriptions, I think, is his account of "the vast Army of
the Mogul," and the lordly manner of its marching. "It is
reckoned," saith he, "that the whole Body of the Camp
amounted to 500,000 if not six. They eat and drank up the
Country as they passed along, the largest stores were exhausted, and the rivers not able to supply them with drink."

The Jahangir Mahall (built, they say, by Jahangir[1] about
1605 A.D., at the very beginning of his reign) is a magnifical
palace of a red sandstone; and the deep crimson colour
thereof greatly augments the wild effect of the strange and
fanciful sculpture.

From the Jahangir Mahall our friends find their way to
the high sandstone wall overlooking the River, and wander
along at the top of it through a succession of lovely white-
marble chambers and pavilions, so marvellously light and
graceful that English seems to have no phrases to fit them;
—and besides (as aforesaid) we do not know in England
what white marble is. Everywhere is sculpture of flowers,
not in the crowded wreaths and bunches that Western taste
delights in, but each plant separated and spread out on the
marble surface as botanists arrange their specimens for
pressing, and generally accompanied by a curious, cloud-like
device which symbolises, may be, the scent thereof. Everywhere too is rich embroidery of more conventional sculpture, and (most admirable of all) beautiful inlayer's work
of delicate floral designs wrought in agate, cornelian, jasper,

---

[1] This seems to be at least a common opinion; but some of the more learned
sort aver that it was built by Akbar for the use of his son Jahangir.

lapis-lazuli, and other precious stones, all set in the white marble so perfectly as to preserve the polished surface absolutely unbroken.

There are fountains too, and channels cut in the marble pavements for sparkling waters to flow in, and clustered arches, and fluted columns, and screens of faëry lace-work shining and light and various like films of melting cloud, yet firm and solid and cool as though carved in frozen snow. Of such is the low balustrade which, supported on sandstone brackets, hangs round the edge of the walls; and over it our friends look down on the courses of deep-red masonry,[1] where brilliant parrots perch on every ledge and nestle in every recess. Smooth and delicate is their plumage of soft, rich emerald-green, and some have crimson beaks and narrow crimson collars. In their long tails are golden feathers which gleam in the glowing sunlight when they spread them out in flight. A charming contrast do the parrots make with the deep-red sandstone walls, but still more radiant are they when they sweep across the marble courts and perch on the shining rail.

The travellers fail not to visit the room wherein died, in December 1666, the Emperor Sháh Jahán. It is a marble chamber, perched near the edge of the wall, whence he could look away across the waters of the Jamna to the Taj Mahall that he himself had builded. There, beneath that stainless dome, lay his well-loved Empress, the beautiful Arjmand Banu,—"Mumtaz Mahall," the Chosen of the Palace,—while their son Aurangzib, keeping his father a prisoner at Agra, exultingly governed in his stead from his lordly court in Dehli. Poor old Sháh Jahán! It was a sad

---

[1] A story is told that there is rubble inside, and that the red-sandstone slabs are only facing-stones. People have no right to say such things as these.

ending for him whose head (so our Persian authority avers) had been "exalted to the Greater and the Lesser Bear," who had been "the sun of the firmament of pomp and glory, the Monarch, bestower of treasures, who is bounteous as the sea," whose "sacred and sublime cavalcade" had been of such marvellous "state and splendour" that the "concussion of the people, together with the sound of the kettle-drums and blasts of trumpets, occasioned an earthquake" whensoever he travelled; who rode "on an elephant swift as the spheres, and firm as a mountain, whilst abundance of money was flung on all sides among the populace;" before whom was carried "an umbrella touching the sky," while behind him marched "the principal officers with chowries and fans inlaid with precious stones, like the shadow after the sun in the firmament of greatness."

Wandering northward along the walls, the visitors reach at length the Khas Mahall, and, passing through it, make their way to the Diwán-i Khás, or Hall of Private Audience, which, if possible, is more beautiful still. Its lovely colonnade looks upon a terrace whereon are two thrones opposite one another, and made, the one of slate, the other of white marble. Each is a large, flat slab, raised above the pavement on a low marble platform. On the black throne sat the Emperor; and some say that his jester sat on the white one, confronting the mighty despot with a parody of his princely state. This place is that "Semblance of Paradise" whither his Majesty the Asylum of the World used to repair at evening, when (saith his chronicler), reclining on "the throne of state, the semblance of the empyrean one," he "exerts his great abilities in arranging the affairs of government; and the pearl of ordinary designs which lies hidden and concealed from

THE DIWAN-I KHAS, AGRA FORT.

others the most intelligent, his Majesty, by diving to the depths of reflection, with the aid of his discerning mind grasps the gem, and makes it an ornament for the ear of the wise."

On the Black Throne Akbar himself may have sat, for it bears a chronogram which, the learned say, gives the date 1011 of the Hegira, which is A.D. 1603. The slab is traversed by a great crack. It was not always so, for of old the surface was smooth and even; but there came an usurping sovereign, a violent Jat who had no right to the Mughal's seat, and when he sat thereon the Black Throne quaked, and it cracked with a thundering noise, and drops of blood oozed forth. To this day the red-brown stain is there, and some have wisely talked of I know not what compound of iron; but in that mechanical explanation I have no faith at all.

Near the Diwán-i Khás is a *pachisi*-board inlaid in the marble pavement. *Pachisi* has been learnedly defined as "a kind of Eastern backgammon." This board is on a large scale, as the pieces which the Mughals employed in the game were slaves.

Thence our friends go on to the Saman Burj, or Jasmine Tower, a pavilion wherein the chief sultana used to live; and thence find their way to a tiny mosque built of white marble and intended for the ladies of the palace to worship in. Its three snowy domes recall the Moti Masjid; and the whole has a delightful air of infancy, as though it would grow up some day.

But one cannot go on for ever enumerating buildings; and besides, it seems to our travellers to be more than time for breakfast. Before finally leaving the Fort, however, they are introduced to the venerable Gates of Som-

nath ; and the Father, who alone can remember Lord Ellenborough's days, presently recounts their history.   Made of
sandal-wood and originally the portals of the famous Hindu
temple at Somnath, they were seized, so long ago as the
year 1024, by the Sultan Mahmoud, and carried away,
together with the temple treasure, to Ghuzni, his capital.
After his death they were set up at his tomb, and there
they remained until Lord Ellenborough, with a great flourish
of trumpets, brought them to Agra on a triumphal car;
and a magniloquent proclamation he boastingly issued about
them.   The romance of this return is somewhat clouded by
the fact that their long residence among the Mussalmans
has strangely affected them.   In fact they (with all their
ornamentation) have turned Muhammadan.   Moreover, they
are of sandal-wood no longer, but only of deodar pine.
Indeed they are sadly changed; but it is very hard work
to hold out against one's environment, especially if one is
made of wood.

Often do the travellers visit the Fort, and they fail not to
pay their respects to other noteworthy buildings, especially the
Jam 'i Masjid, the Great Mosque built by Sháh Jahán, A.D.
1639-1644, to do honour to his daughter Jahánára, that very
lovable Princess who afterwards shared her father's imprison-
ment with such affectionate devotion.   It is a grand erection,
builded of red sandstone and white marble in very pleasing
contrast.   But oftenest our friends are attracted by the Taj ;
and now doth it behove us to celebrate the beauties of that
stately garden-tomb.

The effect of the first impression thereof is greatly height-
ened by the very imposing approach.   One is not allowed
to rush into its presence with unprepared and unexpectant
mind.   Our travellers enter first a grand outer court, and

thence pass beneath the arches of the most majestic gateway they have ever seen. Its height is 140 feet, and it is builded of red sandstone richly inlaid with white marble, and crowned with twenty-two small, white-marble cupolas and four larger ones, all resting on slender sandstone columns. The spandrels of all its arches are of white marble inlaid with floral arabesques; and round the two greater archways run, in a broad band of black marble inlaid in white, long texts from the Koran. Within, beneath the gateway's arches and semi-domes, are lofty spaces filled with shadow.

Through the gloom and the stillness the travellers hasten, and emerge therefrom into dazzling sunshine and a world of verdant loveliness. Before them stretches a long, long vista bordered by cypresses and other trees, and luxuriant clumps of bamboo. Down the centre stretches a broad, marble channel filled with running water, whence many fountains rise. At the far end is a low red-sandstone platform whereon rests that radiant group of marble forms like nothing else in the world,—a great white platform, smooth and shining, its four corners guarded by four strong, snow-white *minars*, each crowned with a gleaming cupola; and in the centre thereof a majestic octagonal building with slender pinnacles, and four large marble cupolas placed round the vast central dome which rises upward and upward yet, swelling in bulbous curves till the topmost point is crowned by a gilded crescent 243½ feet above the garden-level. Each of the four chief arches rises 63 feet from the pavement, and the spandrels thereof, as well as those of the smaller arches to right and left, are inlaid with arabesques drawn in great, sweeping lines, distinctly visible even at so great a distance.

Long do the travellers gaze, and then, to obtain a wider view, ascend to the top of the great gateway, whence they can look abroad over the garden and past the Tomb itself to the wide, green plains beyond the River. Now are more clearly visible the twin mosques (of red sandstone with snow-white marble domes) which, standing to right and left, so nobly support the Taj. Symmetry demanded that they should both face inward to the central group, wherefore only the *mihrab* of one of them can look, as it ought, toward Mecca; whence it follows that only the left-hand building is really a mosque, while the other is nothing particular. This is a pity; but so charming is the general effect that one has not the heart to complain.

As for the Taj itself, from this high standpoint, whence the view is uninterrupted by the trees, it looks fairer and more wonderful than ever. No photograph ever could catch its mystery of enchanting loveliness, for such unearthly and ethereal beauty can hardly be reproduced. They talk of the cost of the Taj being nearly £2,000,000; and they say that for seventeen years there laboured upon it day by day some 20,000 workmen. But I know better! It was built in a night from the moonlit snows that lay on the peaks of Himalaya. Frozen and hard were the gleaming crystals, but the snow-sprites deftly quarried them, and on waggons of cloud they brought them in haste and builded the Tomb therefrom; but the delicate mouldings around the dome are the petals of jasmine - blossoms. Through the hours of night the sprites did labour, and finished their work at dawn, when the spirits of morning came riding on sunbeams around the topmost crescent, and touched it lightly with glittering wings till it turned to radiant gold.

THE TAJ MAHALL, FROM THE TOP OF THE GATEWAY.

Some there are who have dared to blame this bright handiwork of the fairies, and many things have they foolishly alleged against it. Yet still (as one has suggested) it is even as a lovely face that smiles away reproof. "It is wanting in structural form," a learned critic avers, —a somewhat vague accusation, it seems to unlearned me. Does he mean that one cannot discern how the weight of the dome is supported, the thrust of the arches met? Nay, but is it not this which gives so magic a charm, and such unsubstantial lightness, that the building seems not to rest at all, but rather to float without need of support in an unapproachable glory? So pure and fair is the marble, that it seems immeasurably far removed from the dark-red sandstone beneath it, the dark-green trees around. It is like the bright castles in the air that children love to build—not all untrue as the elders think them, and not all unattainable either, but true with a truth that is ideal and cannot be mechanically approached, so that no mere journeying through the years can ever bring them nearer. Just so (as all travellers wonderingly notice, though none can in any wise explain it) the Taj seems to recede as one tries to approach, and its distance can only be judged from the wonderful smallness of the native figures that move like brilliant flies beside its lofty walls.

Happily the Taj does not go on receding for ever, and our friends have at length traversed the garden and mounted first the sandstone platform, and then the higher marble one whereon no Native ever treads except with shoeless feet. Passing beneath the great southern archway, they enter at length the central hall of the Tomb.

Herein is welcome shadow and the hush of perfect stillness. Each ray of light that enters must pass through two several screens of marble lattice-work, and the result is a wondrous twilight wherein is no gloom at all. Exactly under the centre of the dome is the marble tomb of Mumtaz Mahall, the lady for whom the Taj was builded and from whom it takes its name. That of her husband, Shah Jahan, is a little to the left. Both are richly carved and inlaid. They are only cenotaphs, for the bodies rest in a vault far below. Around them is a screen of marble fretwork such as, even in India, is almost too wonderful to be believed in. The mazes of its snowy traceries are intricate and light as the melting foam-wreaths that float and change on deep-blue waves at sea; and round each compartment of marble lace runs a band of inlayer's work, marvellously harmonious designs of semi-conventional flowers.

The dome above the tombs possesses a strangely beautiful echo, and Irene is presently called upon to sing the notes of chords, which are caught up in a wonderful manner and given back in a softened harmony that sounds like the voices of spirits.

Then our friends leave the hall, and descend a sloping marble passage to the real tombs below, each exactly under its ornate representative above.

Thence ascending, and emerging on to the marble platform, they spend a long time in admiring the rich sculpture of flowers and the endless inlaid ornament that adorn the outside of the building. At length, oppressed by overmuch sunshine, they retreat to the western mosque, and, seated on the step beneath its arches, gaze still at the shining Taj from a luxury of cool repose. Overhead, in the curve of the central arch of the mosque, a swarm of bees have built their nest—a dark-brown shapeless mass whose buzzing crowd of inhabitants reminds the travellers beneath of those other

metaphoric bees who live in the boughs of the Tree of
Selfishness; whereupon our friends must needs repeat that
quaintest of Indian similitudes, with its edifying moral of
apathetic inaction which seems peculiarly fitting in this
cool and sheltered retreat.

It was Dattatreya, the wise and illustrious Sage, who told
that story long ago to King Alarka, the tiger-hero. The
Tree of Selfishness is great and high, filling the path of final
emancipation. "Home and lands are its topmost boughs;
children and wife and other relatives are its young shoots;
wealth and corn are its great leaves. . . . It is rich with
festoons of bees, which are the desire to be doing."

Our travellers are much given to haunting the Taj and its
garden, but there is one picture thereof which, more than all
others, will remain vividly impressed on their memories.

It is the afternoon of February 27, the birthday of Shah
Jahan, and a native festival kept in his honour. The gallery
of the great gateway is filled with musicians, and the thunderous native music, somewhat terrible when near at hand,
is heard throughout the far-stretching garden in sweetly
softened rumblings, recalling to mind those splendid days of
Shah Jahan's pre-eminence when his "auspicious approach"
(so the Persian chronicle states) was wont to be proclaimed
aloud by the voice of "the kettle-drum of joy."

On their first visit our friends were too eager for the
splendours of the Taj itself to do justice to its lovely garden;
but to-day they wander far among its lawns and thronging
trees, gaze with wonder at the flowers, and gladly linger
beside the waters, which reflect with glittering clearness
the sunlit domes of the Tomb. Everywhere the trees are
haunted by birds of brilliant plumage. Most beautiful of
all, perhaps, are those which have straight, sharp beaks,

and plumage of the softest emerald green that ever was
seen on earth. But even the birds are outshone to-day by
the gorgeous native dresses. The festal crowd, dispersed
among the trees and lawns of the garden, or moving with
unslippered feet over the snow-white pavement of the Tomb,
is a continual feast to the eyes, and will ever be remembered
by the travellers like some strange and dazzling dream.

Our friends climb up to the marble platform, and descend
to the vaulted chamber, where they find the Emperor's tomb
decked out with freshly gathered flowers and all the air per-
fumed with the breath of fragrant incense. Then, standing
again in the sunshine on the platform's eastern edge, they
watch the shifting rainbow throng gradually concentrating
itself on the sandstone level beneath them, where carpets
have been spread with a view to a natch-dance which will
presently begin. The heat of the day is over, and the golden
light, already tinged with the rosy evening glow, blends into
a wonderful harmony of colour the luxuriant verdure of the
southern vegetation, the countless hues of the native crowd,
the white pavements and walls of marble, and the clear,
blue sky above; while still the faint and far-off sounds
of Indian music swell through the radiant air in dreamy,
monotonous cadence.

To say farewell to the Taj is sad indeed; but it must be
done at last, and late in a moonlit evening the travellers take
their leave of it. The moon is not nearly full, but her light is
wonderfully soft and bright, reminding them of the legendary
childhood of Parîkchita the Son of Kings, who, "loaded with
the cares of his parents, grew swiftly from day to day as grows
the moon throughout the time that fills her radiant orb."[1]

---

[1] From 'Le Bhâgavata Purâna,' . . . traduit . . . par M. Eugène
Burnouf.

If the garden of the Taj is a faëry precinct by day, it is pervaded at night by an elfin mystery enchanting beyond description. The waters glimmer beneath the moonbeams, and between the dark masses of foliage rises in ghostly loveliness the faintly shining dome. The deep stillness is broken only by the deep, grating sound of the bull-frog's mournful croak. So awe-inspiring is all the shadowy scene that one scarcely dares to speak except in whispers; and it is under her breath that Sebaste exclaims—

"Why, Philippa! it is true after all, what Aristophanes says."

"What does Aristophanes say?"

"That there are frogs who say βρεκεκεκέξ! And I have been unhappy about it for years. Every one knows that all common frogs say κοὰξ, κοάξ; but βρεκεκεκέξ I knew they never did, which was terribly distressing to a truthful mind. And after all, he must have meant the bull-frog! What are the commentators thinking about, that they never told us? Of course Aristophanes is true to human nature; but to find him so accurate about froggish nature as well,—it is delightful!"

"My dear," answers Philippa in a crushing whisper, "if I had known that you were coming to India to talk about Greek frogs, I should have suggested your remaining at home! Nothing, it seems to me, can be in worse taste than to trot out scraps of European classics here in the East where they are altogether incongruous with the oriental atmosphere around us, with which we should be trying to bring our minds into harmony."

"But, Philippa dear, it was the bull-frog who began it. There again! Do you not hear him? βρεκεκεκέξ."

"I believe he does it on purpose!" says Philippa wrathfully.   " Let us go away to the mosque, where we can't hear him."

The moonlight falls full on the western face of the Taj, and very lovely is the view of the Tomb from our travellers' favourite seat on the step of the western mosque.   The stillness is wonderful; even the bees, those restless desires to be doing, are fast asleep, and nothing moves at all, except once, when a dark shadow crosses the step of the mosque, and a soft-footed jackal glides swiftly past, away into the darkness within.

Long do the visitors linger; but at length it is time to go, and slowly they move away beside the shimmering waters, where still, at intervals, the bull-frog thoughtfully remarks, βρεκεκεκέξ.

CHAPTER XVI.

GWALIAR.

THE travellers fail not to visit Sikandarah, nor to devote a long day to the architectural wonders of beautiful Fathpur Sikri. Short expeditions from Agra are many and interesting; but our friends soon meditate a somewhat longer flight, and, beginning to despise the comparative civilisation of British India, determine to plunge into downright heathendom and visit a Native State. Their choice falls on the ancient and famous city of Gwaliar; and so, with a merry farewell to white faces and English tongues, thither they take their journey.

Whether the city was really founded (as they say the poet Kharg Rai has recorded) in the year 3101 B.C., I cannot undertake to say; but in any case the place is old, and has a long and tangled history. Therein have reigned I know not how many dynasties of Kings, succeeding one another in a bewildering fashion until even Philippa looks disheartened, and proposes to leave them alone.

Then there is the Muhammadan conquest that ought to be described, and many other things, including the terrible 14th of June in the Mutiny year, and the loyalty of Sindhia, the young Maharaja, and the wonderful capture of 1858.

But Sindhia is dead now, and his son reigns in his stead; nor can any of our friends remember those days except the Father alone; and I must run after the travellers, and cannot stay dreaming here.

Gwaliar lies almost due south of Agra, and the journey (performed, I am sorry to admit, in what cannot honestly be described otherwise than as a railway-train) takes some three hours. About half-way the travellers pass through Dholpúr, and soon after cross, by a long bridge of red sandstone, the river Chambal, which bounds the Gwaliar territory, flowing away north-eastward to pour itself into the Jamna.

Arriving late in the afternoon, the travellers betake them to the Muzafir Khana, which is the Maharaja's guest-house. It is built of white stone, and is a charming specimen of modern native architecture. Most delightful of it all are the elephants who, with their carven trunks turned gracefully upward, support the stone balconies whereon open the upper windows. Within is luxurious furniture, and all else that heart can desire.

Next morning our friends are early astir, and setting forth to visit the Fort. It is perched on the top of a great mass of sandstone rock which rises 300 feet above the plain at its foot. Mr Finch, when he visited "Gualere" nearly three centuries ago, was much impressed by this bold rock, which he calls "the ruggy Cliff on which the Castle is seated." It is indeed a ruggy cliff, steep by nature and scarped as well, so that the position of the fort is perhaps the strongest in India.

Arrived at the foot of the rock, our travellers find, waiting to conduct them to the top, one of the most estimable, and quite the most good-natured, of all their Indian acquaint-

ances. His name is Ham, and he is said to be the largest
and slowest elephant that the Maharaja of Gwaliar possesses.
Strong and stately is he as the mighty elephant Airavata,
who rose of old from the ocean when the gods and demons
were churning it, and who hath ever since belonged to Indra,
the god of thunder. But Ham is much more amiable than
he. Dear Ham will ever be remembered by our friends
with the deepest gratitude and affection. His patience is
something abnormal, and the sweetness of his temper an
unfailing source of astonishment. Even thrusting one's
fingers into his eyes, as he kneels on the ground, elicits
no more emphatic remonstrance than a mildly deprecating
blink.

As soon as the travellers have mounted on his broad and
commodious back, Ham rises to his feet, and proceeds along
the ascending road with a cheerful, swaying motion suggestive of a small boat in a big sea, but in very slow time.
Thus he carries our travellers to the top of the great rock's
eastern face, where rises, on the edge of the precipitous cliff,
the grand façade, 100 feet in height and 300 feet long, of
that most interesting of Hindu palaces, the Man Mandir,
built by Mân Sing, who reigned at Gwaliar from A.D. 1486
to 1516. Its yellow-sandstone walls seem to be a part of
the rock on which they stand, rising from it in lines of
massive strength relieved by ornament of sculpture and
blue-green tiles, while at intervals stand beautiful towers
crowned with cupolas which were originally covered with
plates of gilded copper.

Entering by the Elephant Gate, and leaving for awhile
their gigantic steed, the visitors eagerly explore the interior,
and finally make their way to one of the pillared cupolas of
the eastern wall, whence they look abroad far over the green

plains, and watch a company of the Maharaja's elephants straying about near the foot of the rock, and making, with their few native attendants, a pleasing feature in the landscape. Descending from the wall, the travellers go on to other palaces builded by Vicramaditya and Jahangir and Shah Jahan. Wonderfully grotesque are some of the sculptures therein. Terrific monsters grin and glare from unsuspected corners; and our friends grow so thoroughly accustomed to all marvellous sights that, when they come suddenly on a company of peacocks supporting on their stony tails the weight of massive architraves, they feel no more astonishment thereat than would be the case if they happened to be exploring one of the palaces of Dreamland.

But there are temples as well as palaces within the walls of the fortress; and, sometimes on foot, sometimes with kind Ham's assistance, the travellers wander on from one ruined shrine to another in an ecstasy of archæologic enthusiasm. First they visit the pillared pavilion known as the Gwáli shrine, and then seek out the more interesting Chaturbhuj Mandir, the temple of the Four-armed God. It is carved out of the living rock, and dates from A.D. 876. The Four-armed God is none other than the "immortal, unconquerable Vishnu," who uses his four hands to carry about with him a wheel, a lotus-flower, a conch-trumpet, and a mace,—symbols which (as saith that learned Pandit, Cavali Venkat Ramaswami) signify respectively Universal Supremacy, Creative Power, Preservation, and Destruction. Within the temple is a Sanskrit inscription, which, happily for our unlearned travellers, has been translated at length by that accomplished Sanskrit scholar Bábu Rajendralála Mitra.[1] It begins with the solemn dedication: "Om! Salutation to

[1] See the 'Journal of the Asiatic Society of Bengal,' vol. xxxi. (1862).

Vishnu!" and sets forth how, on the second day of the waxing moon in the month Magha of the Samvat year 933
(which is 876 of our era), a piece of ground lying on the
opposite bank of the Vrischikala river, and measuring "in
length 270 cubits and in breadth 187, is presented on a
fortunate day for the purpose of a flower-garden for the
temple of Rudra, Rudráni, Pushnásá, and others, as also of
the nine Durgas."

Above the entrance to the temple is a great rock-sculpture
of the Boar Avatar, and, in amicable nearness to this Vaishnava scene, a Saiva group of Mahadeo and his wife, who are
such usual forms of Siva and Parvati that we ought long
ago to have recorded their attributes. Mahadeo, it seems,
is lord "of the spirits of ill, of kine, of portents and planets,
of infirmities and diseases," [1] and of "ghosts." He is fond
of wearing a necklace of skulls, and of twisting snakes in his
hair. His consort (like all Hindu goddesses) is the active
manifestation of her husband's qualities.

Not far off is a small building, formerly (as an inscription
announces) "the idol-temple of the vile Gwáli," but transformed, in the reign of the great Prince Aurangzib, the
Enlightener of the World, into "a mosque like a mansion of
Paradise."

One of the most impressive of the fort temples is the Tali
Mandir, a stately pile 60 feet square at the base (exclusive of
a projecting portico), and rising thence at first perpendicu-
larly, but afterwards tapering with graceful curvilinear outlines to the ridge that, 30 feet in length, crowns the whole at
a height of 80 feet from the ground. The lines of the building are wonderfully grand and beautiful, and there is much
adornment of richly elaborated sculpture. Over the majestic

---

[1] Wilson, quoted by Poley in his "Devimahatmyam."

doorway, which is 35 feet high, appears Garuda, the brown kite whereon Vishnu rides abroad; and there seems to be no doubt that the building is of Vaishnava origin, although in the fifteenth century it was turned into a Saiva temple. Its date is uncertain, the learned say, but it may well be as early as the tenth or eleventh century.

Thence the visitors go on to the two temples named Sasbahu (or "Mother-in-law and Daughter-in-law"), because of some vague tradition about the family of an ancient king of Gwaliar, which our travellers do not succeed in unravelling. The larger of the two dates from 1092 A.D., and is dedicated to Vishnu the Lord of the Lotus. Originally it was a towering pile 100 feet long, and probably not less than 100 feet high, with a greatest breadth of 63 feet. All that remains of it now is the stately, cruciform porch builded in three massive storeys, with numberless small pillars whose bracket-capitals seem flattened and bulging beneath the weight of the heavy courses of masonry. Everywhere are horizontal bands of richly varied sculpture. The plinth of the building is from 10 to 12 feet high, and, though its surface is terribly shattered, the elaborate sculpture-ornament thereof may still be partly traced,—round the top a band of small human figures; then one of elephants; and below, line upon line of more conventional patterns. Of the interior, the most astonishing feature is a group of four gigantic pillars—no part, say the learned, of the original design, but introduced of necessity to support the weight of the towering pyramidal roof.

Now doth it behove me to discourse of the smaller Sasbahu temple, and of that Jaina temple discovered by General Cunningham, and dating from about 1108 A.D. But I am tired of describing buildings!

Near the Jaina temple our travellers sit them down to rest

awhile; whereupon all eyes turn upon Philippa, and she finds herself expected (by her unreasonable relatives) to hold forth on the Jains and their history, and to give an accurate account of their beliefs and their sacred books.

Thanks to Professor Jacobi, the Jaina philosophy is no longer shrouded in the hopeless mystery which used to envelop it. At all events, he has established its great antiquity, and dismissed the popular notion of its being a modified form of Buddhism. Of its independent origin there can now be no doubt at all, for the Professor has shown it to be fully as ancient as Buddhism itself. What common elements the two systems possess either have been borrowed by both from ancient Brahmanism, or are such as would naturally be produced simultaneously by the same age and the same conditions of thought. I wish I were old enough to remember what the valley of the Ganges was like in the fifth and sixth centuries B.C. What a great upheaval of thought there must have been, long-continued, maybe, rather than sudden, but all the more irresistible for that, ever increasing in strength until at last it had burst its way through the Brahmans' tyrant system and the intolerable restrictions of caste; a far-reaching, manifold movement whereof the Buddhism and the Jainism of the present day are the long-enduring results.

The historic founder of Jainism is one Vardhamâna; but we are not obliged to call him so, any more than one need call Buddha "Sakyamuni" unless one likes, and Vardhamâna is generally known by his title Mahâvîra. He was a contemporary of the Buddha, but it is quite possible that the Jaina system (or at least the movement that Mahâvîra systematised) had existed long before his days. Mythically he is the twenty-fourth and last of the Jaina Tirthakaras or Prophets, who

appeared at enormous intervals of time, and preached, each
to his own age, the sacred doctrines of Jainism. He alone
emerges into actual history, but the tradition of the others
may well have a nucleus of truth. The life of Mahâvîra, as
told in the ancient Jaina scriptures, is as good as a fairy tale;
and, thanks again to our kind Professor, we can read it without being, like him, able to decipher Prâkrit. In the Pillow
of Righteousness it is written, and in the Kalpa Sûtra as
well.

A wonderful night was that wherein the Venerable Ascetic
was born! "In the conflux of gods the bustle of gods
amounted to confusion." "In that night . . . the gods and
goddesses rained down one great shower of nectar, sandal-
powder, gold, and pearls." So long as his parents were alive,
he seems, like other young princes, to have lived delicately;
but the time came when he determined to retire from the
world and become a holy ascetic. "When the gods and
goddesses had become aware of his intention, they assumed
their proper form, dress, and ensigns," and in "their proper
pomp and splendour" set forth "with that excellent, quick,
swift, rapid, divine motion of the gods," and "crossing
numberless continents and oceans," arrived at the home of
Mahâvîra. Then "Sakra the leader and king of the gods"
(the same is Indra) "produced by magic the great palankin
called Kandraprabhâ," which meaneth "shining like the
moon." A thousand men were required to carry it. "It
shone with heaps and masses of pearls. . . . In the middle
of the palankin was a costly throne covered with a divine
cloth, precious stones, and silver, with a footstool, for the
best of Ginas," who is the Venerable Mahâvîra. . . . "After
a fast of three days, with a glorious resolution he ascended
the supreme palankin, purifying all by his light." Thus,

escorted by all the gods and goddesses, he left his home "by the highway for the park Gnâtra Shanda. There, just at the beginning of night, he caused the palankin Kandraprabhâ to stop quietly on a slightly raised untouched ground, quietly descended from it, sat quietly down on a throne with the face towards the East, and took off all his ornaments and finery . . . Mahâvîra then plucked out with his right and left hands, on the right and left sides of his head, his hair in five handfuls. . . . After the Venerable Ascetic Mahâvîra had plucked out hair in five handfuls, . . . he adopted the holy conduct. At that moment the whole assembly of men and gods stood motionless, like figures in a picture."

Then "for more than twelve years" did the Venerable One perform unheard-of austerities. He would sometimes go six months without drinking. "As water does not adhere to a copper vessel, . . . so sins found no place in him. . . . Like the firmament, he wanted no support; like the wind, he knew no obstacles; . . . his senses were well protected like those of a tortoise; he was single and alone like the horn of a rhinoceros; he was free like a bird, . . . valorous like an elephant, strong like a bull, difficult to attack like a lion, steady and firm like Mount Mandara, deep like the ocean, mild like the moon, refulgent like the sun, pure like excellent gold; like the earth, he patiently bore everything; like a well-kindled fire, he shone in his splendour. . . . He was indifferent alike to . . . straw and jewels, dust and gold, pleasure and pain. . . . With supreme intuition, with supreme conduct, in blameless lodgings, in blameless wandering, . . . the Venerable One meditated on himself for twelve years." Terrible were the persecutions he underwent. When he was sitting immovable, immersed in meditation, "the people, . . . striking the monk, . . . cried 'Khukkhû,' and made the dogs bite him; . . . they tore his hair, . . . or covered him with dust. Throwing him up, they let him fall, or disturbed him in his religious postures."

But all this could not in anywise trouble him, and at length, "during the thirteenth year, in the second month of summer, in the fourth fortnight, . . . not far from a *sâl*-tree, in a squatting position with joined heels, exposing himself to the heat of the sun, with the knees high and the head low, in deep meditation, in the midst of abstract meditation, he reached Nirvâna, the complete and full, the unobstructed, unimpeded, infinite, and supreme. . . . Then when the Venerable Ascetic Mahâvîra had reached the highest know-ledge and intuition, he reflected on himself and on the world. First he taught the law to the gods, and afterwards to men."

So he passed his life in teaching his great philosophy, until "in the town of Pâpâ, in King Hastipâla's office of the writers, the Venerable Ascetic Mahâvîra died, went off, quitted the world, cut asunder the ties of birth, old age, and death; became a Sidha, a Buddha, a Mukta, a maker of the end to all misery, finally liberated, freed from all pains. This occurred in the year called Kandra, . . . in the month called Prîtivardhana. . . . In that night the eighteen con-federate kings of Kâsî and Kasala . . . instituted an illu-mination, . . . for they said, 'Since the light of intelligence is gone, let us make an illumination of material matter.'"

So much for Mahâvîra. But what of the system which he taught? Like Buddhism, it is a development from Brahmanic philosophy; but it cannot, like Buddhism, be called a system of ethics, a principal feature being its mass of metaphysical doctrines. Very prominent is the hylozoist notion that all things are full of multitudinous life—that earth, air, fire, and water are inhabited by invisible beings who must not on any account be neglected. For what saith Mahâvîra in that ancient Jaina book, the Akârânga Sûtra?

"There are beings living in water, many lives; of a truth, to the monks water has been declared to be living matter."

"Considering the injuries done to water-bodies," saith the ordinance, water must be strained before using it. . . . "There are beings living in the earth, living in grass, living on leaves, living on wood, . . . living in dust-heaps."

As for Jaina psychology, it differs not much from Brahmanic notions, and is far less depressing to contemplate than the psychology of Buddhism. Atma, it seems, is an absolute and immortal soul, and it is this (and no mere *karma*, or sum of merits and demerits) that transmigrates from one body into another. Whence it follows that the Jaina Nirvâna is something more tangible and satisfactory than the mere neutralising of existence to which Buddhists longingly aspire.

Jaina Asceticism also owes much to Brahmanism. Its fundamental maxim is this, "Quality is the seat of the root, and the seat of the root is quality;" which meaneth (saith our learned Professor), "In the qualities of external things lies" sin, the primary cause of all misery; "the qualities produce sin, and sinfulness makes us apt to enjoy the qualities." The perfect state of mind attained by the wise man is thus summarised in the Âkârânga Sûtra: "Subduing desire by desirelessness, he does not enjoy the pleasures that offer themselves. Desireless, giving up the world and ceasing to act, he knows and sees, and has no wishes because of his discernment." All who would attain to such perfection must "wisely reject hope and desire" and extract the thorn of pleasure. "A wise man," saith the same discourse, "should not rejoice in the receipt of a gift, nor be sorry when he gets nothing."

The way to this laudable apathy lies through terrible austerities. "Subdue the body," saith the scripture, "chastise thyself, weaken thyself, 'just as fire consumes old wood.'" There are meritorious methods of suicide, too, whereof one consists in sitting absolutely still in the same place, "checking all motions," until one dies.

The most curious feature of Jaina Asceticism is the great merit obtained by refusing to wear clothes. Great is the praise of the "naked monk" whom grass pricks, cold attacks, flies and mosquitoes sting. It is recorded of Mahâvîra that, though Indra, the "wielder of the thunderbolt," the "thousand-eyed one," the "bestrider of the elephant Airavata," had given him a "divine robe," yet, having adopted the holy conduct, he wore it only for one winter, and thenceforward became a "naked, world-relinquishing, houseless sage," a "great Hero" who did no acts at all.

This custom of discarding clothes was at first practised by all the Jaina ascetics, and the Digambaras, or "Sky-clad Ones," are by far the older section of the Jains, seeing that the other party, called Swetambaras, or "White-robed Ones," cannot be traced back beyond the sixth century of our era. The custom is falling now into disuse, and is observed by few besides the statues of the Tirthakaras, whereof there is a multitude at Gwaliar, hewn in the sandstone rock on which the Fort is built. Those in the Happy Valley our travellers hope to see this very morning.

There are many other things that ought to be said about the Jains; and very delightfully they have been said by erudite Professor Jacobi. Specially satisfactory is the conclusiveness wherewith he establishes the great antiquity of the sacred Jaina scriptures. It is true that they were never reduced to writing until the fifth century of our era; but that they should have been correctly handed down for many centuries by word of mouth will astonish no one who knows anything about the ancient books of the East. The Purvas, indeed, those very earliest of the Jaina books, are lost; but we still have those which may well date from 300 B.C. They abound in quaint similitudes, such as that in the Akaranga Sutra: "A lake is full of water, it is in an even plain, it is free from dust, it harbours many fish. Like unto it is a teacher who is full of wisdom."

So doth Philippa discourse in the shade of the Jaina temple, while Ham, with deep solemnity, deferentially listens in the background, until, cooled and refreshed by this soothing stream of instruction, the travellers again bestir themselves, and, mounting the back of their kneeling steed, go swaying and rolling and flopping away to visit the Urwahi Valley, a deep, rocky defile in the western side of the fort-rock. Grave and intent their thoughts should be as they approach the strange old Jaina statues carved in the rock of the valley's southern side by hands that crumbled into dust some four centuries ago. But, as they slowly move along the descending road, Ham's great black shadow is thrown full on the wayside rock, with so quaint a caricature of his solemn expression of countenance that gravity is out of the question; and, before they can in anywise compose their minds, the travellers find themselves in the very presence of the weird and stony giants, all carved between 1440 A.D. and 1474.

The principal figures in the group are twenty-two, all "sky-clad," and all standing or sitting cross-legged in attitudes of an astonishing stiffness which, if not graceful, is all the more delightfully archaic, as no doubt are also the self-satisfied and extremely supercilious expressions of the gigantic and immovable countenances. Each of the larger figures represents one of the Jaina Tirthakaras, among whom there seems to have been a curious family likeness. Most imposing of all is a huge personage 57 feet in height, who seems to have grown 17 feet since the days of the Mughal Emperor Babar; for he came to Gwaliar A.D. 1527, and recorded the fact that this same statue was at that time 40 feet high.

Very interesting too is the colossal portrait of Adináth, first of all the Tirthakaras, and distinguished by the symbol of a bull. On his rocky pedestal is an inscription beginning with: "Salutation to Adinatha!" and giving the date as "the seventh day of the waxing moon when she was in the mansion of Punarvashu in the month Vaisákha in the Samvat year 1497"—that is to say, A.D. 1440.

There are innumerable smaller figures, and many symbolic devices, which take long to examine, so that, by the time our travellers are rolling and flopping back up the valley, the terrible sun, that "illustrious leader of the troop of planets" (as the Jaina scripture calls him), the "thousand-eyed maker of the day," the "destroyer of night," the "lamp of the firmament, throttling, as it were, the mass of cold," is already driving his fiery steeds high up in the blinding sky.

Again entering the Fort, and passing out by the Elephant Gate, our friends descend, by the way they came, to the eastern base of the rock. Here they bid a reluctant fare-well to their dear friend Ham, and then drive away to the guest-house for coolness and rest and tiffin.

When the heat of the day is over, they fare forth again, and take their way through the heart of the town, watch-ing the native life, more wonderful here than even in the

JAINA SCULPTURES IN THE URWAHI VALLEY, GWALIOR.

crowded scenes of the cities of British India. The young
Maharaja gives a state banquet to-day, and our friends
meet many of the guests on their way to the royal Palace,
—dignified gentlemen of dusky countenances, clad in splendid apparel. Preparations, too, for the coming festival of
Vishnu are not wanting, and in one of the streets appear
two gigantic idols of that worthy. They are made of mud,
and at present look somewhat deplorable; but before the
feast-day they will have been duly painted and adorned,
and made ready to receive with fitting dignity the devotion
of their pious worshippers. Proud as their career will be,
however, it will not last long; for, as soon as the festival
is over, the venerated images will be summarily and ruthlessly destroyed.

Stranger than all else are the carriages wherein the native
ladies drive abroad. The picturesque *ekkas* have long been
familiar to our travellers' eyes; but they have never yet
seen the like of these extraordinary equipages. Each of
them is a square platform on wheels, richly hung with
bright-hued and embroidered stuffs, and furnished with a
towering tent of crimson, within whose sheltering curtains
the ladies lurk unseen.

But, fascinating as are the streets of the town, our travellers must not linger long therein, for they have to visit before
sunset the tomb of Muhammad Ghaus, a learned and holy
personage who flourished in the reign of Akbar. The tomb
is an impressive sandstone building, and dates from the early
part of Akbar's reign. It is crowned with a heavy Pathan
dome, which used to reflect the sunshine from a covering of
blue encaustic tiles. The most beautiful part of the building
is the succession of exquisite fretwork screens wherewith the
surrounding corridor is shaded from the glare without.

Hard by is the tomb of Tansen, who, it seems, was a famous musician, well known in Akbar's court. His tomb, which is small, is overshadowed by a tamarind of very remarkable properties; for whoso eateth a leaf therefrom straightway is able to sing as sweetly as Tansen of old. The present tree is only a descendant of the original one, for so many were the singers who came to benefit by the first tree's marvellous virtue, that, having no leaves left, it not unreasonably died,—a fate which probably awaits also its no less magical successor.

Next morning the travellers explore the somewhat barbaric splendours of the Maharaja's modern palace, and, bringing thus to an end their hurried experiences of Gwaliar, set forth therefrom with sorrow, and journey back to Agra.

CHAPTER XVII.

THE PEACOCK CITY AND THE FOREST OF VRINDA.

SOON our travellers are planning another expedition—this time to holy Mathurá, the capital of Braj and the birth-place of "blessed Krishna," who is the Teacher and Soul of the Universe, "destroyer of the race of earth's tyrant-kings,"[1] the "First of Spirits."

Mathurá (one is not allowed to talk of Muttra now) lies north-westward from Agra on the right bank of the Jamna. So holy is the place that some have said, "If a man spend in Benares all his lifetime, he hath earned less merit than if he pass but a single day in the sacred city of Mathurá."[2]

Our friends begin the three hours' railway journey at seven o'clock in the freshest and most radiant morning that mind can imagine. Strange and brilliantly beautiful are the birds that sweep through the sunlit air or perch on the telegraph-wires. There are little birds with plumage of emerald green, and long-tailed kingcrows, and large dove-like birds arrayed in two shades of blue, and the great, brown, white-headed kite which Crawfurd identifies with Garuda, Vishnu's favourite steed; and, resplendent

---

[1] 'Le Bhâgavata Purâna.' M. Eugène Burnouf.
[2] From 'Mathurá: A District Memoir.' By F. S. Growse, B.C.S.

in green and gold, the lively parrots, on one of which Kamadeva, the little god of love, rides often by moonlight over the plain of Mathurá, holding his terrible sugar-cane bow with its string that is made of bees.

There is a legend about that wicked little god, telling how once, with Spring for his companion, he journeyed to Himachal's snowy heights, and when the two came thither the spring flowers bloomed around them, though it was not the season of spring. There did they meet with Siva; and the mischievous love-god drew forth his arrow that was made of the mango-tree, and presumed to aim at the mighty deity just as a lovely maiden, Parvati, the Daughter of the Mountain, had come forth to gather flowers to offer at Siva's shrine. But, in a moment, from Siva's third and central eye beamed forth a terrible stream of fire, and Kamadeva was caught thereby, and in a moment burned to ashes. How it was that he recovered from that disaster I know not, but certain it is that soon he was seen again, merrily riding his parrot through the moonlit plains of Mathurá.

All life is sacred in the Mathurá district, and not even bloodthirsty Britons may in any wise molest the birds. Every sheet of water near the railway is crowded with multitudes of wild-fowl—wild geese and ducks, pelicans and cranes, and other kinds innumerable. Everywhere, too, are wild peacocks perambulating in twos and threes, their brilliant plumage beautifully contrasting with the soft, rich verdure of the background. Well do they know in their regal pride that they are Krishna's sacred birds, who gave their name long centuries ago to Mathurá, the Peacock City.

The trees are mostly tamarinds, wherein hang, each by its slender band of fibre, the light-brown nests of the weaver-

birds. Often too the dark-green foliage is illuminated by
the soft, golden masses of a lovely parasite plant called
Absalom's Hair—or, if it is not called so, it ought to be.
Another beautiful plant is a crimson water - weed which
grows over the surface of pools in the most delectable manner; and there are so many other strange things to be seen
that our travellers are in danger of forgetting to tell each
other the marvellous history of Krishna, though it assuredly
behoves them to do so before the journey is ended.

Krishna, the all-comprising, the pure, the ancient, the
immutable, who by his frown alone can annihilate the
universe, is the eighth incarnation of Vishnu; but he has a
cult that is all his own, and he seems to be considered by his
worshippers as supreme over all other gods, including Vishnu
himself, who sometimes appears in the scriptures as *Krishna's
son*. This is somewhat bewildering, but one gets used to it
in time.

The story of Krishna is worth listening to; for what said
Narada long ago? "It is a history that delivereth man from
all diseases of body and soul, and maketh him wise and
blessed."[1] Some have thought to trace therein vestiges of
Christian influence; yet there seems but little reason therefor (the etymologic fancy about Krishna's name was long ago
disposed of); and in any case, for practical purposes, Krishna's
legends are, in all conscience, quite heathenish enough.

A mighty deity was Krishna, and he lived in an excellent
abode upheld by the wind ten thousand millions of leagues
above the egg of the world. But further and higher yet, in
the exalted paradise of the celestial shepherdesses, dwelt
Radha his lovely bride, reigning among green and sacred

---

[1] See 'Traduction et Commentaire des principaux passages du Brahmâvæ-
varta Purana.' Par L. Leupol.

lawns over numberless choirs of nymphs. Joyful was Radha
of old among her maiden companions. But there arose a
contention betwixt her and Dharman the demon - spirit,
whose eyes were red like the lotus. And Dharman cursed
her, saying in his cruel wrath, "Take thou an human form!
Thou shalt become a woman, and shalt wander on the face
of the earth." Then Radha wept in sorrow, and thus addressed her lord: "Dharman hath cursed me! Tell me, O
thou destroyer of fear, . . . how can I endure life without
thee? Thou art my sight, my strength, mine eye, and my
highest riches." But Krishna, when he heard it, comforted
the fair goddess, saying, "I, too, O thou of the lovely countenance, will go down to the earth. Since thou must there
be born, descend with me. I will walk in the woodland of
Braj when thou comest thither. What canst thou fear when
I am with thee?"

So Radha rode on a boar until she came to the face of the
earth, and with her went Krishna her lord, the ruler of all
the world. Then Radha was born as the daughter of Nanda
and Yasoda his wife; but Krishna came to the city of
Mathurá that is in the region of Braj, near to the Jamna
River, and became the eighth son of Prince Vasudeva and
his lady, Princess Devaki; and his elder brother was Balarama, the hero of many achievements.

Now there reigned at that time in Mathurá the wicked
tyrant Kansa, the brother of Princess Devaki. And he had
thrust from the throne his father Ugrasen, and boastfully
reigned in his stead. But there came to him a Voice out of
the air, saying, "By the eighth son of Vasudeva thou shalt
be slain." Then would Kansa have slain the infant Krishna;
but Vasudeva [1] took him in his arms and fled away through

[1] See Growse, 'District Memoir.'

the stormy night till he came to the river Jamna. The great
river was in flood (for it was the rainy season), and the current was deep and strong; but Vasudeva boldly entered the
stream, and there was no cause of fear, for when the waters
had risen up to the foot of the sleeping Krishna, they could
go no further, and Vasudeva with his little son passed over
the river in safety.

So Krishna grew up to manhood, and did many a mighty
deed; and at length he slew Kansa the tyrant, and restored
to his throne in peace the aged king Ugrasen. And Radha
also grew up a lovely milkmaid, and Krishna made her his
bride.

Much more there is to tell of Krishna's heroic achievements; but legendary rhapsodies are suddenly interrupted
by the arrival at Mathurá. Whereupon the travellers drive
in a gharry away to the travellers' bungalow, and are there
received by a white-turbaned, black-bearded personage whose
name is Wazír. Would that I could in anywise do justice,
O marvellous Wazír, to the altogether extraordinary qualities
of thine intellect and conversation! Never before have the
travellers heard such fluent discourse. It is a never-ending,
voluble stream of infinitely varied sound. The language (in
Wazír's fond imagination) is English, but must be a strange
and unfamiliar form thereof, that philologists ought to investigate. Most Indians are nervous, and poor Wazír is perhaps slightly hysterical. His earnestness and insistence are
something appalling, and his intense excitement is oppressive
as a nightmare. Finding it impossible to silence him, the
travellers wrathfully drive him away; but he is always turning up again with more to say than ever.

At last, the door having been finally shut in his face and
secured on the inside, our friends are free to breakfast in

peace, and discuss their plans of action. Bindraban, with its
venerable temples and its mythical associations, has long
been haunting their minds, and thither they propose to go
forthwith, leaving till to-morrow the nearer sights of the city
of Mathurá itself.

Suddenly through a second and unsuspected door, in sidles
Wazír, pouring forth such a volume of multitudinous words
that his hearers are for the moment subdued and overwhelmed. But, when it becomes evident that he too proposes to go to Bindraban, their indignation knows no bounds.

"No!" says Philippa firmly, "we will not allow it! You
talk too much."

Whereupon Wazír, the picture of injured innocence,
plunges into so violent a stream of protestations, such a
whirling storm of denials, that Philippa sorrowfully deter-
mines never to repeat the accusation. Realising at length
that he really may not go, poor Wazír is for some seconds
silent and dejected; but just as the travellers are entering
their gharry he noiselessly sidles up, climbs in a moment to
the roof thereof, and sits him down there (like a great white
bird), the master of the situation. Commands and threats
and remonstrances are thenceforth all in vain, and it is the
travellers' turn to look dejected as at length they drive away.

"Well," says Irene, trying to cheer the others, "he cannot
do much harm while he is safe overhead. I think, Philippa,
that you had better make the best of the respite, and tell us
some of the legends that belong to Bindraban."

"There would be more legends to tell," says Philippa indignantly, "if those meddlesome scholars would only leave
them alone. Bindraban is the Forest of Vrinda, and Vrinda
used to be a mighty goddess about whom any number of
delightful stories might have been told; but the learned

have turned her into a botanical species, and say that Bind-raban means 'a forest of *tulsi*-trees.'"

"But, Philippa, what about Krishna and Balarama? Didn't they live there as boys, and run wild in the woods thereabout, playing on shepherds' pipes? And what is the legend about the little Krishna stealing butter and curds?"

"Ah, that is a wonderful story!" exclaims Philippa, brightening up. "Krishna, it seems, as a child, was extremely fond of butter; and once on a time he went by stealth to a neighbour's house, and mounted by a ladder to a shelf whereon a great butter-jar stood, and he ate the butter as far as he could reach, and then got into the jar. So, when the master of the house came home, he covered the jar with a plate that Krishna might not escape, and went to his home to complain; but when he arrived, the wonderful child was already there before him. On another day he had stolen curds, and eaten them when no one was looking. 'O thou wicked one!' said his foster-mother, 'come let me see thy mouth, that I may know what thou hast eaten.' Then Krishna opened his mouth, and she looked therein, and lo! there was the Universe—the earth and the sea, and the heavens with the sun and moon, the planets, and all the stars."

"Philippa, what nonsense you are telling us! Are there *no* Krishna legends that have any beauty or sense in them?"

"Oh yes!" answers Philippa, "there is that solemn and impressive story about the flood that Krishna averted. Indra, the King of the Firmament, the God of a Thousand Eyes, was angry with Krishna, and he sent so terrible a storm of rain that the shepherds of these regions must needs have been drowned. But Krishna laid hold on the mountain Govarddhana, and tore it up by the roots, and, supporting the point on his little finger, held up that mighty mountain as an umbrella to shelter the world. But the legend which is far more interesting than all the others——"

Suddenly, in at the window, craning round the corner so that it is frightful to see, comes the turbaned head of Wazír; and with it comes, bursting with terrible force upon the defenceless travellers within, the pent-up torrent of words. Thenceforward conversation is impossible, and great is the relief of mind when the six miles' drive is over.

Bindraban lies due north of Mathurá on the same bank of the Jamna. It stands on a tongue of land surrounded on three sides by the River, which has curved about in a strange fashion that would be hard indeed to account for had not kind Tradition fully explained the matter. Balarama, it seems, the hero of giant strength, once led a dance on the Jamna's bank; but so clumsily moved his giant limbs that the River laughed aloud, and taunted him scornfully on this wise: "Forbear, O clumsy one! How wilt thou strive to move as Krishna, the youth divine?" Then Balarama was very angry with the River; and he laid hold on his own great plough, and traced a furrow therewith from the very brink of the stream; and so deep was that furrow, that Jamna fell thereinto, and Balarama led him far astray so that he could not return.

From time immemorial Bindraban has been a sacred place; but it was not (saith Mr Growse) till the middle of the sixteenth century that certain holy men came thither, who made it their home, and builded there a shrine to the goddess Vrinda. Whereupon other temples were builded too, and there arose a stately city.

There is much to see; but the visitors, who love not hurried sight-seeing, prefer to visit in peace a few of the

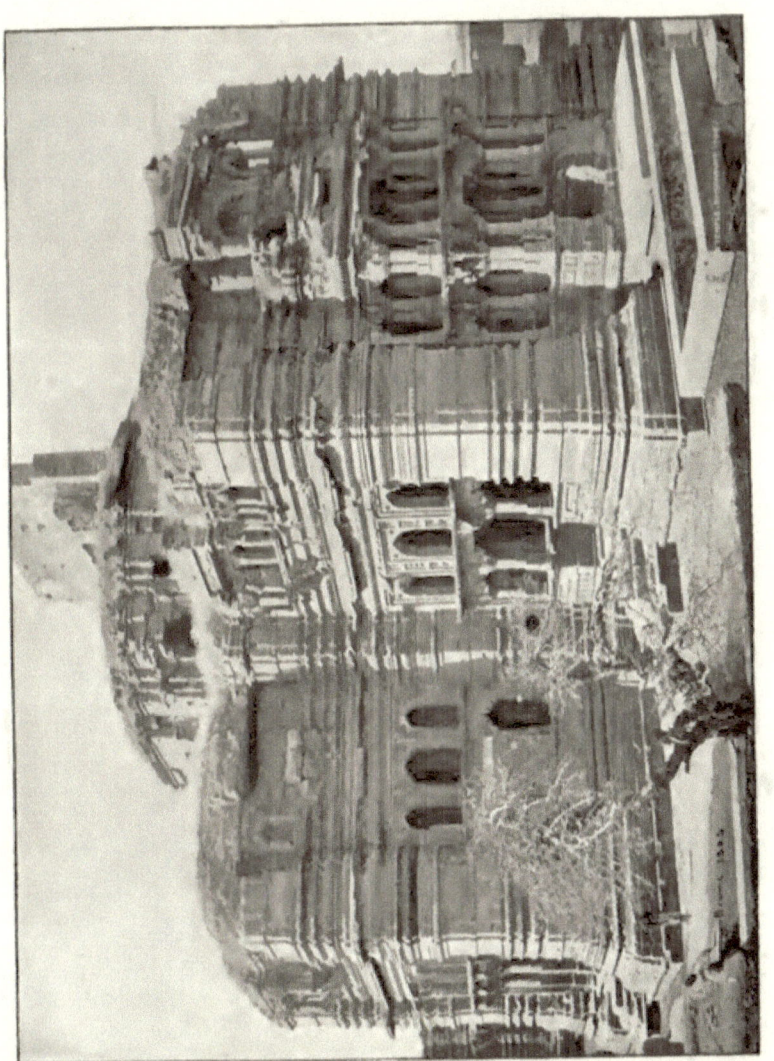

THE TEMPLE OF GOVIND DEO, BINDRABAN.

principal temples, and to regard all for which they have not time as virtually non-existent. They betake them first to the famous temple of Govind Deo, built by Man Sing of Amber, A.D. 1590, in honour of Krishna, of whose titles Govinda is one. It is a massive cruciform pile of red sandstone, and at the first glance looks like a reproduction (on a far grander scale) of the larger of the two Sas-bahu temples in the Fort at Gwaliar. Parts of it have been injured; for the folk used it at one time for a quarry,—even as I am using (and shall use to the end of the chapter) that majestic and ponderous tome published in India and called 'Mathurá, a District Memoir,' wherein most things that anybody could possibly write about the Mathurá district have been written before (and better) by Mr Growse.

The chief loss which the temple has suffered is the destruction of the central dome. The *sikra*, or curvilinear tower, which should have surmounted the cella, was perhaps never built, the learned say. But the temple is still wonderfully grand and impressive,—a lordly pile of massive walls, and clustered pillars with beautiful bracket capitals, and numberless pointed arches opening into the deep shadow that reigns within, and breaking, with a delicious relief, the crimson glare of the sunlit surfaces. Everywhere the walls are covered with bold, horizontal lines of moulding, which produce a delightfully natural effect hardly to be conveyed in words.

"They are like the strata of the cosmic masonry!" exclaims Sebaste. "This temple never can have been built. It *grew*."

Scarcely less majestic is the sombre interior — a Greek cross 100 feet in length and breadth, the Gothic lines of its massive vaulted roof presenting so curiously Christian an appearance that one thinks wistfully what a beautiful church the temple would make, if only the Hindus who worship therein would make haste and get converted. The interior of the temple, and especially the doors, are haunted by the wretched figures of long-haired devotees, their dark skins besmeared with ashes, and changed thereby into a ghastly grey. They recall the figure that Siva presented long since on his wedding-day, when he came "mounted on a cow, having five heads and three eyes, his body rubbed with ashes, and the hair of his head all in a knot after the fashion of the ascetics."[1] So holy are these devotees that they take no food except milk and sweetmeats brought them by pious worshippers; and as the result, perhaps, of this diet, they look scarcely human, and seem to be slowly but surely dwindling down into monkeys.

The walls of the temple are, on an average, 10 feet thick, and the most delightful part of the building is the labyrinth of stairs and passages which they are found to contain. Nothing in the world could be more alluring, more suggestive of mysterious adventure, than these narrow flights of red sandstone steps within the thickness of the walls, leading up and away to giddy heights of triforium and hanging balcony, whence one sometimes looks down into the shadowy depths of the interior, sometimes, clinging to a pillar on the brink of empty space, gazes out into the glowing world of sunshine with a wild desire to bound over the edge and come crashing down on the red pavement lying far below.

Near the Govind Deo temple the travellers visit a great modern pagoda, built, after the pattern of those in the South, by two brothers, Seth Rádhá Kríshn and Seth Govind Dás.

[1] Sheeve Pouran. Halhed.

Its giant courts and *gopuras* look strangely out of place up here in the North.

After this our friends drive away to the older and more interesting temple of Madan Mohan. This, too, is a temple of Krishna, who seems to have had an enormous number of names,—as indeed he had need to have, if all be true that the legends tell of his supernatural power of multiplying himself at pleasure. At one time, it seems, there were sixteen thousand of him.

The legend of this temple is less fanciful than usual. It happened long ago that one Kapurí, a merchant of Multán, was floating down the River in a boat which he had laden with merchandise to be sold at Agra. And when he had reached the place below the height on which now stands the temple, his boat stuck fast on a sandbank. For three days he strove to escape; but the sandbank held him fast. Then he went out of the boat, and climbed up the hill. And he came where the holy Sanátan dwelt, and told him all his trouble. Then said Sanátan, the holy ascetic, "My counsel is that thou pray to Madan Mohan." And when Kapurí had so done, his boat forthwith was floating free. So he went on his way gladly, and coming to Agra, he sold all his merchandise; and he returned with the price thereof to the place where his prayer had been answered, and builded there a temple of red sandstone, which remaineth unto this day.

I ought to describe that venerable ruin, and especially its beautiful curvilinear *sikras* which rise with such fantastic grace, stately forms of glowing crimson, against the blue of the sky. But I would much rather not! I am tired, like the travellers, and gladly turn away to follow them back to Mathurá, the travellers' bungalow, and tea. The heat is so great that even Wazír is subdued, and, sitting enthroned on the top of the gharry, passes in strange, unnatural silence the time of the homeward drive.

Next morning our friends set forth to explore the city of Mathurá. It is holy and picturesque beyond imagination. Everywhere rollicking monkeys haunt the streets, galloping in and out of the temples, trotting along on the tops of walls, grinning at the white-faced intruders, and very conscious the while of their own inviolable sanctity.

The temples are numberless, and at the door of one of them the travellers linger long, watching the worship within. An important part of the ritual is the striking, by each worshipper, of a bell which hangs from above. The mystic significance thereof I know not, nor do the Hindu scriptures seem to expound it; but they often speak of the bell as a sacred and venerable thing. For what said Indra, and Vanhi, the god of fire, long ago when "with joyful countenances" they hymned the great goddess Durga because she had gloriously conquered the army of the great-cheeked demons ? "May the bell of the goddess," they cried, "the sound of which has appalled the energy of the giants, and penetrated through all the worlds, preserve us as its children !"[1]

But more beautiful than the temples are some of the private houses, for they are richly adorned with the lovely native sculpture for which Mathurá city is famous,—beautiful embroideries of stone, mazy and delicate exceedingly.

Then there is the Jam 'i Masjid to visit, a relic of Muhammadan times that must feel sadly out of place in Krishna's sacred town. It was builded A.D. 1661, in the reign, as an inscription puts it, of "the king of the world, Aurangzib,

---

[1] From the 'Sapta-Shati,' . . . translated by Cavali Venkat Rámasswámi, Pandit.

who is adorned with justice." It seems to have replaced an older Hindu temple, for the inscription goes on to relate that " this second ' Holy Temple' caused the idols to bow down and worship." Finally the devout builder thereof thus exclaims in flowing Persian :—

" May this Jam 'i Masjid of majestic structure shine forth for ever like the hearts of the pious !

" Its roof is high like aspirations of love; its courtyard is wide like the arena of thought." [1]

All this is incongruous in this stronghold of Hinduism ; and the travellers soon wander away in search of older sites associated with " blessed Krishna," whose countenance was fair and bright " like the moon in an autumn festival." A small temple marks his birthplace; but more interesting are the scanty remains of what tradition confidently avers to be the Palace of Kansa itself. Herein did that violent usurper long hold his evil court. No human monarch was he in truth, but the mighty demon Kálanemi disguised in the form of a man. No safety was there in his days for priests or for sacred cattle ; for he slew them all alike, till the temples ran with blood. And when he heard how the boys Krishna and Balarama his brother did wondrous deeds at Bindraban, his wicked heart was filled with fear, and he sought to slay them also. Then said he within himself, " If they do but come to Mathurá, then shall they quickly die ; for who can withstand the might of the champions, even Chanur and Mushtika my servants ? " So he sent to the noble brothers by the hand of Akrur the chieftain, saying, " Behold I have set a contest of arms in my royal city of Mathurá. Come ye, therefore, hither, and try your strength before me."

Then Krishna and Balarama were glad, and set forth to-

---

[1] Translated by Blochman (apud Growse).

gether for Mathurá. And when the set day was come, king Kansa sat on a lofty throne hard by the place of contest. Then came Krishna and Balarama. But, as they came in, there went against them the mighty elephant Kuvalayapída; for Kansa urged him on, saying, "Surely he will trample them under foot, and so shall they die." But Krishna seized the beast by his tail, and, swinging him round his head, he cast him down on the earth, so that he died forthwith. Then Krishna and Balarama took each one of his tusks, and said, "Who will fight against us? Let him come forth, for we are ready." Then came Chanur and Mushtika, the mighty champions, and fought with the noble boys. And forthwith Krishna slew Chanur, and Balarama slew Mushtika.

Then Kansa arose in haste, and commanded to slay Krishna and Balarama with Vasudeva their father, and Ugrasen the rightful king. But Krishna sprang up the steps of the throne, and seized Kansa by the hair of his head, and hurled him down from his lofty seat into the deep ravine hard by. So the aged king, Ugrasen, sat again on the throne of Mathurá, and ruled thenceforth his kingdom in peace and great prosperity. And to this day may be seen, hard by the city of Mathurá, the mount where Kansa's throne was set, and the arena wherein were slain the champions and the elephant Kuvalayapída.

After this a visit must be paid to the Museum. To enter the Museum is difficult, because the outside is so beautiful; but, when one is once within, it is harder still to come out again, so fascinating are the ancient sculptures, carrying back the mind to those strange old Buddhist times when Krishna's name was not so much as mentioned in all his sacred city.

Fifteen hundred years ago, in good Fa-hien's days, there were grand times, in Mathurá and the neighbourhood, for

the wearers of the Yellow Robe. Then were kings devout
believers, and humbly brought them offerings. Laying aside
their royal head-dresses, with their own hands they brought
the food that was their gift to the devotees. Then was it
never known that in presence of a Buddhist community a
king should sit on a couch; but he would cause to be spread
for himself on the ground an unassuming carpet. Long did
the Buddhist doctrine flourish; and Hiuen Tsiang has left
us a vivid account of Mathurá's great devotion early in the
seventh century. Then were in this district some twenty
monasteries containing about 2000 monks; and wonderful
then were the scenes enacted on the sacred festivals of the
Buddha. Jewelled banners flashed in the sunlight; "rich
coverings" were "crowded together as network"; the fragrant smoke of incense rose up in clouds continually; and
flowers were scattered like rain, till "the sun and moon
were concealed" as by the mists that veil the valleys.

Little do the learned seem to know of how Buddhism
came to Mathurá and extinguished for a time the ancient
cults. Some say that its coming is shadowed forth in the
legend of Kálá-yavana. A terrible conqueror was Kálá-
yavana, mighty and fierce and cruel. From the far West he
came, and brought a vast army of barbarous folk against the
city of Mathurá. But in the night of his coming, through
the wondrous power of Krishna, there arose, far off on the
shore of the ocean, a city strong and fair, whereof the name
was Dwaraka. And thither did Krishna carry away all
that dwelt in Mathurá, bearing them thence in the night
while they slept, so that they knew it not until they awoke
in the morning, and, lo! they were hard by the sea-shore,
and the sound of the waves was in their ears. But Mathurá
was taken by Kálá-yavana, who reigned there all his days.

And, long after, the soul of that fierce conqueror once more returned to earth; so he lived again, and men called him Aurangzib.

Leaving the Museum at length, the travellers wander long in the intricate streets of the city. Strange are they to Western eyes, even though these be long accustomed to oriental scenes. Strangest of all are the native shops gleaming to right and left with the wealth of Mathurá brass-work. And still the monkeys gambol round, grinning and grinning again at their wonderful, white-faced visitors.

Onward they wander still, ever meeting new and distracting sights, until at last they come to the River, and, walking out to the middle of the bridge, look back in silent wonder at the ancient city on the bank. Many are the pilgrim-bathers, and here and there a monkey has come down to the water to drink. Many, too, are the ghats by the water's edge; and each ghat has its own quaint legend, —too many for me to tell.

Near the centre of the city's river-side face is the famous Visrant Ghat, the Landing-place of Rest, where Krishna and Balarama rested after dragging the body of Kansa down to the water's edge that it might lie on the funeral pyre. Hard by is a water-course,—so the ignorant call it; but no rain or torrent ever scooped that ancient and venerable channel: it is the trace of the body of Kansa himself, left in the river-side ground as they dragged him down to the water; and to this very day they call it Kansa Khar.

Very conspicuous too is the Sati Burj, a tower built on the spot where a widow once was burned along with her husband's body. He, they say, was Raja Bihar Mall, who ruled long since in Jaipur, and the tower was builded A.D. 1570 by their son Bhagavan Das.

At length the travellers leave the bridge, and embark on
a native boat—a shapeless, lumbering thing that one can
scarcely contemplate with gravity. As they glide along the
stream, past ghats and palaces and temples, they are suddenly aware of many eyes watching them with grave intent-
ness,—the eyes not of men but of majestic tortoises who dwell
in the River at home. Long necks they have, and far out of
the water they thrust their snake-like heads, watching the
strangers in solemn silence with a gaze of mild toleration but
of very much qualified approval. Seeing the travellers' admiring glances, one of the bathers seizes and holds up in the air
the most solemn and dignified of all the tortoise company—
a striking example of that Hindu scheme of the universe,
known as the Science of Sank, which asserts that "nothing
is annihilated, but only disappears, the effect being absorbed
in the cause, as the tortoise draws his legs into his shell."[1]

Too soon it is time to hasten away and prepare for the
Agra train. As our friends are leaving the travellers'
bungalow, Wazír comes softly out to wish them a sad farewell. The Father, thankful indeed to take leave of him,
bestows a small remembrance, which Wazír receives with
the utmost dejection, and with such heartrending looks of
disappointment that the Father is compelled, from mere
humanity, to give him a little more. But all is to no purpose. Poor Wazír is broken-hearted at so poor a requital of
his devotion. His manifest misery casts a gloom over the
pleasure of parting; but, as the travellers drive away, there
sounds through the still air a wild, chuckling laugh, and,
looking back, they behold Wazír bounding into the air with
irrepressible exultation, and waving his long, brown arms
overhead in a transport of triumphant joy.

[1] From the 'Ayeen Akbery.' Gladwin.

CHAPTER XVIII.

THE POOL OF IMMORTALITY.

To the cities of Dehli and Lahor our friends devote as much time as they can, and a respectable amount of study; but concerning these places there are not many things to write that have not been written before, and the travellers' experiences therein may safely be left, they think, to the kind and indulgent Reader's graphic imagination.

Toward the end of their stay in Lahor their restless and excitable minds are invaded by visions of Amritsar the Sikhs' most holy city, of the Pool of Immortality, and the far-famed Golden Temple. A long day must be devoted thereto, and early in the morning they set forth with eager expectation. Amritsar lies only thirty-two miles to the east of Lahor, and the railway journey should be a short one; but the engine, despising with a stolid and lumbering contempt our travellers' impatient enthusiasm, breaks down midway on purpose, and our friends must resign themselves as best they may to spending on the journey four long, hot hours, which they beguile by diligently rehearsing the history of Sikhism.

Having duly recalled all the historic events they can remember, having ascertained that the present number of

Sikhs in the Panjab is not much less than 2,000,000, and
having generally done their duty by serious matters of fact,
they begin telling those quaint traditions of the Sikh Gurus
which, thanks to Dr Trumpp, are now within the reach of
even those benighted beings who cannot read Gurmukhi.

Delightful is his account of the manuscripts of various ages
which he has so diligently translated, and particularly of
that oldest of all the lives of Nanak, long ago forgotten even
by the Sikhs themselves, and for many years unknown to
any one except the white ants, who have browsed on its
precious pages and made lamentable gaps therein. • This
early ' Book of Nanak ' is far more to be relied on than the
later accounts at present in use among his followers, and
even the most wonderful stories thereof may rest on a substratum of truth. Nanak, the founder of the Sikh religion,
was born, saith this venerable authority, "in Sambat 1526
[*i.e.,* A.D. 1469], in the month of Vaisakh; in a moonlight
night at an early hour, while yet about a watch of the night
was remaining, he was born. . . . The 330 millions of gods
paid homage to the child Nanak."

A later manuscript tells how Kalu, his father, made
request of the Pandit Hari Dyal that he would give him a
name. Then "the Pandit reflected for thirteen days. When
thirteen days had passed, a coat was put on the child"; and
the name that the Pandit gave him was "Nanak, the Formless One": and, being wise in the wisdom of the stars, he
spake and said, "This one both Hindus and Turks will
worship; his name will be current on earth and in heaven.
Wood and grass will say, ' Nanak! Nanak!' The ocean will
grant him access."

As Nanak grew up he was not like to other children, for
in his spirit he meditated on the Lord. " When he was five

years old he began to talk of the Shastras and the Vedas," and "everybody received comfort from him." When he was seven years old, Kalu his father said to him, "'O Nanak, read!' Then he brought Guru Nanak to the schoolmaster. Kalu said, 'O schoolmaster, teach this one to read!'" Then the schoolmaster wrote on a wooden slate the thirty-five letters of the Gurmukhi alphabet, and gave it to Nanak to read. But forthwith the wondrous child began to instruct his teacher, exhorting him in a discourse of thirty-four verses, which, afterward written in the holy book of the Adi Granth, are called to this day Patti, the Wooden Slate.

Afterward the Guru "went home and sat down. It was the order of the Lord that he did no work whatever." Thus does the 'Book of Nanak' depict the years of his life at home: "When he sits down, he remains seated; when he goes to sleep, he remains asleep. He associates with Fakirs." It was his custom, moreover, to go and sit under trees, and there remain "retired from the world." And one day "at the time of noon" he had fallen asleep in a garden within the shade of a tree. For many hours he slept; and the shadows of the other trees moved round as the day wore on, but that wherein Nanak had laid himself down remained ever steadfast to shield him. Moreover, as the later writings record, a black snake came forth and sat at his head, and spread over him the shelter of its hood. So Nanak "drank the breath of the snake," but took no hurt at all.

When Nanak was grown to be a man he still refused to work, and spake to none except Fakirs. And when he neither ate nor drank for three full months, his kinsfolk said, "He is mad." Then by "the order of the Lord" he departed from Talvandi his birthplace, and came to Sultanpur, where Jairam dwelt who had married his sister; and

there he became a steward of the Nawab Daulat Khan.
Now by the order of the Lord "the river was going continually." And one day Nanak came to the river, having
his servant with him. And when he had entered the river
to bathe, celestial messengers carried him away and set
him at "the threshold of the Lord." But his servant
tarried on the bank "standing and standing"; and when
Nanak came not again he returned home. And they cast
a net into the river, and the fishermen searched for Nanak,
but they found him not. For by the order of the Lord
Nanak stood at the threshold, and beheld the celestial court.
Then a cup was filled with elixir of life and given to him,
and a voice commanded him, saying, "Nanak, this elixir
is a cup of my name, drink it!" Then "Guru Nanak made
a salutation and drank it," and the voice spake to him,
saying, "I have made thee exalted. . . . Go and mutter
my name, and cause others also to mutter it! . . . My
name is the Supreme Brahm, the Supreme Lord." Then "a
dress of honour was given" to Nanak, and those celestial
messengers were commanded that they should bring him
back to the river, whence they had carried him away. So
on the third day they brought him thither, and Nanak
came out from the water. But when they saw him the
people were astonished, and said, "Friends, this one had
fallen into the river! Whence is he come?"

After this Nanak gave all that he had to the poor, and
"removed his abode afar off." And when he had "continued in silence for one day," the next day "he arose and
said, '*There is no Hindu and there is no Musalman.*'" Then
all the people wondered, but Nanak added and said :—

"He is a Musalman who clears away his own self, who
is sincere, patient, of pure words.

"Who does not touch what is standing, who does not eat what is fallen down:

"That Musalman will go to Paradise, says Nanak."

Then the wisdom of Nanak was made manifest to all. "Wherever he looked, there all were saluting him;" the Khan also "came and fell down at his feet." But Nanak began to wander over the earth; and he took with him Mardāna the rebeck-player, and "practised wind-eating." The first journey of Nanak was toward the East. Many things befell him by the way; and on every occasion Nanak exclaimed, "Mardāna, play the rebeck!" And as he played, Nanak chanted forth those poems of wisdom and instruction which all may read to this day in the book of the Adi Granth.

Wandering thus, they came to Dehli, and when they were come thither, behold! an elephant had lately died, and all the folk were lamenting. But Nanak recalled the elephant to life, and there were great rejoicings. And on this same journey he met with certain Thags, and when he spake to them they repented.

But most wonderful of all were the things that befell them in the country of Kauru; for therein was a town where dwelt many women that were conjurers. Now Mardāna went before into the town, for he was hungry; and he came to the door of a woman's house "and stood there." Then she took a thread and bound him therewith, and forthwith Mardāna became a ram. So when Guru Nanak came thither, Mardāna began to bleat; but the woman was gone to fetch water. And when she came back with the water-jar, Guru Nanak caused the jar to remain fixed on her head, and she could in nowise remove it. And the Guru spake to the ram, and said, "Mardāna, say 'Vah

Guru!' and bow thy head." So, when Mardāna bowed his head, the thread brake, and he regained his own form.

Now the chief of the conjurers was Nur Shahi. And when she heard how the water-jar remained immovable, she sent to all the other conjurers, saying, "Come ye, every one; let none remain behind." So all the women that were conjurers "came with their skill. One came mounted on a tree, another came mounted on a deerskin, another on the moon, another on a wall"; and they all began "to practise their jugglery, binding threads"; but all their spells were powerless in the presence of Guru Nanak. Then came Nur Shahi with her wisest disciples, riding on "an apparatus of paper," and began to apply her mightiest spells; but when they were of no avail, she "fell down at the feet of the Guru," and "became a votary of the name," muttering "Guru, Guru!"

On another day, as they wandered, Nanak and Mardāna the rebeck - player "came to a city of ants"; and of the inhabitants thereof the Guru recounted a marvellous history, which no doubt was the attraction which drew their white relatives to evince for this manuscript such enthusiastic affection: Once on a time it happened that a Raja came to this city; for he was marching to war with another Raja, and with "a host of fifty-two complete armies" he passed through the land by the way of the city of ants. Then an ant went out to meet him, and said, "O Raja, remain in this place; march no farther. Or if thou wilt march, my will is this that thou shouldest first eat of my bread, and then shalt thou go thy way." But the Raja was very proud, and said, "I am the Raja of fifty-two complete armies, how should I eat thy bread?" "Then," said the ant, "thou must do battle with us"; and the Raja said,

"So be it." Then he took his fifty-two complete armies,
and "began to fight with the ants. The chief of the ants
gave the order to the ants, 'Go and fetch poison.' Having filled their mouth with poison from the Piyal-tree, they
brought it; every one died to whom they applied it. . . .
The whole host of the fifty-two complete armies died by
the order of the Lord; the Raja alone remained alive. Then
that ant went and said, 'O Raja, hear my word, now thou
wilt eat of my bread.' The Raja, joining his hands, stood
and said, 'Well, be it so!' Then that ant gave the order to
the ants, 'Go and bring nectar!' In the nether regions
there are seven pools of nectar and seven pools of poison.
The ants went, filled their mouth with nectar and brought
it. To whom they applied it, he rose and stood; so the
host of fifty-two complete armies rose and stood by the
order of the Lord." Then the Raja arose and "went to
eat bread with his fifty-two complete armies," and afterward he "returned to his house."

Such was the history that Nanak told, and he added, in
praise of the Lord, the Formless One, this verse:—

"He establishes an ant and gives it dominion, and an army
he reduces to ashes."

So Nanak wandered over the earth, and returned at length
to Talvandi. And the second time he wandered, journeying
toward the South, and came even as far as Singhala dvipa,
the same is Ceylon.

The third time he wandered, journeying toward the North;
and he came into the country of Kashmir, and even to
Mount Sumeru in the far-off northern land.

And the fourth time he wandered, travelling toward the
West, journeying as a pilgrim to Mecca; and as he went a
cloud went with him, floating overhead to give him shade.

And when he came to Mecca, he lay down to sleep, and by chance his feet were directed toward the holy place of the Ka'ba. And at "the time of evening prayer the Kazi Rukn Din came" in to offer his prayers. And "when he beheld Nanak he said, 'O servant of God, why dost thou stretch out thy feet in the direction of the house of God and towards the Ka'ba?'" Then said Nanak, "Where the house of God and the Ka'ba is not, thither direct my feet!" So the Kazi Rukn Din turned away the Guru's feet; but whithersoever he turned them, thither the Ka'ba also moved. Then "the Kazi Rukn Din became astonished and kissed his feet," and "made his salaam and said, 'Vah, Vah! Wonderful, wonderful!'"

And the fifth time Nanak wandered, and journeyed as far as the country which is called Gōrakh-hatari; but where that country is, methinketh no man knows.

So Nanak passed his life until his age was sixty-nine; and the time drew near when the Guru, the "turning-pin of the world," should be absorbed in the Formless One. As his successor he named his faithful disciple who is called Lahana and Angad. And it was the Sambat year 1595 (the same is 1538 of the Christian era), "on the tenth of the light half of the month of Asu." "It was night, towards dawn of day, at the time of his departure." And he "went to a sarih-tree and sat down under it." Now the sarih-tree was dry, and had no leaves; but when the Guru had sat him down, it "became green again; leaves and blossoms came forth." Then "the wife of Nanak began to weep; brothers, relations, all the retainers began to weep. . . . The Society began to sing funeral songs."

And there were many Hindus and Musalmans who were "votaries of the Name." Then the Musalmans began to say,

"We shall bury him"; but the Hindus said, "We shall burn him." And Nanak said, "Put ye flowers beside me; on the right side put those of the Hindus, on the left those of the Musalmans. If the flowers of the Hindus remain fresh till to-morrow, then they shall burn me; and if the flowers of the Musalmans remain fresh, then they shall bury me." Then Nanak lay down to sleep, and they covered him with a sheet, and laid him on a funeral pyre. But in the morning, "when they lifted up the sheet, there was nothing at all"; for, behold! the Guru had been absorbed. And the flowers, both those of the Hindus and those of the Musalmans, were all of them fresh and fragrant. Then "the whole Society fell on their knees," and the Hindus took their flowers and departed, and the Musalmans did likewise.

So much for Guru Nanak; but what has our learned Doctor to say of the nine other Gurus who succeeded him? Angad and Amar-das, the second and third Gurus, were both unlettered men, and did nothing more noteworthy than composing sundry verses afterwards included in the 'Book of the Adi Granth.' The fourth Guru was Ram-das, who succeeded to the Guruship A.D. 1574. He was born in the village Gurūcakk, and in his native place he restored an ancient tank and adorned it with the utmost splendour, and in the midst of it he builded a temple; and he called the tank "Amrita Saras," the Fount of Nectar, the Pool of Immortality; and both it and the great city which surrounds it are to this day called Amritsar. Many verses also did Guru Ram-das compose, and they are written in the 'Adi Granth.' He named as his successor his son Arjun; and thenceforth the Guruship became an hereditary office and acquired much wealth and temporal power.

Arjun, the fifth of the Gurus, succeeded to the Guruship

A.D. 1581; and he it was who collected the verses of his predecessors, and, adding thereto many of his own and many also from the writings of the Bhagats or Saints who lived before Nanak's days, he compiled that holy book of the Sikhs, the far-famed 'Adi Granth.' Guru Arjun, moreover, wore no longer the garb of a Fakir like the earlier Gurus, but kept the state of a prince, and busied himself in trade and politics. Whereupon the Muhammadan Government awoke, and Guru Arjun was slain.

Then succeeded, A.D. 1606, Har Govind, the sixth Guru; and he it was who armed his followers, and first fought against the Muhammadans. And there followed him in the Guruship Har Rāi and Har-Kisan and Tēg-Bahādur; and the tenth of the Gurus was Gōvind Singh.

In the year 1675 of our era Gōvind Singh became Guru. He had been born at Patna, and by the Pandits there his mind had been filled with superstitions of Hinduism. Wherefore he began his military career by cutting off the head of one of his followers (who willingly offered the same) and giving it in sacrifice to the Goddess Durga, who, pleased with this devotion, appeared forthwith, and said, "Go, thy sect will prosper in the world." And so it did, for Gōvind Singh is said to have gained for the Sikh persuasion 120,000 disciples. Many other things he did; and he it was who added to the names of his followers that surname of "Singh," or "Lion," which to this day is characteristic of the Sikhs.

But at length (A.D. 1708) his death drew near, and "his disciples heaped up a pyre of sandal-wood, and kept everything ready" for his cremation. Then "they all joined their hands, and asked, 'O true Guru, whom will you seat, for the sake of our welfare, on the throne of the Guruship?'" He

answered, 'As the nine Kings before me seated at their death
another Guru on their throne, so shall I now not do; I have
intrusted the whole Society to the bosom of the timeless,
divine male. After me you shall everywhere mind the book
of the Granth as your Guru; whatever you shall ask it, it
will show to you.' . . . He then sat himself down on the
funeral pyre, and having meditated on the Supreme Lord,
. . . he closed his eyes and expired. . . . All the Sikhs and
saints who from many parts were assembled there, raised a
shout of 'Victory!' and sang a beautiful song, and the eyes
of many people were filled with tears on account of the
separation of the Guru."

Such histories do the travellers rehearse as the broken
engine crawls puffing along at a rate which a snail would
despise, until at length the journey is nearly over and Amritsar not far off.

"Philippa," exclaims Irene, "you have never told us what
the Sikh religion is like! Do pray be quick, for we are almost there."

"It is a reformed phase of Hinduism," says Philippa; "and
its chief merit is the rejection of idolatry, and the recognition
of one formless, timeless god whom they call Hari. The
system is pantheistic; but it is monotheistic too, and the
Granth abounds with personal epithets addressed to the
Absolute Being who is the root and the ground of all things.
It is interesting to notice that that fundamental and almost
universal instinct which creates a longing to worship some
one who is human as well as divine, and which in Hinduism
expresses itself in the myths of Vishnu's avatars, appears in
Sikhism as a tendency to regard the Gurus as successive
incarnations of the Formless One, and to pay them divine

THE GOLDEN TEMPLE, AMRITSAR.

honours accordingly. The Metaphysic of Sikhism, like that of other pantheistic systems—— But here we are at Amritsar!"

So long time has the journey taken that not many hours remain for sight-seeing; and our travellers, ignoring the other sights of the city, drive straight to the Pool of Immortality. It is surrounded by a square of palaces, the *bungahs* of distinguished chiefs. The pavements are all of marble from Jaipur; and the marble tank itself contains a grand sheet of water 470 feet square. In the midst of the waters, approached by a marble causeway, rises the Golden Temple, nearly cubical in form, and decorated with wonderful richness. In all their wanderings the travellers have never seen the like. The lower part of the walls is faced with snow-white marble slabs (many of them were stolen, they say, by Ranjit Singh from Jahangir's tomb at Shah Darrah) inlaid with arabesques of conventionalised flower-sprays in many-hued precious stones. But above this gleaming dado, all the temple, walls and cornices, dripstone and roof, slender columns, cupolas and finials, are one blaze of gilded copper, reflecting the mighty sunlight with a brightness that is almost terrible. Beautiful is the contrast between the snowy marble and the burnished gold; and every detail is reflected in the glassy waters with scarcely diminished lustre. To ask whether the temple is in good taste, would be as absurd as to inquire whether the martial adornments of the Duke of Diamonds (or any other fairy-tale Prince) were æsthetically correct. I have no patience with those who apply to the fantastic splendours of India the humdrum rules of art which mere mortals have to build by!

Of the palaces our friends only have time to enter one,

the *bungah* of Takht Akál, made conspicuous among its fellows by a resplendent gilded dome. Here they are introduced to the sword of Gōvind Singh, and other relics of the Gurus preserved in a gilded ark.

Thence the visitors betake them to the west side of the tank, and prepare to pass along the causeway into the island-temple. They are now despoiled of their shoes, which they willingly relinquish as a sign of respect to the magic fane of gold; for, though looking as if built by enchantment, it is still a monotheistic temple, and doubtless possesses some weird kind of holiness. The causeway is approached by a grand gateway of marble, wherein the travellers ascend to an upper room and behold the wonderful jewels wherewith the holy Granth is adorned when carried in procession at festivals,—tall chowries with golden handles, and strings of pearls, and a priceless canopy of pure gold thickly set with diamonds, rubies, and emeralds of astonishing size and lustre, and further adorned with pendent tassels of pearls.

Descending thence and passing out on to the causeway, our travellers go on between tall lamps of marble, looking wonderingly the while at the extraordinary scene around them. In the clear waters of the tank some pilgrims are devoutly bathing; and on the bright pavement of the causeway sit many solemn figures of white-robed Sikhs, who mutter under their breath that secret name of Hari which none but the initiate may know. Striking figures are these, and their bearing is far more free and dignified than that of the average Hindu. In their grave faces and steadfast eyes is something which calls to mind that truthfulness and kindness are strictly inculcated by the law of the Sikh religion. The dark, handsome faces are well set off by the full black beards, each ending in two plaits, which are turned back into the silky black cloud of the whiskers. To shave either head or beard is strictly forbidden among Sikhs. The women plait their hair in a compact peak, which stands out like a horn at the back of the head. They also wear gigantic earrings, several in each ear.

But it is hard to look at anything but the temple itself, with its brilliant reflection piercing the clear depths of the water with inverted domes of gold. A sound of deep-toned chanting comes out through the temple door; but, as the visitors enter, the voices cease, and they find themselves in the presence of a silent assemblage of worshippers. Beneath a canopy of state lies the ponderous tome of the Adi Granth, whereof some irreverent scholars have said that in all the world exists not another book so stupid for its size. Resting on cushions, it is wrapped in a rich covering of silk, and fragrant roses are scattered over it. Near it is a little heap of grain, the accumulated offerings of pious worshippers. Before the Granth sits a white-turbaned personage who seems to be presiding over the assembly. He continually waves a chowrie over the holy Book to prevent the flies from settling on the folds of its silken wrappings. Facing him in a semicircle sit on the floor the other worshippers, a solemn company, with one or two musicians among them, who hold in their hands quaint native instruments wherewith to accompany the chanting. The walls and vaulted ceilings of the hall are covered with gilding and with elaborate designs in colours. India is the land of reflected lights, but never have our travellers beheld such a strange effect as is caused by this vaulted ceiling; for, reflecting the mighty glow from without, the golden vaulting throws it downward on the assembly of worshippers, until their snowy robes and turbans are all dyed in gleaming colour.

The presiding dignitary receives the visitors with grave and gracious courtesy, even uncovering the holy Book that they may see the unfamiliar writing. He also presents each of them with a small cup made of what looks like white sugar. No doubt these are specimens of that sacred sweetmeat (consisting of flour and sugar and melted butter) which Guru Gōvind Singh in his dying speech directed his followers to make and distribute, saying, "Whichever disciple wishes to have an interview with me, he shall make for one rupee and a quarter, or for as much as he is able, *Karāh parsād;* then, opening the Book and bowing his head, he will obtain a reward equal to an interview with me."

Next, to each of the travellers is presented a sacred rose from the Book; and then he of the waving chowrie exclaims in the vernacular, "It is enough"; and they find that they are expected to withdraw. As they go out they admire the devotion expressed by the worshippers as they enter and leave the temple. Each one prostrates himself on the threshold, placing his head against the stone, and reverently touches with his hand first the threshold itself and then his own forehead.

The visitors now ascend to a gallery in the upper part of the temple, and thence go up to the roof. Here they wander freely among the dazzling cupolas; only they are not allowed to tread within that sacred circle drawn in the pavement of the roof immediately above the sacred Book and adorned with peacocks' feathers. As they explore the outside of the building, the musicians within again take up their interrupted strains, and the deep voices of the turbaned congregation ring forth, chanting who shall say what passage from the holy Book? Perhaps that solemn hymn of Nanak, which comes

as near as anything else in the Granth to the dignity of true
devotion.

"HYMN TO HARI.[1]

"Thou art the Friend of my heart, and for ever beside me ;
    Thou art my Friend, my Belovèd ;
Thou art my Honour and Jewel ! My soul in Thy presence
    Moment by moment must be.
Thou art my dearest, the breath and the life of my being !
    Who is my Prince, and the Lord of my spirit, but Thee ?

Where wilt Thou set me ? Lo, there will I tarry in silence ;
    What is Thy word ? I will do it.
Whithersoever I look, Thou art there. By Thy servant
    Gladly Thy Name is confessed.
Thou art my treasure, in Thee is the store of my riches ;
    All my delight is in Thee, and in Thee is my rest.

Thou art my glory, my loved one, my shield and my shelter ;
    Lo, Thou art He that upholdeth !
Ever of Thee are the thoughts of my heart ; for the Teacher,
    When to Thy servant he gave
Freely Thy secret, the One in my spirit established.
    Thou art the Helper, O Hari, of Nanak Thy slave ! "

---

[1] From the literal prose translation in 'The Adi Granth' . . . translated
from the original Gurmukhī . . . by Dr Ernest Trumpp.

CHAPTER XIX.

PESHAWAR AND THE KHAIBER PASS.

MARCH is already far advanced when the travellers leave
Lahor and set forth on that northward journey to which
they have long looked forward as the crowning achievement of their Indian wanderings,—an expedition wherein
they hope to penetrate to the north-west frontier of India
and into the wild recesses of the far-off Khaiber Pass.

The first day's journey brings them to Rawal Pindi, and
a very hot journey it is. Already the spring crops are
gathered; and the plains, lately so richly covered with
verdure, are turning, beneath the blazing sun, to a scorched
expanse of yellow. Crossing the Ravi, the railway runs
nearly due north for sixty-two miles, as far as Wazirabad
on the southern bank of the Chenab; then, crossing the
broad stream, arrives at Gujarat, where the travellers
recall that memorable 21st of February in the year 1849
and the great battle that was fought thereon, the death-
blow to the power of the Sikhs. Vividly do they picture
to themselves the headlong flight and the hot pursuit, and
the closing scene at Rawal Pindi, where General Gilbert
received the Sikhs' submission.

Meanwhile the train speeds on north-westward through

the Jetch Doab, and so across the Jhilam and away north-
westward still. Through the hottest hours of the day the
scorched plains glow like a furnace; but on the right,
from the north-eastward horizon, rise up in shining loveliness the snow-clad mountains of Kashmir; and to bear the
burden of the overwhelming heat is worth while, our travellers think, for the sake of that constant vision of ideal
coolness and beauty.

"My dear," says Irene to her youngest sister, " why
do you gaze at the mountains with that wool - gathering
expression of countenance ? "

"'Wool - gathering,' Irene, is scarcely an accurate expression ! I was merely recalling the ancient Buddhist
legends which tell how the land of Kashmir is guarded
by an aged and venerable Dragon—a mighty Naga Prince,
by reason of whose dignity the country is reverenced by
all the surrounding peoples. In ancient days a vast lake
filled all that region of the earth, and in the waters of
that lake the Dragon had made his home. Then came
Madhyantika, the wise and holy Arhat; and he sat in a
wood on a mountain's summit, wrapped in profound meditation. And the Dragon saw him from the lake below, and
being filled with reverence and faith, he besought the Arhat
to tell him what service he might perform. And the Arhat
made request that in the centre of that lake the Naga would
grant him so much dry ground as his knees might securely
rest on. Then the great Naga Prince withdrew the waters,
and granted that spot of ground; but presently the Arhat
began to grow, till his knees filled all the space where that
great lake had been; and the good Naga still kept back the
waters, for he would not break his promise. So that kind
Dragon could dwell no more in his ancient home; and, going

forth in sadness of heart, he abode in a little lake that lies to the north-west of Kashmir. There shall he dwell in silence while the law of Buddha endures; but when the law declines and is no more taught on earth, then shall this land return and become a lake once more, and that good Dragon shall come to his home and dwell therein as aforetime. Nor is that day far distant now, for long years ago in Kashmir the fountains began to rise again, bubbling up ever more and more in token that the time draws near."

"That is a pretty story," says Philippa meditatively, "and its meaning is, I suppose, that, when Buddhism was preached in Kashmir, the old serpent - worship of pre-historic times was suppressed, and those who still adhered to it were obliged to leave the country. It is always well, my dears, to sift these curious legends, and to seek, among worthless accretions, for hidden grains of truth."

"My poor, dear old Dragon!" sighs Sebaste; "I would never, never have mentioned him if I had thought he was to be 'sifted' by Philippa."

At length comes the welcome hour of sunset; and at a quarter to eight in the evening, wearied out with twelve hot hours' travelling, our friends are fain indeed to arrive at Rawal Pindi.

Except Bishop Milman's tomb, the Fort, and the can-tonments, there is very little to see, and the next day the travellers are again rushing away north-westward, eager to reach Peshawar. On their right still lies in stainless glory the lofty chain of mountains. Here and there, between nearer and lower peaks, appear the far-off heights of snow; but more wonderful than even their dazzling and ethereal

beauty are the iridescent opal-hues that rest and change
and melt one into another on the rocky slopes and shadowy
folds of the intervening ranges,—a harmony of exquisitely
tender colours, the glory of many hot climates, but never to
be seen in Europe. In those purple lights and deep-blue
shadows, in the delicate softness of the rainbow lustre, is an
irresistible enchantment as of some land of magic light that
has nothing to do with earth. Above and beyond all the
beauty there seems to be a radiant mystery about that far-
off region, making one long to reach it with a wild and
childish eagerness that is hard to understand.

"And if you could have your wish, my friend," some
unseen moraliser seems to be saying, "how much do you
think you would find there of the wondrous glories you
imagine yourself to be looking at? It is a mere effect of
light which makes that part of the landscape look like a
fairyland of mysterious loveliness. If you could go thither
you would see that those shining heights and dreamy depths
of shadow are nothing in the world but barren rocks and
gullies; and you would find the walking rough and dis-
agreeable, and would very soon wish yourself back again.
It would be a good lesson of experience for you, and would
teach you to realise that 'things are not what they seem.'"

Ah yes, Mr Moralist, I had not thought of that; and it is
indeed a saddening reflection. And in like manner were we
to examine accurately the greatest picture that ever brought
fame to an artist, we should see (if only we could get near
enough) that it is really nothing in the world but blotches of
paint on a canvas ground. Nay, sir, even your own learned
and eloquent books, if their pages were accurately examined
with a microscope and subjected to chemical analysis, would
enforce the same sad moral that "things are not what they

seem." Is it not so with all that is beautiful when we draw
near to look into it? And if so, surely there is no such
thing as real beauty. Beauty exists not, save in the vain
imagination of those who fancy they see it;—unless, indeed,
it were possible to think that beauty is a spiritual thing, and
that it is with the spirit that we must draw near to it.

"What a frown, Sebaste!" exclaims Irene in alarm.
"And what are you muttering under your breath?"

"It is absurd and ridiculous, Irene, what people say!
They had better hold their tongues instead of setting up to
be moralists and philosophers."

"This is serious!" exclaims Philippa; "Sebaste speaks,
and no philosopher or moralist is ever to bark again."

"But, my dear," says patient Irene, "try to tell us! What
have they said lately to hurt your feelings?"

"One of them says that a statue is in the marble block,
only waiting for the sculptor's hand to call it forth, Irene!
To think that it is more than twenty-two centuries since
Aristotle wrote, and that men don't know the difference yet
between matter and form!"

"But, my dear, that saying about the statue is only a
fanciful mode of expression. Why do you consider it a
personal affront?"

"It is an affront, Irene, an insult to the understanding;
and the evil lies much deeper than mere fancy and grace of
expression. Even dear Thomas à Kempis was infected by
it, thanks to his exaggerated asceticism. For, exhorting the
'good monk' to seek no earthly delight but to remain alone
in his cell, in the persuasive cadence of his sweet Church-
Latin he says, 'What canst thou see elsewhere which here
thou seest not? Behold the sky and the earth, and all the
elements; for *of these all things are made.*' The fallacy is so

obvious and childlike that one almost loves him the better for it; but of that same fallacy the moralisers have made to themselves spectacles through which to look, not only at the beauties of Nature, but also at those life-landscapes, the distant views of the future that wayward hope is wont to gaze at, till they see in them nothing but stocks and stones and mists of dull delusion."

"My dear," says the Father, "I do not quite see what such moralisings have to do with the Punjab! We are just arriving at Atak, and here is the Indus that you ought to be looking at, and in a moment more we shall see the Kabul River flowing into it. See what a narrow gorge the great Indus is rushing through, and how bare and rugged the mountains are."

"What a savage landscape it is!" exclaims Philippa. "We *must* be coming to the ends of the earth at last. And how quaintly the little town of Atak is perched up there, with its antique fort, that Akbar built, overlooking the deep, swift river! How wild it all looks, with only the little red-roofed church to seem familiar and home-like!"

So the train rushes on, past the junction of the mighty streams, and up the valley of the Kabul River, westward toward Peshawar. Here the travellers arrive soon after sunset; whereupon two turbaned drivers of gharries fight furiously together for them and their luggage, and have to be forcibly separated by some dark-faced native policemen.

Purushapura, now called Peshawar, is an ancient city; and Fa-hien, who was here about the year 400 of our era, has many things to say of its long and marvellous history, while Hiuen Tsiang, who journeyed to India in 629, tells us still more curious matters of fantastic Buddhist tradition. Here it was that for long centuries was preserved

U

the Buddha's sacred begging-bowl, that venerable fourfold vessel that the four Guardian Deities gave him, coming from the four corners of heaven and presenting each his separate bowl; whereupon the Buddha placed them one within another, and caused them to grow together and to form one single vessel. And of old it happened that a great conqueror had subdued the land, and in the pride of his boastful heart would carry away in triumph that bowl of far-famed virtue. So, when he and his captains had made to the Three Precious Ones abundant offerings with great devotion, he caused to be caparisoned a mighty elephant, and placed the bowl on its back; but the great elephant fell on his knees beneath that holy burden, and could not rise or move. Then in a four-wheeled waggon they reverently set the bowl, and eight elephants were yoked thereto and dragged it with all their strength, but they could not move it at all. So the mighty conqueror was ashamed, and the alms-bowl abode in peace at sacred Purushapura. There it still resided at the time of Fa-hien's visit; and well hath he described the worship it daily received, and how, when poor folk cast therein an offering of but very few blossoms, the bowl was straightway full, but how rich men might throw in thousands of bushels of flowers and never be able to fill it.

But the venerable antiquities of Purushapura are now no more. Gone is that ancient pipal-tree which Hiuen Tsiang describes as about 100 feet high, and under which, Tradition avers, the Buddha discoursed of old. The very name is almost forgotten of the mighty King Kanishka, who at first "had no faith either in wrong or right," and "lightly esteemed the law of Buddha," but who was eventually converted to the faith, and held, about 79 A.D., the fourth great Buddhist Council;—and vanished from the city is that great *stupa* of his that once reared its towering summit to a height of 400 feet,—the grandest and most majestic building that Fa-hien saw in his journeyings. Gone, too, is the famous Buddhist Monastery, and that other most sacred building wherein was enshrined in solemn splendour the Buddha's begging-bowl. Muhammadanism reigns supreme; and the chief interest of Peshawar lies now in the variety of the unfamiliar races that haunt its winding streets.

Our travellers love the native town with its encircling walls of mud, and find wandering through the crowded ways thereof an intensely interesting occupation. Never before have they found themselves in such unconventional company. There are mighty Afghans arrayed in sheepskins, and wild-looking Afridis, and shaggy specimens of those other unconquered mountain-tribes who, owning allegiance to none, have favoured the British with their friendship.

It is a strange city, and our travellers have time to explore it while awaiting an opportunity to visit the Khaiber Pass, for only on certain days do the Afridis undertake to guard the Pass so that it may be safe for travellers. But at length the day arrives, and early in the morning, while the sunshine is as yet innocent of the cruel fierceness to come, our friends drive westward across the plain, gazing the while at the grand amphitheatre of rocky heights that hems the lowland round with so stern and immovable a barrier. Wonderful is the colouring thereof,—deep purples and browns, and luminous depths of azure shadow, with now and then a radiant glimpse of far-off snow-clad peaks.

About ten miles and a half the travellers drive, to the

Fort of Jamrud, a point in that line, visible only on maps, which is the boundary of British India. Here they find awaiting them their picturesque mounted escort, two turbaned Afridis, bearing themselves with martial dignity, and riding on horses so beautiful that our friends feel envious, and eye with ungracious contempt the *tumtums* to which they are fated. Now a *tumtum*—— But no! let me not disperse with impertinent explanations the glamour of that mystic word. *Tumtums* are *tumtums;* and in them our travellers dispose their tiffin-basket and themselves, and so set forth in procession. Crossing the invisible border, they speed on westward still, and enter with eager expectation the mouth of the rugged Pass. Many and uncouth are the figures which they meet or overtake,—wild, shaggy men free as their own rude mountains, and proud as untamed lions. And there are journeying caravans with hundreds of lordly camels—no sleek, meek-spirited creatures, but rough and unkempt as their masters, with thick masses of curling mane. Those from Afghanistan are doubtless laden with silk and nuts and dyes; those journeying toward Kabul, with salt and tea and spices, and stuffs from Indian looms.

The rocky sides of the narrowing Pass are almost wholly bare of vegetation, and, as mile after mile the sun pours down an ever more merciless heat, they glow like the sides of an oven. But at length the watershed is passed, and a refreshing line of verdure marks the course of the Khaiber stream, as it flows away north-westward to pour itself into the Kabul. And now the fort of Ali Masjid is visible, towering aloft on its isolated height, beyond which, alas! the Pass is not safe for Europeans.

Presently the travellers pass some of the dwellings of

the mountain-folk, many of them mere holes in the mountain-sides like the lairs of wild beasts; and then, arriving at the foot of the rock whereon Ali Masjid stands, they leave their *tumtums,* and, in the cheerful warmth of the noonday sun, climb up some 400 feet to the top, guided by a wild man clad in white and carrying a very long gun. Starting merrily, they arrive subdued, and, with eyes too nearly blinded to look at anything, creep feebly into the fort. Presently they find themselves in a shady verandah, whence they look abroad at their leisure on a panorama more absolutely rude and savage in its grandeur than any they have ever seen.

Around and above them rise in endless variety of form tall crags and masses of rock, while at their feet, far, far below, winds on, north-westward still, the narrowest part of the Pass, a deep way shut in by the rugged cliffs which rise to right and left. Onward it winds, and onward march the caravans in long procession, moving slowly along the narrow passage, and away on the road to Kabul; but our travellers may not follow. The shaggy camels may go onward and onward still; but they, on the very verge of that alluring country which is ever a little beyond, must sadly turn away and retrace their wasted steps. Oh, these turnings back! What strange disappointment they bring! what a ridiculous bitterness of spirit, what perversity of vague discontent! They make one to think that all travel is vanity, to suspect that those eager longings for the Beyond, which are the very essence of the travelling spirit, are after all the expression of an instinct too deep to be satisfied by mere fresh mountains and valleys, fresh streams and plains and cities.

Wistfully the travellers gaze along the Pass, and away

into the northern mountains.   To think that they have
come all this way for nothing!—that they have journeyed
over those thousands of miles to be turned away at last from
the gate of that enchanted region on whose very borders they
seem to stand.

"Oh, how impatient it makes one," exclaims Sebaste, "to
reach that other pass toward which we are journeying, and to
get through it and out into a wider world where barriers of
time are not, and where perhaps (who knows?) we may have
the whole universe before us, and explore it all at our
leisure!"

"You talk wildly, my dear," says Philippa, reprovingly,
"and flippantly too, I think."

"Flippantly!" cries Sebaste.   "Do you think that death
is a graver matter than life, Philippa?   Would you like me
to copy those good people who pull a long face when they
talk of their souls,—just as if all the rest of them were not
exceedingly serious too?   Oh, it is dreadful to be stopped
like this!   *Why* can't we be disguised as camels, and go
to Kabul in a caravan?"

In a dejected frame of mind, but laughing too at their own
dejection, the travellers eat a picnic tiffin, and, having rested
through the fiercest heat of the afternoon, descend at length
to their waiting *tumtums*, and begin the return journey to
Peshawar.   But as the overpowering glare is softened, and
the air grows cooler and yet more cool, their drooping spirits
revive; and when the sun is low and all things shine transfigured in the glow of the evening light, they are lost in
wondering admiration of the wild beauty of form, the gorgeous richness of colour, which on every side surround them.
Though the rocky crags are bare and dry, yet are they so

brightly bathed in vivid and changing hues that they seem
to breathe and live, until it is hard to believe it possible for
any reverent mind to look upon material Nature as a lifeless, mechanical thing. It is a scene such as makes the
soul spring up in sudden exultation, exclaiming, The world
is Thought; and thought is Life; and life is Light, and
Love !

CHAPTER XX.

RETURNING toward Lahor through the wide, scorched-up plains of the Panjab, the travellers begin to understand what is meant in India by "the hot weather." For one Sunday they stay at Lahor, helpless victims to mosquitoes and the still more terrible sand-flies; and then, unable to bear it any longer, set forth for exalted Simla and the breezes of the Himalaya. South-eastward they travel as far as Ambala, and northward thence to Kalka, where, surrounded by pomegranate-trees bright with scarlet blossoms, they rest for one day at the very foot of the mighty hills, which rear themselves up to their lofty height with slopes of wonderful abruptness.

Next morning at three o'clock, through the heavy and fragrant night-air, they set forth by starlight on the upward drive of fifty-seven miles to Simla, passing by the way long strings of camels, who carry on their backs the baggage of the Government and of all other Europeans who can escape from Calcutta for the hot weather. When the dawn overtakes them they are far above the plains, and around them is a whole forest of cactuses, their thick, green arms all covered with yellow blossoms. The way is haunted by wild monkeys,

VIEW FROM JAKO, SIMLA.

and there are many other things to see as the mountain-views become grander and less confined. Hour after hour the air grows fresher, until, at more than 7000 feet above the sea, the ridge of Simla is reached at length.

And now follow for our travellers days of peace and coolness and freedom, and a rest from sight-seeing which they will long remember. Far they ride on mountain-paths, through the blue-green shade of majestic deodars, or by forests of rhododendrons ablaze with crimson blossoms, mingling with the silvery foliage of the beautiful Himalayan oak-trees. Sometimes the path lies along the edges of abysmal valleys, sometimes in a far-off glory of sunshine appear the perpetual snows of the higher ranges to the northward. As for the little heights whereon Simla itself is builded, they would be called mountains in Europe, but in the Himalaya they almost resemble those hills of nursery fame which were "so low as to look like hollows."

One of them, who rejoices in the name of Jako, reaches a height of 8048 feet; and to his summit our travellers walk before breakfast one morning when the air is full of dewy freshness and overflowing with sunshine. On the top lives an ascetic, a holy *yogi*, said to have a strange understanding with the wild monkeys who haunt the surrounding forests. As the travellers approach his little hermitage, they hear his voice reading aloud in chanting monotone from some volume of ancient scripture. Presently he comes forth, a wild figure in strange attire, his face covered with a pigment of the brightest yellow imaginable. Perceiving that the visitors desire to see not only himself but also his monkey friends, he looks abroad among the deodars, and gives forth a peculiar cry. The monkeys are far away, and at first no answer comes; but presently, swiftly gliding up the mountain-slope from below, rising noiselessly from the deep shadows of the trees, the monkeys begin to assemble. Wonderfully varied is the group they form. There are old monkeys and young monkeys, stout and mighty monkeys, and monkeys slim and graceful, and one charming baby in arms no bigger than a kitten. The visitors regale them with grain and native sweetmeat, which delicacies the beasts snatch out of their hands in a defiant and ungrateful fashion that gives a bad impression of monkey manners. Evidently our travellers' white faces have excited suspicion and dislike, for toward their friend the *yogi* the monkeys are far more gracious. With his yellow countenance he stands in the midst of the excited crowd, and beyond is a background of tall, dark trees,—a picture to be long remembered.

Too soon comes the day of departure, and the downward plunge into glowing heat and the oppressive air of the plains. Dreadful, after the breezes of the heights, is the glare of the sun on the vast, scorched-up expanses of yellow; and, as they journey southward toward Dehli, our travellers begin to realise the meaning of that terrible similitude of Holy Writ, "I will make your heaven as iron, and your earth as brass: and your strength shall be spent in vain."

Travelling in such weather would hardly be safe without many mitigating precautions. All Indian railway-trains are furnished with a broad eaves of wood, but now must be drawn up as well the deeply-tinted window-panes, which darken and deaden the tremendous glow without into something nearly as faint as our own so-called sunshine; and now is the time to keep continually drenched with water the round tatties of *khas-khas* grass through which alone the air from without should enter. By such means our travellers succeed in keeping the temperature within down to about 106° Fahr., and very triumphant they feel about it. It does not *sound* very cool; but step outside for a moment into the outer blaze, and you will come in again with a sense of delicious relief, and be thankful indeed for the contrast.

Still, if the day is somewhat trying, it is compensated for by the glory and the beauty of the night. Then the soft air is heavy with the sweetness of flowers, and resplendent with moonlight,—no cold and ghostly radiance as with us, but a living glory of almost golden light, which yet, wherever it falls, seems to cover the ground with snow. April weather in India almost tempts one to think with regret of those long-past days of the wicked Tareke, that "mighty injurer of men,"[1] for then the sun, "out of fear of that ill-fated, violent monster, altogether desisted from his heat; the moon also, in terror of that passionate, bloodthirsty fiend, appeared always at full." Certainly he was not an estimable character, for he "stretched out the arm of tyranny and oppression"; but then what austerities he had performed whereby he gained his power! It is recorded of him that "for a hundred years he held up his two arms and one foot towards heaven, and *fixed his eyes upon the sun* for the whole time."

For two days our travellers rest at Dehli; and then they set forth south-westward to cross once more the boundary of British India, and to visit that most wonderful of native cities, Jaipur in Rajputana. To spend Holy Week and Easter in a place so thoroughly oriental is the strangest of strange experiences. The church is so small, and the Christians are so few, that it seems hardly credible that the number of Easter days that have been is already between eighteen and nineteen hundred.

[1] From Halhed's 'Sheeve Pouran.'

In exploring the city our friends are assisted by a white-turbaned, grave-faced Muhammadan whose name is Fakir-ud-din, and who speaks very creditable English. Many wonderful things hath he to tell — as that the precipitous rock which, crowned by the Tiger Fort, overlooks the city on its north-western side, is hollow, and that therein is safely stored the Maharaja's countless treasure. Such things are easy to believe among surroundings so unfamiliar. The extraordinary buildings, the gorgeous Eastern colouring, the exuberant intensity of the native life, all unite to produce a sense of dream-like unreality which makes it no longer possible to be astonished at anything.

Of brilliant scenes there is plenty in Jaipur; and most brilliant of all are those of the hour before sunset, when the broad streets overflow with sacred cows and thronging human life, and when all the Maharaja's innumerable elephants come forth to take the air. Then doth the great Hall of the Winds, with its multitudinous array of cupolas, glow softly in the reddening light; and all aglow in like manner are the other palaces, and that central Íshwarí Minár Swarga Sul, "the Tower that pierceth Heaven." Then many dark-faced citizens ride past on bullocks or camels, or are borne by their servants in *jhampans*, or speed gaily along in *ekkas*, while the ladies drive forth in curtained *bahlis* drawn by oxen, or in those glittering tents on wheels, ablaze with crimson and embroidery, called *khása raths*, "select chariots," as indeed they well may be. Wonderfully lively is the cease-less motion of the crowds of humbler folk, who buy and sell for ever, and hasten always hither and thither in vivid streams and eddies of ever-varying colour.

Often the throng is parted to let a procession pass through, — perhaps a wedding-train of bronze-faced girls robed in

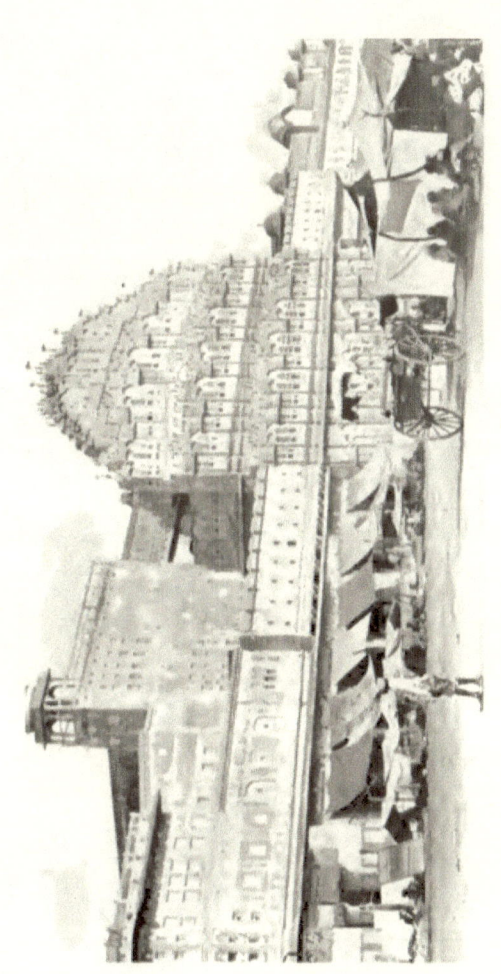

crimson, and carrying on their heads in open baskets goodly presents from the house of the bride to be bestowed on the bridegroom's father; or a wailing funeral-train on its way to the burning-place, whence the dead man's ashes will be carried away to be thrown into the far-off Ganges.

But grave and decorous amid all the stir, the numberless elephants move slowly along, towering in their solemn dignity like massive rocks above the eddying crowds; and high on their necks the mahouts are set, and look down upon all the world. Most amiable of all the elephant worthies is a dear little fellow whose age is two. In a sprightly manner he makes a salaam to the travellers, and then puts out his baby-trunk in the most endearing way, as though he said, "Have you got a banana about you that you don't require?"

Most of the private houses in Jaipur are painted a bright strawberry-pink. Other buildings there are in plenty, imposing palaces, and temples with many worshippers, and little idol-shrines built in the middle of the broad streets.

Then there are choice collections of native art-work to be visited; and our travellers gaze with delight at the enamel-work for which Jaipur is renowned,—rich harmonies of deep-blue and scarlet, or more brilliant shades of blue combined with wondrous mazes of delicate gold arabesque.

Our friends fail not to visit the far-famed alligator-tank, nor to feed with welcome lumps of meat its eager and voracious inhabitants. It is wonderful to see the monsters thrusting high above the surface of the water their great, gaping jaws bristling with saw-like teeth. Truly was it said of the crocodile, long ago in the days of Job—

> " Who can open the doors of his face?
> Round about his teeth is terror."

The travellers, moreover, go to pay their respects to the Maharaja's lions and tigers,—and very charming beasts they find them to be. They are in charge of a one-armed native keeper, who, to gain the visitors' applause, thrusts his hand into the lions' mouths, and pulls their whiskers, and pinches them, until they growl and snarl in fury. In this way he lost his arm one day, and it seems likely that the other one will soon follow down one of the lions' throats. In another place are kept several great tigers who used to be man-eaters. Some say that man-eating entails a shabby coat with mangy patches of bare skin; but if so, these particular delinquents have remained in captivity long enough to regain their good looks, for their fur is smooth and glossy, and only a greedy fierceness of the eyes recalls their former misdoings. Two of them are known to have eaten some half-a-dozen men apiece, and of such achievement they look fully capable. The bars of their cage are so close together that there is no danger of a paw being thrust out between them, and to place one's own face within a few inches of theirs, and to gaze into their savage eyes, is a possible and instructive amusement. The travellers have never seen such eyes before. They seem to have a curious magnetic power, and with a sullen implacable gleam they say, as clearly as ever eyes said anything, "I *should* like to eat you!"

On another morning our friends explore the great Palace of the Maharaja, which, with the gardens belonging to it, covers one-seventh of the whole area of the city. Over many of the gateways are hung long wreaths of mango-leaves. These, as Fakir-ud-din explains, prevent the entrance of evil spirits.

Presently the visitors are introduced to the Maharaja's horses, three hundred princely steeds of all imaginable nationalities. Their stables are built round the exercising-ground, in the middle of which a wild boar is tethered with a view to accustoming the horses beforehand to the terrors of boar-hunting. It is breakfast-time, and the three hundred horses have been led forth to be fed, and placed in two long rows facing each other. Each has a humble native attendant who carries a large bowl of brass, wherein is a delectable compound of gram and milk and sugar and liquid butter. The horses are far too proud to help themselves, and the rich mass is crammed down their throats by the hands of their obsequious servants. It is an absurd scene, and the travellers, as they pass between the long rows of banqueters, find it hard to maintain the requisite solemnity. But suddenly they come upon one solitary horse who, though handsome and dignified, has none of the supercilious airs of his companions. No sugar and butter for him! He is eating plain and wholesome grain from an unassuming nosebag.

"Fakir-ud-din, what is this? Why is not that horse fed like the others?"

Fakir-ud-din inquires into the matter, and then explains, with a look of solemn wonder at the grave countenance of the steed in question, "This is an English horse, and he becomes ill if fed on sugar!"

With a smile of pardonable pride the travellers leave their compatriot, and go in search of the Maharaja's elephants. Many of them they have already seen parading through the streets at evening; but there are some who never go out, twenty or thirty gigantic beasts, kept only for fighting, and poisoned into raging madness by some pernicious native drug. They are terrible to behold as that awful steed of "Indra, the Lord of the Sky," even the "infuriated elephant

Airavata, whose eyes were dim with inebriety." [1] Furiously they toss up their trunks, and make wild grimaces at the travellers, and stamp their mighty limbs, each of which is secured by a great iron cable. Sometimes, says Fakir-uddin, these strong chains burst, and then the maddened elephants wreak deadly vengeance on their cruel tyrant-masters. Truly it would seem as though Jaipur were one of those three magic cities (built long ago for the sons of Tareke) wherein were excellent wells and tanks, and chariots and drunken elephants.

On the day before their departure our friends rise early, and at five o'clock set forth to visit the ancient city of Amber, the seat of the former Kings of the State whereof Jaipur is now the capital. Northward they drive among the hills, through seas of ethereal moonlight at first, and then through the sudden dawn. Dazzlingly shines the morning sunlight as they come among Amber's stately buildings, now all deserted, and half buried in luxuriant leafage. What the travellers most desire to see is the great Palace of the Maharajas; but up the long and sacred ascent thereto no wheeled thing may rumble, and they look round anxiously for the elephants who should be awaiting them. Those worthies, it seems, have not yet arrived; and our friends start on foot, wondering, as they go, at the dense forest of tall cactuses growing wild by the roadside. They are in full blossom, and very beautiful is the crimson colour of the small flowers wherewith they are covered. Along the road, and in and out among the cactuses, stray many wild peacocks. Secure in their sanctity, they have no fear of native wayfarers; but the white faces of the English travellers inspire them with vague uneasiness, and at their ap-

[1] From the 'Vishnu Purana,' translated by H. H. Wilson.

proach they glide swiftly into the shade among the thronging cactus-stems. So regal are they in their jewelled plumage that one feels tempted to steal pot-herbs for the rest of one's life, in the hope of incurring the penalty allotted to that misdeed, and being born next time as a peacock.

Presently advances, from behind, a soft but ponderous tread; and, turning round, the travellers are met by their welcome elephants, two solemn and dignified personages who humbly kneel before them. The name of the one is Ganga, and that of the other Jawāhur Kuli, whereof the significa-tion is "Perfect Jewel." Each has his face and trunk elaborately painted, and their countenances are benign and affable. As soon as the travellers have mounted, the great beasts rise to their feet, and go swinging and rolling and flopping along toward the venerable deserted Palace. It was built, the learned say, by that Man Singh who began to reign A.D. 1592 (whose is also the great temple at Bindra-ban, but who must not be confounded with that earlier Man Singh who built the palace at Gwaliar), and was finished by Sawai Jai Singh II., who afterward builded Jaipur, and called it after his own name, and in 1728 removed thither, and made it thenceforth his capital. A striking group of buildings is the Amber Palace, perched picturesquely on a rock overlooking the waters of a lake wherein alligators are said to live.

Passing the outer gate, the travellers enter a spacious court, and then, leaving their gigantic steeds, wander far through the palace-buildings—halls and chambers, corridors and marble baths, with here and there a balcony whence they look forth on the lake and far over the sunlit land-scape. At last they find their way to the small palace-temple dedicated to Shilá Devi, who is none other than their old acquaintance the goddess Durga herself. From Ambika, another of her many appellations, the name of Amber is said to be derived. Very hideous is the image of her which sits enthroned in the palace-temple; and over the whole place seems still to linger the horror of those human sacrifices which were daily offered in past days before that dreadful image. The goddess sits in a recess, not looking straight before her, but with her head turned aside. In the good old times, they say, when she daily feasted on a human victim, she looked forth into the temple with open and gracious countenance; but there came a day when men presumed to cheat her of her rightful tribute, and, when the hour of the daily sacrifice came round, to bring her nought but a goat. Then, in high disdain, the dread goddess turned her head away, and ever since has eyed with scornful, sidelong glance her miserable, makeshift kid. Nor can she now be persuaded to relent even by the great yearly sacrifice wherein, at the feast of the Dasahra, are slain for her delectation a hundred buffaloes and five hundred goats or sheep.

Among the unholy shadows of the haunted temple our travellers linger long, telling those old legends of the Devi's wondrous achievements which are written in the 'Sapta-Shati,'[1] that most curious of Hindu scriptures, and are solemnly chanted day by day in Durga's numberless temples.

Long, long ago it was that the goddess came into existence. It was the terrible time of the demon-war, when the

---

[1] The 'Sapta-Shati,' or 'Chandi-Pat,' has been translated into English by that learned Pandit, Cavali Venkat Rámasswámi, who says in his preface that, "as an orthodox Hindu," he "firmly and devoutly" believes "that the theomachy described in this sacred volume is to be taken in its plain and literal sense."

great-cheeked demons Madhu and Kaitabh, that were born from the wax of Vishnu's ear, fought furiously against the gods, and drove them from their heavenly thrones. Then from all the deities proceeded "a great mass of light," and being conglomerate it "appeared as a flaming mountain," and the demons, when they saw it, receded to the extremities of the regions. Then that "effulgent lustre," that "peerless light," was transformed into the figure of a glorious goddess "extending through the three worlds. The energy of Siva created her face; the brightness of Yama made her hair; her arms were formed by the light of Vishnu. . . . Her feet were made by the energy of Brahma; her toes by the rays of the sun. . . . Her teeth were created by the brightness of Prajápati; her three eyes by the energy of Parvak."

Then all the deities vied one with another in bestowing fair gifts on the goddess. Vishnu gave her a *chakra*, that mystic circle, the symbol of universal supremacy. Indra, the God of a Thousand Eyes, gave her a thunderbolt; he took also the bell from the elephant Airavata and bestowed it on Durga the mighty. "The maker of day filled his rays in the roots of her hair. . . . Jaladhi the Ocean conferred on her a prosperous chaplet of lotus." Himavant, King of the Dewy Mountain, "gave her a lion" whereon she should ride to battle. The Earth also "granted a necklace of snakes, and the other deities gave her jewels and arms," and Shesha, the King of Snakes, "gave her a necklace of serpents' ornaments."

Then Durga shouted "with a terrible voice, the sound of which filled the sky. The eternal vault echoed with the terrific sound, . . . all the world was alarmed, the ocean trembled. The earth quaked, . . . the deities joyfully exclaimed, 'Victory to the rider of the lion!'" Terrible was

the goddess to the hosts of the demons; "she indented the
earth occupied by her foot, her crown struck the sky: the
sound of her bowstring terrified the whole subterraneous
world. She grasped all the space of the regions by her one
thousand arms; fierce war was waged between the goddess
and the enemies of the gods."

"The great demons encountered the goddess with a thousand times ten million millions of chariots, and with elephants
and horses of like number;" but Durga "sportively cut them
in pieces by the shower of her powerful shafts and arrows.
By the trident, by the mace, by the *shaktiristi*, by the sword,
she killed immense numbers of demons, and made others to
fall by the ringing of the bell. The lion made an excessive
roar, it produced a concussion among the . . . foes of the
gods. . . . The gods were gratified, and poured down am-
aranthine flowers from heaven." Then came against her
Chámara, the general of the demon-host, riding on an elephant. But she "leapt from the lion to the globular forehead of the elephant, and directly wrestled" with the
enemy of the gods. "During the combat, they both dis-
mounted and began furiously to beat one another." But
the lion of the goddess, that mighty "enemy of beasts,"
swiftly attacked the dreadful demon, "and separated the
head of Chámara from his body, by the strokes of his
paws."

"The band of deities with the magnificent sages applauded
the goddess," Devi the "Three-eyed," the "Matron of the
World," who bore "wrathful redness of the eyes. . . . The
eloquent Indra and the crowd of gods, after the death of the
demons, bowing their heads, were delighted," and making
obeisance to the goddess, implored her "to rule the universe," saying: "Thou art the instigating cause of the

universal earth, . . . thou art . . . the proprietor of this
world; thou art indefinable, inscrutable, and the excellent
principle of matter. . . . O Ambiká! preserve us by thy
trident and sword; preserve us by the ringing of thy bell,
and by the sound of thy bowstring."

Many other battles did the valiant goddess fight. For it
happened on a time that "Sumbha, lord of the demons," and
"the mighty demon Nisumbha" were suitors for Durga's
hand. But when Sumbha asked her to be his bride, "the
goddess with a disdainful smile replied to him, 'How can I
repeal my determined vow that I formerly swore to without
consideration, that whoever can vanquish me in combat,
whoever can oppress my pride, whoever is equal to me in
vigour, he shall be my husband?'"

Then Nisumbha sent against Durga Dhumralochan the
Smoky-eyed Giant, with an army of 60,000 demons. But
the "supreme goddess," the "Supporter of the World," "became mightily enraged; she furiously rose and destroyed the
force of the demons by her lion. Grasping some of them,
she dashed them against each other and killed the great
demons; she demolished some by the blows of her hand.
The lion tore some with his claws, and some by the strokes
of his paws, separating their heads. In a moment all that
army was destroyed by the magnanimous and enraged lion
of the goddess," and Dhumralochan was reduced to ashes by
the breath of the wrathful Durga.

Then "Sumbha, king of the demons, with agitated lips
thus commanded the great demons Chand and Mund:
'O Chand and Mund, go ye with a great army against
the Devi; kill ye the wicked lion quickly.'" So Chand
and Mund, "attended by four sorts of armies," marched
forth in anger to the fight. "Ambiká then became terribly

angry at her enemies; rage changed her face into a hideous black," she was transformed in a moment and became "the terrific-faced Kali." "Her contracting brows overshadowed her forehead; . . . her mouth expanded, she had a lolling tongue, a horrible red-tinged eye; her front filled the regions. She furiously fell upon the demons, and destroyed the foes of the deities and devoured their forces. . . . The troopers' chariots with their drivers she threw into her mouth, and chewed them with her teeth horribly. . . . The magnanimous goddess . . . killed some with the sword, and struck some with the *khatwanga* weapon; the giants died with the pressure of her teeth." "Chand beheld it," and rushed on the frightful Kali. "The dreadful-eyed goddess . . . angrily shouted: her voice was horrible, her mouth became distended and frightful, and she gnashed with her tremendous teeth. The goddess made her lion to rise, ran at Chand, and laying hold on him by his hair, she cut off his head with her sword. After this, Mund, seeing the fall of Chand, marched against her; she made him to fall on the earth, and instantaneously killed him with her sword. The surviving forces perceived the fall of Chand and the valiant Mund, and through fear retreated in all directions. . . . The lion roared tremendously; the goddess rang the bell; Ambiká shouted. The sound of the roar penetrated to the extremities of the regions, the mouth of Devi expanded hideously."

Such things the travellers tell in the gloom of the blood-stained temple, gazing the while at the hideous image of the goddess, until a half-superstitious horror begins to fill their minds. It is a strange sensation, often experienced in India by our not very imaginative travellers, but hard to make intelligible to those who have never entered idol-temples, or who have made acquaintance only with the fossil-gods of Egypt, whose life and worship were over and done with thousands of years ago. Here in India the gods are still alive, endowed with a hideous and personal vitality which, fancy though it be, yet makes itself felt and feared. Absurd and unreasonable as the feeling is (springing perhaps from some mysterious influence of unconscious suggestion set in motion by the ardent conviction of the surrounding multitudes of believers), yet is it strong enough to give rise to a curious notion, a half-felt suspicion that millions of human minds concentrated in one deep-seated belief may be strong enough to project into something like objective existence the thought they have made their own.

"I wish," exclaims Philippa, "that those who talk so glibly about 'the vandalism of the early Christians' would but live for a while among these demon-deities, until they realise that there may be such a thing as a condition of thought and feeling in which there is no possible compromise between believing in the power of idol-gods, and straightway knocking them to pieces!"

"Oh, hush, Philippa!" cries Sebaste, shivering. "She is listening! She has fixed her sidelong glance upon you, and surely her eyes are gleaming!"

At this moment enters the temple a group of Brahmans leading a black kid. It is the time of the daily sacrifice. Moving to a little distance, the travellers sit down to watch the performance of the rite. The pretty little kid is made to stand before the goddess, and a cord is fastened to his horns and held by one of the priests. Then an ancient chopper — a large and curious implement of sacrifice — is laid on the ground beside him. Rice and flowers and Ganges water are sprinkled on the blade of the chopper and on the unresisting head of the innocently unconscious kid. All is now ready for the slaying of the victim, and the chopper should be raised in the air and brought down on the kid's black neck. But the chopper is old, and no doubt blunted and jagged with hacking at something other than the necks of kids; and, as severing the head with a single blow is an essential part of the sacrifice, it is necessary now to use a newer and sharper sword. This is brought by one of the attendant Brahmans, who, lifting it above his head, brings it down with a rushing sound,—and all is over for the poor little kid. The head is caught up by the cord before it can touch the ground and placed in a basin of brass, whereinto, with a gurgling noise, the blood of the victim is made to flow, while a stately Brahman holds down with his bare brown foot the still violently struggling limbs. Then the brimming basin, with the head still lying therein, is borne into the recess where sits the expectant goddess with a look of greedy discontent on her half-averted face; and over her hideous lips the warm blood of the victim is smeared. But to hide this concluding rite a Brahman draws across the recess the folds of a crimson curtain.

Throughout the ceremony our travellers are haunted with visions of former more horrible sacrifices, and at its conclusion they come forth into the sunlight shuddering in spite of the heat. Silently they return to the great court of the Palace, and so go rolling and flopping away, enthroned on the high and spacious backs of Ganga and Jawāhur Kuli.

CHAPTER XXI.

BOMBAY—THE CAVES OF ELEPHANTA.

Our travellers' last railway journey in India is a south-westward rush lasting two nights and a long, hot day. Awaking in an atmosphere of tropical moisture and heat, they find themselves surrounded by a forest of coco-nut palms, and presently arrive in the city of Bombay.

Hence they are to sail for England in the good ship Clyde, and the time of their stay is but a very few days. There are many things in Bombay that are worthy to be studied; but by resolutely ignoring the existence of whatever they have not time to see, our friends gain in the short time at their command a very satisfactory impression; and this closing scene of their Indian wanderings will always be remembered as a bright, many-coloured picture wherein are blended in pleasant and dream-like confusion majestic buildings and picturesque streets, and thronging multitudes of people with faces of many different hues and garments of endless variety. Specially animated are the scenes in the markets, and the travellers are fond of lingering in that famous fruit-market where is massed and piled together a marvellous wealth of tropical produce. What a pity to be leaving India when the mangos are just in their glory!

But the island of Elephanta and the great cave-temple therein are haunting our travellers' imagination, and before long they set forth in a steam-launch to explore those ancient wonders. Eastward they steam for an hour, and then land on the western side of a rocky island whereon corinda-bushes grow. Ghárapúri the natives call it, "the Town of the Rock"; but the Portuguese named it Elephanta by reason of a great elephant of stone that they found here, and so it is called by Europeans even to this day. On their way to the cave-temple the visitors fall in with some very attractive beetles in a brilliant livery of scarlet; but otherwise the way is lonely, leading upward with many steps to a height of about 250 feet above high-water mark.

Here at length the travellers reach the great cave-temple, hewn into the hard trap-rock to a depth of 130 feet. A thousand years old it is, the learned say, or maybe a little older, and the ghosts of the centuries haunt it. As the travellers enter its gloomy depths, the desolate silence wraps them round with a heavy, irresistible oppression. So dreary are the shadowy spaces, so hopeless the massive rock-hewn columns, so daunting the immovable weight of the darkly impending roof, that the visitors can hardly rouse themselves to find out what manner of place they are in.

The first to recover the power of speech is the ever strong-minded Philippa, who remarks (with the more vehemence because she has herself to convince as well as the others) that they are not in a bad dream, but, on the contrary, in a Brahmanic rock-temple well worthy of careful study.

"You see," she continues cheerfully, "the temple consists mainly of a square pillared hall of which the side measures about 90 feet, and this is approached on the North and the

East and the West by pillared porticoes, at the sides of which
are left considerable masses of unhewn rock. The principal
entrance, by which we came in, is the northern, and only on
that side was there originally a free surface to work upon.
On the east and west sides of the temple the solid rock has
been laboriously hewn away,—a tedious piece of work that it
tires one only to think of!"

"What tires me," says Sebaste dolefully, "is to look at
these oppressively heavy columns! What an extraordinary
kind of pillar it is!—first a great square pedestal 8 feet high,
with queer little gods sitting on the corners; and then a
short, round, fluted shaft; and then a great bulging cushion!
Why could they not carve out slim graceful columns here
like those in the rock-temples at the Seven Pagodas?"

"Because they had learned better," answers Philippa
severely. "The work at the Seven Pagodas belongs to an
earlier stage of rock-cut architecture. In those days they
copied structural forms exactly, and did not realise that
pillars which have thousands of tons of solid rock to support
ought not to waste their strength in trying to look elegantly
slim and graceful as if they had only a wooden roof to think
about. Even this Elephanta Cave is, of course, copied from
structural architecture,— those great beams of rock left
attached to the roof are unmistakably wooden in form; but
at the Seven Pagodas the analogy is much closer, and very
disastrous were the results of it. Have you forgotten
Bhima's Rath, and how the roof settled and cracked, so that
the work was given up in despair? But you never had an
architectural mind!"

"I would rather not, Philippa, if it would require such
pillars as these to bolster up the roof of it!"

"But let us hear the rest of your lecture, Philippa!" ex-

claims Irene. "You have not even told us yet to what god
the temple is dedicated."

"It is a Saiva temple," says Philippa, "and here on our
right is the shrine or *garbha*, in the middle of which stands
that symbol of Siva which is the central object of worship in
whose honour the temple was made. They say that it is
still adored by crowds of worshippers on Siva's festival-days."

The shrine is a square rock-hewn chamber filling the space
included by four of the massive pillars. Each of its four
doors is approached by a flight of six steps, and is guarded
by two gigantic *dwârpâlas*, or Doorkeepers, about 15 feet
high. These rocky personages are supported by those curious
figures of dwarf-demons which are so striking a feature of
this temple, and are thought by some to represent aboriginal
races of India, while their tall and lordly neighbours are
supposed to symbolise the mightier and conquering Aryans.

Having sufficiently admired these worthies, and long
enough contemplated the central symbol of stone (which
stands on a square base of rock awaiting the libations of
liquid butter which its worshippers devoutly pour over it),
the travellers go on through deepening shadows, until, reaching at length the southern wall of the temple, they find
themselves confronted by that most solemn and impressive
of all the Elephanta sculptures, a colossal three-faced bust,
the far-famed Trimurti. It is carved from the living rock,
in a recess whereof the depth is 10½ feet. The height of
the sculpture is 19 feet, and its breadth is 21½ feet. It
represents Siva in the threefold character of Brahma the
Creator, Vishnu the Preserver, and Rudra the Destroyer.
Very solemn, in the dim light of the gloomy temple, look
those three gigantic countenances, each crowned with a high
head-dress elaborately wrought with sculptured ornament.

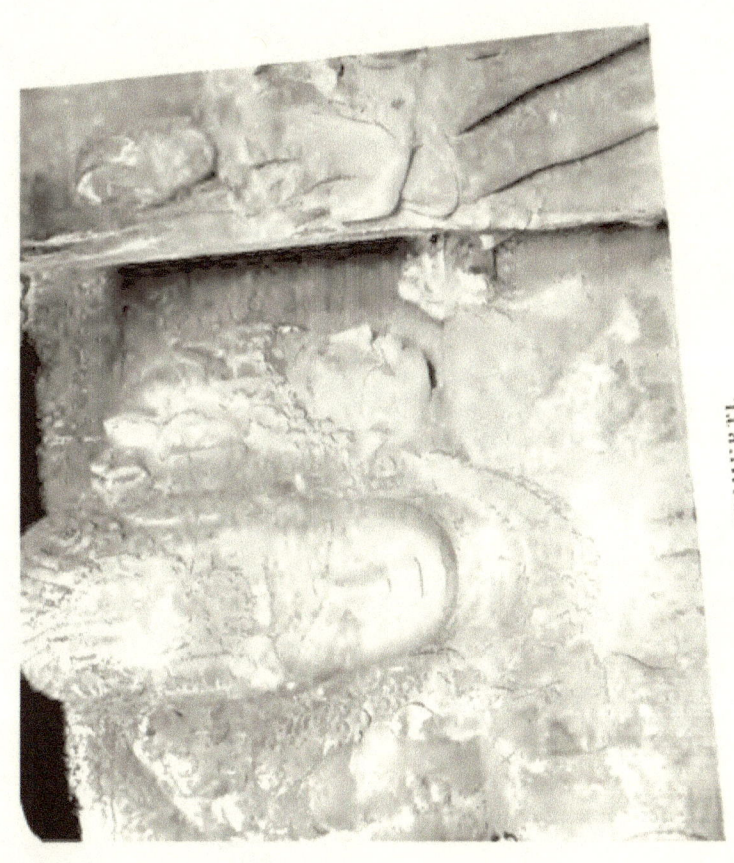

ELEPHANTA. TRIMURTI.

The central face, looking northward into the cave, is that
of Brahma, the **Father of the Vedas.** His head-dress is the
tallest of the three, and he wears a pendent breast-ornament
of beautiful and elaborate design. In his left hand he holds
what is probably a gourd, the characteristic drinking-vessel
of a Hindu ascetic. The face on the right, which looks westward, is that of Vishnu, who holds in his right hand his well-
known symbol, a full-blown lotus-flower.

Rudra, the Destroyer, faces eastward. He is an ancient
Vedic deity who in later times became identified with Siva.
He is "the god of the roaring storm, terrible as a wild beast";
but, notwithstanding his destructive powers, he is described
as "the promoter of the desires of the two worlds, and the
gratifier of the inclinations of the Universe." He holds in
his right hand a cobra which, with hood uplifted, gazes into
his eyes. His lips are parted in a terrible smile, and between
them the tongue is visible. A projection at the corner of the
mouth is said by the learned to be a tusk, and a mysterious
lump in the middle of the forehead represents that third and
vertical eye wherein Siva so constantly rejoices. From that
third eye a flame will blaze forth one day, and all the world
will be burned to ashes.

Strangely impressed by the silent majesty of the mystic
Trimurti, the travellers, with eyes growing used to the darkness, gaze awhile in silence; but presently the immovable
expression of the colossal countenances above them seems to
cast a spell on their vague imaginings, and to carry away
their minds as captives into a mythic region of ancient
fable where the light is more dim, the shadows are more
confused than even in the gloomy depths of this abysmal
rock-hewn temple. So, in the solemn presence of the
faintly seen Trimurti, our friends begin to tell old legends

of Brahma and Vishnu and Siva, and of how the world was made.

The beginning of all things, it seems, is Bráhmá the Imperishable and the Supreme; for, in that far-off day when the universe was yet undiscerned, the self-existent Spirit "created the waters by meditation"; and in the waters there floated a golden egg whereinto the self-existent Spirit entered, and from that egg he was born as Brahmá "the forefather and creator of all things." Of old, they say that Brahma had five heads; but Siva offended him, and there was battle, and Siva cut off one of the heads, so that there remained but four; and the head that was cut off gave chase to Siva, so that he fled before it and hardly escaped at the last. But from the mouths of the four heads that were left the four Vedas came forth; and many other benefits did Brahma confer on the world. Cool is "the water of the knowledge of Brahma,"[1] bringing life and refreshment when duly sprinkled on minds "disordered with pain through the heat of the sun of mundane existence."

But Brahma must not be overmuch praised in a temple dedicated to Siva. The "three-eyed lord" is here supreme, and all other gods must be regarded as manifestations of his power; wherefore the travellers bethink them of the wild myths of the Siva Purana, and begin to rehearse a wondrous history wherein Siva is greatly exalted.

Long, long ago, when neither the four castes nor yet any of the other creatures had as yet been brought into "the field of existence," there was shining in stainless splendour a "ray of essential light." And "out of the body of that ray" there bubbled forth "water like a boiling froth," which forthwith "enveloped the surface of the earth." And from the midst

[1] Markandeya Purána. Pargiter.

of the boundless waters sprang a lotus-plant whereon grew a
flower the length of whose petals was hundreds of thousands
of miles. With a light as it had been thousands of millions
of suns the sacred flower shone, and from it did Brahma
come into existence. Having been born from the flower, he
marvelled greatly, saying, "Who am I? and whence came
I? and how should I employ myself? and who is my
creator?" And being unable to trace his origin, he began
to descend the stem of the lotus, climbing downward and
downward still, in hope to reach its root. But when he had
descended for a hundred years, nor yet could see the end,
he returned to that place whence he had set forth. Then
he began to ascend the stem of the lotus, climbing upward
and upward still, in hope to reach the top. But when for
a hundred years he had "measured upward" the "road of
his desires," nor yet could see the summit, he fell into a
"trance of thoughtfulness and perplexity."

Then, after twelve years, Vishnu sprang on a sudden into
existence. He had four arms and "a skin entirely black; a
crown of jewels on his head, and a yellow garment on his
breast;" his eyes were "large as the flower of the lotus, his
body splendid as the purest gold;" around his neck "cor-
nelians and diamonds were sparkling; he appeared smiling
and simpering with a heavenly beauty that surpassed all
imagination." And forthwith Brahma "made a sign with
his hand and said, 'Who art thou, and from whence? Arise,
and be at a distance.'" But Vishnu was very angry at that
word, and "the fire of wrath began to blaze high" between
them, and they two prepared to do battle.

Then suddenly "shone out into view another luminous
figure, whose splendour was like that of a dazzling flame
and his rays more bright than a thousand suns." He was

"exempt from defect and increase, and from the past, present, and future;" and his form was that of the symbol of Siva. Then said Vishnu to Brahma, "Why dost thou hold forth the signal of war? Lo! a third excellence is now produced. Let us attain to its extremities." After this Vishnu, for a thousand years, in the shape of a boar, descended into the nether regions, while Brahma "for the same space of time, assuming the figure of a goose, soared to the world above." So for a thousand years they "travelled over the superior and inferior worlds," but still they sought in vain. Returning therefore to the place whence they had come, they performed devotions for a hundred years to that third excellence. And at the end of that time Siva himself was seen proceeding from the essential light which formed the figure of his symbol. He had "five heads and ten arms," he was "as white as camphor" and "of great strength," endowed with all beauty and clad in "majestic garments." So Brahma and Vishnu doubted no longer concerning their origin, for they both exclaimed, exulting, "This same is our Creator!" and opened their mouths in his praise with sacred *mantras* of the Veda.

And Siva told them, saying, "Another figure, in this same form of mine, shall appear from a wrinkle of Brahma's forehead, and be named Rudra; he shall possess power not inferior to my own. Between him and me there is no distinction."

After this Brahma "earnestly took him to the work of creation," and from the golden egg of the world all creatures came into existence; but that, methinks, is too long a tale to tell,—which is a pity; for such wondrous virtue is it said to possess, that only to listen to it "will atone for the blackest crimes," and heap up merit for the hearer.

The Trimurti is guarded by colossal *dwárpálas*, who lean on dwarf-demons of hideous aspect.   These figures contrast strangely with the majestic calm of the great central bust, and the whole group is one of the most extraordinary sculptures that the travellers have ever seen.

Adjoining it on the east side, carved in this same south wall of the cave, is a group wherein the principal figure is 16 feet 9 inches high, and calls itself Arddhanáríshwar.   This too is a form of Siva, and is attended by Nandi his sacred bull, while around him appear Brahma seated on a lotus-flower upheld by five swans, and Vishnu riding on Garuda, and Indra, "the king of gods," mounted on his elephant Airavata.

There are so many quaint stories to be told about Indra, if only my book would hold them!   He is an ancient Vedic god, and his very name, methinks, has a ring of Aryan dignity.   He is the god of winds and rains, and something of nature-worship lingers about his legends.   Very curious is the history of how the might of the wind is derived from Indra, set forth in that holy book of the illustrious Markandeya :—

"Then uprose Vritra, the mighty demon, encircled with flame, huge in body, with great teeth. . . . He, the enemy of Indra, of immeasurable soul, . . . mighty in valour, increased daily a bow-shot in stature."   But Indra, when he saw the mighty demon Vritra eager to slay him, trembled with fear, and sent unto him seven Sages, desiring peace.   Then the "affectionate-minded" Sages, "who delighted in benevolence towards all creatures, brought about friendship and treaties between him and Vritra."   But Indra violated that sacred treaty, and slew Vritra the demon; and forthwith Indra's might was "overwhelmed by the sin" of that slaying, and

Y

ebbed away from his powerful limbs; and "that might which quitted Indra's body entered the wind" which pervadeth all things, invisible to the eyes of men.

There is another legend which tells how "Indra the king of gods" once walked the earth in the form of "a bird mighty in size, with broken wings, stricken with age, with eyes of a copperish colour, downcast in soul." Thus he came to the four sons of a Rishi, and said—— But what he said, and what they answered, and all that befell thereupon, is more than I can relate just now; for my travellers have moved away, and I perforce must follow.

In another part of the temple Siva's wedding has been carved in the rocky wall, and there are many other groups of sculpture which ought to be minutely studied. Then the supplementary excavations have to be explored, and there are other rock-temples in the neighbourhood which ought to be visited.

For these last no time remains, and, as the travellers steam back to Bombay Island, the night is falling fast.

CHAPTER XXII.

BY the city of Bombay the travellers have as yet not half done their duty. There is the Cathedral of S. Thomas to be visited, and the history of the Diocese to be studied; and time must be left wherein to rejoice over the fact that in the Bombay Presidency (including the native states appertaining thereto) the number of Christians is already no less than 170,651. In Bombay city the Society for the Propagation of the Gospel is hard at work, having therein five schools, four Clergy, and fifteen lay-agents. That other most admirable and useful institution, the Society for the Promotion of Christian Knowledge, has been at home in Bombay for more than seventy years, and the Church Missionary Society is also working vigorously. There are, moreover, a Mission to Seamen, Church-work among the Jews, many Church-schools, and I know not how many other kinds of devoted Christian labour. Of the interesting and prosperous work at Puna the travellers hear much, with many regrets that they have no time to go and see it for themselves.

But to such pleasant studies our friends can devote but a very little while, for soon their inconstant minds are attracted by a fresh object of interest. Continually, dur-

ing their walks in the city, they meet the strange figures of
the Parsis,—men in unfamiliar costume, whereof the most
curious part is the stiff, curving head-dress; and ladies
arrayed in silken robes, with beautiful unmuffled faces whose
expression fits admirably with the well-known fact that their
owners enjoy more respect, and are more worthy of the same,
than any other gentile women outside of Christendom.

Very cheerful are all Parsi countenances, and they wear a
look of good-humoured enjoyment which recalls that condemnation of asceticism uttered long ago by Ahura Mazda,
the Lord of Light: "Verily I say unto thee, O Spitama
Zarathustra! . . . he who has riches is far above him who
has none. And of two men, he who fills himself with meat
is filled with the good spirit much more than he who does
not do so; the latter is all but dead; the former is above him
by the worth of a *dirhem*, by the worth of a sheep, by the
worth of an ox, by the worth of a man. It is this man that
can strive against the onsets of the Astô-vîdhôtu; that can
strive against the self-moving arrow [of death]; that can
strive against the winter fiend, with thinnest garment on;
that can strive against the wicked tyrant and smite him on
the head."[1]

In Bombay the Parsis number some 74,000, and this is the
great bulk of the Zarathustrians, though some smaller bodies
still remain in cities of Guzerât, and there is also a remnant
in their original Persian home, living at Kermân and Yazd
and Teherân. Of these last, according to Professor Darmesteter, there may still be 8000 or 9000; but their numbers
are fast diminishing.

Very delightfully has that same learned Professor set forth

[1] Sacred Books of the East. 'The Vendidad,' translated by Professor
Darmesteter.

the origin of the migration which brought the Parsis into
Guzerât and thence as far as Bombay.   Until the fall of the
Sassanian Dynasty all Persia followed the religion of Zarathustra (one is not allowed to call him Zoroaster now, for
that form is a Greek invention); but in the seventh century
of our era the Muhammadan invasion befell, and the great
battle of Nihâvand, and before the second successor of the
Prophet the Sassanian Dynasty went down.   Then was
Persia brought over to the Muslim religion, and such as
were faithful to the teaching of Zarathustra must leave their
ancestral home.   So forth they fared, and came to Guzerât,
and adopted the language thereof, bringing it with them on
their further journey to their present home in Bombay.   It
is a romantic history, and a beautiful one, but too modern
for the fastidious minds of our travellers, who, with a somewhat childish and unreasonable preference, love rather to let
their fancy wander away into the far-off past, where, in the
first faint dawn of history, with a fair halo around him of
age-long tradition, stands in majestic grandeur Zarathustra's
mighty form.

He was born in ancient Media, who shall say how long
ago?   Was it the fourteenth century B.C., as some have
thought, and was he really a contemporary of Moses?   I
know not; and what matters it so long as his birth took
place indeed, putting to flight the Daêvas, those fiends of
darkness, and that evil Drug, the Nasu, the demon of
death?   "They rush,"[1] cries the birth-hymn of Zarathustra,
"they run away, the wicked, evil-doing Daêvas; they run
away with shouts, the wicked, evil-doing Daêvas; they run
away casting the evil eye, the wicked, evil-doing Daêvas:
'Let us gather together at the head of Arezûra, at the gate

[1] From Professor Darmesteter's translation.

of hell! For he is just born the holy Zarathustra, in the house of Pourushaspa. How can we procure his death? He is the stroke that fells the fiends; he is a Drug to the Drug. Down are the Daêva worshippers, the Nasu made by the Daêva, the false-speaking Lie!' They run away, they rush away, the wicked, evil-doing Daêvas, into the depths of the dark, horrid world of hell. Ashem vohu: Holiness is the best of all good!"

And who was Vistaspa, that great King of Bactria, "the mighty-speared and the lordly one," at whose court Zarathustra rose to power? Hystaspes we call him after the Greek manner, and try to think we know something about him; but that he was not Hystaspes the father of Darius seems to be all that is historically certain, except that he supported Zarathustra, and encouraged the religion he taught. "We sacrifice," saith an ancient liturgy, "to the awful kingly Glory made by Mazda, that clave unto king Vistaspa, so that he thought according to the Law, spake according to the Law, and did according to the Law, destroying his foes and causing the Daêvas to retire. Who, driving the Drug before him, sought wide room for the holy religion; who, driving the Drug before him, made wide room for the holy religion; who made himself the arm and support of this law of Ahura, of this law of Zarathustra; who took her (Daêna, the Religion), standing bound, from the hands of Hunus, and established her to sit in the middle of the world, high ruling, never falling back, holy, nourished with plenty of cattle and pastures."

Zarathustra himself has fared but ill at the hands of the learned. First they discover that the meaning of his sonorous name is "Keeper of Old Camels," and then they do their utmost to explain him away into a storm-god. From this latter undesirable fate Professor Geldner has rescued him, setting aside the myths that grew up among his successors the Magi, and showing how his supernatural attributes are to be found only in the "later Avesta," while the Zarathustra of the Gathas (those earliest of the Avesta scriptures) emerges as a struggling, sorrowing Prophet with a personality that is intensely human.   But shall Zarathustra now be left in peace?   Ah no!   Professor Geldner is a valiant champion; but he is out-professored, alas! by Zarathustra's relentless foe, Professor Darmesteter the learned and the terrible.   Did the ancient Prophet live indeed?   Well, be it so; but the ground shall be cut away from beneath his feet till he falls to the depths of insignificance.   A great work he cannot have done,—there was none such for him to do.   Was he the founder of a new religion?   Nay, for Zarathustrianism is but a natural development of the ancient Aryan faith.   Did he even revolutionise the old?   Nay, for the development was long and gradual, and we can trace no sudden changes.   Can he be called a great Reformer?   Nay, there was no Reformation, but an age-long, insensible growth, with never a violent reaction.

O venerable Zarathustra!   If from some transcendental home thy spirit yet looks down on this small planet whence, more than three thousand years ago, it soared away to the holy stars, what dost thou think of us now?   Of old thou didst tell how, when the world was in making, all the holy creatures, all animals and plants that are good, were fashioned by Ahura Mazda,[1] the Lord of Light and Life; but Angra Mainyu,[1] who is Death and the Lord of Darkness, made all creatures that are destructive and evil.   In which catalogue,

---

[1] "Ormazd" and "Ahriman" are now, alas! no more; and although the correct forms of the names look sadly unfamiliar, yet what am I that I should presume to fly in the face of the learned?

couldest thou have foreseen the ages that were to come, would European Professors have been placed?

It is the Magi's fault. They it was who opened the door to the ancient Aryan gods, and allowed a whole multitude of beautiful myths to obscure the simplicity and the grandeur of Zarathustra's sublime conceptions. The Gathas alone— the work of Zarathustra himself and his immediate disciples —can show us Zarathustra and his teaching as they really were. But the Gathas are obscure and difficult; and for me, who know nothing of Eastern languages, only to speak of them is presumption.

Yet, thanks to the labours of oriental scholars, the most unlearned now can read the Avesta in English, and it is truly a pity that they do not. The task is a sad one; for the Avesta, as we have it, is but a precious fragment of a far larger and richer literature, and the more we study what remains, the more we shall grieve for what is lost, and glow with anger against him who, they say, burned all that price- less treasure, Sikander Rûmi, the mighty conqueror of Persian tradition whom we call Alexander the Great. Still we may be thankful that something escaped him; and the writings of the Avesta, as we know them now, are truly a great posses- sion. There is, indeed, no universality about them; to com- pare them for a moment with our own inspired Scriptures— to liken, for instance, the Gathas to the Psalms—would be mere trifling and absurdity. But (setting aside the sacred Hebrew books) they are, I suppose, more beautiful and more exalted than any other ancient literature of the East. In any case, no one can hope to understand anything of the Parsi religion until he has read the Avesta.

There is so much to say about that religion and its history! Would that I could stay to trace its long development,—to

see the uncompromising Dualism of Zarathustra's original
teaching gradually changing to the definite Monotheism of
the present day; to disentangle the elements of Nature-
worship so conspicuous in the writings of the Magi, and the
myths that they borrowed from the old Indo-Iranian faith,
from Zarathustra's simpler creed. But my poor little book
is a feeble beast of burden, and such overlading with heavy
materials would hardly be kind or wise.

And where are my travellers all this while? I had almost
forgotten them, and now they have driven away without me
to visit the Parsi Towers of Silence. Let us overtake them
as quickly as may be, and indulge in no more reveries.
South-westward they drive through the sunlight of early
morning, and eagerly converse by the way.

" Philippa," exclaimed Sebaste, " you are treating us very
badly indeed. What is the use of knowing everything if
you don't instruct your sisters? Pray tell us at once what
these Towers of Silence mean! Why can't the Parsis bury
their dead or burn them like other folk, instead of building
these extraordinary places for them?"

" Because of the holiness of the material world!" says
Philippa. "That is one of the most beautiful of all the
Zarathustrian doctrines, and if it is connected with Nature-
worship, that is no proof that it has not a great truth at the
bottom of it. But if Water, and Earth, and 'Fire the son of
Ahura Mazda' are holy things, then they must not be pol-
luted by contact with the dead, and there is nothing for it
but to get the vultures to make their graves for them. There
is a passage in the 'Vendidad' which tells how Zarathustra inquired of Ahura Mazda the All-knowing Lord, and said: 'O
Maker of the material world, thou Holy One! if a man shall
bury in the earth either the corpse of a dog or the corpse of

a man, and if he shall not disinter it within the second year, what is the penalty for it? What is the atonement for it? What is the cleansing from it?' And Ahura Mazda answered, 'For that deed there is nothing that can pay, nothing that can atone, nothing that can cleanse from it: it is a trespass for which there is no atonement, for ever and ever.' I am glad to say that there is added the comforting doctrine, 'The law of Mazda indeed, O Spitama Zarathustra! . . . takes away the sin of deeds for which there is no atonement, . . . as a swift-rushing mighty wind cleanses the plain.'"

So doth Philippa discourse, until, arriving in the southwest corner of Bombay Island, the travellers reach the height whereon stand the Dakhmas, or Towers of Silence. As they ascend the hill where the sea-breeze blows, they call to mind that ancient ordinance for the disposal of the dead, given of old, say the Avesta scriptures, by Ahura Mazda, the Lord of Life, to his righteous servant the holy Zarathustra. For Zarathustra inquired and said: "O Maker of the material world, thou Holy One! whither shall we bring, where shall we lay, the bodies of the dead, O Ahura Mazda?" And Ahura Mazda answered, "On the highest summits where they know there are always corpse-eating dogs and corpse-eating birds, O holy Zarathustra! There shall the worshippers of Mazda fasten the corpse, by the feet and by the hair, with brass, stones, or lead, lest the corpse-eating dogs and the corpse-eating birds shall go and carry the bones to the water and to the trees. . . . The worshippers of Mazda shall erect a building out of the reach of the dog, of the fox, and of the wolf, and wherein rain-water cannot stay. Such a building shall they erect, if they can afford it, with stones, mortar, and earth; if they cannot afford

ONE OF THE TOWERS OF SILENCE, NEAR BOMBAY.

it, they shall lay down the dead man on the ground, on his carpet and his pillow, clothed with the light of heaven, and beholding the sun."

Presently the travellers pass a small temple, which they are not allowed to enter. Herein is the sacred fire brought long centuries ago from Persia, and kept perpetually burning. Fire, the "Beneficent," the "Valiant Warrior," is holy in its commonest forms, much more this symbolic flame devoutly worshipped day by day with the consecrated bundles of *baresma*,[1] with stately ritual, and with chanted hymns such as that solemn formula used thousands of years ago in the cities of ancient Iran :—

"Bring libations unto the Fire, bring hard wood unto the Fire, bring incense of Vohu-gaona unto the Fire. Offer up the sacrifice to the Vâzista Fire, which smites the fiend Spengaghra: bring unto it the cooked meat and the offerings of boiling milk."

There are other fire-temples in Bombay, and there is a story that into one of them, as a great and unprecedented favour, an American traveller was once admitted. Solemnly he was led by the priest to the sacred flame, and told that for thousands of years that fire had never been extinguished. "Is that so?" said the visitor. "*Puff!*—I guess it's out now!"

But my travellers have passed on, and see before them at length those five mysterious towers in one of which the body of every Parsi in Bombay must sooner or later be laid. The largest tower measures 25 feet in height and 276 feet in circumference. Each tower is entered by a square open-

[1] These were bundles of twigs,—originally, I suppose, symbolic fuel for the sacred Fire, but now represented by lengths of wire bound together in bundles.

ing at the top of a flight of steps. The travellers are not allowed to enter themselves; but a model is shown them whereby it is easy to understand the internal arrangements. In the centre is a well, round which, rising from it in an incline, is a circular platform filled with shallow grooves wherein the bodies of the dead are placed. The grooves are disposed in three circles, the outermost reserved for men, the next for women, and the innermost for children.

Round the top of the encircling walls of the towers huge vultures sit expectant, portentous forms looming dark against the sky. Very drowsy they look and indolent, until a funeral is seen approaching. Then suddenly they are all on the alert, watching with greedy eyes till the dead is left alone. Whereupon down they swoop in thronging companies, and feast to their hearts' content. In a very short time a bare skeleton only is left, and this is afterwards dragged away with tongs and cast into the central well.

Round the Dakhmas are planted palms and other pleasant trees, forming a luxuriant garden which, if those awful vultures did not haunt it, might be delightful to wander in. As it is, the very sunlight seems infected, and it is not hard to believe that ancient saying, "Nor is the Earth happy at that place whereon stands a Dakhma with corpses upon it; for that patch of ground will never be clean again till the day of resurrection." Long do the travellers linger near the towers, watching the ways of those evil birds, and recalling the discourse which Ahura Mazda spake of old to Zara-thustra "the wisest of all beings": "Those Dakhmas that are built upon the face of the earth, O Spitama Zara-thustra! and whereon are laid the corpses of dead men, that is the place where the fiends are, that is the place whereon

the troops of fiends come rushing along, that is the place
whereon they rush together to kill their fifties and their
hundreds, their hundreds and their thousands, their thousands and their tens of thousands, their tens of thousands
and their myriads of myriads. On those Dakhmas, O
Spitama Zarathustra! those fiends take food. . . . It is,
as it were, the smell of their feeding that you smell there,
O men! Thus the fiends revel on there, . . . thus from
the Dakhmas arise the infection of diseases . . . and hair
untimely white. There death has most power on man, from
the hour when the sun is down."

As our friends wander about recalling such fragments of
the Magi's ancient lore, a funeral procession draws near,
and, passing between the trees, moves slowly toward that
nearest Dakhma whereon the giant birds of prey do more
especially congregate. The body of the dead is carried
openly, muffled only in a white sheet, which, when the
last resting-place is reached, will be taken away, so that
the dead man may lie, according to the ordinance, clothed
only in "the light of heaven." The mourners are clad in
white robes, and walk in twos and threes, linked together
by cloths of white, whereof they hold the ends in their
hands. With them goes a dog, that most sacred of Ahura
Mazda's creatures, whose very look is enough to put to
flight the "corpse-drug" that haunts the helpless dead.

To find, here in the East of all places, such reverence for
the dog is very curious. Hinduism regards him as unclean,
and it is written in the book of Virtuous Custom that if
raiment have been looked at by dogs it is no longer fit
to be worn. But what said Ahura Mazda of old to Zarathustra the wisest of men? "The dog, O Spitama Zarathustra! I, Ahura Mazda, have made self - clothed and

self-shod, watchful, wakeful, and sharp-toothed, born to take his food from man and to watch over man's goods. I, Ahura Mazda, have made the dog strong of body against the evil-doer, and watchful over your goods, when he is of sound mind. And whosoever shall awake his voice, neither shall the thief nor the wolf steal anything from his house, without his being warned; the wolf shall be smitten and torn in peaces; he is driven away, he flies away."

To injure dogs, or to offer them bad food, is to Zarathustrians a terrible crime, and in sickness they must be carefully tended. Long ago Zarathustra asked, and said: "O Maker of the material world, thou Holy One! if there be in the house of a worshipper of Mazda . . . a mad dog, what shall the worshippers of Mazda do?" And Ahura Mazda answered: "They shall attend him to heal him, in the same manner as they would do for one of the faithful."

The dog used to scare away the corpse-Drug should be "a yellow dog with four eyes," or "a white dog with yellow ears;" but as four-eyed dogs are not easy to find in these latter days, and even a white dog with yellow ears may not always be forthcoming, there prevails in this matter a great deal of laxity, and the present funeral is followed by a dark-brown specimen who, though not fully qualified for the office, looks quite equal to the occasion. He must be led three times at least along the way whereon the corpse has been carried, else that way is Drug-haunted and unclean, and never again may it be passed through "by flocks and herds, by men and women, by Fire, the son of Ahura Mazda, by the consecrated bundles of *baresma*, nor by the faithful." But "when either the yellow dog with the four eyes, or the white dog with the yellow ears, is brought there, then the Drug Nasu flies away to the regions of the north in the

shape of a raging fly, with knees and tail sticking out, all
stained with stains." And before the dog the priest must
walk, chanting as he goes "these fiend - smiting words:
'*Yathâ ahû vairyô . . . Kem nâ mazdâ . . . Ke verethrem
gâ.* . . . Perish, O fiendish Drug! Perish, O brood of the
fiend! Perish, O world of the fiend! Perish away, O Drug!
Rush away, O Drug! Perish away, O Drug! Perish away
to the regions of the north, never more to give unto death
the living world of the holy spirit!' Then the worshippers
of Mazda may at their will bring by those ways sheep and
oxen, men and women, and Fire the son of Ahura Mazda, the
consecrated bundles of *baresma*, and the faithful."

The funeral train moves on, the great birds begin to bestir
themselves, and our travellers turn away and begin to descend the hill, telling as they go that strange Zarathustrian
myth concerning the far journey that the souls of the dead
must make. When one of the faithful departs, for three
nights the soul abides hard by the head of the corpse, singing the Ustavaiti Gâtha: "Happy is he, happy the man,
whoever he be, to whom Ahura Mazda gives the full accom-
plishment of his wishes!" In those nights "his soul tastes
as much pleasure as the whole of the living world can taste.
And at the end of the third night, when the dawn appears
. . . and makes Mithra, the god with the beautiful weapons,
reach the all-happy mountains, . . . then the soul enters
the way made by Time, and open both to the wicked and the
righteous," and comes to the Kinvad Bridge, the holy bridge
made by Mazda. There do the dead "ask for their spirits
and souls the reward for the worldly goods which they gave
away here below." Then "it seems to the soul of the faithful one as if it were brought amidst plants and scents: it
seems as if a wind were blowing from the region of the

south, . . . a sweet-scented wind, sweeter-scented than any other wind in the world. And it seems to the soul of the faithful as if he were inhaling that wind with his nostrils, and he thinks, 'Whence does that wind blow, the sweetest-scented wind I ever inhaled with my nostrils?' And it seems as if his own conscience were advancing to him in that wind, in the shape of a maiden fair, bright, white-armed, . . . as fair as the fairest things in the world." And the soul of the faithful one addresses her, asking, "What maid art thou, who art the fairest maid I have ever seen?" And she, being his own conscience, answers him: "O thou youth of good thoughts, good words, and good deeds, of good religion, I am thy own conscience! Everybody did love thee for that greatness, fairness, sweet-scentedness, victorious strength and freedom from sorrow, in which thou didst appear to me. . . . I was lovely, and thou madest me still lovelier; I was fair, and thou madest me still fairer." So the soul of the faithful passes on in felicity across the Kinvad Bridge. And "the first step that the soul of the faithful man makes" brings him into the "Good Thought Paradise"; "the second step that the soul of the faithful man makes" brings him into the "Good Word Paradise"; "the third step that the soul of the faithful man makes" brings him into the "Good Deed Paradise"; "the fourth step that the soul of the faithful man makes" brings him into the "Endless Lights." So with gladness "pass the souls of the righteous to the golden seat of Ahura Mazda," to Garô Nmânem the House of Songs.

But "when one of the wicked perishes," for three nights the soul abides hard by the head of the corpse, singing the Kima Gatha, "*Kâm nemê zâm:* To what land shall I turn, O Ahura Mazda? To whom shall I go with praying?" "In those nights he tastes as much suffering as the whole living world can taste." And when he comes to the Kinvad Bridge, "the holy bridge made by Mazda, the bridge that leads to Paradise, then it seems to the soul of the wicked . . . as if a wind were blowing from the region of the north, a foul-scented wind, the foulest-scented of all the winds in the world. And it seems to the soul of the wicked man as if he were inhaling that wind with his nostrils, and he thinks, 'Whence does that wind blow, the foulest-scented wind that I ever inhaled with my nostrils?'" Then there comes to meet him a horrible old woman who is none other than his own evil conscience; and the Kinvad Bridge, when he would cross it, shrinks to a single thread, and he falls therefrom, and goes down through the Evil Thought Hell and the Evil Word Hell and the Evil Deed Hell, until he comes at length to the Endless Darkness and the abode of Angra Mainyu, the deadly, the fiend of fiends.

Such legends the travellers recall on this their last day in India; and when, on the morning of their departure, the dawning light glows brightly, and the world is transfigured in that golden radiance which heralds the coming of the "undying, shining, swift-horsed Sun," then seems to ring in their ears that sweetest of ancient Zarathustrian hymns chanted by the faithful in the early morning, before the day has fully come, when the dawn appears in the East:—

"GÂH USHAHIN[1]—HYMN TO THE DAWN.

" We worship the lord Ushahina that rules our devotion
    In th' order of ritual reigning !
  We worship the breaking of day ; and the upspringing motion
    We praise, of the glorious morn.
  We worship the Dawn that in splendour appeareth, refraining
    Her glittering steeds, in the brightness of heaven upborne.

[1] That division of the day which extends from midnight to 6 A.M.

The brave among men and the prudent thy glories are telling,
  As servants to thee they are given.
Of thee is the brightness that shines in our innermost dwelling !
  Hail, hail to the manifold light !
Hail, hail to the Dawn, and her steeds that so swiftly are driven
  Far over the sevenfold Earth in all-radiant flight !"[1]

So at length comes the last farewell, and then the Arabian
Sea and long, bright days of rest. Far beneath the eastern
horizon lie the vanished shores of India. That strange part
of our travellers' lives when they rode upon elephants and
met wild peacocks by the way, when stately palm-trees waved
overhead and the green parrots fluttered in the sun, when
they wandered through lordly cities among bright-robed
native crowds,—those days have receded already to the immeasurably long ago. India has faded back into dreamland,
leaving behind but a radiant vision of verdant plains and
purple mountains, and faëry gardens of tropical foliage where
strange birds of brilliant plumage soar and sweep through
the golden sunshine, and through all the haunted night the
glorious moonlight glows; a vision of magic palace-halls
with walls of dazzling marble inlaid with precious gems; a
vision of ancient cities, and weird temples filled with worshippers who, clad in gorgeous robes, bring fragrant garlands of
all bright hues to honour their idol-king; a vision of sacred
Rivers gliding hard by palace-walls and bearing with them to
the far-off ocean a fragrant wealth of floral offerings. The
darkness of foul superstitions, the horrors of a degrading
worship, the nameless evils of a pagan civilisation,—all
these are for the moment forgotten, and India is a magic

[1] From the prose version in 'The Zend Avesta,' Part iii.; translated
by L. H. Mills. Sacred Books of the East.

Fairyland far removed in elfin light, shining with a glow of all rich colours, transfigured with enchantment of radiant mystery.

Slowly it faded away, sinking beneath the deep-blue waters; and now all the world is golden sunshine and azure sea and sky. Day after day the same wide plain is traversed, a vast and shining pavement whereon rests in unchanging splendour the great dome of stainless blue. India is vanished for ever; and our travellers gaze not long on its grave in the eastern waters. Eagerly they turn away, to look with homesick longing toward the far-off horizon before them whence, after many days, the dear white cliffs will rise.

Hardly can they know the loveliness of home who have never beheld it from far-off deserts or the strange wastes of foreign seas! Gazed at thence in the shadowy distance, it shines with an ideal brightness which can only be seen afar off. It is like those dream-homes which fanciful minds so often build for themselves in the sunny, far-off plains of a dim and indefinite future. Each one is an enchanted palace in the eyes of its wistful architect, and full of all good things that the heart of man can desire. And when, after long toil, he reaches it, and finds it after all but an inn on the great high-road, then he builds him another farther on, and thereafter another yet; and seldom do such travellers bethink them that Home, being no merely physical thing, is not to be reached, or even approached, by walking through miles or years.

"Ah, well," says Philippa kindly, "it is quite right to end with a Moral; but the really original parts of your book, Sebaste, are the quotations."

PRINTED BY WILLIAM BLACKWOOD AND SONS.

www.ingramcontent.com/pod-product-compliance
Lightning Source LLC
Chambersburg PA
CBHW030822110726
47900CB00006B/1713